SUMMER SHADOWS

The Right Path

and

Partners

ANTHOLOGIES

From the Heart • *A Little Magic* • *A Little Fate*

Moon Shadows
(with Jill Gregory, Ruth Ryan Langan, and Marianne Willman)

The Once Upon Series
(with Jill Gregory, Ruth Ryan Langan, and Marianne Willman)
Once Upon a Castle • *Once Upon a Star* • *Once Upon a
Dream* • *Once Upon a Rose* • *Once Upon a Kiss* • *Once Upon
a Midnight*

Silent Night
(with Susan Plunkett, Dee Holmes, and Claire Cross)

Out of This World
(with Laurell K. Hamilton, Susan Krinard, and Maggie Shayne)

Bump in the Night
(with Mary Blayney, Ruth Ryan Langan, and Mary Kay McComas)

SUMMER SHADOWS

The Right Path

and

Partners

TWO NOVELS IN ONE

NORA ROBERTS

St. Martin's Paperbacks

This is a work of fiction. All of the characters, organizations, and events portrayed in this book are either products of the author's imagination or are used fictitiously.

Published in the United States by St. Martin's Paperbacks, an imprint of St. Martin's Publishing Group

SUMMER SHADOWS: THE RIGHT PATH copyright © 1985 by Nora Roberts and PARTNERS copyright © 1985 by Nora Roberts.

For information, address St. Martin's Publishing Group, 120 Broadway, New York, NY 10271.

www.stmartins.com

ISBN: 978-1-250-84714-0

Our books may be purchased in bulk for promotional, educational, or business use. Please contact your local bookseller or the Macmillan Corporate and Premium Sales Department at 1-800-221-7945, ext. 5442, or by email at MacmillanSpecialMarkets@macmillan.com.

Printed in the United States of America

St. Martin's Paperbacks edition / June 2022

10 9 8 7 6 5 4 3 2 1

The Right Path

CHAPTER 1

The sky was cloudless—the hard, perfect blue of a summer painting. A breeze whispered through the roses in the garden. Mountains were misted by distance. A scent—flowers, sea, new grass—drifted on the air. With a sigh of pure pleasure, Morgan leaned farther over the balcony rail and just looked.

Had it really only been yesterday morning that she had looked out on New York's steel and concrete? Had she run through a chill April drizzle to catch a taxi to the airport? One day. It seemed impossible to go from one world to another in only a day.

But she was here, standing on the balcony of a villa on the Isle of Lesbos. There was no gray drizzle at all, but strong Greek sunlight. There was quiet, a deep blanketing stillness that contrasted completely with the fits and starts of New York traffic. If I could paint, Morgan mused, I'd paint this view and call it *Silence*.

"Come in," she called when there was a knock on the door. After one last deep breath, she turned, reluctantly.

"So, you're up and dressed." Liz swept in, a small, golden fairy with a tray-bearing maid in her wake.

"Room service." Morgan grinned as the maid placed the

tray on a glass-topped table. "I'll begin to wallow in luxury from this moment." She took an appreciative sniff of the platters the maid uncovered. "Are you joining me?"

"Just for coffee." Liz settled in a chair, smoothing the skirts of her silk and lace robe, then took a long survey of the woman who sat opposite her.

Long loose curls in shades from ash blond to honey brown fell to tease pale shoulders. Almond-shaped eyes, almost too large for the slender face, were a nearly transparent blue. There was a straight, sharp nose and prominent cheekbones, a long, narrow mouth and a subtly pointed chin. It was a face of angles and contours that many a model starved herself for. It would photograph like a dream had Morgan ever been inclined to sit long enough to be captured on film.

What you'd get, Liz mused, would be a blur of color as Morgan dashed away to see what was around the next corner.

"Oh, Morgan, you look fabulous! I'm so glad you're here at last."

"Now that I'm here," Morgan returned, shifting her eyes back to the view, "I can't understand why I put off coming for so long. *Efxaristo*," she added as the maid poured her coffee.

"Show-off," Liz said with mock scorn. "Do you know how long it took me to master a simple Greek hello, how are you? No, never mind." She waved her hand before Morgan could speak. The symphony of diamonds and sapphires in her wedding ring caught the flash of sunlight. "Three years married to Alex and living in Athens and Lesbos, and I still stumble over the language. Thank you, Zena," she added in English, dismissing the maid with a smile.

"You're simply determined not to learn." Morgan bit enthusiastically into a piece of toast. She wasn't hungry, she discovered. She was ravenous. "If you'd open your mind, the words would seep in."

"Listen to you." Liz wrinkled her nose. "Just because you speak a dozen languages."

"Five."

"Five is four more than a rational person requires."

"Not a rational interpreter," Morgan reminded her and dug wholeheartedly into her eggs. "And if I hadn't spoken Greek, I wouldn't have met Alex, and you wouldn't be *Kryios* Elizabeth Theoharis. Fate," she announced with a full mouth, "is a strange and wonderful phenomenon."

"Philosophy at breakfast," Liz murmured into her coffee. "That's one of the things I've missed about you. Actually, I'd hate to think what might have happened if I hadn't been home on layover when Alex popped up. You wouldn't have introduced us." She commandeered a piece of toast, adding a miserly dab of plum jelly. "I'd still be serving miniature bottles of bourbon at thirty thousand feet."

"Liz, my love, when something's meant, it's meant." Morgan cut into a fat sausage. "I'd love to take credit for your marital bliss, but one brief introduction wasn't responsible for the fireworks that followed." She glanced up at the cool blond beauty and smiled. "Little did I know I'd lose my roommate in less than three weeks. I've never seen two people move so fast."

"We decided we'd get acquainted after we were married." A grin warmed Liz's face. "And we have."

"Where is Alex this morning?"

"Downstairs in his office." Liz moved her shoulders absently and left half her toast untouched. "He's building another ship or something."

Morgan laughed outright. "You say that in the same tone you'd use if he were building a model train. Don't you know you're supposed to become spoiled and disdainful when you marry a millionaire—especially a foreign millionaire?"

"Is that so? Well, I'll see what I can do." She topped off her coffee. "He'll probably be horribly busy for the next few weeks, which is one more reason I'm glad you're here."

"You need a cribbage partner."

"Hardly," Liz corrected as she struggled with a smile. "You're the worst cribbage player I know."

"Oh, I don't know," Morgan began as her brows drew together.

"Perhaps you've improved. Anyway," Liz went on, concealing with her coffee cup what was now a grin, "not to be disloyal to my adopted country, but it's just so good to have my best friend, and an honest-to-God American, around."

"Spasibo."

"English at all times," Liz insisted. "And I know that wasn't even Greek. You aren't translating government hyperbole at the U.N. for the next four weeks." She leaned forward to rest her elbows on the table. "Tell me the truth, Morgan, aren't you ever terrified you'll interpret some nuance incorrectly and cause World War Three?"

"Who me?" Morgan opened her eyes wide. "Not a chance. Anyway, the trick is to think in the language you're interpreting. It's that easy."

"Sure it is." Liz leaned back. "Well, you're on vacation, so you only have to think in English. Unless you want to argue with the cook."

"Absolutely not," Morgan assured her as she polished off her eggs.

"How's your father?"

"Marvelous, as always." Relaxed, content, Morgan poured more coffee. When was the last time she had taken the time for a second cup in the morning? Vacation, Liz had said. Well, she was damn well going to learn how to enjoy one.

"He sends you his love and wants me to smuggle some ouzo back to New York."

"I'm not going to think about you going back." Liz rose and swirled around the balcony. The lace border at the hem of her robe swept over the tile. "I'm going to find a suitable mate for you and establish you in Greece."

"I can't tell you how much I appreciate your handling things for me," Morgan returned dryly.

"It's all right. What are friends for?" Ignoring the sarcasm, Liz leaned back on the balcony. "Dorian's a likely candidate. He's one of Alex's top men and really attractive. Blond and bronzed with a profile that belongs on a coin. You'll meet him tomorrow."

"Should I tell Dad to arrange my dowry?"

"I'm serious." Folding her arms, Liz glared at Morgan's grin. "I'm not letting you go back without a fight. I'm going to fill your days with sun and sea, and dangle hordes of gorgeous men in front of your nose. You'll forget that New York and the U.N. exist."

"They're already wiped out of my mind . . . for the next four weeks." Morgan tossed her hair back over her shoulders. "So, satiate and dangle. I'm at your mercy. Are you going to drag me to the beach this morning? Force me to lie on the sand and soak up rays until I have a fabulous golden tan?"

"Exactly." With a brisk nod, Liz headed for the door. "Change. I'll meet you downstairs."

Thirty minutes later, Morgan decided she was going to like Liz's brand of brainwashing. White sand, blue water. She let herself drift on the gentle waves. *Too wrapped up in your work.* Isn't that what Dad said? *You're letting the job run you instead of the other way around.* Closing her eyes, Morgan rolled to float on her back. Between job pressure and the nasty breakup with Jack, she mused, I need a peace transfusion.

Jack was part of the past. Morgan was forced to admit that he had been more a habit than a passion. They'd suited each other's requirements. She had wanted an intelligent male companion; he an attractive woman whose manners would be advantageous to his political career.

If she'd loved him, Morgan reflected, she could hardly think of him so objectively, so . . . well, coldly. There was no ache, no loneliness. What there was, she admitted, was relief. But with the relief had come the odd feeling of being at loose ends. A feeling Morgan was neither used to nor enjoyed.

Liz's invitation had been perfectly timed. And this, she thought, opening her eyes to study that perfect sweep of sky, was paradise. Sun, sand, rock, flowers—the whispering memory of ancient gods and goddesses. Mysterious Turkey was close, separated only by the narrow Gulf of Edremit. She closed her eyes again and would have dozed if Liz's voice hadn't disturbed her.

"Morgan! Some of us have to eat at regular intervals."

"Always thinking of your stomach."

"And *your* skin," Liz countered from the edge of the water. "You're going to fry. You can overlook lunch, but not sunburn."

"All right, Mommy." Morgan swam in, then stood on shore and shook like a wet dog. "How come you can swim and lie in the sun and still look ready to walk into a ballroom?"

"Breeding," Liz told her and handed over the short robe. "Come on, Alex usually tears himself away from his ships for lunch."

I could get used to eating on terraces, Morgan thought after lunch was finished. They relaxed over iced coffee and fruit. She noted that Alexander Theoharis was still as fascinated with his small, golden wife as he had been three years before in New York.

Though she'd brushed off Liz's words that morning, Morgan felt a certain pride at having brought them together. A perfect match, she mused. Alex had an old-world charm—dark aquiline looks made dashing by a thin white scar above his eyebrow. He was only slightly above average height but with a leanness that was more aristocratic than rangy. It was the ideal complement for Liz's dainty blond beauty.

"I don't see how you ever drag yourself away from here," Morgan told him. "If this were all mine, nothing would induce me to leave."

Alex followed her gaze across the glimpse of sea to the mountains. "But when one returns, it's all the more magnificent. Like a woman," he continued, lifting Liz's hand to kiss, "paradise demands constant appreciation."

"It's got mine," Morgan stated.

"I'm working on her, Alex." Liz laced her fingers with his. "I'm going to make a list of all the eligible men within a hundred miles."

"You don't have a brother, do you, Alex?" Morgan asked, sending him a smile.

"Sisters only. My apologies."

"Forget it, Liz."

"If we can't entice you into matrimony, Alex will have to offer you a job in the Athens office."

"I'd steal Morgan from the U.N. in a moment," Alex reminded her with a move of his shoulders. "I couldn't lure her away three years ago. I tried."

"We have a month to wear her down this time." She shot Alex a quick glance. "Let's take her out on the yacht tomorrow."

"Of course," he agreed immediately. "We'll make a day of it. Would you like that, Morgan?"

"Oh, well, I'm constantly spending the day on a yacht on

the Aegean, but"—her lake-blue eyes lit with laughter—
"since Liz wants to, I'll try not to be too bored."

"She's such a good sport," Liz confided to Alex.

* * *

It was just past midnight when Morgan made her way down
to the beach again. Sleep had refused to come. Morgan wel-
comed the insomnia, seeing it as an excuse to walk out into
the warm spring night.

The light was liquid. The moon was sliced in half but
held a white, gleaming brightness. Cypresses that flanked
the steps down to the beach were silvered with it. The scent
of blossoms, hot and pungent during the day, seemed more
mysterious by moonlight.

From somewhere in the distance, she heard the low rumble
of a motor. A late-night fisherman, she thought, and smiled.
It would be quite an adventure to fish under the moon.

The beach spread in a wide half circle. Morgan dropped
both her towel and wrap on a rock, then ran into the water.
Against her skin it was so cool and silky that she toyed with
the idea of discarding even the brief bikini. Better not, she
thought with a low laugh. No use tempting the ghosts of the
gods.

Though the thought of adventure appealed to her, she
kept to the open bay and suppressed the urge to explore
the inlets. They'd still be there in the daylight, she reminded herself. She swam lazily, giving her strokes just
enough power to keep her afloat. She hadn't come for the
exercise.

Even when her body began to feel the chill, she lingered.
There were stars glistening on the water, and silence. Such
silence. Strange, that until she had found it, she hadn't known
she was looking for it.

New York seemed more than a continent away; it seemed centuries away. For the moment, she was content that it be so. Here she could indulge in the fantasies that never seemed appropriate in the rush of day-to-day living. Here she could let herself believe in ancient gods, in shining knights and bold pirates. A laugh bubbled from her as she submerged and rose again. Gods, knights, and pirates . . . well, she supposed she'd take the pirate if she had her pick. Gods were too bloodthirsty, knights too chivalrous, but a pirate . . .

Shaking her head, Morgan wondered how her thoughts had taken that peculiar turn. It must be Liz's influence, she decided. Morgan reminded herself she didn't want a pirate or any other man. What she wanted was peace.

With a sigh, she stood knee-deep in the water, letting the drops stream down her hair and skin. She was cold now, but the cold was exhilarating. Ignoring her wrap, she sat on the rock and pulled a comb from its pocket and idly ran it through her hair. Moon, sand, water. What more could there be? She was, for one brief moment, in total harmony with her own spirit and with nature's.

Shock gripped her as a hand clamped hard over her mouth. She struggled, instinctively, but an arm was banded around her waist—rough cloth scraping her naked skin. Dragged from the rock, Morgan found herself molded against a solid, muscular chest.

Rape? It was the first clear thought before the panic. She kicked out blindly as she was pulled into the cover of trees. The shadows were deep there. Fighting wildly, she raked with her nails wherever she could reach, feeling only a brief satisfaction at the hiss of an indrawn breath near her ear.

"Don't make a sound." The order was in quick, harsh Greek. About to strike out again, Morgan felt her blood freeze. A glimmer of knife caught the moonlight just before she was thrust to the ground under the length of the man's body. "Wildcat," he muttered. "Keep still and I won't have to hurt you. Do you understand?"

Numb with terror, Morgan nodded. With her eyes glued to his knife, she lay perfectly still. I can't fight him now, she thought grimly. Not now, but somehow, somehow I'll find out who he is. He'll pay.

The first panic was gone, but her body still trembled as she waited. It seemed an eternity, but he made no move, no sound. It was so quiet, she could hear the waves lapping gently against the sand only a few feet away. Over her head, through the spaces in the leaves, stars still shone. It must be a nightmare, she told herself. It can't be real. But when she tried to shift under him, the pressure of his body on hers proved that it was very, very real.

The hand over her mouth choked her breath until vague colors began to dance before her eyes. Morgan squeezed them tight for a moment to fight the faintness. Then she heard him speak again to a companion she couldn't see.

"What do you hear?"

"Nothing yet—in a moment." The voice that answered was rough and brisk. "Who the devil is she?"

"It doesn't matter. She'll be dealt with."

The roaring in her ears made it difficult to translate the Greek. Dealt with? she thought, dizzy again from fear and the lack of air.

The second man said something low and furious about women, then spat into the dirt.

"Just keep your ears open," Morgan's captor ordered. "And leave the woman to me."

"Now."

She felt him stiffen, but her eyes never left the knife. He was gripping it tighter now; she saw the tensing of his fingers on the handle.

Footsteps. They echoed on the rock steps of the beach. Hearing them, Morgan began to struggle again with the fierce strength of panic and of hope. With a whispered oath, he put more of his weight on her. He smelt faintly of the sea. As he shifted she caught a brief glimpse of his face in a patchy stream of moonlight. She saw dark, angular features, a grim mouth, and narrowed jet eyes. They were hard and cold and ruthless. It was the face of a man prepared to kill. *Why?* she thought as her mind began to float. I don't even know him.

"Follow him," he ordered his companion. Morgan heard a slight stirring in the leaves. "I'll take care of the woman."

Morgan's eyes widened at the sharp glimmer of the blade. She tasted something—bitter, copper—in her throat, but didn't recognize it as terror. The world spun to the point of a pin, then vanished.

The sky was full of stars, silver against black. The sea whispered. Against her back, the sand was rough. Morgan rose on her elbow and tried to clear her head. Fainted? Good God, had she actually fainted? Had she simply fallen asleep and dreamed it all? Rubbing her fingers against her temple, she wondered if her fantasies about pirates had caused her to hallucinate.

A small sound brought her swiftly to her feet. No, it had been real, and he was back. Morgan hurled herself at the shadow as it approached. She'd accepted the inevitability of death once without a struggle. This time, he was going to have a hell of a fight on his hands.

The shadow grunted softly as she struck, then Morgan found herself captured again, under him with the sand scraping her back.

"*Diabolos!* Be still!" he ordered in furious Greek as she tried to rip at his face.

"The hell I will!" Morgan tossed back in equally furious

English. She fought with every ounce of strength until he pinned her, spread-eagle beneath him. Breathless, fearless in her rage, she stared up at him.

Looking down, he studied her with a frown. "You're not Greek." The statement, uttered in surprised and impatient English, stopped her struggles. "Who are you?"

"None of your business." She tried, and failed, to jerk her wrists free of his hold.

"Stop squirming," he ordered roughly, as his fingers clamped down harder. He wasn't thinking of his strength or her fragility, but that she wasn't simply a native who had been in the wrong place at the wrong time. His profession had taught him to get answers and adjust for complications. "What were you doing on the beach in the middle of the night?"

"Swimming," she tossed back. "Any idiot should be able to figure that out."

He swore, then shifted as she continued to struggle beneath him. "Damn it, be still!" His brows were lowered, not in anger now but concentration. "Swimming," he repeated as his eyes narrowed again. He'd watched her walk out of the sea—perhaps it was as innocent as that. "American," he mused, ignoring Morgan's thrashing. Weren't the Theoharises expecting an American woman? Of all the ill-timed . . . "You're not Greek," he murmured again.

"Neither are you," Morgan said between clenched teeth.

"Half." His thoughts underwent some rapid readjustments. The Theoharises' American houseguest, out for a moonlight swim—he'd have to play this one carefully or there'd be hell to pay. Quite suddenly, he flashed her a smile. "You had me fooled. I thought you could understand me."

"I understand perfectly," she retorted. "And you won't find it an easy rape now that you don't have your knife out."

"Rape?" Apparently astonished, he stared at her. His

laughter was as sudden as the smile. "I hadn't given that much thought. In any case, Aphrodite, the knife was never intended for you."

"Then what do you mean by dragging me around like that? Flashing a knife in my face and nearly suffocating me?" Fury was much more satisfying than fear, and Morgan went with it. "Let me go!" She pushed at him with her body, but couldn't nudge him.

"In a moment," he said pleasantly. The moonlight played on her skin, and he enjoyed it. A fabulous face, he mused, now that he had time to study it. She'd be a woman accustomed to male admiration. Perhaps charm would distract her from the rather unique aspect of their meeting. "I can only say that what I did was for your own protection."

"Protection!" she flung back at him and tried to wrench her arms free.

"There wasn't time for amenities, fair lady. My apologies if my . . . technique was unrefined." His tone seemed to take it for granted that she would understand. "Tell me, why were you out alone, sitting like Lorelei on the rock and combing your hair?"

"That's none of your business." His voice had dropped, becoming low and seductive. The dark eyes had softened and appeared depthless. She could almost believe she had imagined the ruthlessness she'd glimpsed in the shadows. But she felt the light throbbing where his fingers had gripped her flesh. "I'm going to scream if you don't let me go."

Her body was tempting now that he had time to appreciate it, but he rose with a shrug. There was still work to be done that night. "My apologies for your inconvenience."

"Oh, is that right?" Struggling to her feet, Morgan began to brush at the sand that clung to her skin. "You have your nerve, dragging me off into the bushes, smothering me, brandishing a knife in my face, then apologizing like you've just stepped on my toe." Suddenly cold, she wrapped her arms around herself. "Just who are you and what was this all about?"

"Here." Stooping, he picked up the wrap he had dropped in order to hold her off. "I was bringing this to you when you launched your attack." He grinned as she shrugged into the wrap. It was a pity to cover the lengthy, intriguing body. "Who I am at the moment isn't relevant. As for the rest"—again the smooth, easy shrug—"I can't tell you."

"Just like that?" With a quick nod, Morgan turned and stalked to the beach steps. "We'll see what the police have to say about it."

"I wouldn't if I were you."

The advice was quiet, but vibrated with command. Hesitating, Morgan turned at the base of the steps to study him. He wasn't threatening now. What she felt wasn't fear, but his authority. He was quite tall, she noticed suddenly. And the moonlight played tricks with his face, making it almost cruel one moment, charming the next. Now it held all the confidence of Lucifer regrouping after the Fall.

Looking at him, she remembered the feel of hard, wiry muscles. He was standing easily, hands thrust into the pockets of jeans. The aura of command fit him perfectly. His smile didn't disguise it, nor did his casual stance. Damn pirates, she thought, feeling a quick twinge. Only lunatics find them attractive. Because she felt vulnerable, Morgan countered with bravado.

"Wouldn't you?" She lifted her chin and walked back to him.

"No," he answered mildly. "But perhaps, unlike me, you look for complications. I'm a simple man." He took a long, searching look at her face. *This is not,* he decided instantly, *a simple woman.* Though in his mind he cursed her, he went on conversationally. "Questions, reports to fill out, hours wasted on red tape. And then, even if you had my name"—he shrugged and flashed the grin again—"no one would believe you, Aphrodite. No one."

She didn't trust that grin—or the sultry way he called her by the goddess's name. She didn't trust the sudden warmth in her blood. "I wouldn't be so sure," Morgan began, but he cut her off, closing the slight distance between them.

"And I didn't rape you." Slowly, he ran his hands down her hair until they rested on her shoulders. His fingers didn't bite into her flesh now, but skimmed lazily. She had the eyes of a witch, he thought, and the face of a goddess. His time was short, but the moment was not to be missed. "Until now, I haven't even given in to the urge to do this."

His mouth closed over hers, hot and stunningly sweet. She hadn't been prepared for it. She pushed against him, but it was strictly out of reflex and lacked strength. He was a man who knew a woman's weakness. Deliberately, he brought her close, using style rather than force.

The scent of the sea rose to surround her, and heat—such a furnace heat that seemed to come from within and without at the same time. Almost leisurely, he explored her mouth until her heart thudded wildly against the quick, steady beat of his. His hands were clever, sliding beneath the wide sleeves of her robe to tease and caress the length of her arms, the slope of her shoulders.

When her struggles ceased, he nibbled at her lips as if he would draw out more taste. Slow, easy. His tongue tempted hers, then retreated, then slipped through her parted lips again to torment and savor. For a moment, Morgan feared she would faint for a second time in his arms.

"One kiss," he murmured against her lips, "is hardly a criminal offense." She was sweeter than he had imagined and, he realized as desire stirred hotly, deadlier. "I could take another with little more risk."

"No." Coming abruptly to her senses, Morgan pushed away from him. "You're mad. And you're madder still if you think I'm going to let this go. I'm going—" She broke off as her hand lifted to her throat in a nervous gesture. The chain that always hung there was missing. Morgan glanced down, then brought her eyes back to his, furious, glowing.

"What have you done with my medal?" she demanded. "Give it back to me."

"I'm afraid I don't have it, Aphrodite."

"I want it back." Bravado wasn't a pose this time; she was livid. She stepped closer until they were toe to toe. "It's not worth anything to you. You won't be able to get more than a few drachmas for it."

His eyes narrowed. "I didn't take your medal. I'm not a thief." The temper in his voice was cold, coated with control. "If I were going to steal something from you, I would have found something more interesting than a medal."

Her eyes filled in a rush, and she swung out her hand to slap him. He caught her wrist, adding frustration to fury.

"It appears the medal is important," he said softly, but his hand was no longer gentle. "A token from a lover?"

"A gift from someone I love," Morgan countered. "I wouldn't expect a man like you to understand its value." With a jerk, she pulled her wrist from his hold. "I won't forget you," she promised, then turned and flew up the stairs.

He watched her until she was swallowed by the darkness. After a moment he turned back to the beach.

CHAPTER 2

The sun was a white flash of light. Its diamonds skimmed the water's surface. With the gentle movement of the yacht, Morgan found herself half-dozing.

Could the moonlit beach and the man have been a dream? she wondered hazily. Knives and rough hands and sudden draining kisses from strangers had no place in the real world. They belonged in one of those strange, half-remembered dreams she had when the rush and demands of work and the city threatened to become too much for her. She'd always considered them her personal release valve. Harmless, but absolutely secret—something she'd never considered telling Jack or any of her coworkers.

If it hadn't been for the absence of her medal, and the light trail of bruises on her arms, Morgan could have believed the entire incident had been the product of an overworked imagination.

Sighing, she shifted her back to the sun, pillowing her head on her hands. Her skin, slick with oil, glistened. Why was she keeping the whole crazy business from Liz and Alex? Grimacing, she flexed her shoulders. They'd be horrified if she told them she'd been assaulted. Morgan could all but see Alex placing her under armed guard for the rest of her stay

on Lesbos. He'd make certain there was an investigation—
complicated, time-consuming, and, in all probability, fruit-
less. Morgan could work up a strong hate for the dark man
for being right.

And what, if she decided to pursue it, could she tell the
police? She hadn't been hurt or sexually assaulted. There'd
been no verbal threat she could pin down, not even the slimmest motivation for what had happened. And what had happened? she demanded of herself. A man had dragged her into
the bushes, held her there for no clear reason, then had let
her go without harming her.

The Greek police wouldn't see the kiss as a criminal offense. She hadn't been robbed. There was no way on earth to
prove the man had taken her medal. And damn it, she added
with a sigh, as much as she'd like to assign all sorts of evil
attributes to him, he just didn't fit the role of a petty thief.
Petty anything, she thought grudgingly. Whatever he did,
she was certain he did big . . . and did well.

So what was she going to do about it? True, he'd frightened and infuriated her—the second was probably a direct
result of the first—but what else was there?

If and when they caught him, it would be his word against
hers. Somehow, Morgan thought his word would carry more
weight.

So I was frightened—my pride took a lump. She shrugged
and shifted her head on her hands. It's not worth upsetting Liz
and Alex. Midnight madness, she mused. Another strange adventure in the life and times of Morgan James. File it and
forget it.

Hearing Alex mount the steps to the sun deck, Morgan
rested her chin on her hands and smiled at him. On the
lounger beside her, Liz stirred and slept on.

"So, the sun has put her to sleep." Alex mounted the last
of the steps, then settled into the chair beside his wife.

"I nearly dozed off myself." With a yawn, Morgan stretched luxuriously before she rolled over to adjust the lounger to a sitting position. "But I didn't want to miss anything." Gazing over the water, she studied the clump of land in the distance. The island seemed to float, as insubstantial as a mist.

"Chios," Alex told her, following her gaze. "And"—he gestured, waiting for her eyes to shift in the direction of his— "the coast of Turkey."

"So close," Morgan mused. "It seems as though I could swim to it."

"At sea, the distance can be deceiving." He flicked a lighter at the end of a black cigarette. The fragrance that rose from it was faintly sweet and exotic. "You'd have to be a hardy swimmer. Easy enough with a boat, though. There are some who find the proximity profitable." At Morgan's blank expression, Alex laughed. "Smuggling, innocence. It's still popular even though the punishment is severe."

"Smuggling," she murmured, intrigued. Then the word put her in mind of pirates again and her curious expression turned into a frown. A nasty business, she reminded herself, and not romantic at all.

"The coast." Alex made another sweeping gesture with the elegant cigarette held between two long fingers. "The many bays and peninsulas, offshore islands, inlets. There's simple access from the sea to the interior."

She nodded. Yes, a nasty business—they weren't talking about French brandy or Spanish lace. "Opium?"

"Among other things."

"But, Alex." His careless acceptance caused her frown to deepen. Once she'd sorted it through, Morgan's own sense of right and wrong had little middle ground. "Doesn't it bother you?"

"Bother me?" he repeated, taking a long, slow drag on the cigarette. "Why?"

Flustered with the question, she sat up straighter. "Aren't you concerned about that sort of thing going on so close to your own home?"

"Morgan." Alex spread his hands in an acceptance of fate. The thick chunk of gold on his left pinky gleamed dully in the sunlight. "My concern would hardly stop what's been going on for centuries."

"But still, with crime practically in your own backyard . . ." She broke off, thinking about the streets of Manhattan. Perhaps she was the pot calling the kettle black. "I supposed I'd thought you'd be annoyed," she finished.

His eyes lit with a touch of amusement before he shrugged. "I leave the matter—and the annoyance—to the patrols and authorities. Tell me, are you enjoying your stay so far?"

Morgan started to speak again, then consciously smoothed away the frown. Alex was old-world enough not to want to discuss unpleasantries with a guest. "It's wonderful here, Alex. I can see why Liz loves it."

He flashed her a grin before he drew in strong tobacco. "You know Liz wants you to stay. She's missed you. At times, I feel very guilty because we don't get to America to see you often enough."

"You don't have to feel guilty, Alex." Morgan pushed on sunglasses and relaxed again. After all, she reflected, smuggling had nothing to do with her. "Liz is happy."

"She'd be happier with you here."

"Alex," Morgan began with a smile for his indulgence of his wife. "I can't simply move in as a companion, no matter how much both of us love Liz."

"You're still dedicated to your job at the U.N.?" His tone had altered slightly, but Morgan sensed the change. It was business now.

"I like my work. I'm good at it, and I need the challenge."

"I'm a generous employer, Morgan, particularly to one with your capabilities." He took another long, slow drag, studying her through the mist of smoke. "I asked you to come work for me three years ago. If I hadn't been"—he glanced down at Liz's sleeping figure—"distracted"—he decided with a mild smile—"I would have taken more time to convince you to accept."

"Distracted?" Liz pushed her sunglasses up to her forehead and peered at him from under them.

"Eavesdropping," Morgan said with a sniff. A uniformed steward set three iced drinks on the table. She lifted one and drank. "Your manners always were appalling."

"You have a few weeks yet to think it over, Morgan." Tenacity beneath a smooth delivery was one of Alex's most successful business tactics. "But I warn you, Liz will be more persistent with her other solution." He shrugged, reaching for his own drink. "And I must agree—a woman needs a husband and security."

"How very Greek of you," Morgan commented dryly.

His grin flashed without apology. "I'm afraid one of Liz's candidates will be delayed. Dorian won't join us until tomorrow. He's bringing my cousin Iona with him."

"Marvelous." Liz's response was drenched in sarcasm. Alex sent her a frown.

"Liz isn't fond of Iona, but she's family." The quiet look he sent his wife told Morgan the subject had been discussed before. "I have a responsibility."

Liz took the last glass with a sigh of acceptance. Briefly she touched her hand to his. "We have a responsibility," she corrected. "Iona's welcome."

Alex's frown turned into a look of love so quickly, Morgan gave a mock groan. "Don't you two ever fight? I mean, don't you realize it isn't healthy to be so well balanced?"

Liz's eyes danced over the rim of her glass. "We have our moments, I suppose. A week ago I was furious with him for at least—ah, fifteen minutes."

"That," Morgan said positively, "is disgusting."

"So," Alex mused, "you think a man and woman must fight to be . . . healthy?"

Shaking back her hair, Morgan laughed. "*I* have to fight to be healthy."

"Morgan, you haven't mentioned Jack at all. Is there a problem?"

"Liz." Alex's disapproval was clear in the single syllable.

"No, it's all right, Alex." Taking her glass, Morgan rose and moved to the rail. "It's not a problem," she said slowly. "At least I hope it's not." She stared into her drink, frowning, as if she wasn't quite sure what the glass contained. "I've been running on this path—this very straight, very defined path. I could run it blindfolded." With a quick laugh, Morgan leaned out on the rail to let the wind grab at her hair. "Suddenly, I discovered it wasn't a path, but a rut and it kept getting deeper. I decided to change course before it became a pit."

"You always did prefer an obstacle course," Liz murmured. But she was pleased with Jack's disposal, and took little trouble to hide it.

The sea churned in a white froth behind the boat. Morgan turned from her study of it. "I don't intend to fall at Dorian's feet, Liz—or anyone else you might have in mind—just because Jack and I are no longer involved."

"I should hope not," Liz returned with some spirit. "That would take all the fun out of it."

With a sigh of exasperated affection, Morgan turned back to the rail.

The stark mountains of Lesbos rose from the sea. Jagged, harsh, timeless. Morgan could make out the pure white lines of Alex's villa. She thought it looked like a virgin offering to the gods—cool, classic, certainly feminine. Higher still was a rambling gray structure that seemed hewn from the rock itself. It faced the sea; indeed, it loomed over it. As if challenging Poseidon to claim it, it clung to the cliff. Morgan saw it as arrogant, rough, masculine. The flowering vines that grew all around it didn't soften the appearance, but added a haunted kind of beauty.

There were other buildings—a white-washed village, snuggled cottages, one or two other houses on more sophisticated lines, but the two larger structures hovered over the rest. One was elegant; one was savage.

"Who does that belong to?" Morgan called over her shoulder. "It's incredible."

Following her gaze, Liz grinned and rose to join her. "I should have known that would appeal to you. Sometimes I'd swear it's alive. Nicholas Gregoras, olive oil, and more recently, import-export." She glanced at her friend's profile. "Maybe I'll include him for dinner tomorrow if he's free, though I don't think he's your type."

Morgan gave her a dry look. "Oh? And what is my type?"

"Someone who'll give you plenty to fight about. Who'll give you that obstacle course."

"*Hmm.* You know me too well."

"As for Nick, he's rather smooth and certainly a charmer." Liz tapped a fingernail against the rail as she considered. "Not as blatantly handsome as Dorian, but he has a rather basic sort of sex appeal. Earthier, and yet . . ." She trailed off, narrowing her eyes as she tried to pigeonhole him. "Well, he's an odd one. I suppose he'd have to be to live in a house like that. He's in his early thirties, inherited the olive oil empire almost ten years ago. Then he branched into import-export. He seems to have a flair for it. Alex is very fond of him because they go back to short pants together."

"Liz, I only wanted to know who owned the house. I didn't ask for a biography."

"These facts are part of the service." She cupped her hands around her lighter and lit a cigarette. "I want to give you a clear picture of your options."

"Haven't you got a goatherd up your sleeve?" Morgan demanded. "I rather like the idea of a small, white-washed cottage and baking black bread."

"I'll see what I can do."

"I don't suppose it occurs to you or Alex that I'm content to be single—the modern, capable woman on her own? I know how to use a screwdriver, how to change a flat tire . . ."

" 'Methinks she doth protest too much,' " Liz quoted mildly.

"Liz—"

"I love you, Morgan."

On a frustrated sigh, Morgan lifted her drink again. "Damn it, Liz," she murmured.

"Come on, let me have my fun," she coaxed, giving Morgan a friendly pat on the cheek. "As you said yourself, it's all up to fate anyway."

"Hoist by my own petard. All right, bring on your Dorians and your Nicks and your Lysanders."

"Lysander?"

"It's a good name for a goatherd."

With a chuckle, Liz flicked her cigarette into the churning water. "Just wait and see if I don't find one."

"Liz . . ." Morgan hesitated for a moment, then asked casually, "do many people use the beach where we swam yesterday?"

"*Hmm?* Oh." She tucked a pale blond strand behind her ear. "Not really. It's used by us and the Gregoras villa for the most part. I'd have to ask Alex who owns it; I've never given it any thought. The bay's secluded and only easily accessible by the beach steps that run between the properties. Oh, yes, there's a cottage Nick owns which he rents out occasionally," she remembered. "It's occupied now by an American. Stevens . . . no," she corrected herself. "Stevenson. Andrew Stevenson, a poet or a painter or something. I haven't met him yet." She gave Morgan a frank stare. "Why? Did you plan for an all-over tan?"

"Just curious." Morgan rearranged her thoughts. If she was going to file it and forget it, she had to stop letting the incident play back in her mind. "I'd love to get a close look at that place." She gestured toward the gray villa. "I think the architect must have been just a little mad. It's fabulous."

"Use some charm on Nick and get yourself an invitation," Liz suggested.

"I might just do that." Morgan studied the villa consideringly. She wondered if Nick Gregoras was the man whose footsteps she had heard when she had been held in the bushes. "Yes, I might just."

* * *

That evening, Morgan left the balcony doors wide. She wanted the warmth and scents of the night. The house was quiet but for the single stroke of a clock that signaled the hour. For the second night in a row she was wide awake. Did people really sleep on vacations? she wondered. What a waste of time.

She sat at the small rosewood desk in her room, writing a letter. From somewhere between the house and the sea, an owl cried out twice. She paused to listen, hoping it would call again, but there was only silence. How could she describe how it felt to see Mount Olympus rising from the sea? Was it possible to describe the timelessness, the strength, the almost frightening beauty?

She shrugged, and did what she could to explain the sensation to her father on paper. He'd understand, she mused as she folded the stationery. Who understood better her sometimes whimsical streaks of fancy than the man she'd inherited them from? And, she thought with a lurking smile, he'd get a good chuckle at Liz's determination to marry her off and keep her in Greece.

She rose, stretched once, then turned and collided with a hard chest. The hand that covered her mouth used more gentleness this time, and the jet eyes laughed into hers. Her heart rose, then fell like an elevator with its cable clipped.

"*Kalespera*, Aphrodite. Your word that you won't scream, and you have your freedom."

Instinctively she tried to jerk away, but he held her still without effort, only lifting an ironic brow. He was a man who knew whose word to accept and whose word to doubt.

Morgan struggled for another moment, then finding herself outmatched, reluctantly nodded. He released her immediately.

She drew in the breath to shout, then let it out in a frustrated huff. A promise was a promise, even if it was to a devil. "How did you get in here?" she demanded.

"The vines to your balcony are sturdy."

"You climbed?" Her incredulity was laced with helpless admiration. The walls were sheer, the height was dizzying. "You must be mad."

"That's a possibility," he said with a careless smile.

He seemed none the worse for wear after the climb. His hair was disheveled, but then she'd never seen it otherwise. There was a shadow of beard on his chin. His eyes held no strain or fatigue, but rather a light of adventure that drew her no matter how hard she tried to resist. In the lamplight she could see him more clearly than she had the night before. His features weren't as harsh as she had thought and his mouth wasn't grim. It was really quite beautiful, she realized with a flood of annoyance.

"What do you want?"

He smiled again, letting his gaze roam down her leisurely with an insolence she knew wasn't contrived but inherent. She wore only a brief cinnamon-colored teddy that dipped low at the breast and rose high at the thighs. Morgan noted the look, and that he stood squarely between her and the closet where she had left her robe. Rather than acknowledge the disadvantage, she tilted her chin.

"How did you know where to find me?"

"It's my business to find things out," he answered. Silently, he approved more than her form, but her courage as well. "Morgan James," he began. "Visiting friend of Elizabeth Theoharis. American, living in New York. Unmarried. Employed at the U.N. as interpreter. You speak Greek, English, French, Italian, and Russian."

She tried not to let her mouth fall open at his careless rundown on her life. "That's a very tidy summary," she said tightly.

"Thank you. I try to be succinct."

"What does any of that have to do with you?"

"That's yet to be decided." He studied her, thinking again. It might be that he could employ her talents and position for his own uses. The package was good, very good. And so, more important at the moment, was the mind.

"You're enjoying your stay on Lesbos?"

Morgan stared at him, then slowly shook her head. No, he wasn't a ruffian or a rapist. That much she was sure of. If he were a thief, which she still reserved judgment on, he was no ordinary one. He spoke too well, moved too well.

What he had was a certain amount of odd charm, a flair that was hard to resist, and an amazing amount of arrogance. Under different circumstances, she might even have liked him.

"You have incredible gall," she decided.

"You continue to flatter me."

"All right." Tight-lipped, Morgan strode over to the open balcony doors and gestured meaningfully. "I gave you my word I wouldn't scream, and I didn't. But I have no intention of standing here making idle conversation with a lunatic. Out!"

With his lips still curved in a smile, he sat on the edge of the bed and studied her. "I admire a woman of her word." He stretched out jean-clad legs and crossed his feet. "I find a great deal to admire about you, Morgan. Last night you showed good sense and courage—rare traits to find together."

"Forgive me if I'm not overwhelmed."

He caught the sarcasm, but more important, noted the change in her eyes. She wasn't as angry as she tried to be. "I did apologize," he reminded her and smiled.

Her breath came out in a long-suffering sigh. She could detest him for making her want to laugh when she should be furious. Just who the devil was he? He wasn't the mad rapist she had first thought—he wasn't a common thief. So just what was he? Morgan stopped herself before she asked—she was better off in ignorance.

"It didn't seem like much of an apology to me."

"If I make a more . . . honest attempt," he began with a bland sincerity that made her lips twitch, "would you accept?"

Firmly, she banked down on the urge to return his smile. "If I accept it, will you go away?"

"But I find your company so pleasant."

An irrepressible light of humor flickered in her eyes. "The hell you do."

"Aphrodite, you wound me."

"I'd like to draw and quarter you. Are you going to go away?"

"Soon." Smiling, he rose again. What was that scent that drifted from her? he wondered. It was not quite sweet, not quite tame. Jasmine—wild jasmine. It suited her. He moved to the dresser to toy with her hand mirror. "You'll meet Dorian Zoulas and Iona Theoharis tomorrow," he said casually. This time Morgan's mouth did drop. "There's little on the island I'm not aware of," he said mildly.

"Apparently," she agreed.

Now he noted a hint of curiosity in her tone. It was what he had hoped for. "Perhaps, another time, you'll give me your impression of them."

Morgan shook her head more from bafflement than offense. "I have no intention of there being another time, or of gossiping with you. I hardly see why—"

"Why not?" he countered.

"I don't *know* you," she said in frustration. "I don't know this Dorian or Iona either. And I don't understand how you could possibly—"

"True," he agreed with a slight nod. "How well do you know Alex?"

Morgan ran a hand through her hair. Here I am, wearing little more than my dignity, exchanging small talk with a maniac who climbed in the third-story window. "Look, I'm not discussing Alex with you. I'm not discussing anyone or anything with you. Go away."

"We'll leave that for later too, then," he said mildly as he crossed back to her. "I have something for you." He reached into his pocket, then opened his hand and dangled a small silver medal by its chain.

"Oh, you did have it!" Morgan grabbed, only to have him whip it out of her reach. His eyes hardened with fury.

"I told you once, I'm no thief." The change in his voice and face had been swift and potent. Involuntarily, she took a step away. His mouth tightened at the movement before he went on in a more controlled tone. "I went back and found it in the grove. The chain had to be repaired, I'm afraid."

With his eyes on hers, he held it out again. Taking it, Morgan began to fasten it around her neck. "You're a very considerate assailant."

"Do you think I enjoyed hurting you?"

Her hands froze at the nape of her neck. There was no teasing banter in his tone now, no insolent light of amusement in his eyes. This was the man she recognized from the shadows. Waves of temper came from him, hardening his voice, burning in his jet eyes. With her hands still lifted, Morgan stared at him.

"Do you think I enjoyed frightening you into fainting, having you think I would murder you? Do you think it gives me pleasure to see there are bruises on you and know that I put them there?" He whirled away, stalking the room. "I'm not a man who makes a habit of misusing women."

"I wouldn't know about that," she said steadily.

He stopped, and his eyes came back to hers. Damn, she was cool, he thought. And beautiful. Beautiful enough to be a distraction when he couldn't afford one.

"I don't know who you are or what you're mixed up in," she continued. Her fingers trembled a bit as she finished fastening the chain, but her voice was calm and unhurried. "Frankly, I don't care as long as you leave me alone. Under different circumstances, I'd thank you for the return of my property, but I don't feel it applies in this case. You can leave the same way you came in."

He had to bank down on an urge to throttle her. It wasn't often he was in the position of having a half-naked woman order him from her bedroom three times in one evening. He might have found it amusing if he hadn't been fighting an overwhelming flood of pure and simple desire.

The hell with fighting it, he thought. A woman who kept her chin lifted in challenge deserved to be taken up on it.

"Courage becomes you, Morgan," he said coolly. "We might do very well together." Reaching out, he fingered the medal at her throat and frowned at it. With a silent oath, he tightened his grip on the chain and brought his eyes back to hers.

There was no fear in those clear blue pools now, but a light, maddening disdain. A woman like this, he thought, could make a man mad, make him suffer and ache. And by God, a woman like this would be worth it.

"I told you to go," she said icily, ignoring the sudden quick thud of her pulse. It wasn't fear—Morgan told herself she was through with fear. But neither was it the anger she falsely named it.

"And so I will," he murmured and let the chain drop. "In the meantime, since you don't offer, I take."

Once again she found herself in his arms. It wasn't the teasing, seductive kiss of the night before. Now he devoured her. No one had kissed her like this before—as if he knew every secret she hoarded. He would know, somehow, where she needed to be touched.

The hot, insistent flow of desire that ran through her left her too stunned to struggle, too hungry to reason. How could she want him? her mind demanded. How could she want a man like this to touch her? But her mouth was moving under his, she couldn't deny it. Her tongue met his. Her hands gripped his shoulders, but didn't push him away.

"There's honey on your lips, Morgan," he murmured. "Enough to drive a man mad for another taste."

He took his hand on a slow journey down her back, pressing silk against her skin before he came to the hem. His fingers were strong, callused, and as clever as a musician's. Without knowing, without caring what she did, Morgan framed his face with her hands for a moment before they dove into his hair. The muttered Greek she heard from him wasn't a love word but an oath as he dragged her closer.

How well she knew that body now. Long and lean and wiry with muscle. She could smell the sea on it, almost taste it beneath that hot demand as his mouth continued to savage hers.

The kiss grew deeper, until she moaned, half in fear of the unexplored, half in delight of the exploration. She'd forgotten who she was, who he was. There was only pleasure, a dark, heavy pleasure. Through her dazed senses she felt a struggle—a storm, a fury. Then he drew her away to study her face.

He wasn't pleased that his heartbeat was unsteady. Or that the thoughts whirling in his head were clouded with passion. This was no time for complications. And this was no woman to take risks with. With an effort, he slid his hands gently down her arms. "More satisfying than a thank-you," he said lightly, then glanced with a grin toward the bed. "Are you going to ask me to stay?"

Morgan pulled herself back with a jolt. He must have hypnotized her, she decided. There was no other rational explanation. "Some other time, perhaps," she managed, as carelessly as he.

Amusement lightened his features. Capturing her hand, he kissed it formally. "I'll look forward to it, Aphrodite."

He moved to the balcony, throwing her a quick grin before he started his descent. Unable to prevent herself, Morgan ran over to watch him climb down.

He moved like a cat, confident, fearless, a shadow clinging to the stark white walls. Her heart stayed lodged in her throat as she watched him. He sprang to the ground and melted into the cover of trees without looking back. Whirling, Morgan shut the doors to the balcony. And locked them.

CHAPTER 3

Morgan swirled her glass of local wine but drank little. Though its light, fruity flavor was appealing, she was too preoccupied to appreciate it. The terrace overlooked the gulf with its hard blue water and scattering of tiny islands. Small dots that were boats skimmed the surface, but she took little notice of them. Most of her mind was occupied in trying to sort out the cryptic comments of her late-night visitor. The rest was involved with following the conversation around her.

Dorian Zoulas was all that Liz had said—classically handsome, bronzed, and sophisticated. In the pale cream suit, he was a twentieth-century Adonis. He had intelligence and breeding, tempered with a golden beauty that was essentially masculine. Liz's maneuvers might have caused Morgan to treat him with a polite aloofness if she hadn't seen the flashes of humor in his eyes. Morgan had realized immediately that he not only knew the way his hostess's mind worked, but had decided to play the game. The teasing challenge in his eyes relaxed her. Now she could enjoy a harmless flirtation without embarrassment.

Iona, Alex's cousin, was to Morgan's mind less appealing.

Her dark, sultry looks were both stunning and disturbing. The gloss of beauty and wealth didn't quite polish over an edge that might have come from poor temperament or nerves. There was no humor in her sloe eyes or pouting mouth. Iona was, Morgan mused, like a volcano waiting to erupt. Hot, smoky, and alarming.

The adjectives brought her night visitor back to her mind. They fit him just as neatly as they fit Iona Theoharis, and yet . . . oddly, Morgan found she admired them in the man and found them disturbing in the woman. Double standard? she wondered, then shook her head. No, the energy in Iona seemed destructive. The energy in the man was compelling. Annoyed with herself, Morgan turned from her study of the gulf and pushed aside her disturbing thoughts.

She gave Dorian her full attention. "You must find it very peaceful here after Athens."

He turned in his chair to face her. With only a smile, he intimated that there was no woman but she on the terrace—a trick Morgan found pleasant. "The island's a marvelous place . . . tranquil. But I thrive on chaos. As you live in New York, I'm sure you understand."

"Yes, but at the moment, tranquility is very appealing." Leaning against the rail, she let the sun play warm on her back. "I've been nothing but lazy so far. I haven't even whipped up the energy to explore."

"There's quite a bit of local color, if that's what you have in mind." Dorian slipped a thin gold case from his pocket, and opening it, offered Morgan a cigarette. At the shake of her head, he lit one for himself, then leaned back in a manner that was both relaxed and alert. "Caves and inlets, olive groves, a few small farms and flocks," he continued. "The village is very quaint and unspoiled."

"Exactly what I want." Morgan nodded and sipped her

drink. "But I'm going to take it very slow. I'll collect shells and find a farmer who'll let me milk his goat."

"Terrifying aspirations," Dorian commented with a quick smile.

"Liz will tell you, I've always been intrepid."

"I'd be happy to help you with your shells." He continued to smile as his eyes skimmed her face with an approval she couldn't have missed. "But as to the goat . . ."

"I'm surprised you're content with so little entertainment." Iona's husky voice broke into the exchange.

Morgan shifted her gaze to her and found it took more of an effort to smile. "The island itself is entertainment enough for me. Remember, I'm a tourist. I've always thought vacations where you rush from one activity to the next aren't vacations at all."

"Morgan's been lazy for two full days," Liz put in with a grin. "A new record."

Morgan cast her a look, thinking of her nighttime activities. "I'm shooting for two weeks of peaceful sloth," Morgan murmured. *Starting today*, she added silently.

"Lesbos is the perfect spot for idleness." Dorian blew out a slow, fragrant stream of smoke. "Rustic, quiet."

"But perhaps this bit of island isn't as quiet as it appears." Iona ran a manicured nail around the rim of her glass.

Morgan saw Dorian's brows lift as if in puzzlement while Alex's drew together in disapproval.

"We'll do our best to keep it quiet during Morgan's visit," Liz said smoothly. "She rarely stays still for long, and since she's determined to this time, we'll see that she has a nice, uneventful vacation."

Morgan made some sound of agreement and managed not to choke over her drink. Uneventful! If Liz only knew.

"More wine, Morgan?" Dorian rose, bringing the bottle to her.

Iona began to tap her fingers on the arm of her wrought iron chair. "I suppose there are people who find boredom appealing."

"Relaxation," Alex said with a slight edge in his voice, "comes in many forms."

"And of course," Liz went on, skimming her hand lightly over the back of her husband's, "Morgan's job is very demanding. All those foreign dignitaries and protocol and politics."

Dorian sent Morgan an appreciative smile as he poured more wine into her glass. "I'm sure someone with Morgan's talents would have many fascinating stories to tell."

Morgan cocked a brow. It had been a long time since she had been given a purely admiring male smile—undemanding, warm without being appraising. She could learn to enjoy it. "I might have a few," she returned.

*   *   *

The sun was sinking into the sea. The rosy light streamed through the open balcony doors and washed the room. Red sky at night, Morgan mused. Wasn't that supposed to mean clear sailing? She decided to take it as an omen.

Her first two days on Lesbos had been a far cry from the uneventful vacation Liz had boasted of, but that was behind her now. With luck, and a little care, she wouldn't run into that attractive lunatic again.

Morgan caught a glimpse of her own smile in the mirror and hastily rearranged her expression. Perhaps when she got back to New York, she'd see a psychiatrist. When you started to find lunatics appealing, you were fast becoming one yourself. Forget it, she ordered herself firmly as she went to the closet. There were more important things to think about— like what she was going to wear to dinner.

After a quick debate, Morgan chose a drifting white dress—thin layers of crepe de chine, full-sleeved, full-skirted. Dorian had inspired her to flaunt her femininity a bit. Jack, she recalled, had preferred the tailored look. He had often offered a stern and unsolicited opinion on her wardrobe, finding her taste both inconsistent and flighty. There might be a multicolored flowing skirt hanging next to a prim business suit. He'd never understood that both had suited who she was. Just another basic difference, Morgan mused as she hooked the line of tiny pearl buttons.

Tonight she was going to have fun. It had been a long while since she'd flirted with a man. Her thoughts swung back to a dark man with tousled hair and a shadowed chin. Hold on, Morgan, she warned herself. *That* was hardly in the same league as a flirtation. Moving over, she closed the balcony doors and gave a satisfied nod as she heard the click of the lock. And that, she decided, takes care of that.

*   *   *

Liz glided around the salon. It pleased her that Morgan hadn't come down yet. Now she could make an entrance. For all her blond fragility, Liz was a determined woman. Loyalty was her strongest trait; where she loved, it was unbendable. She wanted Morgan to be happy. Her own marriage had given her nothing but happiness. Morgan would have the same if Liz had any say in it.

With a satisfied smile, she glanced around the salon. The light was low and flattering. The scent of night blossoms drifting in through the open windows was the perfect touch. The wines she'd ordered for dinner would add the final prop for romance. Now, if Morgan would cooperate . . .

"Nick, I'm so glad you could join us." Liz went to him,

holding out both hands. "It's so nice that we're all on the island at the same time for a change."

"It's always a pleasure to see you, Liz," he returned with a warm, charming smile. "And a relief to be out of the crowds in Athens for a few weeks." He gave her hands a light squeeze, then lifted one to his lips. His dark eyes skimmed her face. "I swear, you're lovelier every time I see you."

With a laugh, Liz tucked her arm through his. "We'll have to invite you to dinner more often. Did I ever thank you properly for that marvelous Indian chest you found me?" Smiling, she guided him toward the bar. "I adore it."

"Yes, you did." He gave her hand a quick pat. "I'm glad I was able to find what you had in mind."

"You never fail to find the perfect piece. I'm afraid Alex wouldn't know an Indian chest from a Hepplewhite."

Nick laughed. "We all have our talents, I suppose."

"But your work must be fascinating." Liz glanced up at him with her wide-eyed smile as she began to fix him a drink. "All those treasures and all the interesting places you travel to."

"There are times it's more exciting just to be home."

She shot him a look. "You make that hard to believe, since you're so seldom here. Where was it last month? Venice?"

"A beautiful city," he said smoothly.

"I'd love to see it. If I could drag Alex away from his ships . . ." Liz's eyes focused across the room. "Oh dear, it looks like Iona is annoying Alex again." On a long breath, she lifted her eyes to Nick's. Seeing the quick understanding, she gave a rueful smile. "I'm going to have to play diplomat."

"You do it charmingly, Liz. Alex is a lucky man."

"Remind him of that from time to time," she suggested.

"I'd hate for him to take me for granted. Oh, here comes Morgan. She'll keep you entertained while I do my duty."

Following Liz's gaze, Nick watched as Morgan entered the room. "I'm sure she will," was his murmured reply. He liked the dress she wore, the floating white that was at once alluring and innocent. She'd left her hair loose so that it fell over her shoulders almost as if it had come off a pillow. Quite beautiful, he thought as he felt the stir. He'd always had a weakness for beauty.

"Morgan." Before Morgan could do any more than smile her hello at Liz, Liz took her arm. "You'll keep Nick happy for a moment; I have a job to do. Morgan James, Nicholas Gregoras." With the quick introduction, Liz was halfway across the room.

Morgan stared in stunned silence. Nick lifted her limp hand to his lips. "You," she managed in a choked whisper.

"Aphrodite, you're exquisite. Even fully dressed."

With his lips lingering over her knuckles, he met her eyes. His were dark and pleased. Regaining her senses, Morgan tried to wrench her hand free. Without changing expression, Nick tightened his grip and held her still.

"Careful, Morgan," he said mildly. "Liz and her guests will wonder at your behavior. And explanations would"—he grinned, exactly as she remembered—"cause them to wonder about your mental health."

"Let go of my hand," she said quietly and smiled with her lips only. "Or I swear, I'll deck you."

"You're magnificent." Making a small bow, he released her. "Did you know your eyes literally throw darts when you're annoyed?"

"Then I've the pleasure of knowing you're riddled with tiny holes," she returned. "Let me know when one hits the heart, *Mr.* Gregoras."

"Nick, please," he said in a polished tone. "We could

hardly start formalities now after all we've . . . been through together."

Morgan gave him a brilliant smile. "Very well, Nick, you odious swine. What a pity this isn't the proper time to go into how detestable you are."

He inclined his head. "We'll arrange for a more appropriate opportunity. Soon," he added with the faintest hint of steel. "Now, let me get you a drink."

Liz breezed up, pleased with the smiles she had seen exchanged. "You two seem to be getting along like old friends."

"I was just telling Mr. Gregoras how enchanting his home looks from the sea." Morgan sent him a quick but lethal glance.

"Yes, Morgan was fascinated by it," Liz told him. "She's always preferred things that didn't quite fit a mold, if you know what I mean."

"Exactly." Nick let his eyes sweep over Morgan's face. A man could get lost in those eyes, he thought, if he wasn't careful. Very careful. "Miss James has agreed to a personal tour tomorrow afternoon." He smiled, watching her expression go from astonishment to fury before she controlled it.

"Marvelous!" Pleased, Liz beamed at both of them. "Nick has so many treasures from all over the world. His house is just like Aladdin's cave."

Smiling, Morgan thought of three particularly gruesome wishes, all involving her intended host. "I can't wait to see it."

* * *

Through dinner, Morgan watched, confused, then intrigued by Nick's manner. This was not the man she knew. This man was smooth, polished. Gone was the intensity, the ruthlessness, replaced by an easy warmth and charm.

Nicholas Gregoras, olive oil, import-export. Yes, she could see the touches of wealth and success—and the authority she'd understood from the first. But command sat differently on him now, with none of the undertones of violence.

He could sit at the elegant table, laughing with Liz and Alex over some island story with the gleam of cut crystal in his hand. The smoky-gray suit was perfectly tailored and fit him with the same ease as the dark sweatshirt and jeans she'd first seen him in. His arrogance had a more sophisticated tone now. All the rough edges were smoothed.

He seemed relaxed, at home—with none of that vital, dangerous energy. How could this be the same man who had flourished a knife, or climbed the sheer wall to her balcony?

Nick handed her a glass of wine and she frowned. But he was the same man, she reminded herself. And just what game was he playing? Lifting her eyes, Morgan met his. Her fingers tightened on the stem of the glass. The look was brief and quickly veiled, but she saw the inner man. The force was vital. If he was playing games, she thought, sipping her wine to calm suddenly tight nerves, it wasn't a pleasant one. And she wanted no part of it—or of him.

Turning to Dorian, Morgan left Nick to Iona. Intelligent, witty, and with no frustrating mysteries, Dorian was a more comfortable dinner companion. Morgan fell into the easy exchange and tried to relax.

"Tell me, Morgan, don't you find the words of so many languages a bit crowded in the mind?"

She toyed with her moussaka, finding her stomach too jittery to accept the rich sauce. Damn the man for interfering even with her appetite. "I do my thinking in one at a time," she countered.

"You take it too lightly," Dorian insisted. "It's an accomplishment to be proud of. Even a power."

"A power?" Her brows drew together for a moment, then cleared as she smiled. "I suppose it is, though I'd never really thought about it. It just seemed too limiting to only be able to communicate and think in one language, then once I got started, I couldn't seem to stop."

"Having the language, you'd be at home in many countries."

"Yes, I guess that's why I feel so—well, easy here."

"Alex tells me he's trying to entice you into his company." With a smile, Dorian toasted her. "I've drafted myself as promoter. Working with you would add to the company benefits."

Iona's rich laughter floated across the table. "Oh, Nicky, you say the most ridiculous things."

Nicky, Morgan thought with a sniff. I'll be ill any minute. "I think I might enjoy your campaign," Morgan told Dorian with her best smile.

"Take me out on your boat tomorrow, Nicky. I simply must have some fun."

"I'm sorry, Iona, not tomorrow. Perhaps later in the week." Nick softened the refusal with the trace of a finger down her hand.

Iona's mouth formed a pout. "I might die of boredom by later in the week."

Morgan heard Dorian give a quiet sigh. Glancing over, she noted the quick look of exasperation he sent Iona. "Iona tells me she ran into Maria Popagos in Athens last week." The look of exasperation was gone, and his voice was gentle. "She has what—four children now, Iona?"

They treat her like a child, Morgan thought with distaste. And she behaves like one—a spoiled, willful, not quite healthy child.

Through the rest of the meal, and during coffee in the salon, Morgan watched Iona's moods go from sullen to fran-
tic. Apparently used to it, or too good mannered to notice,
Dorian ignored the fluctuations. And though she hated to give
him the credit for it, so did Nick. But Morgan noted, with a
flutter of sympathy, that Alex grew more distracted as the
evening wore on. He spoke to his cousin in undertones as she
added more brandy to her glass. Her response was a dramatic
toss of her head before she swallowed the liquor and turned
her back on him.

When Nick rose to leave, Iona insisted on walking with
him to his car. She cast a look of triumph over her shoulder
as they left the salon arm-in-arm. Now who, Morgan mused,
was that aimed at? Shrugging, she turned back to Dorian and
let the evening wind down naturally. There would be time
enough to think things through when she was alone in her
room again.

* * *

Morgan floated with the dream. The wine had brought
sleep quickly. Though she had left the balcony doors
securely locked, the night breeze drifted through the windows. She sighed, and shifted with its gentle caress on her
skin. It was a soft stroking, like a butterfly's wing. It teased
across her lips, then came back to warm them. She stirred
with pleasure. Her body was pliant, receptive. As the phantom kiss increased in pressure, she parted her lips. She drew
the dream lover closer.

Excitement was sleepy. The tastes that seeped into her were
as sweet and as potent as the wine that still misted her brain.
With a sigh of lazy, languid pleasure, she floated with it. In
the dream, her arms wrapped around the faceless lover—the
pirate, the phantom. He whispered her name and deepened

the kiss as his hands drew down the sheet that separated them. Rough fingers, familiar fingers, traced over her skin. A body, too hard, too muscular for a dream, pressed against hers. The lazy images became more tangible, and the phantom took on form. Dark hair, dark eyes, and a mouth that was grimly beautiful and oh, so clever.

Warmth became heat. With a moan, she let passion take her. The stroking along her body became more insistent at her response. Her mouth grew hungry, demanding. Then she heard the breathy whisper of a Greek endearment against her ear.

Suddenly, the filmy curtain of sleep lifted. The weight on her body was real, achingly real—and achingly familiar. Morgan began a confused struggle.

"The goddess awakes. More's the pity."

She saw him in the shaft of moonlight. Her body was alive with needs, her mind baffled with the knowledge that he had induced them. "What are you doing!" she demanded, and found her breathing was quick and ragged. His mouth had been on hers, she knew. She could still taste him. And his hands . . . "This is the limit! If you think for one minute I'm going to sit still for you crawling into my bed while I'm sleeping—"

"You were very agreeable a moment ago."

"Oh! What a despicable thing to do."

"You're very responsive," Nick murmured, and traced her ear with his fingertip. Beneath his hand he could feel the thunder of her heartbeat. He knew, though he fought to slow it, that his own beat as quickly. "It seemed to please you to be touched. It pleased me to touch you."

His voice had lowered again, as she knew it could—dark, seductive. The muscles in her thighs loosened. "Get off of me," she ordered in quick defense.

"Sweet Morgan." He nipped her bottom lip—felt her

tremble, felt a swift rush of power. It would be so easy to persuade her . . . and so risky. With an effort, he gave her a friendly smile. "You only postpone the inevitable."

She kept her eyes level as she tried to steady her breathing. Something told her that if all else he had said had been lies, his last statement was all too true. "I didn't promise not to scream this time."

He lifted a brow as though the possibility intrigued him. "It might be interesting to explain this . . . situation to Alex and Liz. I could claim I was overcome with your beauty. It has a ring of truth. But you won't scream in any case."

"Just what makes you so sure?"

"You'd have given me away—or tried to by now—if you were going to." Nick rolled aside.

Sitting up, Morgan pushed at her hair. Did he always have to be right? she wondered grimly. "What do you want now? And how the hell did you get in this time? I locked . . ." Her voice trailed off as she saw the balcony doors were wide open.

"Did you think a lock would keep me out?" With a laugh, Nick ran a finger down her nose. "You have a lot to learn."

"Now, you listen to me—"

"No, save the recriminations for later. They're understood in any case." Absently, he rubbed a lock of her hair between his thumb and forefinger. "I came back to make certain you didn't develop a convenient headache that would keep you from coming to the house tomorrow. There are one or two things I want to discuss with you."

"I've got a crate full of things to discuss with you," Morgan hissed furiously. "Just what were you doing that night on the beach? And who—"

"Later, Aphrodite. I'm distracted at the moment. That scent you wear, for instance. It's very . . ." He lifted his eyes to hers, "alluring."

"Stop it." She didn't trust him when his voice dropped to that tone. She didn't trust him at all, she reminded herself and gave him a level look. "What's the purpose behind that ridiculous game you were playing tonight?"

"Game?" His eyes widened effectively. "Morgan, my love, I don't know what you're talking about. I was quite natural."

"Natural be damned."

"No need to swear at me," he said mildly.

"There's every need," she countered. How could he manage to be charming under such ridiculous circumstances? "You were the perfect guest this evening," Morgan went on, knocking his hand aside as he began to toy with the thin strap of her chemise. "Charming—"

"Thank you."

"And false," she added, narrowing her eyes.

"Not false," Nick disagreed. "Simply suitable, considering the occasion."

"I suppose it would have looked a bit odd if you'd pulled a knife out of your pocket."

His fingers tightened briefly, then relaxed. She wasn't going to let him forget that—and he wasn't having an easy time blanking out that moment she had gone limp with terror beneath him. "Few people have seen me other than I was tonight," he murmured, and began to give the texture of her hair his attention. "Perhaps it's your misfortune to count yourself among them."

"I don't want to see you *any* way, from now on."

Humor touched his eyes again as they shifted to hers. "Liar. I'll pick you up tomorrow at one."

Morgan tossed out a phrase commonly heard in the less elite portions of Italy. Nick responded with a pleased laugh.

"*Agapetike*, I should warn you, in my business I've had occasion to visit some Italian gutters."

"Good, then you won't need a translation."

"Just be ready." He let his gaze sweep down her, then up again. "You might find it easier to deal with me in the daylight—and when you're more adequately attired."

"I have no intention of dealing with you at all," Morgan began in a furious undertone. "Or of continuing this ridiculous charade by going with you tomorrow."

"Oh, I think you will." Nick's smile was confident and infuriating. "You'd find yourself having a difficult time explaining to Liz why you won't come when you've already expressed an interest in my home. Tell me, what was it that appealed to you about it?"

"The insanity of the architecture."

He laughed again and took her hand. "More compliments. I adore you, Aphrodite. Come, kiss me good night."

Morgan drew back and scowled. "I certainly will not."

"You certainly will." In a swift movement he had her pinned under him again. When she cursed him, he laughed and the insolence was back. "Witch," he murmured. "What mortal can resist one?"

His mouth came down quickly, lingering until she had stopped squirming beneath him. Gradually, the force went out of the kiss, but not the power. It seeped into her, so that she couldn't be sure if it was hers or his. Then it was only passion—clean and hot and senseless. On a moan, Morgan accepted it, and him.

Feeling the change in her, Nick relaxed a moment and simply let himself enjoy.

She had a taste that stayed with him long after he left her. Each time he touched her he knew, eventually, he would have to have it all. But not now. Now there was too much at stake. She was a risk, and he had already taken too many chances with her. But that taste . . .

He gave himself over to the kiss knowing the danger of

letting himself become vulnerable, even for a moment, by losing himself in her. If she hadn't been on the beach that night. If he hadn't had to reveal himself to her. Would things have been different than they were now? he wondered as desire began to claw at him. Would he have been able to coax her into his arms, into his bed, with a bit of flair and a few clever words? If they had met for the first time tonight, would he have wanted her this badly, this quickly?

Her hands were in his hair. He found his mouth had roamed to her throat. Her scent seemed to concentrate there, and the taste was wild and dangerous. He lived with danger and enjoyed it—lived by his wits and won. But this woman, this feeling she stirred in him, was a risk he could calculate. Yet it was done. There was no changing the course he had to take. And no changing the fact that she was involved.

He wanted to touch her, to tear off that swatch of silk she wore and feel her skin warm under his hand. He dared not. He was a man who knew his own limitations, his own weaknesses. Nick didn't appreciate the fact that Morgan James had become a weakness at a time when he could least afford one.

Murmuring his name, Morgan slid her hands beneath the loose sweatshirt, to run them over the range of muscle. Nick felt need shoot like a spear, white-tipped, to the pit of his stomach. Using every ounce of will, he banked down on it until it was a dull ache he could control. He lifted his head and waited for those pale, clouded blue eyes to open. Something dug into his palm, and he saw that he had gripped her medal in his hand without realizing it. Nick had to quell the urge to swear, then give himself a moment until he knew he could speak lightly. "Sleep well, Aphrodite," he told her with a grin. "Until tomorrow."

"You—" She broke off, struggling for the breath and the wit to hurl abuse at him.

"Tomorrow," Nick repeated as he brought her hand to his lips.

Morgan watched him stride to the balcony, then lower himself out of sight. Lying perfectly still, she stared at the empty space and wondered what she had gotten herself into.

CHAPTER 4

The house was cool and quiet in the mid-morning hush. Gratefully, Morgan accepted Liz's order to enjoy the beach. She wanted to avoid Iona's company, and though she hated to admit it, she didn't think she could handle Liz's carefree chatter about the dinner party. Liz would have expected her to make some witty observations about Nick that Morgan just didn't feel up to. Relieved that Dorian had business with Alex, and wouldn't feel obliged to keep her company, she set out alone.

Morgan wanted the solitude—she did her best thinking when she was alone. In the past few days she had accumulated quite a bit to think about. Now she decided to work it through one step at a time.

What had Nicholas Gregoras been doing that night on the beach? He'd had the scent of the sea on him, so it followed that he had been out on the water. She remembered the sound of a motor. She'd assumed it belonged to a fisherman but Nick was no fisherman. He'd been desperate not to be seen by someone . . . desperate enough to have been carrying a knife. She could still see the look on his face as she had lain beneath him in the shadows of the cypress. He'd been prepared to use the knife.

Somehow the knowledge that this was true disturbed her more now than it had when he'd been a stranger. Kicking bad-temperedly at a stone, she started down the beach steps.

And who had been with him? Morgan fretted. Someone had followed his orders without any question. Who had used the beach steps while Nick had held her prisoner in the shadows? Alex? The man who rented Nick's cottage? Frustrated, Morgan slipped out of her shoes and began to cross the warm sand. Why would Nick be ready to kill either one of them rather than be discovered by them? By anyone, she corrected. It could have been a servant of one of the villas, a villager trespassing.

One question at a time, Morgan cautioned herself as she kicked idly at the sand. First, was it logical to assume that the footsteps she had heard were from someone who had also come from the sea? Morgan thought it was. And second, she decided that the person must have been headed to one of the villas or a nearby cottage. Why else would they have used that particular strip of beach? Logical, she concluded, walking aimlessly. So why was Nick so violently determined to go unseen?

Smuggling. It was so obvious. So logical. But she had continued to push the words aside. She didn't want to think of him involved in such a dirty business. Somewhere, beneath the anger and resentment she felt for him, Morgan had experienced a totally different sensation. There was something about him—something she couldn't really pinpoint in words. Strength, perhaps. He was the kind of man you could depend on when no one else could—or would—help. She wanted to trust him. There was no logic to it, it simply was.

But was he a smuggler? Had he thought she'd seen something incriminating? Did the footsteps she'd heard belong to a patrol? Another smuggler? A rival? If he'd believed her to be a threat, why hadn't he simply used the knife on her? If he were a cold-blooded killer . . . no. Morgan shook her head at the description. While she could almost accept that Nick would kill, she couldn't agree with the adjective. And that led to hundreds of other problems.

Questions and answers sped through her mind. Stubborn questions, disturbing answers. Morgan shut her eyes on them. I'm going to get some straight answers from him this afternoon, she promised herself. It was his fault she was involved. Morgan dropped to the sand and brought her knees to her chest. She had been minding her own business when he had literally dragged her into it. All she had wanted was a nice, quiet vacation.

"Men!"

"I refuse to take that personally."

Morgan spun her head around and found herself staring into a wide, friendly smile.

"Hello. You seem to be angry with my entire gender." He rose from a rock and walked to her. He was tall and very slender, with dark gold curls appealingly disarrayed around a tanned face that held both youth and strength. "But I think it's worth the risk. I'm Andrew Stevenson." Still smiling, he dropped to the sand beside her.

"Oh." Recovering, Morgan returned the smile. "The poet or the painter? Liz wasn't sure."

"Poet," he said with a grimace. "Or so I tell myself."

Glancing down, she saw the pad he held. It was dog-eared and covered with a fine, looping scribble. "I've interrupted your work, I'm sorry."

"On the contrary, you've given me a shot of inspiration. You have a remarkable face."

"I think," Morgan considered, "that's a compliment."

"Dear lady, yours is a face a poet dreams of." He let his eyes roam it for a moment. "Do you have a name, or are you going to vanish in a mist and leave me bewitched?"

"Morgan." The fussy compliment, delivered with bland sincerity made her laugh. "Morgan James, and are you a good poet, Andrew Stevenson?"

"I can't say no." Andrew continued to study her candidly. "Modesty isn't one of my virtues. You said Liz. I assume that's Mrs. Theoharis. You're staying with them?"

"Yes, for a few weeks." A new thought crossed her mind. "You're renting Nicholas Gregoras's cottage?"

"That's right. Actually, it's a free ride." Though he set down the pad, he began to trace patterns in the sand as if he couldn't keep his hands quite still. "We're cousins." Andrew noted the surprise on her face. His smile deepened. "Not the Greek side. Our mothers are related."

"Oh, so his mother's American." This at least explained his ease with the language.

"A Norling of San Francisco," he stated with a grin for the title. "She remarried after Nick's father died. She's living in France."

"So, you're visiting Lesbos and your cousin at the same time."

"Actually, Nick offered me the retreat when he learned I was working on an epic poem—a bit Homeric, you see." His eyes were blue, darker than hers, and very direct on her face. Morgan could see nothing in the open, ingenuous look to link him with Nick. "I wanted to stay on Lesbos awhile, so it worked out nicely. The home of Sappho. The poetry and legend have always fascinated me."

"Sappho," Morgan repeated, turning her thoughts from Nick. "Oh, yes, the poetess."

"The Tenth Muse. She lived here, in Mitilini." His gaze, suddenly dreamy, swept down the stretch of beach. "I like to think Nick's house is on the cliff where she hurled herself into the sea, desperate for Phaon's love."

"An interesting thought." Morgan looked up to where a portion of a gray stone wall was visible. "And I suppose her spirit floats over the house searching for her love." Somehow, she liked the idea and smiled. "Lord knows, it's the perfect house for a poetic haunting."

"Have you been inside?" Andrew asked her, his tone as dreamy as his eyes now. "It's fantastic."

"No, I'm getting a personal tour this afternoon." Morgan kept her voice light as she swore silently in several languages.

"A personal tour?" Abruptly direct again, Andrew tilted his head, with brows lifted in speculation. "You must have made quite an impression on Nick. But then," he added with a nod, "you would. He sets great store by beauty."

Morgan gave him a noncommital smile. He could hardly know that it wasn't her looks or charm that had secured the invitation. "Do you often write on the beach? I can't keep away from it myself." Morgan hesitated briefly, then plunged. "I came down here a couple of nights ago and swam by moonlight."

There was no shock or anxiety in his eyes at this information. Andrew grinned. "I'm sorry I missed that. You'll find me all over this part of the island. Here, up on the cliffs, in the olive groves. I go where the mood strikes me."

"I'm going to do some exploring myself." She thought wistfully of a carefree hour in the inlets.

"I'm available if you'd like a guide." His gaze skimmed over her face again, warm and friendly. "By now, I know this part of the island as well as a native. If you find you want company, you can usually find me wandering around or in the cottage. It isn't far."

"I'd like that." A gleam of amusement lit her eyes. "You don't happen to keep a goat, do you?"

"Ah—no."

Laughing at his expression, Morgan patted his hand. "Don't try to understand," she advised. "And now I'd better go change for my tour."

Andrew rose with her and captured her hand. "I'll see you again." It was a statement, not a question. Morgan responded to the gentle pressure.

"I'm sure you will; the island's very small."

Andrew smiled as he released her hand. "I'd rather call it kismet." He watched Morgan walk away before he settled back on his rock, facing the sea.

*   *   *

Nicholas Gregoras was very prompt. By five minutes past one, Morgan found herself being shoved out the door by an enthusiastic Liz. "Have fun, darling, and don't hurry back. Nick, Morgan will adore your house; all those winding passages and the terrifying view of the sea. She's very courageous, aren't you, Morgan?"

"I'm practically stalwart," she muttered while Nick grinned.

"Well, run along and have fun." Liz shooed them out the door as if they were two reluctant children being sent to school.

"You should be warned," Morgan stated as she slid into Nick's car, "Liz considers you a suitable candidate for my hand. I think she's getting desperate picturing me as her unborn child's maiden aunt."

"Aphrodite." Nick settled beside her and took her hand. "There isn't a male alive who could picture you as anyone's maiden aunt."

Refusing to be charmed, Morgan removed her hand from his, then studied the view out the side window. "I met your poet in residence this morning on the beach."

"Andrew? He's a nice boy. How did you find him?"

"Not like a boy." Turning back to Nick, Morgan frowned. "He's a very charming man."

Nick lifted a brow fractionally. "Yes, I suppose he is. Somehow, I always think of him as a boy, though there's barely five years between us." He moved his shoulders. "He does have talent. Did you charm him?"

" 'Inspire' was his word," she returned, annoyed.

Nick flashed her a quick grin. "Naturally. One romantic should inspire another."

"I'm not a romantic." The conversation forced her to give him a great deal more of her attention than she had planned. "I'm very practical."

"Morgan, you're an insatiable romantic." Her annoyance apparently amused him, because a smile continued to hover on his mouth. "A woman who combs her hair on a moon-lit beach, wears filmy white, and treasures a valueless memento thrives on romance."

Uncomfortable with the description, Morgan spoke coolly. "I also clip coupons and watch my cholesterol."

"Admirable."

She swallowed what might have been a chuckle. "You, Nicholas Gregoras, are a first-rate bastard."

"Yes. I hate to be second-rate at anything."

Morgan flounced back in her seat, but lost all resentment as the house came into full view. "Oh, Lord," she murmured. "It's wonderful!"

It looked stark and primitive and invulnerable. The second story lashed out over the sea like an outstretched arm—not offering payment, but demanding it. None of the power she had felt out at sea was diminished at close range. The flowering shrubs and vines that trailed and tangled were placed to disguise the care of their planting. The result was an illusion of wild abandon. Sleeping Beauty's castle, she thought, a century after she pricked her finger.

"What a marvelous place." Morgan turned to him as he stopped the car at the entrance. "I've never seen anything like it."

"That's the first time you've smiled at me and meant it." He wasn't smiling now, but looking at her with a trace of annoyance. He hadn't realized just how much he'd wanted to see that spontaneous warmth in her eyes—directed at him. And now that he had, he wasn't certain what to do about it. With a quick mental oath, Nick slid from the car.

Ignoring him, Morgan climbed out and tried to take in the entire structure at once. "You know what it looks like," she said, half to herself. "It looks like Zeus hurled a lightning bolt into the mountain and the house exploded into existence."

"An interesting theory." Nick took her hand and started up the stone steps. "If you'd known my grandfather, you'd realize how close that is to the truth."

Morgan had primed herself to begin hurling questions and demanding explanations as soon as they had arrived. When she stepped into the entrance hall, she forgot everything.

Wide and speckled in aged white, the hall was sporadically slashed with stark colors from wall hangings and primitive paintings. On one wall, long spears were crossed—weapons for killing, certainly, but with an ancient dignity she had to admire. The staircase leading to the upper floors arched in a half circle with a banister of dark, unvarnished wood. The result was one of earthy magnificence. It was far from elegant, but there was a sense of balance and savage charm.

"Nicholas." Turning a full circle, Morgan sighed. "It's really wonderful. I expect a cyclops to come stalking down the stairs. Are there centaurs in the courtyard?"

"I'll take you through, and we'll see what we can do." She was making it difficult for him to stick to his plan. She wasn't supposed to charm him. That wasn't in the script. Still, he kept her hand in his as he led her through the house.

Liz's comparison to Aladdin's cave was completely apt. Room after room abounded with treasures—Venetian glass, Fabergé boxes, African masks, Native American pottery, Ming vases. All were set together in a hodgepodge of cultures. What might have seemed like a museum was instead a glorious clutter of wonders. As the house twisted and turned, revealing surprise after surprise, Morgan became more fascinated. Elegant Waterford crystal was juxtaposed with a deadly-looking seventeenth-century crossbow. She saw exquisite porcelain and a shrunken head from Ecuador.

Yes, the architect was mad, she decided, noting lintels with wolves' heads or grinning elves carved into them. Wonderfully mad. The house was a fairy tale—not the tame children's version, but with all the whispering shadows and hints of gremlins.

A huge curved window on the top floor gave her the sensation of standing suspended on the edge of the cliff. It jutted out, arrogantly, then fell in a sheer drop into the sea. Morgan stared down, equally exhilarated and terrified.

Nick watched her. There was a need to spin her around and seize, to possess while that look of dazzled courage was still on her face. He was a man accustomed to taking what he wanted without a second thought. She was something he wanted.

Morgan turned to him. Her eyes were still alive with the fascination of the sea and hints of excited fear. "Andrew said he hoped this was the cliff where Sappho hurled herself into the sea. I'm ready to believe it."

"Andrew's imaginative."

"So are you," she countered. "You live here."

"Your eyes are like some mythological lake," he murmured. "Translucent and ethereal. I should call you Circe rather than Aphrodite." Abruptly, he gripped her hair in his hand, tugging it until her face was lifted to his. "I swear you're more witch than goddess."

Morgan stared at him. There was no teasing in his eyes this time, no arrogance. What she saw was longing. And the longing, more than passion, seduced her. "I'm only a woman, Nicholas," she heard herself say.

His fingers tightened. His expression darkened. Then even as she watched, his mood seemed to shift. This time, he took her arm rather than her hand. "Come, we'll go down and have a drink."

As they entered the salon, Morgan reasserted her priorities. She had to get answers—she *would* get answers. She couldn't let a few soft words and a pair of dark eyes make her forget why she'd come. Before she could speak, however, a man slipped through the doorway.

He was small, with creased, leather skin. His hair was gray with age, but thick. So were his arms—thick and muscled. He made her think of a small-scaled, very efficient tank. His moustache was a masterpiece. It spread under his nose to drop free along the sides of his mouth, reaching his chin in two flowing arches. He smiled, showing several gaps in lieu of teeth.

"Good afternoon." He spoke in respectful Greek, but his eyes were dancing.

Intrigued, Morgan gave him an unsmiling stare. *"Yiasou."*

"Stephanos, Miss James. Stephanos is my, ah, caretaker." The checkerboard grin widened at the term. "Your servant, my lady." He bowed, but there was nothing deferential in the gesture. "The matter we discussed has been seen to, Mr. Gregoras." Turning to Nick, the old man spoke with exaggerated respect. "You have messages from Athens."

"I'll tend to them later."

"As you wish." The small man melted away. Morgan frowned. There had been something in the exchange that wasn't quite what it should be. Shaking her head, she watched Nick mix drinks. It wasn't Nick's relationship with his servants that she was interested in.

Deciding that plunging headfirst was the most direct route, Morgan leaped. "What were you doing on the beach the other night?"

"I rather thought we'd concluded I was assaulting you." His voice was very mild.

"That was only part of the evening's entertainment." She swallowed and took another dive. "Had you been smuggling?"

To his credit, Nick hesitated only briefly. As his back was to her, Morgan didn't see his expression range from surprise to consideration. A very sharp lady, he mused. Too damn sharp.

"And how did you come by such an astonishing conclusion?" He turned to hand her a delicate glass.

"Don't start that charade with me," Morgan fumed, snatching the glass. "I've seen you stripped." She sat down and aimed a level stare.

Nick's mouth twitched. "What a fascinating way you have of putting things."

"I asked if you were a smuggler."

Nick sat across from her, taking a long study of her face as he ticked off possibilities. "First, tell me why you think I might be."

"You'd been out on the water that night. I could smell the sea on you."

Nick gazed down into the liquid in his glass, then sipped. "It's fanciful, to say the least, that my being out on the water equals smuggling."

Morgan ground her teeth at the cool sarcasm and continued. "If you'd been out on a little fishing trip, you'd hardly have dragged me into the trees waving a knife."

"One might argue," he murmured, "that fishing was precisely my occupation."

"The coast of Turkey is very convenient from this part of the island. Alex told me smuggling was a problem."

"Alex?" Nick repeated. There was a quick, almost imperceptible change in his expression. "What was Alex's attitude toward smuggling?"

Morgan hesitated. The question had broken into her well-thought-out interrogation. "He was . . . resigned, like one accepts the weather."

"I see." Nick swirled his drink as he leaned back. "And did you and Alex discuss the intricacies of the procedure?"

"Of course not!" she snapped, infuriated that he had cleverly turned the interrogation around on her. "Alex would hardly be intimate with such matters. But," she continued, "I think you are."

"Yes, I can see that."

"Well?"

He sent her a mildly amused smile that didn't quite reach his eyes. "Well what?"

"Are you going to deny it?" She wanted him to, Morgan realized with something like a jolt. She very, very badly wanted him to deny it.

Nick considered her for a moment. "If I deny it, you won't believe me. It's easy to see you've already made up your mind." He tilted his head, and now the amusement crept into his eyes. "What will you do if I admit it?"

"I'll turn you over to the police." Morgan took a bold sip of her drink. Nick exploded with laughter.

"Morgan, what a sweet, brave child you are." He leaned over to take her hand before she could retort. "You don't know my reputation, but I assure you, the police would think you mad."

"I could prove—"

"What?" he demanded. His eyes were steady on hers, probing. The polished veneer was slowly fading. "You can't prove what you don't know."

"I know that you're not what you pretend to be." Morgan tried to pull her hand from his, but he held it firm. "Or maybe it's more accurate to say you're something you pretend not to be."

Nick watched her in silence, torn between annoyance and admiration. "Whatever I am, whatever I'm not, has nothing to do with you."

"No one wishes more than I that that was the truth."

Battling a new emotion, he sat back and studied her over the rim of his glass. "So your conclusions that I might be involved in smuggling would prompt you to go to the police. That wouldn't be wise."

"It's a matter of what's right." Morgan swallowed, then blurted out what was torturing her mind. "The knife—would you have used it?"

"On you?" he asked, his eyes as expressionless as his voice.

"On anyone."

"A general question can't be given a specific answer."

"Nicholas, for God's sake—"

Nick set down his drink, then steepled his fingers. His expression changed, and his eyes were suddenly dangerous. "If I were everything you seem to think, you're incredibly brave or incredibly foolish to be sitting here discussing it with me."

"I think I'm safe enough," she countered and straightened her shoulders. "Everyone knows where I am."

"I could always dispose of you another time if I considered

you an obstacle." Morgan's eyes flickered with momentary fear, quickly controlled. It was one more thing he could admire her for.

"I can take care of myself."

"Can you?" he murmured, then shrugged as his mood shifted again. "Well, in any case, I have no intention of wasting beauty especially when I intend to enjoy its benefits. Your talents could be useful to me."

Her chin shot up. "I have no intention of being your tool. Smuggling opium is a filthy way to make money. It's a far cry from crossing the English Channel with French silks and brandy."

"With mists curling and eye-patched buccaneers?" Nick countered with a smile. "Is that how your practical mind sees it, Morgan?"

She opened her mouth to retort, but found herself smiling. "I refuse to like you, Nicholas."

"You don't have to like me, Morgan. Like is too tame for my tastes in any case." Outwardly relaxed, he picked up his glass again. "Don't you like your drink?"

Without taking her eyes from his, Morgan set it down. "Nicholas, I only want a straight answer—I deserve one. You're perfectly right that I can't go to the police, no matter what you tell me. You really have nothing to fear from me."

Something flashed in his eyes at her final statement, then was quickly banked. He considered his options before he spoke. "I'll tell you this much, I am—concerned with smuggling. I'd be interested to know of any conversations you might hear on the subject."

Frowning, Morgan rose to wander the room. He was making it difficult for her to remember the straight and narrow path of right and wrong. The path took some confusing twists and turns when emotions were involved. Emotions!

She brought herself up short. No, no emotions here. She had no feelings toward him.

"Who was with you that night?" Keep to the plan, she told herself. Questions and answers. Save the introspection for later. "You were giving someone orders."

"I thought you were too frightened to notice." Nick sipped at his drink.

"You were speaking to someone," Morgan went on doggedly. "Someone who did precisely what you told him without question. Who?"

Nick weighed the pros and cons before he answered. With her mind she'd figure it out for herself soon enough. "Stephanos."

"That little old man?" Morgan stopped in front of Nick and stared down. Stephanos was not Morgan's image of a ruthless smuggler.

"That little old man knows the sea like a gardener knows a rose bush." He smiled at her incredulous expression. "He also has the advantage of being loyal. He's been with me since I was a boy."

"How convenient all this is for you." Depressed, Morgan wandered to a window. She was getting her answers, but she discovered they weren't the ones she wanted. "A home on a convenient island, a convenient servant, a convenient business to ease distribution. Who passed by the grove that night whom you wanted to avoid?"

Frightened or not, he thought angrily, she'd been far too observant. "That needn't concern you."

Morgan whirled. "You got me into this, Nicholas. I have a right to know."

"Your rights end where I say they do." He rose as his temper threatened. "Don't push me too far, Morgan. You wouldn't like the results. I've told you all I intend to for now. Be content with it."

She backed away a step, furious with herself for being frightened. He swore at the movement, then gripped her shoulders.

"I have no intention of harming you, damn it. If I had, there's already been ample opportunity. What do you picture?" he demanded, shaking her. "Me cutting your throat or tossing you off a cliff?"

Her eyes were dry and direct, more angry now than frightened. "I don't know what I picture."

Abruptly he realized he was hurting her. Cursing himself, he eased the grip to a caress. He couldn't keep letting her get under his skin this way. He couldn't let it matter what she thought of him. "I don't expect you to trust me," he said calmly. "But use common sense. Your involvement was a matter of circumstance, not design. I don't want to see you hurt, Morgan. That much you can take as the truth."

And that much she believed. Intrigued, she studied his face. "You're a strange man, Nicholas. Somehow, I can't quite see you doing something as base as smuggling opium."

"Intuition, Morgan?" Smiling, Nick tangled his fingers in her hair. It was soft, as he remembered, and tempting. "Are you a woman who believes in her intuition, or in her reason?"

"Nicholas—"

"No. No more questions or I'll have to divert you. I'm very"—a frown hovered, then flashed into a grin—"very susceptible to beauty. You have a remarkable supply. Coupled with a very good mind, the combination is hard to resist." Nick lifted the medal at her throat, examined it, then let it fall before he moved back from her. "Tell me, what do you think of Dorian and Iona?"

"I resent this. I resent all of this." Morgan spun away from him. He shouldn't be allowed to affect her so deeply, so easily, then switch off like a light. "I came to Lesbos to get away from pressures and complications."

"What sort of pressures and complications?"

She turned back to him, eyes hot. "They're my business. I had a life before I went down to that damned beach and ran into you."

"Yes," he murmured and picked up his drink. "I'm sure you did."

"Now, I find myself tossed into the middle of some grade-B thriller. I don't like it."

"It's a pity you didn't stay in bed that night, Morgan." Nick drank deeply, then twirled his glass by the stem. "Maybe I'm Greek enough to say the gods didn't will it so. For the moment your fate's linked with mine, and there's nothing either of us can do about it."

She surprised him by laying a hand on his chest. He didn't like the way his heart reacted to the touch. Needs . . . he couldn't need. Wants were easily satisfied or ignored, but needs ate at a man.

"If you feel that way, why won't you give me a straight answer?"

"I don't choose to." His eyes locked on hers, cementing her to the spot. In them she saw desire—his and a mirror of her own. "Take me for what I am, Morgan."

She dropped her hand. Frightened not of him now, but of herself. "I don't want to take you at all."

"No?" He pulled her close, perversely enjoying her resistance. "Let's see just how quickly I can make a liar of you."

She could taste anger on his mouth, and just as clearly she could taste need. Morgan stopped resisting. The path of right and wrong took a few more confusing twists when she was in his arms. Whoever, whatever he was, she wanted to be held by him.

Her arms wound around his neck to draw him closer. She heard him murmur something against her mouth; the kiss held a savageness, a demand she was answering with equal abandon.

Had this passion always been there, sleeping inside her? It wasn't asleep any longer. The force of it had her clinging to him, had her mouth urgent and hungry against his. Something had opened inside her, letting him pour through. His hands were in her hair, then running down her back in a swift stroke of possession. She arched against him as if daring him to claim her—taunting him to try.

Somehow she knew, as her body fit truly to his, that they would come back to each other, again and again, against their will, against all reason. She might fight it from moment to moment, but there would be a time. The knowledge filled her with hunger and fear.

"Morgan." Her name wrenched from him on a sigh of need. "I want you—by the gods, I want you. Come, stay here with me tonight. Here, where we can be alone."

His mouth was roaming her face. She wanted to agree. Her body was aching to agree to anything—to everything. Yet, she found herself drawing back. "No."

Nick lifted his face. His expression was amused and confident. "Afraid?"

"Yes."

His brows rose at the unexpected honesty, then drew together in frustration. The look in her eyes made it impossible for him to press his advantage. "*Diabolos*, you're an exasperating woman." He strode away and poured more liquor into his glass. "I could toss you over my shoulder, haul you up to the bedroom, and be done with it."

Though her legs were watery, Morgan forced herself to remain standing. "Why don't you?"

He whirled back, furious. She watched as he slowly pulled out the control. "You're more accustomed to a wine and candlelight seduction, I imagine. Soft promises. Soft lies." Nick drank deep, then set down his glass with a bang. "Is that what you want from me?"

"No." Morgan met his fury steadily while her hand reached instinctively for the medal at her throat. "I don't want you to make love to me."

"Don't take me for a fool!" He took a step toward her, then stopped himself. Another step and neither of them would have a choice. "Your body betrays you every time I touch you."

"That has nothing to do with it," she said calmly. "I don't want you to make love to me."

He waited a beat until the desire and frustration could be tamed a bit. "Because you believe I'm an opium smuggler?"

"No," she said, surprising both of them. She felt her strength waver a moment, then told him the truth. "Because I don't want to be one of your amusements."

"I see." Carefully, Nick dipped his hands into his pockets. "I'd better take you back before you discover I find nothing amusing in lovemaking."

A half-hour later, Nick slammed back into the house. His temper was foul. He stalked into the salon, poured himself another drink, and slumped into a chair. Damn the woman, he didn't have the time or patience to deal with her. The need for her was still churning inside him like a pain, sharp and insistent. He took a long swallow of liquor to dull it. Just physical, he told himself. He'd have to find another woman—any other woman—and release some of the tension.

"Ah, you're back." Stephanos entered. He noted the black temper and accepted it without comment. He'd seen it often enough in the past. "The lady is more beautiful than I remembered." Nick's lack of response left him unperturbed. He moved to the bar and poured himself a drink. "How much did you tell her?"

"Only what was necessary. She's sharp and remarkably

bold." Nick eyed the liquid in his glass with a scowl. "She accused me flat out of smuggling." At Stephanos's cackle of laughter, Nick drained more liquor. "Your sense of humor eludes me at the moment, old man."

Stephanos only grinned. "Her eyes are sharp—they linger on you." Though Nick made no response, Stephanos's grin remained. "Did you speak to her of Alex?"

"Not at length."

"Is she loyal?"

"To Alex?" Nick frowned into his drink. "Yes, she would be. Where she cares, she'd be loyal." He set down the glass, refusing to give in to the urge to hurl it across the room. "Getting information out of her won't be easy."

"You'll get it nonetheless."

"I wish to hell she'd stayed in bed that night," Nick said savagely.

The gap-toothed grin appeared before Stephanos tossed back the drink in one long swallow. He let out a wheezy sigh of appreciation. "She lingers in your mind. That makes you uncomfortable." He laughed loud and long at Nick's scowl, then sighed again with the effort of it. "Athens is waiting for your call."

"Athens can fry in hell."

CHAPTER 5

Morgan's frame of mind was as poor as Nick's when she entered the Theoharis villa. Somewhere on the drive back from Nick's she had discovered that what she was feeling wasn't anger. It wasn't fear or even resentment. In a few days Nick had managed to do something Jack hadn't done in all the months she had known him. He'd hurt her.

It had nothing to do with the bruises that were already fading on her arms. This hurt went deeper, and had begun before she had even met him. It had begun when he had chosen the life he was leading.

Nothing to do with me. Nothing to do with me, Morgan told herself again and again. But she slammed the front door as she swept into the cool white hall. Her plans to go immediately to her room before she could snarl at anyone were tossed to the winds by a call and a wave from Dorian.

"Morgan, come join us."

Fixing on a smile, Morgan strolled out to the terrace. Iona was with him sprawled on a lounge in a hot-pink playsuit that revealed long, shapely legs but covered her arms with white lace cuffs at the wrists. She sent Morgan a languid greeting, then went back to her sulky study of the gulf. Morgan felt the tension hovering in the air and wondered if it had been there before or if she had brought it with her.

"Alex is on a transatlantic call," Dorian told her as he held out a chair. "And Liz is dealing with some domestic crisis in the kitchen."

"Without an interpreter?" Morgan asked. She smiled, telling herself Nick wasn't going to ruin her mood and make her as sulky as Alex's cousin.

"It's ridiculous." Iona gestured for Dorian to light her cigarette. "Liz should simply fire the man. Americans are habitually casual with servants."

"Are they?" Morgan felt her back go up at the slur on her friend and her nationality. "I wouldn't know."

Iona's dark eyes flicked over her briefly. "I don't imagine you've had many dealings with servants."

Before Morgan could retort, Dorian stepped in calmly. "Tell me, Morgan, what did you think of Nick's treasure trove?"

The expression in his eyes asked her to overlook Iona's bad manners, and told her something she'd begun to suspect the night before. He's in love with her, she mused, and felt a stab of pity. With an effort, Morgan relaxed her spine. "It's a wonderful place, like a museum without being regimented or stiff. It must have taken him years to collect all those things."

"Nick's quite a businessman," Dorian commented. Another look passed between him and Morgan. This time she saw it was gratitude. "And, of course, he uses his knowledge and position to secure the best pieces for himself."

"There was a Swiss music box," she remembered. "He said it was over a hundred years old. It played *Für Elise.*" Morgan sighed, at ease again. "I'd kill for it."

"Nick's a generous man—when approached in the proper manner." Iona's smile was sharp as a knife. Morgan turned her head and met it.

"I wouldn't know anything about that either," she said coolly. Deliberately, she turned back to Dorian. "I met Nick's cousin earlier this morning."

"Ah, yes, the young poet from America."

"He said he wanders all over this part of the island. I'm thinking of doing the same myself. It's such a simple, peaceful place. I suppose that's why I was so stunned when Alex said there was a problem with smuggling."

Dorian merely smiled as if amused. Iona stiffened. As Morgan watched, the color drained from her face, leaving it strained and cold and anything but beautiful. Surprised by the reaction, Morgan studied her carefully. Why, she's afraid, she realized. Now why would that be?

"A dangerous business," Dorian commented conversationally. Since his eyes were on Morgan, Iona's reaction went unnoticed by him. "But common enough—traditional in fact."

"An odd tradition," Morgan murmured.

"The network of patrols is very large, I'm told, and closely knotted. As I recall, five men were killed last year, gunned down off the Turkish coast." He lit a cigarette of his own. "The authorities confiscated quite a cache of opium."

"How terrible." Morgan noticed that Iona's pallor increased.

"Just peasants and fishermen," he explained with a shrug. "Not enough intelligence between them to have organized a large smuggling ring. It's rumored the leader is brilliant and ruthless. From the stories passed around in the village, he goes along on runs now and then, but wears a mask. Apparently, not even his cohorts know who he is. It might even be a woman." He flashed a grin at the idea. "I suppose that adds an element of romance to the whole business."

Iona rose and dashed from the terrace.

"You must forgive her." Dorian sighed as his eyes followed her. "She's a moody creature."

"She seemed upset."

"Iona's easily upset," he murmured. "Her nerves . . ."

"You care for her quite a lot."

His gaze came back to lock on Morgan's before he rose and strode to the railing.

"I'm sorry, Dorian," Morgan began immediately. "I didn't mean to pry."

"No, forgive me." He turned back and the sun streamed over his face, gleaming off the bronzed skin, combing through his burnished gold hair. Adonis, Morgan thought again, and for the second time since she had come to Lesbos wished she could paint. "My feelings for Iona are . . . difficult and, I had thought, more cleverly concealed."

"I'm sorry," Morgan said again, helplessly.

"She's spoiled, willful." With a laugh, Dorian shook his head. "What is it that makes one person lose his heart to another?"

Morgan looked away at the question. "I don't know. I wish I did."

"Now I've made you sad." Dorian sat back down beside Morgan and took her hands. "Don't pity me. Sooner or later, what's between Iona and me will be resolved. I'm a patient man." He smiled then, his eyes gleaming with confidence. "For now, we'll talk of something else. I have to confess, I'm fascinated by the smuggling legends."

"Yes. It is interesting. You said the rumor is that no one, not even the men who work for him, know who the leader is."

"That's the story. Whenever I'm on Lesbos, I keep hoping to stumble across some clue that would unmask him."

Morgan murmured something as her thoughts turned uncomfortably to Nick. "Yet you don't seem terribly concerned about the smuggling itself."

"Ah, the smuggling." Dorian moved his shoulders. "That's

something for the authorities to worry about. But the thrill of the hunt, Morgan." His eyes gleamed as they moved past her. "The thrill of the hunt."

"You wouldn't believe it!" Liz bustled out and plopped into a chair. "A half-hour with a temperamental Greek cook. I'd rather face a firing squad. Give me a cigarette, Dorian." Her smile and everyday complaint made the subject of smuggling absurd. "So tell me, Morgan, how did you like Nick's house?"

* * *

Pink streaks joined sky and sea as dawn bloomed. The air was warm and moist. After a restless night, it was the best of beginnings.

Morgan strolled along the water's edge and listened to the first serenading of birds. This was the way she had planned to spend her vacation—strolling along the beach, watching sunrises, relaxing. Isn't that what her father and Liz had drummed into her head?

Relax, Morgan. Get off the treadmill for a while. You never give yourself any slack.

She could almost laugh at the absurdity. But then, neither Liz nor her father had counted on Nicholas Gregoras.

He was an enigma, and she couldn't find the key. His involvement in smuggling was like a piece of a jigsaw puzzle that wouldn't quite fit. Morgan had never been able to tolerate half-finished puzzles. She scuffed her sandals in the sand. He was simply not a man she could categorize, and she wanted badly to shake the need to try.

On the other hand, there was Iona. Morgan saw the puzzle there as well. Alex's sulky cousin was more than a woman with an annoying personality. There was some inner agitation—something deep and firmly rooted. And Alex knows something of it, she mused. Dorian, too, unless she missed her guess. But what? And how much? Iona's reaction to talk of smuggling had been a sharp contrast to both Alex's and Dorian's. They'd been resigned—even amused. Iona had been terrified. Terrified of discovery? Morgan wondered. But that was absurd.

Shaking her head, Morgan pushed the thought aside. This morning she was going to do what she had come to Greece to do. Nothing. At least, nothing strenuous. She was going to look for shells, she decided, and after rolling up the hem of her jeans and taking off her sandals, splashed into a shallow inlet.

They were everywhere. The bank of sand and the shallow water were glistening with them. Some had been crushed underfoot or beaten smooth by the slow current. Crouching, she stuffed the pockets of her jacket with the best of them.

She noticed the stub of a black cigarette half-buried in the sand. So, Alex comes this way, she thought with a smile. Morgan could see Liz and her husband strolling hand in hand through the shallows.

As the sun grew higher, Morgan became more engrossed. If only I'd brought a tote, she thought, then shrugged and began to pile shells in a heap to retrieve later. She'd have them in a bowl on her windowsill at home. Then, whenever she was trapped indoors on a cold, rainy afternoon, she could look at them and remember Greek sunshine.

There were dozens of gulls. They flapped around her, circled, and called out. Morgan found the high, piercing sound the perfect company for a solitary morning. As the time passed, she began to find that inner peace she had experienced so briefly on the moonlit beach.

The hunt had taken her a good distance from the beach. Glancing up, she saw, with pleasure, the mouth of a cave. It wasn't large and was nearly hidden from view, but she thought it was entitled to an exploration. With a frown for her white jeans, Morgan decided to take a peek inside the entrance and come back when she was more suitably dressed. She moved to it with the water sloshing up to her calves. Bending down, she tugged another shell from its bed of sand. As her gaze swept over toward the cave, her hand froze.

The face glistened white in the clear water. Dark eyes stared back at her. Her scream froze in her throat, locked there by terror. She had never seen death before—not unpampered, staring death. Morgan stepped back jerkily, nearly slipping on a rock. As she struggled to regain her balance, her stomach heaved up behind the scream so that she could only gag. Even through the horror, she could feel the pressure of dizziness. She couldn't faint, not here, not with that only a foot away. She turned and fled.

She scrambled and spilled over rocks and sand. The only clear thought in her head was to get away. On a dead run, breath ragged, she broke from the concealment of the inlet out to the sickle of beach.

Hands gripped her. Blindly, Morgan fought against them with the primitive fear that the thing in the inlet had risen up and come after her.

"Stop it! Damn it, I'll end up hurting you again. Morgan, stop this. What's wrong with you?"

She was being shaken roughly. The voice pierced the first layer of shock. She stared and saw Nick's face. "Nicholas?" The dizziness was back and she went limp against him as waves of fear and nausea wracked her. Trembling—she couldn't stop the trembling—but knew she'd be safe now. He was there. "Nicholas," she managed again as though his name alone was enough to shield her.

Nick caught her tighter and shook her again. Her face was

deathly pale, her skin clammy. He'd seen enough of horror to recognize it in her eyes. In a moment, he knew, she'd faint or be hysterical. He couldn't allow either.

"What happened?" he demanded in a voice that commanded an answer.

Morgan opened her mouth, but found she could only shake her head. She buried her face against his chest in an attempt to block out what she had seen. Her breath was still ragged, coming in dry sobs that wouldn't allow for words. She'd be safe now, she told herself as she fought the panic. He'd keep her safe.

"Pull yourself together, Morgan," Nick ordered curtly, "and tell me what happened."

"Can't . . ." She tried to burrow herself into him.

In one quick move he jerked her away, shaking her. "I said tell me." His voice was cold, emotionless. He knew only one way to deal with hysteria, and her breath was still rising in gasps.

Dazed by the tone of his voice, she tried again, then jolted, clinging to him when she heard the sound of footsteps.

"Hello. Am I intruding?" Andrew's cheerful voice came from behind her, but she didn't look back. The trembling wouldn't stop.

Why was he angry with her? Why wasn't he helping her? The questions whirled in her head as she tried to catch her breath. Oh, God, she needed him to help her.

"Is something wrong?" Andrew's tone mirrored both concern and curiosity as he noted Nick's black expression and Morgan's shaking form.

"I'm not sure." Nick forced himself not to curse his cousin and spoke briefly. "Morgan was running across the beach. I haven't been able to get anything out of her yet." He drew her away, his fingers digging roughly in her skin as she tried to hold firm. She saw nothing in his face but cool curiosity. "Now, Morgan"—there was an edge of steel now—"tell me."

"Over there." Her teeth began to chatter as the next stage of reaction set in. Swallowing, she clamped them together while her eyes pleaded with him. His remained hard and relentless on hers. "Near the cove." The effort of the two short sentences swam in her head. She leaned toward him again. "Nicholas, please."

"I'll have a look." He grabbed her arms, dragging them away from him, wishing he didn't see what she was asking of him—knowing he couldn't give it to her.

"Don't leave, please!" Desperate, she grabbed for him again only to be shoved roughly into Andrew's arms.

"Damn it, get her calmed down," Nick bit off, tasting his own fury. She had no right—no right to ask for things he couldn't give. He had no right—no right to want to give them to her. He swore again, low and pungent under his breath as he turned away.

"Nicholas!" Morgan struggled out of Andrew's arms, but Nick was already walking away. She pressed a hand to her mouth to stop herself from calling him again. He never looked back.

Arms encircled her. Not Nick's. She could feel the gentle comfort of Andrew as he drew her against his chest. Her fingers gripped his sweater. Not Nick. "Here now." Andrew brought a hand to her hair. "I had hoped to entice you into this position under different circumstances."

"Oh, Andrew." The soft words and tender stroking had the ice of shock breaking into tears. "Andrew, it was so horrible."

"Tell me what happened, Morgan. Say it fast. It'll be easier then." His tone was quiet and coaxing as he stroked her hair. Morgan gave a shuddering sigh.

"There's a body at the mouth of the cave."

"A body!" He drew her back to stare into her face. "Good God! Are you sure?"

"Yes, yes, I saw— I was . . ." She covered her face with her hands a moment until she thought she could speak.

"Easy, take it easy," he murmured. "And let it come out."

"I was collecting shells in the inlet. I saw the cave. I was going to peek inside, then I . . ." She shuddered once, then continued. "Then I saw the face—under the water."

"Oh, Morgan." He drew her into his arms again and held her tight. He didn't say any more, but in silence gave her everything she had needed. When the tears stopped, he kept her close.

Nick moved rapidly across the sand. His frown deepened as he saw Morgan molded in his cousin's arms. As he watched, Andrew bent down to kiss her hair. A small fire leaped inside him that he smothered quickly.

"Andrew, take Morgan up to the Theoharis villa and phone the authorities. One of the villagers has had a fatal accident."

Nodding, Andrew continued to stroke Morgan's hair. "Yes, she told me. Terrible that she had to find it." He swallowed what seemed to be his own revulsion. "Are you coming?"

Nick looked down as Morgan turned her face to his. He hated the look in her eyes as she stared at him—the blankness, the hurt. She wouldn't forgive him easily for this. "No, I'll stay and make sure no one else happens across it. Morgan . . ." He touched her shoulders, detesting himself. There was no response, her eyes were dry now, and empty. "You'll be all right. Andrew will take you home."

Without a word, Morgan turned her face away again.

His control slipped a bit as Nick shot Andrew a hard glance. "Take care of her."

"Of course," Andrew murmured, puzzled by the tone. "Come on, Morgan, lean on me."

Nick watched them mount the beach steps. When they were out of sight, he went back to search the body.

* * *

Seated in the salon, her horror dulled with Alex's best brandy, Morgan studied Captain Tripolos of Mitilini's police department. He was short, his build spreading into comfortable lines that stopped just short of fat. His gray hair was carefully slicked to conceal its sparseness. His eyes were dark and sharp. Through the haze of brandy and shock, Morgan recognized a man with the tenacity of a bulldog.

"Miss James." The captain spoke in quick, staccato English. "I hope you understand, I must ask you some questions. It is routine."

"Couldn't it wait?" Andrew was stationed next to Morgan on the sofa. As he spoke he slipped an arm around her shoulders. "Miss James has had a nasty shock."

"No, Andrew, it's all right." Morgan laid her hand over his. "I'd rather be done with it. I understand, Captain." She gave him a straight look that he admired. "I'll tell you whatever I can."

"Efxaristo." He licked the end of his pencil, settled himself in his chair, and smiled with his mouth only. "Perhaps you could start by telling me exactly what happened this morning, from the time you arose."

Morgan began to recount the morning as concisely as she could. She spoke mechanically, with her hands limp and still in her lap. Though her voice trembled once or twice, Tripolos noted that her eyes stayed on his. She was a strong one, he decided, relieved that she wasn't putting him to the inconvenience of tears or jumbled hysterics.

"Then I saw him under the water." Morgan accepted Andrew's hand with gratitude. "I ran."

Tripolos nodded. "You were up very early. Is this your habit?"

"No. But I woke up and had an impulse to walk on the beach."

"Did you see anyone?"

"No." A shudder escaped, but her gaze didn't falter. She went up another notch in Tripolos's admiration. "Not until Nicholas and Andrew."

"Nicholas? Ah, Mr. Gregoras." He shifted his eyes to where Nick sprawled on a sofa across the room with Alex and Liz. "Had you ever seen the . . . deceased before?"

"No." Her hand tightened convulsively on Andrew's as the white face floated in front of her eyes. With a desperate effort of will, she forced the image away. "I've only been here a few days and I haven't been far from the villa yet."

"You're visiting from America?"

"Yes."

He made a quiet cluck of sympathy. "What a pity a murder had to blight your vacation."

"Murder?" Morgan repeated. The word echoed in her head as she stared into Tripolos's calm eyes. "But I thought . . . wasn't it an accident?"

"No." Tripolos glanced idly down at his notepad. "No, the victim was stabbed—in the back," he added with distaste. It was as if he considered murder one matter and back-stabbing another. "I hope I won't have to disturb you again." He rose and bowed over her hand. "Did you find many shells this morning, Miss James?"

"Yes I—I gathered quite a few." She felt compelled to reach in her jacket pocket and produce some. "I thought they were . . . lovely."

"Yes." He smiled, then turned to the others. "I regret we will have to question everyone on their whereabouts from last evening to this morning. Of course," he continued with a shrug, "we will no doubt find the murder was a result of a village quarrel, but with the body found so close to both villas . . ." He trailed off as he pocketed his pad and pencil. "One of you might recall some small incident that will help settle the matter."

Settle the matter? Morgan thought on a wave of hysteria. Settle the matter? But a man's dead. I'm dreaming. I must be dreaming.

"Easy, Morgan," Andrew whispered in her ear. "Have another sip." Gently, he urged the brandy back to her lips.

"You have our complete cooperation, Captain," Alex stated, and rose. "It isn't pleasant for any of us to have such a thing happen so near our homes. It's particularly upsetting that a guest of mine should have found the man."

"I understand, of course." Tripolos nodded wearily, rubbing a hand over his square chin. "It would be less confusing if I spoke with you one at a time. Perhaps we could use your office?"

"I'll show you where it is." Alex gestured to the door. "You can speak to me first if you like."

"Thank you." Tripolos gave the room a general bow before retreating behind Alex. Morgan watched his slow, measured steps. He'd haunt a man to the grave she thought, and shakily swallowed the rest of the brandy.

"I need a drink," Liz announced, moving toward the liquor cabinet. "A double. Anyone else?"

Nick's eyes skimmed briefly over Morgan. "Whatever you're having." He gestured with his hand, signaling Liz to refill Morgan's glass.

"I don't see why he has to question us." Iona moved to the bar, too impatient to wait for Liz to pour. "It's absurd. Alex should have refused. He has enough influence to avoid all of this." She poured something potent into a tall glass and drank half of it down.

"There's no reason for Alex to avoid anything." Liz handed Nick his drink before splashing another generous portion of brandy into Morgan's glass. "We have nothing to hide. What can I fix you, Dorian?"

"Hide? I said nothing about hiding," Iona retorted as she swirled around the room. "I don't want to answer that policeman's silly questions just because *she* was foolish enough to stumble over some villager's body," she said, gesturing toward Morgan.

"A glass of ouzo will be fine, Liz," Dorian stated before Liz could fire a retort. His gaze lit on Iona. "I hardly think we can blame Morgan, Iona. We'd have been questioned in any case. As it is, she's had to deal with finding the man as well as the questions. Thank you, Liz," he added as she placed a glass in his hand and shot him a grim smile.

"I cannot stay in this house today." Iona prowled the room, her movements as jerky as a nervous finger on a trigger. "Nicky, let's go out in your boat." She stopped and dropped to the arm of his chair.

"The timing's bad, Iona. When I'm finished here, I have paperwork to clear up at home." He sipped his drink and patted her hand. His eyes met Morgan's briefly, but long enough to recognize condemnation. Damn you, he thought furiously, you have no right to make me feel guilty for doing what I have to do.

"Oh, Nicky." Iona's hand ran up his arm. "I'll go mad if I stay here today. Please, a few hours on the sea?"

Nick sighed in capitulation while inside he fretted against a leash that was too long, and too strong, for him to break. He had reason to agree, and couldn't let Morgan's blank stare change the course he'd already taken. "All right, later this afternoon."

Iona smiled into her drink.

The endless questioning continued. Liz slipped out as Alex

came back in. And the waiting went on. Conversation came in fits and starts, conducted in undertones. As Andrew left the room for his conference, Nick wandered to Morgan's new station by the window.

"I want to talk to you." His tone was quiet, with the steel under it. When he put his hand over hers, she jerked it away.

"I don't want to talk to you."

Deliberately, he slipped his hands into his pockets. She was still pale. The brandy had steadied her but hadn't brought the color back to her cheeks. "It's necessary, Morgan. At the moment, I haven't the opportunity to argue about it."

"That's your problem."

"We'll go for a drive when the captain's finished. You need to get away from here for a while."

"I'm not going anywhere with you. Don't tell me what I need now." She kept her teeth clamped and spoke without emotion. "I needed you then."

"Damn it, Morgan." His muttered oath had all the power of a shout. She kept her eyes firmly on Liz's garden. Some of the roses, she thought dispassionately, were overblown now. The hands in his pockets were fists, straining impotently. "Don't you think I know that? Don't you think I—" He cut himself off before he lost control. "I couldn't give you what you needed—not then. Don't make this any more impossible for me than it is."

She turned to him now, meeting his fury with frost. "I have no intention of doing that." Her voice was as low as his but with none of his vibrating emotion. "The simple fact is I don't want anything from you now. I don't want anything to do with you."

"Morgan . . ." There was something in his eyes now that threatened to crack her resolve. Apology, regret, a plea for understanding where she'd never expected to see one. "Please, I need—"

"I don't care what you need," she said quickly, before he could weaken her again. "Just stay away from me. Stay completely away from me."

"Tonight," he began, but the cold fury in her eyes stopped him.

"Stay away," Morgan repeated.

She turned her back on him and walked across the room to join Dorian. Nick was left with black thoughts and the inability to carry them out.

CHAPTER 6

Morgan was surprised she'd slept. She hadn't been tired when Liz and Alex had insisted she lie down, but had obeyed simply because her last words with Nick had sapped all of her resistance. Now as she woke she saw it was past noon. She'd slept for two hours.

Groggy, heavy-eyed, Morgan walked into the bath to splash cool water on her face. The shock had passed, but the nap had brought her a lingering weariness instead of refreshment. Beneath it all was a deep shame—shame that she had run, terrified, from a dead man. Shame that she had clung helplessly to Nick and been turned away. She could feel even now that sensation of utter dependence—and utter rejection.

Never again, Morgan promised herself. She should have trusted her head instead of her heart. She should have known better than to ask or expect anything from a man like him. A man like him had nothing to give. You'd always find hell if you looked to a devil. And yet . . .

And yet it had been Nick she had needed, and trusted— him she had felt safe with the moment his arms had come around her. My mistake, Morgan thought grimly, and studied herself in the mirror over the basin. There were still some lingering signs of shock—the pale cheeks and too wide eyes, but she felt the strength returning.

"I don't need him," she said aloud, wanting to hear the words. "He doesn't mean anything to me."

But he's hurt you. Someone who doesn't matter can't hurt you.

I won't let him hurt me again, Morgan promised herself. Because I won't ever go to him again, I won't ever ask him again, no matter what.

She turned away from her reflection and went downstairs.

Even as she entered the main hall, Morgan heard the sound of a door closing and footsteps. Glancing behind her, she saw Dorian.

"So, you've rested." He came to her and took her hand. In the gesture was all the comfort and concern she could have asked for.

"Yes. I feel like a fool." At his lifted brow, Morgan moved her shoulders restlessly. "Andrew all but carried me back up here."

With a low laugh, he slipped an arm around her shoulders and led her into the salon. "You American women—do you always have to be strong and self-reliant?"

"I always have been." She remembered weeping in Nick's arms—clinging, pleading—and straightened her spine. "I have to depend on myself."

"I admire you for it. But then, you don't make a habit of stumbling over dead bodies." He cast a look at her pale cheeks and gentled his tone. "There, it was foolish of me to remind you. Shall I fix you another drink?"

"No— No, I've enough brandy in me as it is." Morgan managed a thin smile and moved away from him.

Why was it she was offered a supporting arm by everyone but the one who mattered? No, Nick couldn't matter, she reminded herself. She couldn't let him matter, and she didn't need a supporting arm from anyone.

"You seem restless, Morgan. Would you rather be alone?"

"No." She shook her head as she looked up. His eyes were calm. She'd never seen them otherwise. There'd be strength in him, she thought, and wished bleakly it had been Dorian she had run to that morning. Going to the piano, she ran a finger over the keys. "I'm glad the captain's gone. He made me nervous."

"Tripolos?" Dorian drew out his cigarette case. "I doubt he's anything to worry about. I doubt even the killer need worry," he added with a short laugh. "The Mitilini police force isn't known for its energy or brilliance."

"You sound as if you don't care if the person who killed that man is caught."

"Village quarrels mean nothing to me," he countered. "I'm concerned more with the people I know. I don't like to think you're worried about Tripolos."

"He doesn't worry me," she corrected, frowning as he lit a cigarette. Something was nagging at the back of her mind, struggling to get through. "He just has a way of looking at you while he sits there, comfortable and not quite tidy." She watched the column of smoke curl up from the tip of the long, black cigarette. With an effort, Morgan shook off the feeling of something important, half remembered. "Where is everyone?"

"Liz is with Alex in his office. Iona's gone on her boat ride."

"Oh, yes, with Nicholas." Morgan looked down at her hands, surprised that they had balled into fists. Deliberately, she opened them. "It must be difficult for you."

"She needed to escape. The atmosphere of death is hard on her nerves."

"You're very understanding." Disturbed and suddenly headachy, Morgan wandered to the window. "I don't think I would be—if I were in love."

"I'm patient, and I know that Nick means less than nothing to her. A means to an end." He paused for a moment, before he spoke again, thoughtfully. "Some people have no capacity for emotion—love or hate."

"How empty that would be," Morgan murmured.

"Do you think so?" He gave her an odd smile. "Somehow, I think it would be comfortable."

"Yes, comfortable perhaps but . . ." Morgan trailed off as she turned back. Dorian was just lifting the cigarette to his lips. As Morgan's eyes focused on it, she remembered, with perfect clarity, seeing the stub of one of those expensive brands in the sand, only a few yards from the body. A chill shot through her as she continued to stare.

"Morgan, is something wrong?" Dorian's voice broke through so that she blinked and focused on him again.

"No, I—I suppose I'm not myself yet. Maybe I'll have that drink after all."

She didn't want it, but needed a moment to pull her thoughts together. The stub of a cigarette didn't have to mean anything, she told herself as Dorian went to the bar. Anyone from the villa could have wandered through that inlet a dozen times.

But the stub had been fresh, Morgan remembered—half in, half out of the sand, unweathered. The birds hadn't picked at it. Surely if someone had been that close to the body, they would have seen. They would have seen, and they would have gone to the police. Unless . . .

No, that was a ridiculous thought, she told herself as she felt a quick tremor. It was absurd to think that Dorian might have had anything to do with a villager's murder. Dorian or Alex, she thought as that sweet, foreign smoke drifted over her.

They were both civilized men—civilized men didn't stab

other men in the back. Both of them had such beautiful, manicured hands and careful manners. Didn't it take something evil, something cold and hard to kill? She thought of Nick and shook her head. No, she wouldn't think of him now. She'd concentrate on this one small point and work it through to the end.

It didn't make any sense to consider Dorian or Alex as killers. They were businessmen, cultured. What possible dealings could they have had with some local fisherman? It was an absurd thought, Morgan told herself, but couldn't quite shake the unease that was creeping into her. There'd be a logical explanation, she insisted. There was always a logical explanation. She was still upset, that was all. Blowing some minor detail out of proportion.

Whose footsteps were on the beach steps that first night? a small voice insisted. Who was Nick hiding from? Or waiting for? That man hadn't been killed in a village quarrel, her thoughts ran on. She hadn't believed it for a moment, any more than she'd really believed the man had died accidentally. Murder . . . smuggling. Morgan closed her eyes and shuddered.

Who was coming in from the sea when Nick had held her in the shadow of the cypress? Nick had ordered Stephanos to follow him. Alex? Dorian? The dead man perhaps? She jolted when Dorian offered her the snifter.

"Morgan, you're still so pale. You should sit."

"No . . . I guess I'm still a little jumpy, that's all." Morgan cupped the snifter in both hands but didn't drink. She would ask him, that was all. She would simply ask him if he'd been to the inlet. But when her eyes met his, so calm, so concerned, she felt an icy tremor of fear. "The inlet—" Morgan hesitated, then continued before her courage failed her. "The inlet was so beautiful. It seemed so undisturbed." But so many shells had been crushed underfoot, she remembered abruptly. Why hadn't she thought of that before? "Do you—do a lot of people go there?"

"I can't speak for the villagers," Dorian began, watching as she perched on the arm of a divan. "But I'd think most of them would be too busy with their fishing or in the olive groves to spend much time gathering shells."

"Yes." She moistened dry lips. "But still, it's a lovely spot, isn't it?"

Morgan kept her eyes on his. Was it her imagination, or had his eyes narrowed? A trick of the smoke that wafted between them? Her own nerves?

"I've never been there," Dorian said lightly. "I suppose it's a bit like a native New Yorker never going to the top of the Empire State Building." Morgan's gaze followed his fingers as he crushed out the cigarette in a cut-glass ashtray. "Is there something else, Morgan?"

"Something—no." Hastily, she looked back up to meet his eyes. "No, nothing. I suppose like Iona, the atmosphere's getting to me, that's all."

"Small wonder." Sympathetic, he crossed to her. "You've been through too much today, Morgan. Too much talk of death. Come out in the garden," he suggested. "We'll talk of something else."

Refusal was on the tip of her tongue. She didn't know why, only that she didn't want to be with him. Not then. Not alone. Even as she cast around for a reasonable excuse, Liz joined them.

"Morgan, I'd hoped you were resting."

Grateful for the interruption, Morgan set down her untouched brandy and rose. "I rested long enough." A quick scan of Liz's face showed subtle signs of strain. "You look like you should lie down awhile."

"No, but I could use some air."

"I was just taking Morgan out to the garden." Dorian touched a hand to Liz's shoulder. "You two go out and relax. Alex and I have some business we should clear up."

"Yes." Liz lifted her hand to his. "Thank you, Dorian. I don't know what Alex or I would have done without you today."

"Nonsense." He brushed her cheek with his lips. "Go, take your mind off this business."

"I will. See if you can get Alex to do the same." The plea was light, but unmistakable before Liz hooked her arm through Morgan's.

"Dorian." Morgan felt a flush of shame. He'd been nothing but kind to her, and she'd let her imagination run wild. "Thank you."

He lifted a brow at the gratitude, then smiled and kissed her cheek in turn. He smelt of citrus groves and sunshine. "Sit with the flowers for a while, and enjoy."

As he walked into the hall, Liz turned and headed toward the garden doors. "Should I order us some tea?"

"Not for me. And stop treating me like a guest."

"Good Lord, was I doing that?"

"Yes, ever since—"

Liz shot Morgan a quick look as she broke off, then grimaced. "This whole business really stinks," Liz stated inelegantly, and plopped down on a marble bench.

Surrounded by the colors and scents of the garden, isolated from the house and the outside world by vines, Morgan and Liz frowned at each other.

"Damn, Morgan, I'm so sorry that you had to be the one. No, don't shrug and try to look casual," she ordered as Morgan did just that. "We've known each other too long and too well. I know what it must have been like for you this morning. And I know how you must be feeling right now."

"I'm all right, Liz." She chose a small padded glider and curled her legs under her. "Though I'll admit I won't be admiring seashells for a while. Please," she continued as Liz's frown deepened. "Don't do this. I can see that you and Alex are blaming yourselves. It was just—just a horrible coincidence that I happened to take a tour of that inlet this morning. A man was killed; someone had to find him."

"It didn't have to be you."

"You and Alex aren't responsible."

Liz sighed. "My practical American side knows that, but . . ." She shrugged, then managed to smile. "But I think I'm becoming a bit Greek. You're staying in my house." Liz lit a cigarette resignedly as she rose to pace the tiny court-yard.

A black cigarette, Morgan noticed with a tremor of anxiety—slim and black. She'd forgotten Liz had picked up the habit of occasionally smoking one of Alex's brand.

She stared up into Liz's oval, classic face, then shut her eyes. She must be going mad if she could conceive, even for an instant, that Liz was mixed up in smuggling and back-stabbing. This was a woman she'd known for years—lived with. Certainly if there was one person she knew as well as she knew herself, it was Liz.

But how far—how far would Liz go to protect the man she loved?

"And I have to admit," Liz went on as she continued to pace, "though it sticks me in the same category as Iona, that policeman made me nervous. He was just too"—she searched for an adjective—"respectful," she decided. "Give me a good old American grilling."

"I know what you mean," Morgan murmured. She had to stop thinking, she told herself. If she could just stop think-ing, everything would be all right again.

"I don't know what he expected to find out, questioning us that way." Liz took a quick, jerky puff, making her wed-ding ring flash with cold, dazzling light.

"It was just routine, I suppose." Morgan couldn't take her eyes from the ring—the light, the stones. Love, honor, and obey—forsaking all others.

"And creepy," Liz added. "Besides, none of us even knew this Anthony Stevos."

"The captain said he was a fisherman."

"So is every second man in the village."

Morgan allowed the silence to hang. Carefully, she reconstructed the earlier scene in the salon. What were the reactions? If she hadn't been so dimmed with brandy and shock, would she have noticed something? There was one more person she'd seen lighting one of the expensive cigarettes. "Liz," she began slowly, "don't you think Iona went a little overboard? Didn't she get a bit melodramatic about a few routine questions?"

"Iona thrives on melodrama," Liz returned with grim relish. "Did you see the way she fawned all over Nick? I don't see how he could bear it."

"He didn't seem to mind," Morgan muttered. No, not yet, she warned herself. You're not ready to deal with that yet. "She's a strange woman," Morgan continued. "But this morning . . ." And yesterday, she remembered. "Yesterday when I spoke of smuggling . . . I think she was really afraid."

"I don't think Iona has any genuine feelings," Liz said stubbornly. "I wish Alex would just cross her off as a bad bet and be done with it. He's so infuriatingly conscientious."

"Strange, Dorian said almost the same thing." Morgan plucked absently at an overblown rose. It was Iona she should concentrate on. If anyone could do something deadly and vile, it was Iona. "I don't see her that way."

"What do you mean?"

"Iona." Morgan stopped plucking at the rose and gave Liz her attention. "I see her as a woman of too many feelings rather than none at all. Not all healthy certainly, perhaps even destructive—but strong, very strong emotions."

"I can't abide her," Liz said with such unexpected venom, Morgan stared. "She upsets Alex constantly. I can't tell you how much time and trouble and money he's put into that woman. And he gets nothing back but ingratitude, rudeness."

"Alex has very strong family feelings," Morgan began. "You can't protect him from—"

"I'd protect him from anything," Liz interrupted passionately. "Anything and anyone." Whirling, she hurled her cigarette into the bushes where it lay smoldering. Morgan found herself staring at it with dread. "Damn," Liz said in a calmer tone. "I'm letting all this get to me."

"We all are." Morgan shook off the sensation of unease and rose. "It hasn't been an easy morning."

"I'm sorry, Morgan, it's just that Alex is so upset by all this. And as much as he loves me, he just isn't the kind of man to share certain areas with me. His trouble—his business. He's too damn Greek." With a quick laugh, she shook her head. "Come on, sit down. I've vented my spleen."

"Liz, if there were something wrong—I mean, something really troubling you, you'd tell me, wouldn't you?"

"Oh, don't start worrying about me now." Liz nudged Morgan back down on the glider. "It's just frustrating when you love someone to distraction and they won't let you help. Sometimes it drives me crazy that Alex insists on trying to keep the less-pleasant aspects of his life away from me."

"He loves you," Morgan murmured and found she was gripping her hands together.

"And I love him."

"Liz . . ." Morgan took a deep breath and plunged. "Do you and Alex walk through the inlet often?"

"Hmmm?" Obviously distracted, Liz looked back over her shoulder as she walked toward her bench. "Oh, no, actually, we usually walk on the cliffs—if I can drag him away from his office. I can't think when's the last time I've been near there. I only wish," she added in a gentler tone, "I'd been with you this morning."

Abruptly and acutely ashamed at the direction her thoughts had taken, Morgan looked away. "I'm glad you weren't. Alex had his hands full enough with one hysterical female."

"You weren't hysterical," Liz corrected in a quiet voice. "You were almost too calm by the time Andrew brought you in."

"I never even thanked him." Morgan forced herself to push doubts and suspicions aside. They were as ugly as they were ridiculous. "What did you think of Andrew?"

"He's a very sweet man." Sensing Morgan's changing mood, Liz adjusted her own thoughts. "He appeared to put himself in the role of your champion today." She smiled, deliberately looking wise and matronly. "I'd say he was in the first stages of infatuation."

"How smug one becomes after three years of marriage."

"He'd be a nice diversion for you," Liz mused, unscathed. "But he's from the genteel-poor side of Nick's family. I rather fancy seeing you set up in style. Then again," she continued as Morgan sighed, "he'd be nice company for you . . . for a while."

Dead on cue, Andrew strolled into the courtyard. "Hello. I hope I'm not intruding."

"Why, no!" Liz gave him a delighted smile. "Neighboring poets are always welcome."

He grinned, a flash of boyishness. With that, he went up several notches on Liz's list. "Actually, I was worried about Morgan." Bending over, he cupped her chin and studied her. "It was such an awful morning, I wanted to see how you were doing. I hope you don't mind." His eyes were dark blue, like the water in the bay—and with the same serenity.

"I don't." She touched the back of his hand. "At all. I'm really fine. I was just telling Liz I hadn't even thanked you for everything you did."

"You're still pale."

His concern made her smile. "A New York winter has something to do with that."

"Determined to be courageous?" he asked with a tilted smile.

"Determined to do a better job of it than I did this morning."

"I kind of liked the way you held on to me." He gave her hand a light squeeze. "I want to steal her for an evening," he told Liz, shifting his gaze from Morgan's face. "Can you help me convince her a diversion is what she needs?"

"You have my full support."

"Come have dinner with me in the village." He bent down to Morgan again. "Some local color, a bottle of ouzo, and a witty companion. What more could you ask for?"

"What a marvelous idea!" Liz warmed to Andrew and the scheme. "It's just what you need, Morgan."

Amused, Morgan wondered if she should just let them pat each other on the back for a while. But it was what she needed—to get away from the house and the doubts. She smiled at Andrew. "What time should I be ready?"

His grin flashed again. "How about six? I'll give you a tour of the village. Nick gave me carte blanche with his Fiat while I'm here, so you won't have to ride on an ass."

Because her teeth were tight again, Morgan relaxed her jaw. "I'll be ready."

* * *

The sun was high over the water when Nick set his boat toward the open sea. He gave it plenty of throttle, wanting the speed and the slap of the wind.

Damn the woman! he thought on a new surge of frustration. Seething, he tossed the butt of a slender black cigarette into the churning waves. If she'd stay in bed instead of wandering on beaches at ridiculous hours, all of this could have been avoided. The memory of the plea in her voice, the horror in her eyes flashed over him. He could still feel the way she had clung to him, needing him.

He cursed her savagely and urged more speed from the motor.

Shifting his thoughts, Nick concentrated on the dead man. Anthony Stevos, he mused, scowling into the sun. He knew the fisherman well enough—what he had occasionally fished for—and the Athens phone number he had found deep inside Stevos's pants pocket.

Stevos had been a stupid, greedy man, Nick thought dispassionately. Now he was a dead one. How long would it take Tripolos to rule out the village brawl and hit on the truth? Not long enough, Nick decided. He was going to have to bring matters to a head a bit sooner than he had planned.

"Nicky, why are you looking so mean?" Iona called to him over the motor's roar. Automatically, he smoothed his features.

"I was thinking about that pile of paperwork on my desk." Nick cut the motor off and let the boat drift in its own wake. "I shouldn't have let you talk me into taking the afternoon off."

Iona moved to where he sat. Her skin glistened, oiled slick, against a very brief bikini. Her bosom spilled over in invitation. She had a ripe body, rounded and full and arousing. Nick felt no stir as she swung her hips, moving toward him.

"*Agapetikos*, we'll have to take your mind off business matters." She wound herself into his lap and pressed against him.

He kissed her mechanically, knowing that, after the bottle

of champagne she'd drunk, she'd never know the difference. But her taste lingered unpleasantly on his lips. He thought of Morgan, and with a silent, furious oath, crushed his mouth against Iona's.

"Mmm." She preened like a stroked cat. "Your mind isn't on your paperwork now, Nicky. Tell me you want me. I need a man who wants me."

"Is there a man alive who wouldn't want a woman such as you?" He ran a hand down her back as her mouth searched greedily for his.

"A devil," she muttered with a slurred laugh. "Only a devil. Take me, Nicky." Her head fell back, revealing eyes half closed and dulled by wine. "Make love to me here, in the open, in the sun."

And he might have to, he thought with a grinding disgust in his stomach. To get what he needed. But first, he would coax what he could from her while she was vulnerable.

"Tell me, *matia mou*," he murmured, tasting the curve of her neck while she busily undid the buttons of his shirt. "What do you know of this smuggling between Lesbos and Turkey?"

Nick felt her stiffen, but her response—and, he knew, her wits—were dulled by the champagne. In her state of mind, he thought, it wouldn't take much more to loosen her tongue. She'd been ready to snap for days. Deliberately, he traced his tongue across her skin and felt her sigh.

"Nothing," she said quickly and fumbled more desperately at his buttons. "I know nothing of such things."

"Come, Iona," he murmured seductively. She was a completely physical woman, one who ran on sensations alone. Between wine and sex and her own nerves, she'd talk to him. "You know a great deal. As a businessman"—he nipped at her earlobe—"I'm interested in greater profit. You won't deny me a few extra drachmas, will you?"

"A few million," she murmured, and put her hand on his to show him what she wanted. "Yes, there's much I know."

"And much you'll tell me?" he asked. "Come, Iona. You and the thought of millions excite me."

"I know the man that stupid woman found this morning was murdered because he was greedy."

Nick forced himself not to tense. "But greed is so difficult to resist." He went with her as she stretched full length on the bench. "Do you know who murdered him, Iona?" She was slipping away from him, losing herself to the excess of champagne. On a silent oath, Nick nipped at her skin to bring her back.

"I don't like murder, Nicky," she mumbled, "and I don't like talking to the police even more." She reached for him, but her hands fumbled. "I'm tired of being used," she said pettishly, then added, "Perhaps it's time to change allegiance. You're rich, Nicky. I like money. I need money."

"Doesn't everyone?" Nick asked dryly.

"Later, we'll talk later. I'll tell you." Her mouth was greedy on his. Forcing everything from his mind, Nick struggled to find some passion, even the pretense of passion, in return. God, he needed a woman; his body ached for one. And he needed Iona. But as he felt her sliding toward unconsciousness, he did nothing to revive her.

Later, as Iona slept in the sun, Nick leaned over the opposite rail and lit a cigarette from the butt of another. The clinging distaste both infuriated and depressed him. He knew that he would have to use Iona, be used by her—if not this time, then eventually. He had to tap her knowledge to learn what he wanted to know. It was a matter of his own safety— and his success. The second had always been more important to him than the first.

If he had to be Iona's lover to gain his own end, then he'd be her lover. It meant nothing. Swearing, he drew deeply on the cigarette. It meant nothing, he repeated. It was business.

He found he wanted a shower, a long one, something to cleanse himself of the dirt that wouldn't wash away. Years of dirt, years of lies. Why had he never felt imprisoned by them until now?

Morgan's face slipped into his mind. Her eyes were cold. Flinging the cigarette out to sea, he went back to the wheel and started the engine.

CHAPTER 7

During a leisurely drink after a leisurely tour, Morgan decided the village was perfect. White-washed houses huddled close together, some with pillars, some with arches, still others with tiny wooden balconies. The tidiness, the freshness of white should have lent an air of newness. Instead, the village seemed old and timeless and permanent.

She sat with Andrew at a waterfront *kafenion*, watching the fishing boats sway at the docks, and the men who spread their nets to dry.

The fishermen ranged from young boys to old veterans. All were bronzed, all worked together. There were twelve to each net—twenty-four hands, some wrinkled and gnarled, some smooth with youth. All strong. As they worked they shouted and laughed in routine companionship.

"Must have been a good catch," Andrew commented. He watched Morgan's absorption with the small army of men near the water's edge.

"You know, I've been thinking." She ran a finger down the side of her glass. "They all seem so fit and sturdy. Some of those men are well past what we consider retirement age in the States. I suppose they'll sail until they die. A life on the water must be a very satisfying existence." Pirates . . . would she ever stop thinking of pirates?

"I don't know if any of these people think much about satisfaction. It's simply what they do. They fish or work in Nick's olive groves. They've been doing one or the other for generations." Toying with his own drink, Andrew studied them too. "I do think there's a contentment here. The people know what's expected of them. If their lives are simple, perhaps it's an enviable simplicity."

"Still, there's the smuggling," Morgan murmured.

Andrew shrugged. "It's all part of the same mold, isn't it? They do what's expected of them and earn a bit of adventure and a few extra drachmas."

She shot him a look of annoyed surprise. "I didn't expect that attitude from you."

Andrew looked back at her, both brows raised. "What attitude?"

"This—this nonchalance over crime."

"Oh, come on, Morgan, it's—"

"Wrong," she interrupted. "It should be stopped." Morgan swallowed the innocently clear but potent ouzo.

"How do you stop something that's been going on for centuries in one form or another?"

"It's current form is ugly. I should think the men of influence like Alex and . . . Nicholas, with homes on the island, would put pressure on whoever should be pressured."

"I don't know Alex well enough to comment," Andrew mused, filling her glass again. "But I can't imagine Nick getting involved in anything that didn't concern himself or his business."

"Can't you?" Morgan murmured.

"If that sounds like criticism, it's not." He noted he had Morgan's full attention, but that her eyes were strangely veiled. "Nick's been very good to me, lending me the cottage and the money for my passage. Lord knows when I'll be able to pay him back. And it irks quite a bit to have to borrow, but poetry isn't the most financially secure career."

"I think I read somewhere that T.S. Eliot was a bank teller."

Andrew returned her understanding smile with a wry grimace. "I could work out of Nick's California office." He shrugged and drank. "His offer wasn't condescending, just absentminded. It's rough on the ego." He looked past her, toward the docks. "Maybe my ship will come in."

"I'm sure it will, Andrew. Some of us are meant to follow dreams."

His gaze came back to her. "And artists are meant to suffer a bit, rise beyond the more base needs of money and power?" His smile was brittle, his eyes cool. "Let's order." Morgan watched him shake off the mood and smile with his usual warmth. "I'm starved."

The evening sky was muted as they finished their meal. There were soft, dying colors flowing into the western sea. In the east, it was a calm, deep violet waiting for the first stars. Morgan was content with the vague glow brought on by spiced food and Greek ouzo. There was intermittent music from a mandolin. Packets of people shuffled in and out of the café, some of them breaking into song.

Their waiter cum proprietor was a wide man with a thin moustache and watery eyes. Morgan figured the eyes could be attributed to the spices and cook smoke hanging in the air. American tourists lifted his status. Because he was impressed with Morgan's easily flowing Greek, he found opportunities to question and gossip as he hovered around their table.

Morgan toyed with a bit of *psomaki* and relaxed with the atmosphere and easy company. She'd found nothing but comfort and good will in the Theoharis villa, but this was something different. There was an earthier ambience she had missed in Liz's elegant home. Here there would be lusty laughter and spilled wine. As strong as Morgan's feelings were for both Liz and Alex, she would never have been content with the lives they led. She'd have rusted inside the perpetual manners.

For the first time since that morning, Morgan felt the nagging ache at the base of her skull begin to ease.

"Oh, Andrew, look! They're dancing." Cupping her chin on her hands, Morgan watched the line of men hook arms.

As he finished up the last of a spicy sausage, Andrew glanced over. "Want to join in?"

Laughing, she shook her head. "No, I'd spoil it—but you could," she added with a grin.

"You have," Andrew began as he filled her glass again, "a wonderful laugh. It's rich and unaffected and trails off into something sensuous."

"What extraordinary things you say, Andrew." Morgan smiled at him, amused. "You're an easy man to be with. We could be friends."

Andrew lifted his brows. Morgan was surprised to find her mouth briefly captured. There was a faint taste of the island on him—spicy and foreign. "For starters." At her stunned expression, he leaned back and grinned. "That face you're wearing doesn't do great things for my ego, either." He pulled a pack of cigarettes out of his jacket pocket, then dug for a match. Morgan stopped staring at him to stare at the thin black box.

"I didn't know you smoked," she managed after a moment.

"Oh, not often." He found a match. The tiny flame flared, flickering over his face a moment, casting shadows, mysteries, suspicions. "Especially since my taste runs to these. Nick takes pity on me and leaves some at my cottage whenever he happens by. Otherwise, I suppose I'd do without altogether."

When he noticed Morgan's steady stare, he gave her a puzzled smile. "Something wrong?"

"No." She lifted her glass and hoped she sounded casual. "I was just thinking—you'd said you roam all over this part of the island. You must have been in that inlet before."

"It's a beautiful little spot." He reached over for her hand. "Or it was. I guess I haven't been there in over a week. It might be quite a while before I go back now."

"A week," Morgan murmured.

"Don't dwell on it, Morgan."

She lifted her eyes to his. They were so clear, so concerned. She was being a fool. None of them—Alex, Dorian, Andrew—none of them was capable of what was burning into her thoughts. How was she to know that some maniac from the village hadn't had a taste for expensive tobacco and back-stabbing? It made more sense, a great deal more sense than her ugly suspicions.

"You're right." She smiled again and leaned toward him. "Tell me about your epic poem."

"Good evening, Miss James, Mr. Stevenson."

Morgan twisted her head and felt the sky cloud over. She looked up into Tripolos's pudgy face. "Hello, Captain."

If her greeting lacked enthusiasm, Tripolos seemed unperturbed. "I see you're enjoying a bit of village life. Do you come often?"

"This is Morgan's first trip," Andrew told him. "I convinced her to come out to dinner. She needed something after this morning's shock."

Tripolos clucked sympathetically. Morgan noted the music and laughter had stilled. The atmosphere in the café was hushed and wary.

"Very sensible," the captain decided. "A young lady must not dwell on such matters. I, unfortunately, must think of little else at the moment." He sighed and looked wistfully at the ouzo. "Enjoy your evening."

"Damn, damn, *damn!*" she muttered when he walked away. "Why does he affect me this way? Every time I see him, I feel like I've got the Hope Diamond in my pocket."

"I know what you mean." Andrew watched people fall back to create a path for Tripolos. "He almost makes you wish you had something to confess."

"Thank God, it's not just me." Morgan lifted her glass again, noticed her hands were trembling, and drained it. "Andrew," she began in calm tones, "unless you have some moral objection, I'm going to get very drunk."

Sometime later, after learning Andrew's views on drinking were flexible, Morgan floated on a numbing cloud of ouzo. The thin light of the moon had replaced the colors of sunset. As the hour grew later, the café crowd grew larger, both in size and volume. Music was all strings and bells. If the interlude held a sheen of unreality, she no longer cared. She'd had enough of reality.

The waiter materialized with yet another bottle. He set it on the table with the air of distributing a rare wine.

"Busy night," Morgan commented, giving him a wide if misty, smile.

"It is Saturday," he returned, explaining everything.

"So, I've chosen my night well." She glanced about, seeing a fuzzy crush of people. "Your customers seem happy."

He followed her survey with a smug smile, wiping a hand on his apron. "I feared when the Mitilini captain came, my business would suffer, but all is well."

"The police don't add to an atmosphere of enjoyment. I suppose," she added slowly, "he's investigating the death of that fisherman."

He gave Morgan a quick nod. "Stevos came here often, but he was a man with few companions. He was not one for dancing or games. He found other uses for his time." The waiter narrowed his eyes. "My customers do not like to answer questions." He muttered something uncomplimentary, but Morgan wasn't sure if it was directed at Stevos or Tripolos.

"He was a fisherman," she commented, struggling to concentrate on the Greek's eyes. "But it appears his comrades don't mourn him."

The waiter moved his shoulders eloquently, but she saw her answer. There were fishermen, and fishermen. "Enjoy your evening, *kyrios*. It is an honor to serve you."

"You know," Andrew stated when the waiter drifted to another table, "it's very intimidating listening to all that Greek. I couldn't pick up on it. What was he saying?"

Not wanting to dwell on the murder again, Morgan merely smiled. "Greek males are red-blooded, Andrew, but I explained that I was otherwise engaged for this evening." She locked her hands behind her head and looked up at the stars. "Oh, I'm glad I came. It's so lovely. No murders—no smuggling tonight. I feel marvelous, Andrew. When can I read some of your poetry?"

"When your brain's functioning at a normal level." Smiling, he tilted more ouzo into her glass. "I think your opinion might be important."

"You're a nice man." Morgan lifted her glass and studied him as intensely as possible. "You're not at all like Nicholas."

"What brought that on?" Andrew frowned, setting the bottle back down again.

"You're just not." She held out her glass. "To Americans," she told him. "One hundred percent pure."

After tapping her glass with his, Andrew drank and shook his head. "I have a feeling we weren't toasting the same thing."

She felt Nick begin to push into her thoughts and she thrust him away. "What does it matter? It's a beautiful night."

"So it is." His finger traced lightly over the back of her hand. "Have I told you how lovely you are?"

"Oh, Andrew, are you going to flatter me?" With a warm laugh, she leaned closer. "Go ahead, I love it."

With a wry grin, he tugged her hair. "You're spoiling my delivery."

"Oh, dear . . . how's this?" Morgan cupped her chin on her hands again and gave him a very serious stare.

On a laugh, Andrew shook his head. "Let's walk for a while. I might find a dark corner where I can kiss you properly."

Rising, he helped Morgan to her feet. She exchanged a formal and involved good night with the proprietor before Andrew could navigate her away from the crowd.

Those not gathered in the *kafenion* were long since in bed. The white houses were closed and settled for the night. Now and then a dog barked, and another answered. Morgan could hear her own footsteps echo down the street.

"It's so quiet," she murmured. "All you can really hear is the water and the night itself. Ever since that first morning when I woke up on Lesbos, I've felt as if I belonged. Nothing that's happened since has spoiled that for me. Andrew." She whirled herself around in his arms and laughed. "I don't believe I'm *ever* going home again. How can I face New York and the traffic and the snow again? Rushing to work, rushing home. Maybe I'll become a fisherman, or give in to Liz and marry a goatherd."

"I don't think you should marry a goatherd," Andrew said

practically, and drew her closer. Her scent was tangling his senses. Her face, in the moonlight, was an ageless mystery. "Why don't you give the fishing a try? We could set up housekeeping in Nick's cottage."

It would serve him right, her mind muttered. Lifting her mouth, Morgan waited for the kiss.

It was warm and complete. Morgan neither knew nor cared if the glow was a result of the kiss or the liquor. Andrew's lips weren't demanding, weren't urgent and possessive. They were comforting, requesting. She gave him what she could.

There was no rocketing passion—but she told herself she didn't want it. Passion clouded the mind more successfully than an ocean of ouzo. She'd had enough of hunger and passions. They brought pain with disillusionment. Andrew was kind, uncomplicated. He wouldn't turn away when she needed him. He wouldn't give her sleepless nights. He wouldn't make her doubt her own strict code of right and wrong. He was the knight—a woman was safe with a knight.

"Morgan," he murmured, then rested his cheek on her hair. "You're exquisite. Isn't there some man I should consider dueling with?"

Morgan tried to think of Jack, but could form no clear picture. There was, however, a sudden, atrociously sharp image of Nick as he dragged her close for one of his draining kisses.

"No," she said too emphatically. "There's no one. Absolutely no one."

Andrew drew her away and tilted her chin with his finger. He could see her eyes in the dim glow of moonlight. "From the strength of your denial, I'd say my competition's pretty formidable. No"—he laid a finger over her lips as she started to protest—"I don't want to have my suspicions confirmed tonight. I'm selfish." He kissed her again, lingering over it. "Damn it, Morgan, you could be habit forming. I'd better take you home while I remember I'm a gentleman and you're a very drunk lady."

* * *

The villa shimmered white under the night sky. A pale light glowed in a first-floor window for her return.

"Everyone's asleep," Morgan stated unnecessarily as she let herself out of the car. Andrew rounded the hood. "I'll have to be very quiet." She muffled irrepressible giggles with a hand over her mouth. "Oh, I'm going to feel like an idiot tomorrow if I remember any of this."

"I don't think you'll remember too much," Andrew told her as he took her arm.

Morgan managed the stairs with the careful dignity of someone who no longer feels the ground under her feet. "It would never do to disgrace Alex by landing on my face in the foyer. He and Dorian are *so* dignified."

"And I," Andrew returned, "will have to resume my drive with the utmost caution. Nick wouldn't approve if I ran his Fiat off a cliff."

"Why, Andrew." Morgan stood back and studied him owlishly. "You're almost as sloshed as I am."

"Not quite, but close enough. However"—he let out a long breath and wished he could lie down—"I conducted myself with the utmost restraint."

"Very nicely done." She went off into a muffled peal of giggles again. "Oh, Andrew." She leaned against him so heavily that he had to shift his balance to support her. "I did have a good time—a wonderful time. I needed it more than I realized. Thank you."

"In you go." He opened the door and gave her a nudge

inside. "Be careful on the stairs," he whispered. "Should I wait and listen for the sounds of an undignified tumble?"

"Just be on your way and don't take the Fiat for a swim." She stood on her toes and managed to brush his chin with her lips. "Maybe I should make you some coffee."

"You'd never find the kitchen. Don't worry, I can always park the car and walk if worse comes to worse. Go to bed, Morgan, you're weaving."

"That's you," she retorted before she closed the door.

Morgan took the stairs with painful caution. The last thing she wanted to do was wake someone up and have to carry on any sort of reasonable conversation. She stopped once and pressed her hands to her mouth to stop a fresh bout of giggles. Oh, it felt so good, so good not to be able to think. But this has to stop, she told herself firmly. No more of this, Morgan. Straighten up and get upstairs before all is discovered.

She managed to pull herself to the top landing, then had to think carefully to remember in which direction her room lay. To the left, of course, she told herself with a shake of the head. But which way is left, for God's sake? She spent another moment working it out before she crept down the hall. She gripped the doorknob, then waited for the door to stop swaying before she pushed it open.

"Ah, success," she murmured, then nearly spoiled it by stumbling over the rug. Quietly, she shut the door and leaned back against it. Now, if she could just find the bed. A light switched on, as if by magic. She smiled absently at Nick.

"*Yiasou*, you seem to be a permanent fixture."

The fury in his eyes rolled off the fog as she stepped unsteadily out of her shoes.

"What the hell have you been up to?" he demanded. "It's nearly three o'clock in the morning!"

"Oh, how rude of me not to have phoned to tell you I'd be late."

"Don't get cute, damn it, I'm not in the mood." He stalked over to her and grabbed her arms. "I've been waiting for you half the night, Morgan, I . . ." His voice trailed off as he studied her. His expression altered from fury to consideration, then reluctant amusement. "You're totally bombed."

"Completely," she agreed, and had to take a deep breath to keep from giggling again. "You're so observant, Nicholas."

Amusement faded as her hand crept up his shirt front. "How the hell am I supposed to have a rational conversation with a woman who's seeing two of everything?"

"Three," she told him with some pride. "Andrew's only up to two. I quite surpassed him." Her other hand slid up to toy with one of his buttons. "Did you know you have wonderful eyes. I've never seen eyes so dark. Andrew's are blue. He doesn't kiss anything like you do. Why don't you kiss me now?"

He tightened his grip for a moment, then carefully released her. "So, you've been out with young Andrew." He wandered the room while Morgan swayed and watched him.

"*Young* Andrew and I would have asked you to join us, but it just slipped our minds. Besides, you can be really boring when you're proper and charming." She had a great deal of trouble with the last word and yawned over it. "Do we have to talk much longer? My tongue's getting thick."

"I've had about enough of being proper and charming myself," he muttered, picking up a bottle of her scent and setting it down again. "It serves its purpose."

"You do it very well," she told him and struggled with her zipper. "In fact, you're nearly perfect at it."

"Nearly?" His attention caught, he turned in time to see her win the battle with the zipper. "Morgan, for God's sake, don't do that now. I—"

"Yes, except you do slip up from time to time. A look in your eyes—the way you move. I suppose it's convincing all around if I'm the only one who's noticed. Then again, it might be because everyone else knows you and expects the inconsistency. Are you going to kiss me or not?" She dropped the dress to the floor and stepped out of it.

He felt his mouth go dry as she stood, clad only in a flimsy chemise, watching him mistily. Desire thudded inside him, hot, strong, and he forced himself back to what she was saying.

"Noticed what?"

Morgan made two attempts to pick up the dress. Each time she bent, the top of the chemise drifted out to show the swell of her breasts. Nick felt the thud lower to his stomach. "Noticed what?" she repeated as she left the dress where it was. "Oh, we're back to that. It's definitely the way you move."

"Move?" He struggled to keep his eyes on her face and away from her body. But her scent was already clouding his brain, and her smile—her smile challenged him to do something about it.

"It's like a panther," Morgan told him, "who knows he's being hunted and plans to turn the attack to his advantage when he's ready."

"I see." He frowned, not certain he liked her analogy. "I'll have to be more careful."

"Your problem," Morgan said cheerfully. "Well, since you don't want to kiss me, I'll say good night, Nicholas. I'm going to bed. I'd see you down your vine, but I'm afraid I'd fall off the balcony."

"Morgan, I need to talk to you." He moved quickly and took her arm before she could sink onto the bed. That, he knew, would be too much pressure for any man. But she lost her already uncertain balance and tumbled into his arms.

Warm and pliant, she leaned against him, making no objection as he molded her closer.

"Have you changed your mind?" she murmured, giving him a slow, sleepy-eyed smile. "I thought of you when Andrew kissed me tonight. It was very rude of me—or of you, I'm not sure which. Perhaps I'll think of Andrew if you kiss me now."

"The hell you will." He dragged her against him, teetering on the edge. Morgan let her head fall back.

"Try me," she invited.

"Morgan—the hell with all of it!"

Helplessly, he devoured her mouth. She was quickly and totally boneless, arousing him to desperation by simple surrender. Desire was a fire inside him, spreading dangerously.

For the first time, he let himself go. He could think of nothing, nothing but her and the way her body flowed in his hands. She was softer than anything he'd ever hoped to know. So soft, she threatened to seep into him, become a part of him before he could do anything to prevent it. The need was raging, overpowering, taking over the control he'd been master of for as long as he could remember. But now, he burned to forfeit it.

With her, everything could be different. With her, he'd be clean again. Could she turn back the clock?

He could feel the brush of the bedspread against his thigh and knew, in one movement, he could be on it with her. Then nothing would matter but that he had her—a woman. But it wasn't any woman he wanted. It had been her since the first night she had challenged him on that deserted beach. It had been her since the first time those light, clear eyes had dared him. He was afraid—and he feared little—that it would always be her.

Mixed with the desire came a quick twist of pain. With

a soft oath, he pulled her away, keeping his grip firm on her arms.

"Pay attention, will you?" His voice was rough and unsteady, but she didn't seem to notice. She smiled up at him and touched his cheek with her palm.

"Wasn't I?"

He checked the urge to shake her and spoke calmly. "I need to talk to you."

"Talk?" She smiled again. "Do we have to talk?"

"There are things I need to tell you—this morning . . ." He fumbled with the words, no longer certain what he wanted to say, what he wanted to do. How could her scent be stronger than it had been a moment ago? He was drowning in it.

"Nicholas." Morgan sighed sleepily. "I drank an incredible amount of ouzo. If I don't sleep it off, I may very well die. I'm sure the body only tolerates a certain amount of abuse. I've stretched my luck tonight."

"Morgan." His breath was coming too quickly. His own pulse like thunder in his ears. He should let her go, he knew. He should simply let her go—for both their sakes. But his arms stayed around her. "Straighten up and listen to me," he demanded.

"I'm through listening." She gave a sleepy, sultry laugh. "Through listening. Make love with me or go."

Her eyes were only slits, but the clear, mystical blue pulled him in. No struggle, no force would drag him out again. "Damn you," he breathed as they fell onto the bed. "Damn you for a witch."

It was all hell smoke and thunder. He couldn't resist it. Her body was as fluid as wine—as sweet and as potent. Now he could touch her wherever he chose and she only sighed. As his mouth crushed possessively on hers, she yielded, but in yielding held him prisoner. Even knowing it, he was helpless. There'd be a payment—a price in pain—for succumbing to the temptation. He no longer cared for tomorrows. Now, this moment, he had her. It was enough.

He tore the filmy chemise from her, too anxious, too desperate, but she made no protest as the material ripped away. On a groan of need, he devoured her.

Tastes—she had such tastes. They lingered on his tongue, spun in his head. The crushed wild honey of her mouth, the rose-petal sweetness of her skin, drove him to search for more, and to find everything. He wasn't gentle—he was long past gentleness, but the quiet moans that came from her spoke of pleasure.

Words, low and harsh with desire, tumbled from him. He wasn't certain if he cursed her again or made her hundreds of mad promises. For the moment, it was all the same. Needs ripped through him—needs he understood, needs he'd felt before. But there was something else, something stronger, greedier. Then his flesh was against her flesh, and everything was lost. Fires and flames, a furnace of passion engulfed him, driving him beyond control, beyond reason. She was melting into him. He felt it as a tangible ache but had no will to resist.

Her hands were hot on his skin, her body molten. He could no longer be certain who led and who followed. Beneath his, her mouth was soft and willing, but he tasted her strength. Under him, her body was pliant, unresisting, but he felt her demand. Her skin would be white, barely touched by the sun. He burned to see it, but saw only the glimmer of her eyes in the darkness.

Then she pulled his mouth back to hers and he saw nothing, nothing but the blur of raging colors that were passion. The wild, sweet scent of jasmine seeped into him, arousing, never soothing, until he thought he'd never smell anything else.

With a last force of will, he struggled for sanity. He wouldn't lose himself in her—to her. He couldn't. Without self-preservation he was nothing, vulnerable. Dead.

Even as he took her in a near violent rage, he surrendered.

CHAPTER 8

The sunlight that poured through the windows, through the open balcony doors, throbbed and pulsed in Morgan's head. With a groan she rolled over, hoping oblivion would be quick and painless. The thudding only increased. Morgan shifted cautiously and tried for a sitting position. Warily she opened her eyes, then groaned at the flash of white morning sun. She closed them again in self-preservation. Slowly, gritting her teeth for courage, she allowed her lids to open again.

The spinning and whirling that had been enjoyable the night before, now brought on moans and mutters. With queasy stomach and aching eyes, she sat in the center of the bed until she thought she had the strength to move. Trying to keep her head perfectly still, she eased herself onto the floor.

Carelessly, she stepped over her discarded dress and found a robe in the closet. All she could think of were ice packs and coffee. Lots of coffee.

Then she remembered. Abruptly, blindingly. Morgan whirled from the closet to stare at the bed. It was empty—maybe she'd dreamed it. Imagined it. In useless defense she pressed her hands to her face. No dream. He had been there, and everything she remembered was real. And she remembered . . . the anger in his eyes, her own misty, taunting invitation. The way his mouth had pressed bruisingly to hers, her own unthinking, abandoned response.

The passion—it had been all she had thought it would be. Unbearable, wonderful, consuming. He'd cursed her. She could remember his words. Then he had taken her places she'd never even glimpsed before. She'd given him everything, then mindlessly challenged him to take more. She could still feel those taut, tensing muscles in his back, hear that ragged, desperate breathing at her ear.

He had taken her in fury, and it hadn't mattered to her. Then he had been silent. She had fallen asleep with her arms still around him. And now he was gone.

On a moan, Morgan dropped her hands to her sides. Of course he was gone. What else did she expect? The night had meant nothing to him—less than nothing. If she hadn't had so much to drink . . .

Oh, convenient excuse, Morgan thought on a wave of disgust. She still had too much pride to fall back on it. No, she wouldn't blame the ouzo. Walking to the bed, she picked up the torn remains of her chemise. She'd wanted him. God help her, she cared for him—too much. No, she wouldn't blame the ouzo. Balling the chemise in her fist, Morgan hurled it into the bottom of the closet. She had only herself to blame.

With a snap, Morgan closed the closet door. It was over, she told herself firmly. It was done. It didn't have to mean any more to her than it had to Nick. For a moment, she leaned her forehead against the smooth wooden panel and fought the urge to weep. No, she wouldn't cry over him. She'd never cry over him. Straightening, Morgan told herself it was the headache that was making her feel so weak and weepy. She was a grown woman, free to give herself, to take a man, when and where she chose. Once she'd gone down and had some coffee, she'd be able to put everything in perspective.

She swallowed the threatening tears and walked to the door.

"Good morning, *kyrios*." The tiny maid greeted Morgan with a smile she could have done without. "Would you like your breakfast in your room now?"

"No, just coffee." The scent of food didn't agree with her stomach or her disposition. "I'll go down for it."

"It's a beautiful day."

"Yes, beautiful." With her teeth clenched, Morgan moved down the hall.

The sound of crashing dishes and a high-pitched scream had Morgan gripping the wall for support. She pressed her hand to her head and moaned. Did the girl have to choose this morning to be clumsy!

But when the screaming continued, Morgan turned back. The girl knelt just inside the doorway. Scattered plates and cups lay shattered over the rug where the food had splattered.

"Stop it!" Leaning down, Morgan grabbed her shoulders and shook Zena out of self-defense. "No one's going to fire you for breaking a few dishes."

The girl shook her head as her eyes rolled. She pointed a trembling finger toward the bed before she wrenched herself from Morgan's hold and fled.

Turning, Morgan felt the room dip and sway. A new nightmare crept in to join the old. With her hand gripping the doorknob; she stared.

A shaft of sunlight spread over Iona as she lay on her back, flung sideways across the bed. Her head hung over the edge, her hair streaming nearly to the floor. Morgan shook off the first shock and dizziness and raced forward. Though her fingers trembled, she pressed them to Iona's throat. She felt a flutter, faint, but she felt it. The breath she hadn't been aware she'd held came out in a rush of relief. Moving on instinct, she pulled Iona's unconscious form until she lay back on the bed.

It was then she saw the syringe lying on the tumbled sheets. "Oh, my God."

It explained so much. Iona's moodiness, those tight, jerky nerves. She'd been a fool not to suspect drugs before. She's overdosed, Morgan thought in quick panic. What do I do? There must be something I'm supposed to do.

"Morgan— Dear God!"

Turning her head only, Morgan looked at Dorian standing pale and stiff in the doorway. "She's not dead," Morgan said quickly. "I think she's overdosed—get a doctor—an ambulance."

"Not dead?"

She heard the flat tone of his voice, heard him start to come toward her. There was no time to pamper his feelings. "Do it quickly!" she ordered. "There's a pulse, but it's faint."

"What's Iona done now?" Alex demanded in a tone of strained patience. "The maid's hysterical, and—oh, sweet Lord!"

"An ambulance!" Morgan demanded as she kept her fingers on Iona's pulse. Perhaps if she kept them there, it would continue to beat. "In the name of God, *hurry!*" She turned then in time to see Alex rush from the room as Dorian remained frozen. "There's a syringe," she began with studied calm. She didn't want to hurt him, but continued as his gaze shifted to her. His eyes were blank. "She must have OD'd. Did you know she used drugs, Dorian?"

"Heroin." And a shudder seemed to pass through him. "I thought it had stopped. Are you sure she's—"

"She's alive." Morgan gripped his hand as he came to the bed. A wave of pity washed over her—for Iona, for the man whose hand she held in her own. "She's alive, Dorian. We'll get help for her."

His hand tightened on hers for a moment so that Morgan

had to choke back a protest. "Iona," he murmured. "So beautiful—so lost."

"She's not lost, not yet!" Morgan said fiercely. "If you know how to pray, pray that we found her in time."

His eyes came back to Morgan's, clear, expressionless. She thought as she looked at him she'd never seen anything so empty. "Pray," he said quietly. "Yes, there's nothing else to be done."

It seemed to take hours, but when Morgan watched the helicopter veer off to the west, the morning was still young. Iona, still unconscious, was being rushed to Athens. Dorian rode with her and the doctor while Alex and Liz began hurried preparations for their own flight.

Still barefoot and in her robe, Morgan watched the helicopter until it was out of sight. As long as she lived, she thought, she'd never forget that pale, stony look on Dorian's face—or the lifeless beauty on Iona's. With a shudder, she turned away and saw Alex just inside the doorway.

"Tripolos," he said quietly. "He's in the salon."

"Oh, not now, Alex." Overcome with pity, she held out both hands as she went to him. "How much more can you stand?"

"It's necessary." His voice was tight with control and he held her hands limply. "I apologize for putting you through all this, Morgan—"

"No." She interrupted him and squeezed his hands. "Don't treat me that way, Alex. I thought we were friends."

"Diabolos," he murmured. "Such friends you have. Forgive me."

"Only if you stop treating me as though I were a stranger."

On a sigh, he slipped his arm around her shoulders. "Come, we'll face the captain."

Morgan wondered if she would ever enter the salon without seeing Captain Tripolos seated in the wide, high-back chair. She sat on the sofa as before, faced him, and waited for the questions.

"This is difficult for you," Tripolos said at length. "For all of you." His gaze roamed over the occupants of the room, from Morgan to Alex to Liz. "We will be as discreet as is possible, Mr. Theoharis. I will do what I can to avoid the press, but an attempted suicide in a family as well known as yours . . ." He let the rest trail off.

"Suicide," Alex repeated softly. His eyes were blank, as if the words hadn't penetrated.

"It would seem, from the preliminary report, that your cousin took a self-induced overdose. Heroin. But I hesitate to be more specific until the investigation is closed. Procedure, you understand."

"Procedure."

"You found Miss Theoharis, Miss James?"

Morgan gave a quick, nervous jolt at the sound of her name, then settled. "No, actually, the maid found her. I went in to see what was wrong. Zena had dropped the tray and was carrying on . . . When I went in, I saw Iona."

"And you called for an ambulance?"

"No." She shook her head, annoyed. He knew Alex had called, but wanted to drag the story from her piece by piece. Resigned, Morgan decided to accommodate him. "I thought at first she was dead—then I felt a pulse. I got her back into bed."

"Back into bed?"

Tripolos's tone had sharpened, ever so faintly, but Morgan caught it. "Yes, she was half out of it, almost on the floor. I wanted to lay her down." She lifted her hands helplessly. "I honestly don't know what I wanted to do, it just seemed like the right thing."

"I see. Then you found this?" He held up the syringe, now in a clear plastic bag.

"Yes."

"Did you know your cousin was a user of heroin, Mr. Theoharis?"

Alex stiffened at the question. Morgan saw Liz reach out to take his hand. "I knew Iona had a problem—with drugs. Two years ago she went to a clinic for help. I thought she had found it. If I had believed she was still . . . ill," he managed, "I wouldn't have brought her into my home with my wife and my friend."

"Mrs. Theoharis, were you unaware of Miss Theoharis's problem?"

Morgan heard the breath hiss out between Alex's teeth, but Liz spoke quickly. "I was perfectly aware of it." Alex's head whipped around but she continued calmly. "That is, I was aware that my husband arranged for her to have treatment two years ago, though he tried to shield me." Without looking at him, Liz covered their joined hands with her free one.

"Would you, Mr. Theoharis, have any notion where your cousin received her supply?"

"None."

"I see. Well, since your cousin lives in Athens, perhaps it would be best if I worked with the police there, in order to contact her close friends."

"Do what you must," Alex said flatly. "I only ask that you spare my family as much as possible."

"Of course. I will leave you now. My apologies for the intrusion, yet again."

"I must phone my family," Alex said dully when the door closed behind Tripolos. As if seeking comfort, his hand went to his wife's hair. Then he rose and left without another word.

"Liz," Morgan began. "I know it's a useless phrase, but if there's anything I can do . . ."

Liz shook her head. She shifted her eyes from the doorway back to her friend's. "It's all so unbelievable. That she's lying there, so near death. What's worse, I never liked her. I made no secret of it, but now . . ." She rose and walked to the window. "She's Alex's family, and he feels that deeply. Now, in his heart, he's responsible for whatever happens to her. And all I can think of is how cold I was to her."

"Alex is going to need you." Morgan rose and walked over to put a hand on her shoulder. "You can't help not liking her, Liz. Iona isn't an easy person to like."

"You're right, of course." With a deep breath Liz turned and managed a weak smile. "It's been a hell of a vacation so far, hasn't it? No, don't say anything." She squeezed Morgan's hand. "I'm going to see if Alex needs me. There'll be arrangements to be made."

The villa was silent as Morgan went up to change. As she buttoned her shirt, she stood by the terrace doors, staring out at the view of garden, sea, and mountain. How could it be that so much ugliness had intruded in such a short time? she wondered. Death and near death. This wasn't the place for it. But even Paradise named its price, she thought, and turned away.

The knock on her door was quiet. "Yes, come in."

"Morgan, am I disturbing you?"

"Oh, Alex." As she looked up, Morgan's heart welled with sympathy. The lines of strain and grief seemed etched into his face. "I know how horrible all this is for you, and I don't want to add to your problems. Perhaps I should go back to New York."

"Morgan." He hesitated for a moment. "I know it's a lot to ask, but I don't do it for myself. For Liz. Will you stay for Liz? Your company is all I can give her for a time." He released Morgan's hands and moved restlessly around the room. "We'll have to fly to Athens. I can't say how long—until Iona is well or—" He broke off as if he wasn't yet prepared for the word. "I'll have to stay with my family for a few days.

My aunt will need me. If I could send Liz back knowing you'd be here with her, it would make it so much easier."

"Of course, Alex. You know I will."

He turned and gave her a phantom of a smile. "You're a good friend, Morgan. We'll have to leave you for at least a day and a night. After that, I'll send Liz back. I can be sure she'll leave Athens if you're here." With a sigh, he took her hand absently. "Dorian might choose to stay in Athens as well. I believe he . . . has feelings for Iona I didn't realize before. I'll ask Nick to look after you while we're gone."

"No." She bit her tongue on the hurried protest. "No, really, Alex, I'll be fine. I'm hardly alone, with the servants in the house. When will you leave?"

"Within the hour."

"Alex, I'm sure it was an accident."

"I'll have to convince my aunt of that." He held out his hands, searching his own palms for a moment. "Though as to what I believe . . ." His look had hardened when he lifted his eyes again. "Iona courts disaster. She feeds on misery. I'll tell you now, because I won't ever be able to speak freely to anyone else. Not even Liz." His face was a grim mask now. Cold. "I detest her." He spit the words out as if they were poison. "Her death would be nothing but a blessing to everyone who loves her."

* * *

When Alex, Liz, and Dorian were gone, Morgan left the villa. She needed to walk—needed the air. This time she avoided her habit of heading for the beach. She was far from ready for that. Instead, she struck out for the cliffs, drawn to their jagged, daring beauty.

How clean the air was! Morgan wanted no floral scents

now, just the crisp tang of the sea. She walked without destination. Up, only up, as if she could escape from everything if she could only get higher. If the gods had walked here, she thought, they would have come to the cliffs, to hear the water beat against rock, to breathe the thin, pure air.

She saw, to her pleasure, a scruffy, straggly goat with sharp black eyes. He stared at her a moment as he gnawed on a bit of wild grass he'd managed to find growing in between the rocks. But when she tried to get closer, he scrambled up, lightly, and disappeared over the other side of the cliff.

With a sigh, Morgan sat down on a rock perched high above the water. With some surprise, she saw tiny blue-headed flowers struggling toward the sun out of a crevice hardly wider than a thumbnail. She touched them, but couldn't bring herself to pluck any. Life's everywhere, she realized, if you only know where to look.

"Morgan."

Her hand closed over the blooms convulsively at the sound of his voice. She opened it slowly and turned her head. Nick was standing only a short distance away, his hair caught by the breeze that just stirred the air. In jeans and a T-shirt, his face unshaven, he looked more like the man she had first encountered. Undisciplined. Unprincipled. Her heart gave a quick, bounding leap before she controlled it.

Without a word, Morgan rose and started down the slope.

"Morgan." He caught her quickly, then turned her around with a gentleness she hadn't expected from him. Her eyes were cool, but beneath the frost, he saw they were troubled. "I heard about Iona."

"Yes, you once told me there was little that happened on the island you didn't know."

Her toneless voice slashed at him, but he kept his hands easy on her arms. "You found her."

She wouldn't let that uncharacteristic caring tone cut through her defenses. She could be—would be—as hard and cold as he had been. "You're well informed, Nicholas."

Her face was unyielding, and he didn't know how to begin. If she would come into his arms, he could show her. But the woman who faced him would lean on no one. "It must have been very difficult for you."

She lifted a brow, as though she were almost amused. "It was easier to find someone alive than to find someone dead."

He winced at that—a quick jerk of facial muscles, then dropped his hands. She'd asked him for comfort once, and now that he wanted to give it, needed to give it, it was too late. "Will you sit down?"

"No, it's not as peaceful here as it was."

"Stop slashing at me!" he exploded, grabbing her arms again.

"Let me go."

But the faint quaver in her voice told him something her words hadn't. She was closer to her own threshold than perhaps even she knew. "Very well, if you'll come back to the house with me."

"No."

"Yes." Keeping a hand on her arm, Nick started up the rough path. "We'll talk."

Morgan jerked her arm but his grip was firm. He propelled her up the rough path without looking at her. "What do you want, Nicholas? More details?"

His mouth thinned as he pulled her along beside him. "All right. You can tell me about Iona if you like."

"I don't like," she tossed back. They were already approaching the steps to his house. Morgan hadn't realized they were so close. What devil had prompted her to walk that way? "I don't want to go with you."

"Since when have I cared what you want?" he asked

bitterly and propelled her through the front door. "Coffee," he demanded as Stephanos appeared in the hall.

"All right, I'll give you the details," Morgan raged as she whirled inside the door of the salon. "And then, by God, you'll leave me be! I found Iona unconscious, hardly alive. There was a syringe in bed with her. It seems she was an addict." She paused, unaware that her breath was starting to heave. "But you knew that, didn't you, Nicholas? You know all manner of things."

She'd lost all color, just as she had when she'd run across the beach and into his arms. He felt a twinge, an ache, and reached out for her.

"Don't touch me!" Nick's head jerked back as if she'd slapped him. Morgan pressed her hands against her mouth and turned away. "Don't touch me."

"I won't put my hands on you," Nick managed as they balled into fists. "Sit down, Morgan, before you keel over."

"Don't tell me what to do." Her voice quavered, and she detested it. Making herself turn back, she faced him again. "You have no right to tell me what to do."

Stephanos entered, silent, watchful. As he set the coffee tray down, he glanced over at Morgan. He saw, as Nick couldn't, her heart in her eyes. "You'll have coffee, miss," he said in a soft voice.

"No, I—"

"You should sit." Before Morgan could protest, Stephanos nudged her into a chair. "The coffee's strong."

Nick stood, raging at his impotence as Stephanos clucked around her like a mother hen.

"You'll have it black," he told her. "It puts color in your cheeks."

Morgan accepted the cup, then stared at it. "Thank you."

Stephanos gave Nick one long, enigmatic look, then left them.

"Well, drink it," Nick ordered, furious that the old man had been able to hack through her defenses when he felt useless. "It won't do you any good in the cup."

Because she needed to find strength somewhere, Morgan drank it down quickly. "What else do you want?"

"Damn it, Morgan, I didn't bring you here to grill you about Iona."

"No? You surprise me." Steadier, she set the cup aside and rose again. "Though why anything you do should surprise me, I don't know."

"There's nothing too vile you wouldn't attribute to me, is there?" Ignoring the coffee, Nick strode to the bar. "Perhaps you think I killed Stevos and left the body for you to find."

"No," she said calmly, because she could speak with perfect truth. "He was stabbed in the back."

"So?"

"You'd face a man when you killed him."

Nick turned away from the bar, the glass still empty in his hand. His eyes were black now, as black as she'd ever seen them. There was passion in them barely, just barely, suppressed. "Morgan, last night—"

"I won't discuss last night with you." Her voice was cold and final, cutting through him more accurately than any blade.

"All right, we'll forget it." This time he filled the glass. He'd known there would be a price to pay; somehow he hadn't thought it would be quite so high. "Would you like an apology?"

"For what?"

He gave a short laugh as his hand tightened on the glass. He tossed back the liquor. "God, woman, you've a streak of ice through you I hadn't seen."

"Don't talk to me of ice, Nicholas." Her voice rose with

a passion she'd promised herself she wouldn't feel. "You sit here in your ancestral home, playing your dirty chess games with lives. I won't be one of your pawns. There's a woman barely alive in an Athens hospital. You make your money feeding her illness. Do you think you're remote from the blame because you cross the strait in the dead of night like some swashbuckling pirate?"

Very carefully, he set down the glass and turned. "I know what I am."

She stared at him until her eyes began to fill again. "So do I," she whispered. "God help me."

Turning, she fled. He didn't go after her.

Moments later, Stephanos came back into the room. "The lady's upset," he said mildly.

Nick turned his back to fill his glass again. "I know what the lady is."

"The past two days have been difficult for her." He clucked his tongue. "She came to you for comfort?"

Nick whirled but managed to bite back the words. Stephanos watched calmly. "No, she didn't come to me. She'd go to the devil himself before she came to me again." With an effort, he controlled the rage and his tone. "And it's for the best, I can't let her interfere now. As things stand, she'll be in the way."

Stephanos caressed his outrageous moustache and whistled through his teeth. "Perhaps she'll go back to America."

"The sooner the better," Nick muttered and drained his glass. At the knock on the door, he swore. "See who the hell it is and get rid of them if you can."

"Captain Tripolos," Stephanos announced a few moments later. There was a gleam in his eye as he melted out of sight.

"Captain." Nick fought off the need to swear again. "You'll join me for coffee?"

"Thank you." Tripolos settled into a chair with a few wheezes and sighs. "Was that Miss James I just saw going down the cliff path?"

"Yes." With some effort, Nick prevented his knuckles from whitening against the handle of the pot. "She was just here."

Both men watched each other with what seemed casual interest. One was Morgan's panther—the other a crafty bear.

"Then she told you about Miss Theoharis."

"Yes." Nick offered the cream. "A nasty business, Captain. I intend to call Athens later this morning to see what news there is. Is Iona's condition why you're here?"

"Yes. It's kind of you to see me, Mr. Gregoras. I know you are a very busy man."

"It's my duty to cooperate with the police, Captain," Nick countered as he sat back with his coffee. "But I don't know how I can help you in this case."

"As you were with Miss Theoharis all of yesterday afternoon, I hoped you could shed some light on her frame of mind."

"Oh, I see." Nick sipped his coffee while his mind raced with possibilities. "Captain, I don't know if I can help you. Naturally, Iona was distressed that the man's murder was practically on her doorstep? She was edgy—but then, she often is. I can't say I saw anything different in her."

"Perhaps you could tell me what you did on your boat trip?" Tripolos suggested. "If Miss Theoharis said anything which seemed to indicate she was thinking of suicide?"

Nick lifted a brow. "We weren't overly engaged in conversation."

"Of course."

Nick wondered how long they could continue to fence. He decided to execute a few flourishes of his own. "I will say that Iona seemed a trifle nervous. That is, as I said, however, a habitual trait. You'll find that the people who know her will describe Iona as a . . . restive woman. I can say with complete honesty that it never entered my mind that she was contemplating suicide. Even now, to be candid, I find the idea impossible."

Tripolos settled back comfortably. "Why?"

Generalities, Nick concluded, would suffice. "Iona's too fond of herself to seek death. A beautiful woman, Captain, and one greedy for life's pleasures. It's merely an opinion, you understand. You know much more about this sort of thing." He shrugged. "My opinion is that it was an accident."

"An accident, Mr. Gregoras, is unlikely." He was fishing for a reaction, and Nick gave him another curious lift of brow. "There was too much heroin in her system for any but an amateur to take by mistake. And Miss Theoharis is no stranger to heroin. The marks of the needle tell a sad story."

"Yes, I see."

"Were you aware that Miss Theoharis was an addict?"

"I didn't know Iona very well, Captain. Socially, of course, but basically, she's a cousin of a friend—a beautiful woman who isn't always comfortable to be around."

"Yet you spent the day with her yesterday."

"A beautiful woman," Nick said again, and smiled. "I'm sorry I can't help you."

"Perhaps you'd be interested in a theory of mine."

Nick didn't trust those bland eyes but continued to smile. "Of course."

"You see, Mr. Gregoras," Tripolos went on. "If it was an accident, and if your instincts are correct, there is only one answer."

"One answer?" Nick repeated, then allowed his expression to change slowly. "Do you mean you think someone attempted to . . . murder Iona?"

"I'm a simple policeman, Mr. Gregoras." Tripolos looked plumply humble. "It is my nature to look at such matters from a suspicious point of view. May I be frank?"

"By all means," Nick told him, admiring the captain's plodding shrewdness. Frank be damned, Nick mused, he's going to try to give me enough rope to hang myself.

"I am puzzled, and as a man who knows the Theoharis family well, I would like your opinion."

"Whatever I can do."

Tripolos nodded. "I will tell you first—and of course, you understand this cannot leave this room?"

Nick merely inclined his head and sipped his coffee.

"I will tell you Anthony Stevos was part of a smuggling ring operating on Lesbos."

"I must admit, the thought had crossed my mind." Amused, Nick took out a box of cigarettes, offering one to Tripolos.

"It's no secret that a group has been using this island's nearness to Turkey to smuggle opium across the strait." Tripolos admired the thin wisp of elegant tobacco before he bent closer to Nick for a light.

"You think this Stevos was murdered by one of his cohorts?"

"That is my theory." Tripolos drew in the expensive smoke appreciatively. "It is the leader of this group that is my main concern. A brilliant man, I am forced to admit." Reluctant respect crossed his face. "He is very clever and has so far eluded any nets spread for his capture. It is rumored he rarely joins in the boat trips. When he does, he is masked."

"I've heard the rumors, naturally," Nick mused behind a mist of smoke. "I put a great deal of it down to village gossip and romance. A masked man, smuggling—the stuff of fiction."

"He is real, Mr. Gregoras, and there is nothing romantic about back-stabbing."

"No, you're quite right."

"Stevos was not a smart man. He was being watched in hopes he would lead us to the one we want. But . . ." As was his habit, Tripolos let the sentence trail off.

"I might ask, Captain, why you're telling me what must be police business."

"As an important man in our community," Tripolos said smoothly, "I feel I can take you into my confidence."

The old fox, Nick thought, and smiled. "I appreciate that. Do you think this masked smuggler is a local man?"

"I believe he is a man who knows the island." Tripolos gave a grim smile in return. "But I do not believe he is a fisherman."

"One of my olive pickers?" Nick suggested blandly, blowing out a stream of smoke. "No, I suppose not."

"I believe," Tripolos continued, "from the reports I have received on Miss Theoharis's activities in Athens, that she is aware of the identity of the man we seek."

Nick came to attention. "Iona?"

"I am of the opinion that Miss Theoharis is very involved in the smuggling operation. Too involved for her own safety. If . . . When," he amended, "she comes out of her coma, she'll be questioned."

"It's hard for me to believe that Alex's cousin would be a part of something like that." *He's getting entirely too close*, Nick realized, and swore silently at the lack of time. "Iona's a bit untamed," he went on, "but smuggling and murder. I can't believe it."

"I am very much afraid someone tried to murder Miss Theoharis because she knew too much. I will ask you, Mr. Gregoras, as one who is acquainted with her, how far would Miss Theoharis have gone for love—or for money?"

Nick paused as if considering carefully while his mind raced at readjustments to plans already formed. "For love,

Captain, I think Iona would do little. But for money"—he looked up—"for money, Iona could justify anything."

"You are frank," Tripolos nodded. "I am grateful. Perhaps you would permit me to speak with you again on this matter. I must confess"—Tripolos's smile was sheepish, but his eyes remained direct—"it is a great help to discuss my problems with a man like yourself. It allows me to put things in order."

"Captain, I'm glad to give you any help I can, of course." Nick gave him an easy smile.

For some time after Tripolos left, Nick remained in his chair. He scowled at the Rodin sculpture across the room as he calculated his choices.

"We move tonight," he announced as Stephanos entered.

"It's too soon. Things are not yet safe."

"Tonight," Nick repeated and shifted his gaze. "Call Athens and let them know about the change in plan. See if they can't rig something up to keep this Tripolos off my back for a few hours." He laced his fingers together and frowned. "He's dangled his bait, and he's damn well expecting me to bite."

"It's too dangerous tonight," Stephanos insisted. "There's another shipment in a few days."

"In a few days, Tripolos will be that much closer. We can't afford to have things complicated with the local police now. And I have to be sure." Jet eyes narrowed, and his mouth became a grim line. "I haven't gone through all this to make a mistake at this point. I have to speed things up before Tripolos starts breathing down the wrong necks."

CHAPTER 9

The cove was blanketed in gloom. Rocks glistened, protecting it from winds—and from view. There was a scent—lush wet leaves, wild blossoms that flourished in the sun and hung heavy at night. But somehow it wasn't a pleasant fragrance. It smelt of secrets and half-named fears.

Lovers didn't hold trysts there. Legend said it was haunted. At times, when a man walked near enough on a dark, still night, the voices of spirits murmured behind the rocks. Most men took another route home and said nothing at all.

The moon shed a thin, hollow light over the face of the water, adding to rather than detracting from the sense of whispering stillness, of mystic darkness. The water itself sighed gently over the rocks and sand. It was a passive sound, barely stirring the air.

The men who gathered near the boat were like so many shadows—dark, faceless in the gloom. But they were men, flesh and blood and muscle. They didn't fear the spirits in the cove.

They spoke little, and only in undertones. A laugh might be heard from time to time, quick and harsh in a place of secrets, but for the most part they moved silently, competently. They knew what had to be done. The time was nearly right.

One saw the approach of a new shadow and grunted to his companion. Stealthily, he drew a knife from his belt, gripping its crude handle in a strong, work-worn hand. The blade glittered dangerously through the darkness. Work stopped; men waited.

As the shadow drew closer, he sheathed the knife and swallowed the salty taste of fear. He wouldn't have been afraid to murder, but he was afraid of this man.

The thick, sturdy fingers trembled as they released the knife. "We weren't expecting you."

"I do not like to always do the expected." The answer was in brisk Greek as a pale finger of moonlight fell over him. He wore black—all black, from lean black slacks to a sweater and leather jacket. Lean and tall, he might have been god or devil.

A hood concealed both his head and face. Only the gleam of dark eyes remained visible—and deadly.

"You join us tonight?"

"I am here," he returned. He wasn't a man who answered questions, and no more were asked. He stepped aboard as one used to the life and sway of boats.

It was a typical fishing vessel. Its lines were simple. The decks were clean but rough, the paint fresh and black. Only the expense and power of its motor separated it from its companions.

Without a word, he crossed the deck, ignoring the men who fell back to let him pass. They were hefty, muscled men with thick wrists and strong hands. They moved away from the lean man as if he could crush them to bone with one sweep of his narrow hand. Each prayed the slitted eyes would not seek him out.

He placed himself at the helm, then gazed casually over his shoulder. At the look, the lines were cast off. They would row until they were out to sea and the roar of the motor would go unnoticed.

The boat moved at an easy pace, a lone speck in a dark sea. The motor purred. There was little talk among the men. They were a silent group in any case, but when the man was with them, no one wanted to speak. To speak was to bring attention to yourself—not many dared to do so.

He stared out into the water and ignored the wary glances thrown his way. He was remote, a figure of the night. His hood rippled in the salt-sprayed wind—a carefree, almost adventurous movement. But he was still as a stone.

Time passed; the boat listed with the movement of the sea. He might have been a figurehead. Or a demon.

"We are short-handed." The man who had greeted him merged with his shadow. His voice was low and coarse. His stomach trembled. "Do you wish me to find a replacement for Stevos?"

The hooded head turned—a slow, deliberate motion. The man took an instinctive step in retreat and swallowed the copper taste that had risen to his throat.

"I will find my own replacement. You would all do well to remember Stevos." He lifted his voice on the warning as his eyes swept the men on deck. "There is no one who cannot be . . . replaced." He used a faint emphasis on the final word, watching the dropping of eyes with satisfaction. He needed their fear, and he had it. He could smell it on them. Smiling beneath the hood, he turned back to the sea.

The journey continued, and no one else spoke to him—or about him. Now and then a sailor might cast his eyes toward the man at the helm. The more superstitious crossed themselves or made the ancient sign against evil. When the devil was with them, they knew the full power of fear. He ignored them, treated them as though he were alone on the boat. They thanked God for it.

Midway between Lesbos and Turkey, the motor was shut off. The sudden silence resounded like a thunderclap. No one spoke as they would have done if the figure hadn't been at the helm. There were no crude jokes or games of dice.

The boat shifted easily in its own wake. They waited, all but one swatting in the cool sea breeze. The moon winked behind a cloud, then was clear again.

The motor of an approaching boat was heard as a distant cough, but the sound grew steadier, closer. A light signaled twice, then once again before the glow was shut off. The second motor, too, gave way to silence as another fishing vessel drifted alongside the first. The two boats merged into one shadow.

The night was glorious—almost still and silvered by the moon. Men waited, watching that dark, silent figure at the helm.

"The catch is good tonight," a voice called out from the second boat. The sound drifted, disembodied over the water.

"The fish are easily caught while sleeping."

There was a short laugh as two men leaned over the side and hauled a dripping net, pregnant with fish, onto the deck. The vessel swayed with the movement, then steadied.

The hooded man watched the exchange without word or gesture. His eyes shifted from the second vessel to the pile of fish lying scattered and lifeless on the deck. Both motors roared into life again and separated; one to the east, one to the west. The moon glimmered white. The breeze picked up. The boat was again a lone speck on a dark sea.

"Cut them open."

The men looked up sharply into the slitted eyes. "Now?" one of them dared to ask. "Don't you want them taken to the usual place?"

"Cut them open," he repeated. His voice sent a chill through the quiet night. "I take the cache with me."

Three men knelt beside the fish. Their knives worked swiftly and with skill while the scent of blood and sweat and fear prickled the air. A small pile of white packets grew as they were torn from the bellies of fish. The mutilated corpses were tossed back into the sea. No one would bring that catch to their table.

He moved quickly but without any sense of hurry, slipping packets into the pockets of his jacket. To a man they scrambled back from him, as if his touch might bring death—or worse. Satisfied, he gave them a brief survey before he resumed his position at the helm.

Their fear brought him a grim pleasure. And the cache was his for the taking. For the first time, he laughed—a long, cold sound that had nothing to do with humor. No one spoke, in even a whisper, on the journey back.

Later, a shadow among shadows, he moved away from the cove. He was wary that the trip had gone so easily, exhilarated that it was done. There had been no one to question him, no one with the courage to follow, though he was one man and they were many. Still, as he crossed the strip of beach, he moved with caution, for he wasn't a fool. He had more than just a few frightened fishermen to consider. And he would have more to deal with before he was done.

The walk was long, and steep, but he took it at an easy pace. The hollow call of an owl caused him to pause only briefly to scan the trees and rocks through the slits in the mask. From his position, he could see the cool white lines of the Theoharis villa. He stood where he was a moment—watching, thinking. Then he spun away to continue his climb.

He moved over rocks as easily as a goat—walking with a sure, confident stride in the darkness. He'd covered that route a hundred times without a light. And he kept clear of the path—a path meant men. He stepped around the rock where Morgan had sat that morning, but he didn't see the flowers. Without pausing, he continued.

There was a light in the window. He'd left it burning himself before he had set out. Now for the first time he thought of comfort—and a drink to wash the taste of other men's fear from his throat.

Entering the house, he strode down the corridor and entered a room. Carelessly, he dumped the contents of his pockets on an elegant Louis XVI table, then removed his hood with a flourish.

"Well, Stephanos." Nick's teeth flashed in a grin. "The fishing was rich tonight."

Stephanos acknowledged the packets with a nod. "No trouble?"

"One has little trouble with men who fear the air you breathe. The trip was as smooth as a whore's kiss." Moving away, he poured two drinks and handed one to his companion. The sense of exhilaration was still on him—the power that comes from risking death and winning. He drained his drink in one swallow. "A seedy crew, Stephanos, but they do their job. They're greedy, and"—he lifted the hood, then let it fall on the cache of opium, black on white—"terrified."

"A terrified crew is a cooperative one," Stephanos commented. He poked a stubby finger at the cache of opium. "Rich fishing indeed. Enough to make a man comfortable for a long time."

"Enough to make him want more," Nick stated with a grin. "And more. *Diabolos*, the smell of fish clings to me." He wrinkled his nose in disgust. "Send our cache to Athens, and see they send a report to me of its purity. I'm going to wash off this stink and go to bed."

"There's a matter you might be interested in."

"Not tonight." Nick didn't bother to turn around. "Save your gossip for tomorrow."

"The woman, Nicholas." Stephanos saw him stiffen and pause. There was no need to tell him which woman. "I learned she doesn't go back to America. She stays here while Alex is in Athens."

"Diabolos!" Nick swore and turned back into the room. "I can't be worried about a woman."

"She stays alone until Alex sends his lady back."

"The woman is not my concern," he said between his teeth.

As was his habit, Stephanos sniffed the liquor to add to his appreciation. "Athens was interested," he said mildly. "Perhaps she could still be of use."

"No." Nick took an agitated turn around the room. Nerves that had been cold as ice began to thaw. Damn her, he thought, she'll make me careless even thinking of her. "That woman is more trouble than use. No," he repeated as Stephanos lifted his brows. "We'll keep her out of it."

"Difficult, considering—"

"We'll keep her out of it," Nick repeated in a tone that made Stephanos stroke his moustache.

"As you wish, *kyrios.*"

"Go to the devil." Annoyed with the mock respectful tone, Nick picked up his glass, then set it down again. "She's no use to us," he said with more calm. "More of a stumbling block. We'll hope she keeps her elegant nose inside the villa for a few days."

"And if she pokes her elegant nose out?" Stephanos inquired, enjoying his liquor.

Nick's mouth was a grim line. "Then I'll deal with her."

"I think perhaps," he murmured as Nick strode from the room, "she has already dealt with you, old friend." He laughed and poured himself another drink. "Indeed, the lady's dealt you a killing blow."

After he had bathed, Nick couldn't settle. He told himself it was the excess energy from the night, and his success. But he found himself standing at his window, staring down at the Theoharis villa.

So she was alone, he thought, asleep in that big soft bed. It meant nothing to him. He'd climbed that damn wall to her room for the last time. He'd gone there the night before on impulse, something he'd known better than to do. He'd gone to see her, with some mad idea of justifying his actions to her.

Fool, he called himself as his hands curled tight around the stone railing. Only a fool justifies what he does. He'd gone to her and she'd taunted him, driven him to give up something he had no business giving up. His heart. Damn her, she'd wrenched it out of him.

His grip tightened as he remembered what it had been like to have her—to taste her and fill himself with her. It had been a mistake, perhaps the most crucial one he'd ever made. It was one matter to risk your life, another to risk your soul.

He shouldn't have touched her, Nick thought on yet another wave of anger. He'd known it even as his hands had reached for her. She hadn't known what she was doing, drunk on the ouzo Andrew had bought her. Andrew—he felt a moment's rage and banked it. There'd been moments when he hated Andrew, knowing he'd kissed her. Hated Dorian because Morgan had smiled at him. And Alex because he could touch her in friendship.

And, he knew, Morgan would hate him for what had passed between them that night. Hadn't he heard it in the icy words she'd flung at him? He'd rather have handed her his own knife than to have the words of a woman slash at him that way. She would hate him for taking her when she was vulnerable—while that damn medal hung around her neck. And she would hate him for what he was.

On a rising wave of temper, Nick whirled away from the window. Why should it concern him? Morgan James would slip out of his life like a dream in only a few weeks in any case. He'd chosen his path before, long before he'd seen her. It was his way. If she hated him for what he was, then so be it. He wouldn't allow her to make him feel dirty and soiled.

If she'd touched his heart, he could deal with it. Sprawling into a chair, Nick scowled into the darkness. He would deal with it, he promised himself. After all he'd done, and all he'd faced, no blue-eyed witch would take him under.

* * *

Morgan felt completely alone. The solitude and silence she had so prized only a few days before now weighed down on her. The house was full of servants, but that brought her no comfort, no company. Alex and Liz and Dorian were gone. She wandered listlessly through the morning as she had wandered restlessly through the night. The house felt like a prison—clean and white and empty. Trapped inside it, she was too vulnerable to her own thoughts.

And because her thoughts centered too often on Nick, she found the idea of lying in the bed they had shared too painful. How could she sleep in peace in a place where she could still feel his hands on her, his lips ruthlessly pressing on hers? How could she sleep in a room that seemed to carry that faint sea-smell that so often drifted from him?

So she couldn't sleep, and her thoughts—and needs—haunted her. What could have happened to her to cause her to love such a man? And how long could she fight it? If she surrendered to it, she'd suffer for the rest of her life.

Knowing she was only adding to her own depression, Morgan changed into a bathing suit and headed for the beach.

It was ridiculous to be afraid of the beach, afraid of the

house, she told herself. She was here to enjoy both for the next three weeks. Locking herself in her room wouldn't change anything that had happened.

The sand glistened, white and brilliant. Morgan found that on facing it again, the horror didn't materialize. Tossing aside her wrap, she ran into the sea. The water would ease the weariness, the tension. And maybe, just maybe, she would sleep tonight.

Why should she be keeping herself in a constant state of nerves over the death of a man she didn't even know? Why should she allow the harmless stub of a cigarette to haunt her? It was time to accept the simple explanations and keep her distance. The man had been killed as a result of a village brawl, and that was that. It had nothing to do with her, or anyone she knew. It was tragic, but it wasn't personal.

She wouldn't think about Iona, she told herself. She wouldn't think about smuggling or murders or—here she hesitated a moment and dived under a wave—Nicholas. For now, she wouldn't think at all.

Morgan escaped. In a world of water and sun, she thought only of pleasures. She drifted, letting the tension sink beneath the waves. She'd forgotten, in her own misery, just how clean and alive the water made her feel. For a few moments she would go back to that first day, to that feeling of peace she'd found without even trying.

Liz was going to need her in the next day or two. And Morgan wouldn't be any help at all if she were haggard and tense. Yes, tonight she'd sleep—she'd had enough of nightmares.

More relaxed than she had been in days, Morgan swam back toward shore. The sand shifted under her feet with the gentle current. Shells dotted the shoreline, clean and glistening. She stood and stretched as the water lapped around her knees. The sun felt glorious.

"So Helen rises from the sea."

Lifting her hand, Morgan shielded her eyes and saw Andrew. He sat on the beach by her towel, watching her.

"It's easy to understand how she set kingdoms at odds." He stood and moved to the water's edge to join her. "How are you, Morgan?"

"I'm fine." She accepted the towel he handed her and rubbed it briskly over her hair.

"Your eyes are shadowed. A blue sea surrounded by clouds." He traced her cheek with a fingertip. "Nick told me about Iona Theoharis." He took her hand and led her back to the white sand. Dropping the towel, Morgan sat beside him. "It's a bit soon for you to have to handle something like that, Morgan. I'm sorry you had to be the one to find her."

"It seems to be a talent of mine." She shook her head. "I'm much better today, really." Smiling, she touched his cheek. "Yesterday I felt . . . actually I don't think I felt much of anything yesterday. It was like I was watching everything through a fisheye lens. Everything was distorted and unreal. Today it's real, but I can cope with it."

"I suppose that's nature's way of cushioning the senses."

"I feel this incredible sorrow for Alex and Liz—and for Dorian." She leaned back on her elbows, wanting to feel the sun as it dried the water on her skin. "It's so hard on them, Andrew. It leaves me feeling helpless." She turned her face to his, pushing at her streaming hair. "I hope this doesn't sound hard, but I feel, after these past two days, I think I've just realized how glad I am to be alive."

"I'd say that's a very healthy, very normal reaction." He, too, leaned back on his elbows, narrowing his eyes against the sun as he studied her.

"Oh, I hope so. I've been feeling guilty about it."

"You can't be guilty about wanting to live, Morgan."

"No. Suddenly I realized how much I want to do. How

much I want to see. Do you know, I'm twenty-six, and this is the first time I've been anywhere? My mother died when I was a baby and my father and I moved to New York from Philadelphia. I've never seen anything else." As drops of water trickled down her skin, she shook her damp hair back. "I can speak five languages, and this is the first time I've been in a country where English isn't needed. I want to go to Italy and France." She turned to face him more directly. Her eyes, though still shadowed, were huge with adventure. "I want to see Venice and ride in a gondola. I want to walk on the Cornish moors and on the Champs d'Élysées." She laughed and it felt marvelous. "I want to climb mountains."

"And be a fisherman?" He smiled and laid a hand over hers.

"Oh, I did say that, didn't I?" She laughed again. "I'll do that, too. Jack always said my taste was rather eclectic."

"Jack?"

"He's a man I knew back home." Morgan found the ease with which she put him in the past satisfying. "He was in politics. I think he wanted to be king."

"Were you in love with him?"

"No, I was used to him." She rolled her eyes and grinned. "Isn't that a terrible thing to say?"

"I don't know—you tell me."

"No," she decided. "Because it's the truth. He was very cautious, very conventional, and, I'm sorry to say, very boring. Not at all like . . ." Her voice trailed off.

Andrew followed her gaze and spotted Nick at the top of the cliff. He stood, legs apart, hands thrust in his pockets, staring down at them. His expression was unreadable in the distance. He turned, without a wave or a sign of greeting, and disappeared behind the rocks.

Andrew shifted his gaze back to Morgan. Her expression was totally readable.

"You're in love with Nick."

Morgan brought herself back sharply. "Oh, no. No, of course not. I hardly know him. He's a very disagreeable man. He has a brutal temper, and he's arrogant and bossy and without any decent feelings. He shouts."

Andrew took in this impassioned description with a lifted brow. "We seem to be talking about two different people."

Morgan turned away, running sand through her fingers. "Maybe. I don't like either one of them."

Andrew let the silence hang a moment as he watched her busy fingers. "But you're in love with him."

"Andrew—"

"And you don't want to be," he finished, looking thoughtfully out to sea. "Morgan, I've been wondering, if I asked you to marry me, would it spoil our friendship?"

"What?" Astonished, she spun her head back around. "Are you joking?"

Calmly, he searched her face. "No, I'm not joking. I decided that asking you to bed would put a strain on our friendship. I wondered if marriage would. Though I didn't realize you were in love with Nick."

"Andrew," she began, uncertain how to react. "Is this a question or a proposal?"

"Let's take the question first."

Morgan took a deep breath. "An offer of marriage, especially from someone you care for, is always flattering to the ego. But egos are unstable and friendships don't require flattery." Leaning over, she brushed his mouth with hers. "I'm very glad you're my friend, Andrew."

"Somehow I thought that would be your reaction. I'm a romantic at heart." Shrugging, he gave her a rueful smile. "An island, a beautiful woman with a laugh like a night wind. I could see us setting up house in the cottage. Fires in the winter, flowers in the spring."

"You're not in love with me, Andrew."

"I could be." Taking her hand, he turned it palm up and studied it. "It isn't your destiny to fall in love with a struggling poet."

"Andrew—"

"And it isn't mine to have you." Smiling again, he kissed her hand. "Still, it's a warm thought."

"And a lovely one. Thank you for it."

He nodded before he rose. "I might decide Venice offers inspiration." Andrew studied the protruding section of the gray stone wall before turning back to her. "Maybe we'll see each other there." He smiled, the flashing boyish smile, and Morgan felt a twinge of regret. "Timing, Morgan, is such an essential factor in romance."

She watched him cross the sand and mount the steps before she turned back to the sea.

CHAPTER 10

The villa whispered and trembled like an old woman. Even after all her promises to herself that morning, Morgan couldn't sleep. She rolled and tossed in her bed, frantically bringing herself back from dreams each time she started to drift off. It was too easy for Nick to slip into her mind in a dream. Through sheer force of will, Morgan had blocked him out for most of the day. She wouldn't surrender to him now, for only a few hours' sleep.

Yet awake and alone, she found herself remembering the inlet—the face under the water, the slim black stub of a cigarette. And Iona, pale and barely alive, with her thick mane of hair streaming nearly to the floor.

Why was it she couldn't rid herself of the thought that one had something to do with the other?

There was too much space, too much quiet in the villa to be tolerated in solitude. Even the air seemed hot and oppressive. As fatigue began to take over, Morgan found herself caught between sleep and wakefulness, that vulnerable land where thoughts can drift and tease.

She could hear Alex's voice, cold and hard, telling her that Iona would be better off dead. There were Dorian's eyes, so calm, so cool, as he lifted a thin black cigarette to his lips.

Andrew smiling grimly as he waited for his ship to come in. Liz vowing passionately that she would protect her husband from anyone and anything. And the knife blade, so sharp and deadly. She knew without seeing that Nick's hand gripped the handle.

On a half scream, Morgan sat up and willed herself awake. No, she wouldn't sleep, not alone. She didn't dare.

Before giving herself time to think, she rose and slipped on jeans and a shirt. The beach had given her peace that afternoon. Maybe it would do the same for her tonight.

Outside, she found the openness comforting. There were no walls here or empty rooms. There were stars and the scent of blossoms. She could hear the cypress leaves whisper. The feeling of dread slid from her with every step. She headed for the beach.

The moon was nearly full now, and white as bone. The breeze off the water was degrees cooler than the air had been in her room. She followed the path without hesitation, without fear. Some instinct told her nothing would harm her that night.

After rolling up her pants legs, she stood, letting the water lap over her ankles, warm and silky. Gratefully, she breathed in the moist sea air and felt it soothe her. She stretched her arms toward the stars.

"Will you never learn to stay in bed?"

Morgan spun around to find herself face-to-face with Nick. Had he already been there? she wondered. She hadn't heard him walk behind her. Straightening, she eyed him coolly. Like her, he wore jeans and no shoes. His shirt hung unbuttoned over his bare chest. What madness was it, she wondered, that made her long to go to him. Whatever madness drew her to him, she suppressed.

"That's not your concern." Morgan turned her back on him. Nick barely prevented himself from yanking her back around. He'd been standing sleepless at his window when he'd seen her leave the house. Almost before he had known what he was doing, he was coming down the beach steps to find her. And it was ice, that same ice, she greeted him with.

"Have you forgotten what happens to women who wander night beaches alone?" The words rang with mockery as he tangled his fingers in her hair. He'd touch her if he chose, he thought furiously. No one would stop him.

"If you plan to drag me around this time, Nicholas, I warn you, I'll bite and scratch."

"That should make it interesting." His fingers tightened as she tossed her head to dislodge his grip. "I'd think you'd have had your fill of beaches today, Aphrodite. Or are you expecting Andrew again?"

She ignored the taunt and the peculiar thrill that came whenever he called her by that name. "I'm not expecting anyone. I came here to be alone. If you'd go away, I could enjoy myself."

Hurting, wanting, Nick spun her around. His fingers bruised her skin so that she made a surprised sound of pain before she could clamp it down. "Damn you, Morgan, don't push me any more. You'll find me a different breed from young Andrew."

"Take your hands off me." She managed to control her voice to a hard, cold steadiness. Her eyes glimmered with frost as they stared into his. She wouldn't cower before him again, and she wouldn't yield. "You'd do well to take lessons from Andrew"—deliberately, she tossed her head and smiled—"or Dorian on how to treat a woman."

Nick swore with quick Greek expertise. Unable to do otherwise, he gripped her tighter, but this time she made no sound. Morgan watched as the dark fury took total command of his face. He was half devil now, violent, with barely a trace of the man others knew. It gave her a perverse enjoyment to know she had driven him to it.

"So you offer yourself to Dorian as well?" He bit off the words as he fought to find some hold on his control. "How many men do you need?"

A flood of fury rose, but she stamped it down. "Isn't it strange, Nicholas," she said calmly, "how your Greek half seems to take over when you're angry? I simply can't see how you and Andrew can be related, however remotely."

"You enjoy leading him on, don't you?" The comparison stroked his fury higher. Morgan found she was gritting her teeth to prevent a whimper at the pain. She wouldn't give him the satisfaction. "Heartless bitch," he hissed at her. "How long do you intend to dangle and tease?"

"How dare you!" Morgan pushed against him. Anger, unreasonable and full, welled up in her for all the sleepless hours he'd given her, and all the pain. "How dare you criticize me for anything! You, with the filthy games you play, and the lies. You care about *no one*—no one but yourself. I detest you and everything you are!" Wrenching free, Morgan fled into the sea, blind and senseless with rage.

"Stupid woman!" Nick tore through two sentences of furious Greek before he caught her and pulled her around. The water lapped around her hips as he shook her. When her feet slipped on the bottom, he dragged her back up. He couldn't think now, couldn't reason. His voice whipped out with the violence of his thoughts. "I'll be damned if you'll make me crawl. Damned if I'll beg for your good feelings. I do what I have to do; it's a matter of necessity. Do you think I enjoy it?"

"I don't care about your necessities or your smuggling or your murders! I don't care about anything that has to do with you. I hate you!" She took a swing at his chest and nearly submerged again. "I hate everything about you. I hate myself for ever letting you touch me!"

The words cut at him, deeper than he wanted them to. He fought not to remember what it had felt like to hold her, to press his mouth against her and feel her melt against him. "That's fine. Just keep your distance and we'll get along perfectly."

"There's nothing I want more than to keep away from you." Her eyes glittered as the words brought her a slash of pain. "Nothing I want more than to never see your face again or hear your name."

He controlled himself with an effort—for there was nothing he wanted more at that moment than to crush her against him and beg, as he'd never begged anyone, for whatever she'd give him. "Then that's what you'll have, Aphrodite. Play your games with Dorian if you like, but tread carefully with Andrew. Tread carefully, or I'll break your beautiful neck."

"Don't you threaten me. I'll see Andrew just as often as I like." Morgan pushed at her dripping hair and glared at him. "I don't think he'd appreciate your protection. He asked me to marry him."

In one swift move, Nick lifted her off her feet and dragged her against his chest. Morgan kicked out, succeeding only in drenching both of them. "What did you tell him?"

"It's none of your business." She struggled, and though she was slick as an eel in the water, his hold remained firm. "Put me *down!* You can't treat me this way."

Fury was raging in him, uncontrollable, savage. No, he wouldn't stand by and watch her with another man. "Damn you, I said what did you tell him!"

"No!" she shouted, more in anger than in fear. "I told him *no.*"

Nick relaxed his grip. Morgan's feet met the sea bottom

again as he formed a brittle smile. Her face was white as chalk and he cursed himself. God, would he do nothing but hurt her? Would she do nothing but hurt him? If there weren't so many walls in his way . . . if he could break down even one of them, he'd have her.

"That's fine." His voice was far from steady, but she had no way of knowing it was from panic rather than temper. "I won't stand by and watch you lead Andrew along. He's an innocent yet." He released her, knowing it might be the last time he'd ever touch her. "I don't suppose you chose to tell him about the lover you left behind."

"Lover?" Morgan pushed at her hair as she took a step back. "What lover?"

Nick lifted the medallion at her neck, then let it fall before he gave in to the need to rip it from her. "The one who gave you the trinket you treasure so much. When a woman carries another man's brand, it's difficult to overlook it."

Morgan closed her hand over the small piece of silver. She had thought nothing could make her more angry than she already was. She was blind and trembling with it. "Another man's brand," she repeated in a whisper. "How typical of you. No one brands me, Nicholas. No one, no matter how I love."

"Your pardon, Aphrodite," he returned coolly. "An expression only."

"My father gave me this," she tossed at him. "He gave it to me when I was eight years old and broke my arm falling out of a tree. He's the kindest and most loving person I've ever known. You, Nicholas Gregoras, are a stupid man."

She turned and darted toward the beach, but he caught her again while the water was still around her ankles. Ignoring her curses and struggles, Nick turned her to face him. His eyes bored into hers. His breath was coming in gasps, but not from rage. He needed an answer, and quickly, before he exploded.

"You don't have a lover in America?"

"I said let me *go!*" She was glorious in fury—eyes glittering, skin white as the moonlight. With her head thrown back, she dared him to defy her. In that moment he thought he would have died for her.

"Do you have a lover in America?" Nick demanded again, but his voice was quiet now.

Morgan threw up her chin. "I haven't a lover *anywhere.*"

On an oath that sounded more like a prayer, Nick drew her close. The heat from his body fused through the soaked shirts as if they had been naked. Morgan's breath caught at the pressure and the sudden gleam of triumph in his eyes.

"You do now."

Capturing her mouth, he pulled her to the sand.

His lips were urgent, burning. His talk of branding raced through her head, but Morgan accepted the fire eagerly. And already he was stripping off her shirt as if he couldn't bear even the thin separation between them.

Morgan knew he would always love like this. Intensely, without thought, without reason. She gloried in it. Desire this strong took no denial. Her own fingers were busy with his shirt, ripping at the seam in her hurry to be flesh to flesh. She heard him laugh with his mouth pressed against her throat.

There was no longer any right or wrong. Needs were too great. And love. Even as passion drove her higher, Morgan knew and recognized her love. She had waited for it all of her life. With the heat building, there was no time to question how it could be Nick. She only knew it was, whatever, whoever, he was. Nothing else mattered.

When his hands found her naked breasts, he groaned and crushed his lips to hers again. She was so soft, so slender. He struggled not to bruise her, not again, but desire was wild and free in him. He'd never wanted a woman like this.

Not like this. Even when he had taken her the first time, he hadn't felt this clean silver streak of power.

She was consuming him, pouring inside his mind. And the taste. Dear God, would he never get enough of the taste of her? He found her breast with his mouth and filled himself.

Morgan arched and dove her fingers into his hair. He was murmuring something, but his breathing was as ragged as hers and she couldn't understand. When his mouth was back on hers, there was no need to. She felt him tugging her jeans over her hips, but was too delirious to realize she had pulled at his first. She felt the skin stretched tight over his bones, the surprising narrowness of his body.

Then his lips and hands were racing over her—not in the angry desperation she remembered from the night before, but in unquestionable possession. There was no gentleness, but neither was there a fierceness. He took and took as though no one had a better right. Those strong lean fingers stroked down her, making her gasp out loud in pleasure, then moan in torment when they lay still.

His mouth was always busy, tongue lightly torturing, teeth taking her to the edge of control. There seemed to be no part of her, no inch he couldn't exploit for pleasure. And the speed never slacked.

Cool sand, cool water, and his hot, clever mouth—she was trapped between them. There was moonlight, rippling white, but she was a willing prisoner of the darkness. In the grove of cypresses a night bird called out—one long, haunting note. It might have been her own sigh. She tasted the sea on his skin, knew he would taste it on hers as well. Somehow, that small intimacy made her hold him tighter.

They might have been the only ones, washed ashore, destined to be lovers throughout their lives without the need for anyone else. The scent of the night wafted over her—his scent. They would always be the same to her.

Then she heard nothing, knew nothing, as he drove her beyond reason with his mouth alone.

She was grasping at him, demanding and pleading in the same breathless whispers for him to give her that final, delirious relief. But he held her off, pleasing himself, and pleasing her until she thought her body would simply implode at the pressure that was building.

With a wild, hungry kiss he silenced her while leading her closer to the edge. Though she could feel his heart racing against hers, he seemed determined to hold them there—an instant, an hour—hovering between heaven and hell.

When he drove them over, Morgan wasn't certain on which side they had fallen—only that they had fallen together.

* * *

Morgan lay quiet, cushioned against Nick's bare shoulder. The waves gently caressed her legs. In the aftermath of the demands of passion she was light and cool and stunned. She could feel the blood still pounding in his chest and knew no one, no one had ever wanted her like this. The sense of power it might have given her came as an ache. She closed her eyes on it.

She hadn't even struggled, she thought. Not even a token protest. She had given herself without thought—not in submission to his strength, but in submission to her own desires. Now, as the heat of passion ebbed, she felt the hard edge of shame.

He was a criminal—a hard, self-seeking man who trafficked in misery for profit. And she had given him her body and her heart. Perhaps she had no control over her heart, but Morgan was honest enough to know she ruled her own body. Shivering, she drew away from him.

"No, stay." Nick nuzzled in her hair as he held her against his side.

"I have to go in," she murmured. Morgan drew her body away as far as his arm would permit. "Please, let me go."

Nick shifted until his face hovered over hers. His lips were curved in amusement; his face was relaxed and satisfied. "No," he said simply. "You won't walk away from me again."

"Nicholas, please." Morgan turned her head aside. "It's late. I have to go."

He became still for a moment, then took her face firmly in his hand and turned it back to his. He saw the gleam of tears, tightly controlled, and swore. "It occurs to you suddenly that you've just given yourself to a criminal and enjoyed it."

"Don't!" Morgan shut her eyes. "Just let me go in. Whatever I've done, I've done because I wanted to."

Nick stared down at her. She was dry-eyed now, but her eyes were bleak. Swearing again, he reached for his partially dry shirt and pulled Morgan into a sitting position. Athens, he thought again, could fry in hell.

"Put this on," he ordered, swinging it over her shoulders. "We'll talk."

"I don't want to talk. There's no need to talk."

"I said we'll talk, Morgan." Nick pushed her arm into a sleeve. "I won't have you feeling guilty over what just happened." She could feel the simmering anger pulsing from him as he pulled his shirt over her breasts. "I won't have that," he muttered. "It's too much. I can't explain everything now . . . There are some things I won't ever explain."

"I'm not asking for explanations."

His eyes locked on hers. "You ask every time you look at me." Nick pulled a cigarette from the pocket of the shirt, then lit it. "My business in import-export has made me quite a number of contacts over the years. Some of whom, I imagine, you wouldn't approve of." He mused over this for a moment as he blew out a hazy stream of smoke.

"Nicholas, I don't—"

"Shut up, Morgan. When a man's decided to bare his soul, a woman shouldn't interrupt. God knows how dark you'll find it," he added, as he drew in smoke again. "When I was in my early, impressionable twenties, I met a man who considered me suitable for a certain type of work. I found the work itself fascinating. Danger can become addicting, like any other drug."

Yes, she thought as she stared out over the water. If nothing else, she could understand that.

"I began to—freelance." He smiled at the term, but it had little to do with humor. "For his organization. For the most part I enjoyed it. In any case, I was content with it. It's amazing that a way of life, ten years of my life should become a prison in a week's time."

Morgan had drawn her knees close to her chest while she stared out over the water. Nick laid a hand on her hair, but she still didn't look at him. He was finding it more difficult to tell her than he had imagined. Even after he'd finished, she might turn away from him. He'd be left with nothing—less than nothing. He drew hard on his cigarette, then stared at the red glow at the tip.

"Morgan, there are things I've done . . ." He swore briefly under his breath. "There are things I've done I wouldn't tell you about even if I were free to. You wouldn't find them pleasant."

Now she lifted her face. "You've killed people."

He found it difficult to answer when she was looking at him with tired despair in her eyes. But his voice was cool with control. "When it was necessary."

Morgan lowered her head again. She hadn't wanted to think him a murderer. If he had denied it, she would have

tried to have taken him at his word. She hadn't wanted to believe he was capable of what she considered the ultimate sin.
The taking of a life.

Nick scowled at the cigarette and hurled it into the sea.
I could have lied to her, he thought furiously. Why the hell
didn't I just lie—I'm an expert at it. Because I can't lie to her,
he realized with a tired sigh. Not anymore. "I did what I had
to do, Morgan," he said flatly. "I can't erase the way I've
lived for ten years. Right or wrong, it was my choice. I can't
apologize for it."

"No, I'm not asking you to. I'm sorry if it seems that way."
She drew herself up again and faced him. "Please, Nicholas,
let's leave it at this. Your life's your own. You don't have to
justify it to me."

"Morgan—" If she had hurled abuse at him, stabbed
him with ice, he might have been able to keep silent. But
he couldn't be silent while she struggled to understand. He
would tell her, and the decision he'd been struggling with
for days would be made. "For the last six months, I've been
working on breaking the smuggling ring that runs between
Turkey and Lesbos."

Morgan stared at him as though she'd never seen him before. "Breaking it? But I thought . . . you told me—"

"I've never told you much of anything," he said curtly. "I
let you assume. It was better that way. It was necessary."

For a moment she sat quietly, trying to sort out her
thoughts. "Nicholas, I don't understand. Are you telling me
you're a policeman?"

He laughed at the thought, and part of his anger drained.
"No, Aphrodite, spare me that."

Morgan frowned. "A spy then?"

The rest of his anger vanished. He cupped her face in his
hands. She was so unbearably sweet. "You will romanticize

it, Morgan. I'm a man who travels and follows orders. Be content with that, it's all I can give you."

"That first night on the beach . . ." At last the puzzle pieces were taking a shape she could understand. "You were watching for the man who runs the smuggling ring. That was who Stephanos followed."

Nick frowned and dropped his hands. She believed him without question or hesitation. Already she'd forgotten that he'd killed—and worse. Why, when she was making it so easy for him, did he find it so hard to go on? "I had to get you out of the way. I knew he'd cross that section of beach on his way to Stevos's cottage. Stevos was eliminated because he knew, as I don't yet, the man's exact position in the organization. I think he asked for a raise and got a knife in the back."

"Who is he, Nicholas?"

"No." His eyes came back to hers. His face was hard again, unreachable. "Even if I were sure, I wouldn't tell you. Don't ask me questions I can't answer, Morgan. The more I tell you, the more dangerous your position becomes." His eyes grew darker. "I was ready to use you once, and my organization is very interested in your talent with languages, but I'm a selfish man. You're not going to be involved." His tone was final and just a little furious. "I told my associate you weren't interested."

"That's a bit presumptuous," Morgan began. She frowned until he twisted his head and looked at her again. "I'm capable of making my own decisions."

"You haven't one to make," Nick countered coolly. "And once I know for certain the identity of the head of the ring, my job's finished. Athens will have to learn how to function without me."

"You're not going to do this . . ." She gestured vaguely, not knowing what title to give his work. "This sort of thing any-more?"

"No." Nick stared back out to sea. "I've been in it long enough."

"When did you decide to stop?"

When I first made love with you, he thought, and nearly said it. But it wasn't quite true. There was one more thing he would have to tell her. "The day I took Iona on the boat." Nick let out an angry breath and turned to her. He had his doubts that she would forgive him for what he was going to say. "Iona's in this, Morgan, deeply."

"In the smuggling? But—"

"I can only tell you that she is, and that part of my job was to get information out of her. I took her out on the boat, fully intending to make love to her to help loosen her tongue." Morgan kept her eyes steady and he continued, growing angrier. "She was cracking under pressure. I was there to help her along. That's why someone tried to kill her."

"Kill her?" Morgan tried to keep her voice level as she dealt with what he was telling her. "But Captain Tripolos said it was attempted suicide."

"Iona would no more have committed suicide than she would have tended goats."

"No," she said slowly. "No, of course you're right."

"If I could have worked on her a little longer, I would have had all that I needed."

"Poor Alex," she murmured. "He'll be crushed if it comes out that she was mixed up in this. And Dorian . . ." She remembered his empty eyes and his words. *Poor Iona—so beautiful—so lost.* Perhaps he already suspected. "Isn't there something you can do?" She looked up at Nick, this time with trust. "Do the police know? Captain Tripolos?"

"Tripolos knows a great deal and suspects more." Nick

took her hand now. He wanted the link badly. "I don't work directly with the police, it slows things down. At the moment," he added cheerfully, "Tripolos has me pegged as the prime suspect in a murder, an attempted murder, and sees me in the role of the masked smuggler. Lord, I'd have given him a thrill last night."

"You enjoy your work, don't you?" Morgan studied him, recognizing the light of adventure in his eyes. "Why are you stopping?"

His smile faded. "I told you I was with Iona. It wasn't the first time I used that method. Sex can be a weapon or a tool, it's a fact of life." Morgan dropped her gaze to the sand. "She'd had too much champagne to be cooperative, but there would have been another time. Since that day, I haven't felt clean." He slid his hand under her chin and lifted it. "Not until tonight."

She was studying him closely, searching. In his eyes she saw something she had only seen once before—regret, and a plea for understanding. Lifting her arms, she brought his mouth down to hers. She felt more than his lips—the heady wave of his relief.

"Morgan." He pressed her back to the sand again. "If I could turn back the clock and have this past week to live over . . ." He hesitated, then buried his face in her hair. "I probably wouldn't do anything differently."

"You apologize beautifully, Nicholas."

He couldn't keep his hands off her. They were roaming again, arousing them both. "This thing should come to a head tomorrow night, then I'll be at loose ends. Come away somewhere with me for a few days. Anywhere."

"Tomorrow?" She struggled to keep her mind on his words while her body heated. "Why tomorrow?"

"A little complication I caused last night. Come, we're covered with sand. Let's take a swim."

"Complication?" Morgan repeated as he hauled her to her feet. "What kind of complication?"

"I don't think our man will tolerate the loss of a shipment," he murmured as he slipped his shirt from her shoulders.

"You stole it!"

He was pulling her into the water. His blood was already pounding for her as he saw the moonlight glow white over her body. "With incredible ease." When she was past her waist, he drew her against him. The water lapped around them as he began to explore her again. "Stephanos and I watched the connection from a safe distance on several runs." His mouth brushed over hers, then traced down to her throat. "We'd just come back from one the night I found you on the beach. Now, about those few days."

"What will you do tomorrow night?" Morgan drew back enough to stop his roaming hands and mouth. A hint of fear had worked its way in. "Nicholas, what's going to happen?"

"I'm waiting for some conclusive information from Athens. When it comes, I'll know better how to move. At any rate, I'll be there when the boat docks with its cache tomorrow night."

"Not alone?" She gripped his shoulders. "He's already killed a man."

Nick rubbed his nose against hers. "Do you worry for me, Aphrodite?"

"Don't joke!"

He heard the very real panic in her voice and spoke soothingly. "By late tomorrow afternoon, Tripolos will be brought up to date. If everything goes as planned, I can brief him personally." He smiled down at the frown on her face. "He'll gain all official credit for whatever arrests are made."

"But that's unfair!" Morgan exclaimed. "After all your work, and the time, why shouldn't you—"

"Shut up, Morgan, I can't make love to a woman who's constantly complaining."

"Nicholas, I'm trying to understand."

"Understand this." Impatience shimmered in his voice as he pulled her close again. "I've wanted you from the minute I saw you sitting on that damn rock, and I haven't begun to have enough. You've driven me mad for days. Not anymore, Aphrodite. Not anymore."

He lowered his mouth, and all else was lost.

CHAPTER 11

Her jeans were still damp as Morgan struggled into them laughing. "You would make me so furious I'd run into the water fully dressed."

Nick fastened the snap on his own. "The feeling was mutual."

Turning her head, she looked at him as he stood, naked to the waist, shaking what sand he could from his shirt. A gleam of mischief lit her eyes. "Oh?" Taking a step closer, Morgan ran her palms up his chest—taking her time—enjoying the hard, firm feel of it before she linked them around his neck. "Did it make you furious thinking I was wearing a token from a lover waiting for me back home?"

"No," he lied with a careless smile. Gripping his shirt in both hands, Nick hooked it around her waist to draw her closer. "Why should that concern me?"

"Oh." Morgan nipped lightly at his bottom lip. "Then perhaps you'd like to hear about Jack."

"I damn well wouldn't," he muttered before his mouth crushed down on hers. Even as her lips answered his, Nick heard the low sound of her muffled laughter. "Witch." Then he took her deeper, deeper, until her laughter was only a sigh. "Maybe you prefer me when I'm angry."

"I prefer you," she said simply, and rested her head on his shoulder.

His arms tightened, strong, possessive. Yet somehow he knew strength alone would never keep her. "Dangerous woman," Nick murmured. "I knew it the first time I held you."

With a laugh, Morgan tossed back her head. "The first time you held me, you cursed me."

"And I continue to do so." But his lips sought hers again without an oath.

"I wish there was only tonight." Suddenly, she was clinging to him with her heart racing. "No tomorrows, only now. I don't want the sun to come up."

Nick buried his face in her hair as the guilt swamped him. He'd brought her fear from the first instant. Even loving her, he could bring her nothing else. He had no right to tell her now that his heart was hers for the asking. Once he told her, she might beg him to abandon his responsibility, leave his job half finished. And he would do just as she asked, he realized . . . and never feel like a man again.

"Don't wish your days away, Morgan," he told her lightly. "The sun comes up tomorrow, then goes down. And when it comes up again, we'll have nothing but time."

She had to trust him, had to believe that he would be safe—that the danger he lived with would be over in little more than twenty-four hours.

"Come back with me now." Lifting her head again, Morgan gave him a smile. Her worry and fears wouldn't help him. "Come back to the villa and make love with me again."

"You tempt me, Aphrodite." Bending, he kissed both her cheeks in a gesture she found unbearably gentle and sweet. "But you're asleep on your feet. There'll be other nights. I'll take you back."

She allowed him to turn her toward the beach steps.

"You might not find it as easy to leave me there alone as you think," she commented with another smile.

With a quiet laugh, he drew her closer to his side. "Not easy perhaps, but—" His head whipped up abruptly, as if he were scenting the air. Narrowed and cold, his eyes swept the darkness of the cliffs above them.

"Nicholas, what—"

But his hand clamped over her mouth as he pulled her, once again, into the shadows of the cypress. Her heart leaped to her throat as it had before, but this time Morgan didn't struggle.

"Be still and don't speak," Nick whispered. Removing his hand, he pushed her back against the trunk of a tree. "Not a sound, Morgan."

She nodded, but he wasn't looking at her. His eyes were trained on the cliffs. Standing at the edge of the covering, Nick watched and waited. Then he heard it again—the quiet scrape of boot on rock. Tensing, he strained his eyes and at last saw the shadow. So, he thought with a grim smile as he watched the black form move swiftly over the rocks, he's come for his cache. But you won't find it, Nick told the shadow silently. And I'll be like a hound on your tail.

Soundlessly, he moved back to Morgan. "Go back to the villa and stay there." All warmth had dropped away from him. His voice was as cold as his eyes.

"What did you see?" she demanded. "What are you going to do?"

"Do as I say." Taking her arm, he pulled her toward the beach steps. "Go quickly, I haven't got time to waste. I'll lose him."

Him. Morgan felt a flutter of fear. She swallowed it. "I'm going with you."

"Don't be a fool." Impatient, Nick dragged her along. "Go back to the villa, I'll speak to you in the morning."

"No." Morgan pulled out of his hold. "I said I'm going with you. You can't stop me."

She was standing straight as an arrow, eyes blazing with a combination of fear and determination. Nick swore at her, knowing every second he stayed meant his man was farther away. "I don't have time—"

"Then you'd better stop wasting it," Morgan said calmly. "I'm coming."

"Then come," he said under his breath as he turned away from her. She won't last five minutes on the cliffs without shoes, he thought. She'd limp her way back to the villa in ten. He moved quickly up the beach steps without waiting for her. Gritting her teeth, Morgan raced after him.

As he left the steps to start his scramble up the cliff, Nick paid little attention to her. He cast his eyes to the sky and wished the night were not so clear. A cloud over the moon would allow him to risk getting closer to the man he followed. He gripped a rock and hauled himself up farther—a few pebbles loosened and skidded down. When he glanced back, he was surprised to see Morgan keeping pace with him.

Damn the woman, he thought with a twinge of reluctant admiration. Without a word, he held out his hand and pulled her up beside him. "Idiot," he hissed, wanting to shake her and kiss her all at once. "Will you go back? You don't have any shoes."

"Neither do you," Morgan gritted.

"Stubborn fool."

"Yes."

Cursing silently, Nick continued the climb. He couldn't risk the open path in the moonlight, so kept to the rocks. Though it wouldn't be possible to keep his quarry in sight, Nick knew where he was going.

Morgan clamped her teeth shut as the ball of her foot scraped against a rock. With a quick hiss of breath, she kept going. She wasn't going to whimper and be snapped at. She wasn't going to let him go without her.

On a rough ledge, Nick paused briefly to consider his options. Circling around would take time. If he'd been alone—and armed, he would have taken his chances with the narrow path now. Odds were that the man he followed was far enough ahead and confident enough to continue his journey without looking over his shoulder. But he wasn't alone, he thought on a flare of annoyance. And he had no more than his hands to protect Morgan if they were spotted.

"Listen to me," he whispered, hoping to frighten her as he grabbed her by the shoulders. "The man's killed—and killed more than once, I promise you. When he finds his cache isn't where it should be, he'll know he's being hunted. Go back to the villa."

"Do you want me to call the police?" Morgan asked calmly, though he'd succeeded very well in frightening her.

"No!" The word whipped out, no louder than a breath. "I can't afford to give up the chance to see who he is." Frustrated, he glared at her. "Morgan, I don't have a weapon, if he—"

"I'm not leaving you, Nicholas. You're wasting time arguing about it."

He swore again, then slowly controlled his temper. "All right, damn you. But you'll do exactly as I say or I promise you, I'll knock you unconscious and shove you behind a rock."

She didn't doubt it. Morgan lifted her chin. "Let's go."

Agilely, Nick pulled himself over the ridge and onto the path. Before he could reach back to assist her, Morgan was kneeling on the hard ground beside him. He thought, as he looked into her eyes, that she was a woman men dreamed of. Strong, beautiful, loyal. Taking her hand, he dashed up the path, anxious to make up the time he'd wasted arguing with her. When he felt they'd been in the open long enough, he left the path for the rocks again.

"You know where he's going," Morgan whispered, breathing quickly. "Where?"

"A small cave near Stevos's cottage. He thinks to pick up last night's cache." He grinned suddenly. Morgan heard it in his voice. "He won't find it, and then, by God, he'll sweat. Keep low now—no more talk."

She could see the beauty of the night clearly in the moonlight. The sky was velvet, pierced with stars, flooded by the moon. Even the thin, scruffy bushes working their way through rock held an ethereal allure. The sound of the sea rose from below them, soft with distance. An owl sent up a quiet hooting music of lazy contentment. Morgan thought, if she could look, she might find more blue-headed flowers. Then Nick was pulling her over the next ridge and pressing her to the ground.

"It's just up ahead. Stay here."

"No, I—"

"Don't argue," he said roughly. "I can move faster without you. Don't move and don't make a sound."

Before she could speak, he was scrambling away, silently, half on his belly, half on his knees. Morgan watched him until he was concealed by another huddle of rocks. Then, for the first time since they had begun, she started to pray.

Nick couldn't move quickly now. If he had misjudged the timing, he'd find himself face-to-face with his quarry. He needed to save that pleasure for the following night. But to know—to know who he had been hounding for six months was a bonus Nick couldn't resist.

There were more rocks and a few trees for cover, and he used them as he skirted the dead man's rough cottage. An attempt had been made to clear the ground for a vegetable garden, but the soil had never been worked. Nick wondered

idly what had become of the woman who had sometimes
shared Stevos's bed and washed his shirts. Then he heard
the quiet scrape of boot on rock again. Less than a hundred
yards away, Nick estimated. Eyes gleaming in the darkness,
he crept toward the mouth of the cave.

He could hear the movements inside, quiet, confident. Slipping behind a rock, he waited, patient, listening. The furious
oath that echoed inside the cave brought Nick a rich thrill of
pleasure.

Taste the betrayal, he told the man inside. And choke
on it.

The movements inside the cave became louder. Nick's
smile spread. He'd be searching now, Nick concluded. Looking for signs to tell him if his hiding place had been looted.
But no, you haven't been robbed, Nick thought. Your little
white bags were lifted from right under your nose.

He saw him then, striding out of the cave—all in black,
still masked. Take it off, Nick ordered him silently. Take it
off and let me see your face.

The figure stood in the shadows of the mouth of the
cave. Fury flowed from him in waves. His head turned
from side to side as if he were searching for something . . .
or someone.

They heard the sound at the same instant. The shifting of
pebbles underfoot, the rustling of bushes. Dear God, Morgan! Nick thought and half rose from his concealment. As
he tensed, he saw the black-clad figure draw a gun and melt
back into the shadows.

With his heart beating in his throat, Nick gripped the rock
and prepared to lunge. He could catch the man off-guard,
he thought rapidly, gain enough time to shout a warning to
Morgan so that she could get away. Fear licked at him—not
for himself, but at the thought that she might not run fast
enough.

The bush directly across the path trembled with movement. Nick sucked in his breath to lunge.

Bony, and with more greed than wit, a dusty goat stepped forward to find a more succulent branch.

Nick sunk down behind the rock, furious that he was trembling. Though she had done nothing more than what he had told her, he cursed Morgan fiercely.

With a furious oath, the man in black stuck the gun back in his belt as he strode down the path. As he passed Nick, he whipped off his mask.

Nick saw the face, the eyes, and knew.

Morgan huddled behind the rock where Nick had shoved her, her arms wrapped around her knees. It seemed she'd already waited an eternity. She strained to hear every sound—the whisper of the wind, the sigh of leaves. Her heart hadn't stopped its painful thudding since he'd left her.

Never again, Morgan promised herself. Never again would she sit and wait. Never again would she sit helpless and trembling, on the verge of hot, useless tears. If anything happened—she clamped down on the incomplete thought. Nothing was going to happen to Nick. He'd be back any moment. But the moments dragged on.

When he dropped down beside her, she had to stifle a scream. Morgan had thought her ears were tuned to hear even the dust blow on the wind, but she hadn't heard his approach. She didn't even say his name, just went into his arms.

"He's gone," Nick told her.

The memory of that one shuddering moment of terror washed over him. He crushed his mouth to hers as though he were starving. All of her fears whipped out, one by one, until there was nothing in her but a well of love.

"Oh, Nicholas, I was so frightened for you. What happened?"

"He wasn't pleased." With a grin that was both ruthless and daring, he pulled her to her feet. "No, he wasn't pleased. He'll be on the boat tomorrow."

"But did you see who—"

"No questions." He silenced her again with his mouth, roughly, as though the adventure were only beginning. "I don't want to have to lie to you again." With a laugh, Nick drew her toward the path and the moonlight. "Now, my stubborn, courageous witch, I'll take you back. Tomorrow when your feet are too sore to stand, you'll curse me."

He wouldn't tell her any more, Morgan thought. And for now, perhaps it was best. "Share my bed tonight." She smiled as she hooked her arm around his waist. "Stay another hour with me, and I won't curse you."

Laughing, he ran a hand down her hair. "What man could resist such an ultimatum?"

* * *

Morgan awoke as a soft knock sounded at her door. The small maid peeked inside.

"Your pardon, *kyrios*, a phone call from Athens."

"Oh . . . thank you, Zena, I'll be right there." Rising quickly, Morgan hurried to the phone in Liz's sitting room, belting her robe as she went. "Hello?"

"Morgan, did I wake you? It's past ten."

"Liz?" Morgan tried to shake away the cobwebs. It had been dawn before she had slept.

"Do you know anyone else in Athens?"

"I'm a bit groggy." Morgan yawned, then smiled with memories. "I went for a late-night swim. It was wonderful."

"You sound very smug," Liz mused. "We'll have to discuss it later. Morgan, I feel terrible about it, but I'm going to have to stay here until tomorrow. The doctors are hopeful, but Iona's still in a coma. I can't leave Alex to cope with his family and everything else alone."

"Please, don't worry about me. I'm sorry, Liz. I know it's difficult for both of you." She thought of Iona's involvement in the smuggling and felt a fresh wave of pity. "How is Alex holding up? He seemed so devastated when he left here."

"It would be easier if the whole family didn't look to him for answers. Oh, Morgan, it's so ugly." Strain tightened her voice and Morgan heard her take a deep breath to control it. "I don't know how Iona's mother will handle it if she dies. And suicide—it just makes it harder."

Morgan swallowed the words she wanted to say. Nick had spoken to her in confidence; she couldn't betray it even for Liz. "You said the doctors are hopeful."

"Yes, her vital signs are leveling, but—"

"What about Dorian, Liz? Is he all right?"

"Barely." Morgan heard Liz sigh again. "I don't know how I could have been so blind not to see how he felt about her. He's hardly left her bedside. If Alex hadn't bullied him, I think he might have slept in the chair beside her last night instead of going home. From the way he looks this morning, I don't think he got any sleep anyway."

"Please give him my best—and Alex, too." On a long frustrated breath she sat down. "Liz, I feel so helpless." She thought of smuggling, attempted murder and shut her eyes. "I wish there were something I could do for you."

"Just be there when I get back." Though her tone lightened, Morgan recognized the effort. "Enjoy the beach for me, look for your goatherd. If you're going to take moonlight swims, you should have some company for them." When Morgan was silent Liz continued slowly. "Or did you?"

"Well, actually . . ." Smiling, Morgan trailed off.

"Tell me, have you settled on a goatherd or a poet?"

"Neither."

"It must be Nick then," Liz concluded. "Imagine that—all I had to do was invite him to dinner."

Morgan lifted a brow and found herself grinning. "I don't know what you're talking about." Life was everywhere, she remembered, if you only knew where to look.

"*Mmm-hmmm*. We'll talk about it tomorrow. Have fun. The number's there if you need me for anything. Oh, there's some marvelous wine in the cellar," she added, and for the first time, the smile in her voice seemed genuine. "If you feel like a cozy evening—help yourself."

"I appreciate it, Liz, but—"

"And don't worry about me or any of us. Everything's going to be fine. I just know it. Give Nick my love."

"I will," Morgan heard herself saying.

"I thought so. See you tomorrow."

Smiling, Morgan replaced the receiver.

* * *

And so," Stephanos finished, lovingly stroking his mustache, "after several glasses of ouzo, Mikal became more expansive. The last two dates he gave me when our man joined the fishing expedition were the last week in February and the second week in March. That doesn't include the evening we encountered Morgan James, or when you took the trip in his stead."

Smiling, Nick flipped through the reports on his desk. "And from the end of February to the first week of April, he was in Rome. Even without my stroke of luck last night, that would have ruled him out. With the phone call I just got from Athens, I'd say we've eliminated him altogether from having any part in this. Now we know our man works alone. We move."

"And you move with an easy heart?" Stephanos noted. "What did Athens say?"

"The investigation on that end is complete. He's clean. His books, his records, his phone calls and correspondence. From this end, we know he hasn't been on the island to take part in any of the runs." Nick leaned back in his chair. "I have no doubt that since our man learned of the loss of his last shipment, he'll make the trip tonight. He won't want another to slip through his fingers." He tapped idly on the papers that littered his desk. "Now that I have the information I've been waiting for, we won't keep Athens waiting any longer. We'll have him tonight."

"You were out very late last night," Stephanos commented, taking out an ugly pipe and filling it.

"Keeping tabs on me, Stephanos?" Nick inquired with a lift of brow. "I haven't been twelve for a very long time."

"You are in very good humor this morning." He continued to fill his pipe, tapping the tobacco with patient care. "You haven't been so for many days."

"You should be glad my mood's broken. But then, you're used to my moods, aren't you, old man?"

Stephanos shrugged in agreement or acceptance. "The American lady is fond of walking on the beach. Perhaps you encountered her last night?"

"You're becoming entirely too wise in your old age, Stephanos." Nick struck a match and held it over the bowl of the pipe.

"Not too old to recognize the look of a man satisfied with a night of pleasure," Stephanos commented mildly and sucked to get flame. "A very beautiful lady. Very strong."

Lighting a cigarette, Nick smiled at him. "So you've mentioned before. I'd noticed myself. Tell me, Stephanos, are you also not too old to have ideas about strong, beautiful ladies?"

Stephanos cackled. "Only the dead have no ideas about strong, beautiful ladies, Nicholas. I'm a long way from dead."

Nick flashed him a grin. "Keep your distance, old man. She's mine."

"She is in love with you."

The cigarette halted on its journey to Nick's lips. His smiled faded. Stephanos stood grinning broadly as he was pierced with one of his friend's lancing looks. "Why do you say that?"

"Because it is true, I've seen it." He puffed enjoyably on his pipe. "It is often difficult to see what is standing before your eyes. How much longer is she alone?"

Nick brought his thoughts back and scowled at the papers on his desk. "I'm not certain. Another day or so at least, depending on Iona's condition. In love with me," he murmured and looked back at Stephanos.

He knew she was attracted, that she cared—perhaps too much for her own good. But in love with him. . . . He'd never allowed himself to consider the possibility.

"She will be alone tonight," Stephanos continued blandly, appreciating Nick's stunned look. "It wouldn't do for her to wander from the villa." He puffed a few moments in silence. "If all does not go smoothly, you would want her safely behind locked doors."

"I've already spoken to her. She understands enough to listen and take care." Nick shook his head. Today of all days he had to think clearly. "It's time we invited Captain Tripolos in. Call Mitilini."

*　*　*

Morgan enjoyed a late breakfast on the terrace and toyed with the idea of walking to the beach. He might come, she thought. I could phone and ask him to come. No, she decided, nibbling on her lip as she remembered all he had told her. If tonight is as important as he thinks, he needs to be left alone. I wish I knew more. I wish I knew what he was going to do. What if he gets hurt or . . . Morgan clamped down on the thought and wished it were tomorrow.

"*Kyrios.*" At the maid's quiet summons, Morgan gasped and spun. "The captain from Mitilini is here to speak with you."

"What?" Panic rose and Morgan swallowed it. If Nick had spoken to him, Tripolos would hardly be waiting to see her, she thought frantically. Perhaps Nick wasn't ready yet. What could Tripolos possibly want with her?

"Tell him I'm out," she decided quickly. "Tell him I've gone to the beach or the village."

"Very good, *kyrios*." The maid accepted her order without question, then watched as Morgan streaked from the terrace.

For the second time, Morgan climbed the steep cliff path. This time, she knew were she was going. She could see Tripolos's official car parked at the villa's entrance as she rounded the first bend. She increased her pace, running until she was certain she herself was out of view.

Her approach had been noticed, however. The wide doors of Nick's villa opened before she reached the top step. Nick came out to meet her.

"*Yiasou.* You must be in amazing shape to take the hill at that speed."

"Very funny," she panted as she ran into his arms.

"Is it that you couldn't keep away from me or is something wrong?" He held her close a moment, then drew her back just far enough to see her face. It was flushed with the run, but there was no fear in her eyes.

"Tripolos is at the villa." Morgan pressed her hand to her heart and tried to catch her breath. "I slipped out the back because I didn't know what I should say to him. Nicholas, I have to sit down. That's a very steep hill."

He was searching her face silently. Still struggling for her breath, Morgan tilted her head and returned the survey. She laughed and pushed the hair from her eyes. "Nicholas, why are you staring at me like that?"

"I'm trying to see what's standing in front of my eyes."

She laughed again. "Well, I am, you fool, but I'm going to collapse from exhaustion any minute."

With a sudden grin, Nick swept her off her feet and into his arms. She circled his neck as his mouth came down on hers.

"What are you doing?" she asked, when he let her breathe again.

"Taking what's mine."

His lips came back to hers and lingered. Slowly, almost lazily, he began to tease her tongue with his until he felt her breath start to shudder into his mouth. He promised himself that when everything was over, he would kiss her again, just like this—luxuriously with the heat of the sun warming her skin. When the night's work was finally over, he thought, and for a moment his lips were rough and urgent. Needs rushed through him almost painfully before he banked them.

"So . . ." He strolled into the house, still carrying her. "The captain came to see you. He's very tenacious."

Morgan took a deep breath to bring herself back from the power of the kiss. "You said you were going to speak with him today, but I didn't know if you were ready. If you'd gotten the information you needed. And to confess and humiliate myself, I'm a coward. I didn't want to face him again."

"Coward, Aphrodite? No, that's something you're not." He laid his cheek against hers a moment, making her wonder what was going on in his head. "I called Mitilini," he continued. "I left a message for Tripolos. After our talk, he should lose all interest in you."

"I'll be devastated." He grinned and took her lips again. "Would you put me down? I can't talk to you this way."

"I'm enjoying it." Ignoring her request, he continued into the salon. "Stephanos, I believe Morgan might like something cool. She had quite a run."

"No, nothing really. *Efxaristo*." Faintly embarrassed, she met Stephanos's checkerboard grin. When he backed out of sight, she turned her head back to Nick. "If you know who the man is who's running the smuggling, can't you just tell Captain Tripolos and have him arrested?"

"It's not that simple. We want to catch him when the cache is in his possession. There's also the matter of cleaning up the place in the hills where he keeps his goods stored before he ships them on. That part," he added with an absent interest, "I'll leave to Tripolos."

"Nicholas, what will you do?"

"What has to be done."

"Nicholas—"

"Morgan," he interrupted. Standing her on her feet, he placed his hands on her shoulders. "You don't want a step-by-step description. Let me finish this without bringing you in any more than I already have."

He lowered his mouth, taking hers with uncharacteristic gentleness. He brought her close, but softly, as if he held something precious. Morgan felt her bones turn to water.

"You have a knack for changing the subject," she murmured.

"After tonight, it's the only subject that's going to interest me. Morgan—"

"A thousand pardons." Stephanos hovered in the doorway. Nick looked up impatiently.

"Go away, old man."

"Nicholas!" Morgan drew out of his arms, sending him a look of reproof. "Has he always been rude, Stephanos?"

"Alas, my lady, since he took his thumb out of his mouth."

"Stephanos," Nick began in warning, but Morgan gave a peal of laughter and kissed him.

"Captain Tripolos requests a few moments of your time, Mr. Gregoras," Stephanos said, respectfully and grinned.

"Give me a moment, then send him in, and bring the files from the office."

"Nicholas." Morgan clung to his arm. "Let me stay with you. I won't get in the way."

"No." His refusal was short and harsh. He saw the hurt flicker in her eyes and sighed. "Morgan, I can't allow it even if I wanted to. This isn't going to touch you. I can't let it touch you. That's important to me."

"You're not going to send me away," she began heatedly.

He arched a brow and looked very cool. "I'm not under the same pressure I was last night, Morgan. And I will send you away."

"I won't go."

His eyes narrowed. "You'll do precisely what I say."

"Like hell."

Fury flickered, smoldered, then vanished in a laugh. "You're an exasperating woman, Aphrodite. If I had the time, I'd beat you." To prove his point, he drew her close and touched his lips to hers. "Since I don't I'll ask you to wait upstairs."

"Since you *ask*."

"Mr. Gregoras. Ah, Miss James." Tripolos lumbered into the room. "How convenient. I was inquiring for Miss James at the Theoharis villa when your message reached me."

"Miss James is leaving," Nick told him. "I'm sure you'll agree her presence isn't necessary. Mr. Adonti from Athens has asked me to speak with you on a certain matter."

"Adonti?" Tripolos repeated. Nick watched surprise and interest move across the pudgy face before his eyes became direct. "So, you are acquainted with Mr. Adonti's organization?"

"Well acquainted," Nick returned mildly. "We've had dealings over the years."

"I see." He studied Nick with a thoughtful purse of his lips. "And Miss James?"

"Miss James chose an inopportune time to visit friends," Nick said and took her arm. "That's all. If you'll excuse me, I'll just see her out. Perhaps you'd care for a drink while you're waiting." With a gesture toward the bar, Nick drew Morgan out into the hall.

"He looked impressed with the name you just dropped."

"Forget the name," Nick told her briefly. "You've never heard it."

"All right," she said without hesitation.

"What have I done to deserve this trust you give me?" he demanded suddenly. "I've hurt you again and again. I couldn't make up for it in a lifetime."

"Nicholas—"

"No." He cut her off with a shake of his head. In an uncharacteristic gesture of nerves or frustration, he dragged a hand through his hair. "There's no time. Stephanos will show you upstairs."

"As you wish," Stephanos agreed from behind them. Handing Nick a folder, he turned to the stairs. "This way, my lady."

Because Nick had already turned back to the salon, Morgan followed the old man without a word. She'd been given more time with him, she told herself. She couldn't ask for any more than that.

Stephanos took her into a small sitting room off the master bedroom. "You'll be comfortable here," he told her. "I'll bring you coffee."

"No. No, thank you, Stephanos." She stared at him, and for the second time he saw her heart in her eyes. "He'll be all right, won't he?"

He grinned at her so that his moustache quivered. "Can you doubt it?" he countered before he closed the door behind him.

CHAPTER 12

There was nothing more frustrating than waiting, Morgan decided after the first thirty minutes. Especially for someone who simply wasn't made for sitting still.

The little room was shaped like a cozy box and done in warm, earthy colors with lots of polished wood that gleamed in the early afternoon light. It was filled with small treasures. Morgan sat down and scowled at a Dresden shepherdess. At another time she might have admired the flowing grace of the lines, the fragility. Now she could only think that she was of no more practical use than that pale piece of porcelain. She had, in a matter of speaking, been put on the shelf.

It was ridiculous for Nick to constantly try to . . . shield her. Morgan's sigh was quick and impatient. Hadn't that been Liz's words when she had spoken of Alex's actions? After all, Morgan thought as she rose again, she was hardly some trembling, fainting scatterbrain who couldn't deal with whatever there was to face. She remembered trembling *and* fainting dead away in his arms. With a rueful smile, she paced to the window. Well, it wasn't as though she made a habit of it.

In any case, her thoughts ran on, he should know that she would, and could, face anything now that they were together.

If he understood how she felt about him, then . . . But did he? she thought abruptly. She'd shown him, certainly she'd shown him in every possible way open to her, but she hadn't told him.

How can I? Morgan asked herself as she sunk into another chair. When a man had lived ten years of his life following his own rules, courting danger, looking for adventures, did he want to tie himself to a woman and accept the responsibilities of love?

He cared for her, Morgan reflected. Perhaps more than he was comfortable with. And he wanted her—more than any man had ever wanted her. But love . . . love wouldn't come easily to a man like Nicholas. No, she wouldn't pressure him with hers now. Even the unselfish offer of it would be pressure, she thought, when he had so much on his mind. She was only free to go on showing him, trusting him.

Even that seemed to throw him off-balance a bit, she mused, smiling a little. It was as if he couldn't quite accept that someone could see him as he was, know the way he had lived and still give him trust. Morgan wondered if he would have been more comfortable if she had pulled back from him a little after the things he had told her. He would have understood her condemnations more readily than her acceptance. Well, he'll just have to get used to it, she decided. He'll just have to get used to it because I'm not going to make it easy for him to back away.

Restless, she walked to the window. Here was a different view, Morgan thought, from one she so often looked out on from her bedroom window. Higher, more dangerous. More compelling, she thought with a quick thrill. The rocks seemed more jagged, the sea less tame. How it suited the man she'd given her heart to.

There was no terrace there, and suddenly wanting the air and sun, Morgan went through to his bedroom and opened his balcony doors. She could hear the sea hissing before she reached the rail. With a laugh, she leaned farther out.

Oh, she could live with the challenge of such a view every day, she thought, and never tire of it. She could watch the sea change colors with the sky, watch the gulls swoop over the water and back to the nests they'd built in the cliff walls. She could look down on the Theoharis villa and appreciate its refined elegance, but she would choose the rough gray stone and dizzying height.

Morgan tossed back her head and wished for a storm. Thunder, lightning, wild wind. Was there a better spot on earth to enjoy it? Laughing, she dared the sky to boil and spew out its worst.

"My God, how beautiful you are."

The light of challenge still in her eyes, Morgan turned. Leaning against the open balcony door, Nick stared at her. His face was very still, his gaze like a lance. The passion was on him, simmering, bubbling, just beneath the surface. It suited him, Morgan thought, suited those long, sharp bones in his face, those black eyes and the mouth that could be beautiful or cruel.

As she leaned back on the railing, the breeze caught at the ends of her hair. Her eyes took on the color of the sky. Power swept over her, and a touch of madness. "You want me, I can see it. Come and show me."

It hurt, Nick discovered. He'd never known, until Morgan, that desire could hurt. Perhaps it was only when you loved that your needs ached in you. How many times had he loved her last night? he wondered. And each time, it had been like a tempest in him. Now, he promised himself, this time, he would show her a different way.

Slowly, he went to her. Taking both of her hands, he lifted them, then pressed his lips to the palms. When he brought his gaze to hers, Nick saw that her eyes were wide and

moved, her lips parted in surprise. Something stirred in
him—love, guilt, a need to give.

"Have I shown you so little tenderness, Morgan?" he murmured.

"Nicholas . . ." She could only whisper his name as her
pulses raged and her heart melted.

"Have I given you no soft words, no sweetness?" He kissed
her hands again, one finger at a time. She didn't move, only
stared at him. "And you still come to me. I'm in your debt,"
he said quietly in Greek. "What price would you ask me?"

"No, Nicholas, I . . ." Morgan shook her head, unable to
speak, nearly swaying with the weakness this gentle, quiet
man brought her.

"You asked me to show you how I wanted you." He put
his hands to her face as if she were indeed made of Dresden
porcelain, then touched his lips almost reverently to hers. A
sound came from her, shaky and small. "Come and I will."

He lifted her, not with a flourish as he had on the porch,
but as a man lifts something he cherishes. "Now . . ." He laid
her down with care. "In the daylight, in my bed."

Again, he took her hand, tracing kisses over the back and
palm, then to the wrist where her pulse hammered. All the
while he watched her as she lay back, staring at him with
something like astonished wonder.

How young she looks, Nick thought as he gently drew
her finger into his mouth. And how fragile. Not a witch now,
or a goddess, but only a woman. His woman. And her eyes
were already clouding, her breath already trembling. He'd
shown her the fire and the storm, he thought, but not once—
not once had he given her spring.

Bending, he nibbled lightly at her lips, allowing his hands
to touch no more than her hair.

It might have been a dream, so weak and weightless did
she feel. Nick kissed her eyes closed so that Morgan saw no

more than a pale red glow. Then his lips continued, over her forehead, her temples, down the line of her cheekbones—always soft, always warm. The words he whispered against her skin flowed like scented oil over her. She would have moved to bring him closer if her arms had not been too heavy to lift. Instead, she lay in the flood of his tenderness.

His mouth was at her ear, gently torturing with a trace of tongue, a murmured promise. Even as she moaned in surrender, he moved lower to taste and tease the curve of her neck. With kisses like whispers, and whispers like wine, he took her deeper. Gentleness was a drug for both of them.

Hardly touching her, he loosened the buttons of her blouse and slipped it from her. Though he felt the firm pressure of her breasts against him, he took his mouth to the slope of her shoulder instead. He could feel the strength there, the grace, and he tarried.

Morgan's eyes were closed, weighed down with gold-tipped lashes. Her breath rushed out between her lips. He knew he could watch those flickers of pleasure move over her face forever. With his hands once more buried in her hair, Nick kissed her. He felt the yielding and the hunger before he moved on.

Slowly, savoring, he took his lips down to the soft swell—circling, nibbling until he came to the tender underside of her breast. On a moan, Morgan fretted under him as if she were struggling to wake from a dream. But he kept the pace slow and soothed her with words and soft, soft kisses.

With aching gentleness he stroked his tongue over the peak, fighting a surge of desperation when he found it hot and ready. Her movements beneath him took on a rhythmic sinuousness that had the blood pounding in his brain. Her scent was there, always there on the verge of his senses even when she wasn't with him. Now he wallowed in it. As he suckled, he allowed his hands to touch her for the first time.

Morgan felt the long stroke of his hands, the quick scrape of those strong rough fingers that now seemed sensitive enough to tune violins. They caressed lightly, like a breeze. They made her ache.

Soft, slow, gentle, his mouth traveled down the center of her body, lingering here, exploring there until he paused where her slacks hugged across her stomach. When she felt him unfasten them, she trembled. She arched to help him, but Nick drew them down inch by inch, covering the newly exposed flesh with moist kisses so that she could only lie steeped in a pool of pleasure.

And when she was naked, he continued to worship her with his lips, with his suddenly gentle hands. She thought she could hear her own skin hum. The muscles in her thighs quivered as he passed over them, and her desire leaped from passive to urgent.

"Nicholas," she breathed. "Now."

"You've scratched your feet on the rocks," he murmured, pressing his lips against the ball of her foot. "It's a sin to mar such skin, my love." Watching her face, he ran his tongue over the arch. Her eyes flew open, dazed with passion. "I've longed to see you like this." His voice grew thick as his control began to slip. "With sunlight streaming over you, your hair flowing over my pillow, your body trembling for me."

As he spoke, he began the slow, aching journey back, gradually back to her lips. Needs pressed at him and demanded he hurry, but he wouldn't be rushed. He told himself he could linger over the taste and the feel of her for days.

Her arms weren't heavy now, but strong as they curled around him. Every nerve, every pore of her body seemed tuned to him. The harmony seemed impossible, yet it sung through her. His flesh was as hot and damp as hers, his breath as unsteady.

"You ask how I want you," he murmured, thrilling to her moan as he slipped into her. "Look at me and see."

His control hung by a thread. Morgan pulled his mouth to hers and snapped it.

* * *

Nick held Morgan close, gently stroking her back while her trembles eased. She clung to him, almost as much in wonder as in love. How was she to have known he had such tenderness in him? How was she to have known she would be so moved by it? Blinking back tears, she pressed her lips to his throat.

"You've made me feel beautiful," she murmured.

"You are beautiful." Tilting her head back, Nick smiled at her. "And tired," he added, tracing a thumb over the mauve smudges under her eyes. "You should sleep, Morgan, I won't have you ill."

"I won't be ill." She snuggled against him, fitting herself neatly against the curve of his body. "And there'll be time for sleeping later. We'll go away for a few days, like you said."

Twining a lock of her hair around his finger, Nick gazed up at the ceiling. A few days with her would never be enough, but he still had the night to get through. "Where would you like to go?"

Morgan thought of her dreams of Venice and Cornish moors. With a sigh, she closed her eyes and drew in Nick's scent. "Anywhere. Right here." Laughing, she propped herself on his chest. "Wherever it is, I intend to keep you in bed a good deal of the time."

"Is that so?" His mouth twitched as he tugged on her hair. "I might begin to think you have designs only on my body."

"It is a rather nice one." In a long stroke, she ran her hands down his shoulders, enjoying the feel of firm flesh and strong bone. "Lean and muscled . . ." She trailed off when she spotted a small scar high on his chest. A frown creased her brow as she stared at it. It seemed out of place on that smooth brown skin. "Where did you get this?"

Nick tilted his head, shifting his gaze down. "Ah, an old battle scar," he said lightly.

From a bullet, Morgan realized all at once. Horror ripped through her and mirrored in her eyes. Seeing it, Nick cursed his loose tongue.

"Morgan—"

"No, please." She buried her face against his chest and held tight. "Don't say anything. Just give me a minute."

She'd forgotten. Somehow the gentleness and beauty of their lovemaking had driven all the ugliness out of her mind. It had been easy to pretend for a little while that there was no threat. Pretending's for children, she reminded herself. He didn't need to cope with a child now. If she could give him nothing else, she would give him what was left of her strength. Swallowing fear, she pressed her lips to his chest then rolled beside him again.

"Did everything go as you wanted with Captain Tripolos?"

A strong woman, Nick thought, linking his hand with hers. An extraordinary woman. "He's satisfied with the information I've given him. A shrewd man for all his plodding technique."

"Yes, I thought he was like a bulldog the first time I encountered him."

Chuckling, Nick drew her closer. "An apt description, Aphrodite." He shifted then, reaching to the table beside him for a cigarette. "I think he's one of the few policemen I find it agreeable to work with."

"Why do you—" She broke off as she looked up and

focused on the slim black cigarette. "I'd forgotten," Morgan murmured. "How could I have forgotten?"

Nick blew out a stream of smoke. "Forgotten what?"

"The cigarette." Morgan sat up, pushing at her tumbled hair. "The stub of the cigarette near the body."

He lifted a brow, but found himself distracted by the firm white breasts easily within reach. "So?"

"It was fresh, from one of those expensive brands like you're smoking." She let out an impatient breath. "I should have told you before, but it hardly makes any difference at this point. You already know who killed Stevos—who runs the smuggling."

"I never told you I did."

"You didn't have to." Annoyed with herself, Morgan frowned and missed Nick's considering look.

"Why didn't I?"

"You'd have told me if you hadn't seen his face. When you wouldn't answer me at all, I knew you had."

He shook his head as a reluctant smile touched his lips. *"Diabolos*, it's a good thing I didn't cross you earlier in my career. I'm afraid it would have been over quickly. As it happens," he added, "I saw the cigarette myself."

"I should have known you would," she muttered.

"I can assure you Tripolos didn't miss it either."

"That damn cigarette has driven me to distraction." Morgan gave an exasperated sigh. "There were moments I suspected everyone I knew—Dorian, Alex, Iona, even Liz and Andrew. I nearly made myself sick over it."

"You don't name me." Nick studied the cigarette in his hand.

"No, I already told you why."

"Yes," he murmured, "with an odd sort of compliment I haven't forgotten. I should have eased your mind sooner, Morgan, about what I do. You might have slept better."

Leaning over, she kissed him. "Stop worrying about my sleep. I'm going to start thinking I look like a tired hag."

He slid a hand behind her neck to keep her close. "Will you rest if I tell you that you do?"

"No, but I'll hit you."

"Ah, then I'll lie and tell you you're exquisite."

She hit him anyway, a quick jab in the ribs.

"So, now you want to play rough." Crushing out his cigarette, Nick rolled her beneath him. She struggled for a moment, then eyed him narrowly.

"Do you know how many times you've pinned me down like this?" Morgan demanded.

"No, how many?"

"I'm not sure." Her smile spread slowly. "I think I'm beginning to like it."

"Perhaps I can make you like it better." He muffled her laugh with his lips.

He didn't love her gently now, but fiercely. As desperate as he, Morgan let the passion rule her. Fear that it might be the last time caused her response and demands to be urgent. She lit a fire in him.

Now, where his hands had trailed slowly, they raced. Where his mouth had whispered, it savaged. Morgan threw herself into the flames without a second thought. Her mouth was greedy, searching for his taste everywhere while her hands rushed to touch and arouse.

Her body had never felt so agile. It could melt into his one moment, then slither away to drive him to madness. She could hear his desire in the short, harsh breath, feel it in the tensing and quivering of his muscles as she roamed over them, taste it in the dampness that sheened his skin. It matched her own, and again they were in harmony.

She arched against him as his mouth rushed low—but it was more a demand than an invitation. Delirious with her own strength and power, Morgan dug her fingers into his hair and urged him to take her to that first giddy peak. Even as she cried out with it, she hungered for more. And he gave more, while he took.

But she wasn't satisfied with her own pleasure. Ruthlessly she sought to undermine whatever claim he still held to sanity. Her hands had never been so clever, or so quick. Her teeth nipped at his skin before she soothed the tiny pains with a flick of her tongue. She heard him groan and a low, sultry laugh flowed from her. His breath caught when she reached him, then came out in an oath. Morgan felt the sunlight explode into fragments as he plunged into her.

* * *

Later, much later, when he knew his time with her was nearly up, Nick kissed her with lingering tenderness.

"You're going," Morgan said, struggling not to cling to him.

"Soon. I'll have to take you back to the villa in a little while." Sitting up, he drew her with him. "You'll stay inside. Lock the doors, tell the servants to let no one in. No one."

Morgan tried to promise, and found she couldn't form the words. "When you're finished, you'll come?"

Smiling, he tucked her hair behind her ear. "I suppose I can handle your window vines again."

"I'll wait up for you and let you in the front door."

"Aphrodite." Nick pressed a kiss to her wrist. "Where's your romance?"

"Oh, God!" Morgan threw her arms around his neck and clung. "I wasn't going to say it—I promised myself I wouldn't. Be careful." Biting back tears, she pressed her face against his throat. "Please, please be careful. I'm terrified for you."

"No, don't." Feeling the dampness against his skin, he held her tighter. "Don't cry for me."

"I'm sorry." With a desperate effort, she forced back the tears. "I'm not helping you."

Nick drew her away and looked at the damp cheeks and shimmering eyes. "Don't ask me not to go, Morgan."

"No." She swallowed again. "I won't. Don't ask me not to worry."

"It's the last time," he said fiercely.

The words made her shudder, but she kept her eyes on his. "Yes, I know."

"Just wait for me." He pulled her back against him. "Wait for me."

"With a bottle of Alex's best champagne," she promised in a stronger voice.

He pressed a kiss to her temple. "We'll have some of mine now, before I take you back. A toast," he told her as he drew her away again. "To tomorrow."

"Yes." She smiled. It almost reached her eyes. "I'll drink with you to tomorrow."

"Rest a moment." With another kiss, he laid her back against the pillow. "I'll go bring some up."

Morgan waited until the door had closed behind him before she buried her face in the pillow.

CHAPTER 13

It was dark when she woke. Confused, disoriented, Morgan struggled to see where she was. The room was all shifting shadows and silence. There was a cover over her—something soft and light with a fringe of silk. Beneath it, she was warm and naked.

Nicholas, she thought in quick panic. She'd fallen asleep and he'd gone. On a moan, she sat up, drawing her knees to her chest. How could she have wasted those last precious moments together? How long? she thought abruptly. How long had he been gone? With trembling fingers, she reached for the lamp beside the bed.

The light eased some of her fears, but before she could climb out of bed to find a clock, she saw the note propped against the lamp. Taking it, Morgan studied the bold, strong writing. *Go back to sleep* was all it said.

How like him, she thought, and nearly laughed. Morgan kept the note in her hand, as if to keep Nick close, as she rose to look for her clothes. It didn't take her long to discover they were gone.

"The louse!" Morgan said aloud, forgetting the tender thoughts she had only moments before. So, he wasn't taking any chances making certain she stayed put. Naked, hands

on her hips, she scowled around the room. Where the devil
does he think I'd go? she asked herself. I have no way of
knowing where he is . . . or what he's doing, she thought on
a fresh flood of worry.

Wait. Suddenly cold, Morgan pulled the cover from the
bed and wrapped herself in it. All I can do is wait.

The time dripped by, minute by endless minute. She
paced, then forced herself to sit, then paced again. It would
be morning in only a few more hours, she told herself. In the
morning, the wait would be over. For all of them.

She couldn't bear it, she thought in despair one moment.
She had to bear it, she told herself the next. Would he never
get back? Would morning never come? On a sound of fury,
she tossed the cover aside. She might have to wait, Morgan
thought grimly as she marched to Nick's closet. But she'd be
damned if she'd wait naked.

* * *

Nick shifted the muscles in his shoulders and blocked out
the need for a cigarette. Even the small light would be
dangerous now. The cove was bathed in milky moonlight
and silence. There would be a murmur now and then from
behind a rock. Not from a spirit, but from a man in uniform.
The cove still held secrets. Lifting his binoculars, Nick
again scanned the sea.

"Any sign?" Tripolos seemed remarkably comfortable in
his squat position behind a rock. He popped a tiny mint into
his mouth and crunched quietly. Nick merely shook his head
and handed the glasses to Stephanos.

"Thirty minutes," Stephanos stated, chewing on the stem
of his dead pipe. "The wind carries the sound of the motor."

"I hear nothing." Tripolos gave the old man a doubtful
frown.

Nick chuckled as the familiar feeling of excitement rose. "Stephanos hears what others don't. Just tell your men to be ready."

"My men are ready." His gaze flicked over Nick's profile. "You enjoy your work, Mr. Gregoras."

"At times," Nick muttered, then grinned. "This time, by God."

"And soon it's over," Stephanos said from beside him.

Nick turned his head to meet the old man's eyes. He knew the statement covered more than this one job, but the whole of what had been Nick's career. He hadn't told him, but Stephanos knew. "Yes," he said simply, then turned his eyes to the sea again.

He thought of Morgan and hoped she was still asleep. She'd looked so beautiful—and so exhausted when he'd come back into the room. Her cheeks had been damp. Damn, he couldn't bear the thought of her tears. But he'd felt a wave of relief that she'd been asleep. He didn't have to see her eyes when he left her.

She's safer there than if I'd taken her back, Nick told himself. With luck, she'd still be asleep when he got back and then he'd have spared her hours of worry. Stashing her clothes had been an impulse that had eased his mind. Even Morgan wouldn't go wandering around without a stitch on her back.

His grin flashed again. If she woke and looked for them, she'd curse him. The idea gave him a moment's pleasure. He could see her, standing in the center of his room with only the moonlight covering her as she raged.

He felt the low aching need in the pit of his stomach, and promised himself he'd keep her just that way—naked fire— until the sun went down again.

Lifting the binoculars, he scanned the dark sea. "They're coming."

The moon threw the boat into silhouette. A dozen men watched her approach from clumps of rock and shadows. She came in silence, under the power of oars.

She was secured with little conversation and a few deft movements of rope. There was a scent Nick recognized. The scent of fear. A fresh bubble of excitement rose, though his face was deadly calm. He's there, Nick thought. And we have him.

The crew left the boat to gather in the shadows of the beach. A hooded figure moved to join them. At Nick's signal, the cove was flooded with light. The rocks became men.

"In the King's name," Tripolos stated grandly, "this vessel will be searched for illegal contraband. Put up your weapons and surrender."

Shouts and the scrambling of men shattered the glasslike quiet of the cove. Men seeking to escape, and men seeking to capture tangled in the sudden chaos of sound and light. Gunfire shocked the balmy air. There were cries of pain and fury.

The smugglers would fight with fist and blade. The battle would be short, but grim. The sounds of violence bounced hollowly off the rocks and drifted out on the air.

Nick saw the hooded figure melt away from the confusion and streak from the cove. Swearing, he raced after it, thrusting his gun back in his belt. A burly form collided with him as another man sought escape. Each swore at the obstacle, knowing the only choice was to remove it.

Together, they rolled over the rocks, away from the noise and the light. Thrown into darkness, they tumbled helplessly until the ground leveled. A blade glistened, and Nick grasped the thick wrist with both hands to halt its plunge to his throat.

The crack of shots had Morgan springing up from her

chair. Had she heard, or just imagined? she wondered as her heart began to thud. Could they be so close? As she stared into the darkness, she heard another shot, and the echo. Fear froze her.

He's all right, she told herself. He'll be here soon, and it'll be over. I know he's all right.

Before the sentence had finished racing through her mind, she was running down the steps and out of the villa.

Telling herself she was only being logical, Morgan headed for the beach. She was just going to meet him. He'd be coming along any minute, and she would see for herself that he wasn't hurt. Nick's jeans hung loosely at her hips as she streaked down the cliff path. Her breath was gasping now, the only sound as her feet padded on the hard dirt. Morgan thought it would almost be a relief to hear the guns again. If she heard them, she might be able to judge the direction. She could find him.

Then, from the top of the beach steps, she saw him walking across the sand. With a sob of shuddering relief, she flew down them to meet him.

He continued, too intent on his own thoughts to note her approach. Morgan started to shout his name, but the word strangled in her throat. She stopped running. Not Nicholas, she realized as she stared at the hooded figure. The moves were wrong, the walk. And he'd have no reason to wear the mask. Even as her thoughts began to race, he reached up and tore off the hood. Moonlight fell on golden hair.

Oh God, had she been a fool not to see it? Those calm, calm eyes—too calm, she thought frantically. Had she ever seen any real emotion in him? Morgan took a step in retreat, looking around desperately for some cover. But he turned. His face hardened as he saw her.

"Morgan, what are you doing out here?"

"I—I wanted to walk." She struggled to sound casual. There was no place for her to run. "It's a lovely night. Almost morning, really." As he advanced on her she moistened her lips and kept talking. "I didn't expect to see you. You surprised me. I thought—"

"You thought I was in Athens," Dorian finished with a smile. "But as you see, I'm not. And, I'm afraid, Morgan, you've seen too much." He held up the hood, dangling it a moment before he dropped it to the sand.

"Yes." There was no use dissembling. "I have."

"It's a pity." His smile vanished as though it had never been. "Still, you could be useful. An American hostage," he said thoughtfully as he scanned her face. "Yes, and a woman." Grabbing her arm, Dorian began to pull her across the sand.

She jerked and struggled against his hold. "I won't go with you."

"You have no choice"—he touched the handle of his knife—"unless you prefer to end up as Stevos did."

Morgan swallowed as she stumbled across the beach. He said it so casually. *Some people have no capacity for emotion—love, hate.* He hadn't been speaking of Iona, Morgan realized, but himself. He was as dangerous as any animal on the run.

"You tried to kill Iona too."

"She'd become a nuisance. Greedy not only for money, but to hold me. She thought to blackmail me into marriage." He gave a quick laugh. "I had only to tempt her with the heroin. I had thought the dose I gave her was enough."

Purposely, Morgan fell to her knees as though she'd tripped. "You would have finished her that morning if I hadn't found her first."

"You have a habit of being in the wrong place." Roughly, Dorian hauled her to her feet. "I had to play the worried lover for a time—dashing back and forth between Lesbos and Athens. A nuisance. Still, if I'd been allowed one moment alone with her in the hospital . . ." Then he shrugged, as if the life or the death of a woman meant nothing. "So, she'll live and she'll talk. It was time to move in any case."

"You lost your last shipment," Morgan blurted out, desperate to distract him from his hurried pace toward the beach steps. If he got her up there—up there in the rocks . . . and the dark . . .

Dorian froze and turned to her. "How do you know this?"

"I helped steal it," she said impulsively. "Your place in the hills, the cave—"

The words choked off as his hand gripped her throat. "So you've taken what's mine. Where is it?"

Morgan shook her head.

"Where?" Dorian demanded as his fingers tightened.

A god, she thought staring into his face as the moonlight streamed over it. He had the face of a god. Why hadn't she remembered her own thought that gods were bloodthirsty? Morgan put a hand to his wrist as if in surrender. His fingers eased slightly.

"Go to hell."

Swiftly, he swept the back of his hand across her face, knocking her to the sand. His eyes were a calm empty blue as he looked down at her. "You'll tell me before I'm through with you. You'll beg to tell me. There'll be time," he continued as he walked toward her, "when we're off the island."

"I'll tell you nothing." With the blood singing in her ears, Morgan inched away from him. "The police know who you are, there isn't a hole big enough for you to hide in."

Reaching down, he grabbed her by the hair and hauled her painfully to her feet. "If you prefer to die—"

Then she was free, going down to her knees again as Dorian stumbled back and fell onto the sand.

"Nick." Dorian rubbed the blood from his mouth as his gaze traveled up. "This is a surprise." It dropped again to the revolver Nick held in his hand. "Quite a surprise."

"Nicholas!" Scrambling up, Morgan ran to him. He never looked at her. His arm was rigid as iron when she gripped it. "I thought—I was afraid you were dead."

"Get up," he told Dorian with a quick gesture of the gun. "Or I'll put a bullet in your head while you lie there."

"Were you hurt?" Morgan shook his arm, wanting some sign. She'd seen that cold, hard look before. "When I heard the shots—"

"Only detained." Nick pushed her aside, his gaze fixed on Dorian. "Get rid of the gun. Toss it over there." He jerked his head and leveled his own revolver. "Two fingers. If you breathe wrong, you won't breathe again."

Dorian lifted out his gun in a slow, steady motion and tossed it aside. "I have to admit you amaze me, Nick. It's been you who's been hounding me for months."

"My pleasure."

"And I would have sworn you were a man concerned only with collecting his trinkets and making money. I've always admired your ruthlessness in business—but it seems I wasn't aware of *all* of your business." One graceful brow rose. "A policeman?"

Nick gave a thin smile. "I answer to one man only," he said quietly. "Adonti." The momentary flash of fear in Dorian's eyes gave him great pleasure. "You and I might have come to this sooner. We nearly did last night."

A shadow touched Dorian's face briefly, then was gone. "Last night?"

"Did you think it was only a goat who watched you?" Nick asked with a brittle laugh.

"No." Dorian gave a brief nod. "I smelled something more—foolish of me not to have pursued it."

"You've gotten careless, Dorian. I took your place on your last run and made your men tremble."

"You," Dorian breathed.

"A rich cache," Nick added, "according to my associates in Athens. It might have been over for you then, but I waited until I was certain Alex wasn't involved. It was worth the wait."

"Alex?" Dorian laughed with the first sign of true pleasure. "Alex wouldn't have the stomach for it. He thinks only of his wife and his ships and his honor." He gave Nick a thoughtful glance. "But it seems I misjudged you. I thought you a rich, rather singleminded fool, a bit of a nuisance with Iona this trip, but hardly worth a passing thought. My congratulations on your talent for deceit, and"—he let his gaze travel and rest on Morgan—"your taste."

"Efxaristo."

Morgan watched in confusion, then in terror, as Nick tossed his gun down to join Dorian's. They lay side by side, black and ugly, on the white sand.

"It's my duty to turn you over to Captain Tripolos and the Greek authorities." Calmly, slowly, Nick drew out a knife. "But it will be my pleasure to cut out your heart for putting your hands on my woman."

"No! Nicholas, don't!"

Nick stopped Morgan's panicked rush toward him with a terse command. "Go back to the villa and stay there."

"Please," Dorian interrupted with a smile as he got to his feet. "Morgan must stay. Such an interesting development." He pulled out his own knife with a flourish. "She'll be quite a prize for the one who lives."

"Go," Nick ordered again. His hand tensed on the knife. He was half Greek, and Greek enough to have tasted blood when he had seen Dorian strike her. Morgan saw the look in his eyes.

"Nicholas, you can't. He didn't hurt me."

"He left his mark on your face," he said softly, and turned the knife in his hand. "Stay out of the way."

Touching her hand to her cheek, she stumbled back.

They crouched and circled. As she watched, the knives caught the moonlight and held it. Glittering silver, dazzling and beautiful.

At Dorian's first thrust, Morgan covered her mouth to hold back a scream. There was none of the graceful choreography of a staged fight. This was real and deadly. There were no adventurous grins or bold laughs with the thrusts and parries. Both men had death in his eyes. Morgan could smell the sweat and the sweet scent of blood from both of them.

Starlight dappled over their faces, giving them both a ghostly pallor. All she could hear was the sound of their breathing, the sound of the sea, the sound of steel whistling through the air. Nick was leading him closer to the surf— away from Morgan. Emotion was frozen in him. Anger, such anger, but he knew too much to let it escape. Dorian fought coldly. An empty heart was its own skill.

"I'll pleasure myself with your woman before the night's over," Dorian told him as blade met blade. His lips curved as he saw the quick, naked fury in Nick's eyes.

Morgan watched with horror as a bright stain spread down Nick's sleeve where Dorian had slipped through his guard. She would have screamed, but there was no breath in her. She would have prayed, but even her thoughts were frozen.

The speed with which they came together left her stunned. One moment they were separate, and the next they were locked together as one tangled form. They rolled to the sand, a confusion of limbs and knives. She could hear the labored breathing and grunted curses. Then Dorian was on top of him. Morgan watched, numb with terror, as he plunged his knife. It struck the sand, a whisper away from Nick's face. Without thought, Morgan fell on the guns.

Once, the revolver slipped through her wet hands, back onto the sand. Gritting her teeth, she gripped it again. As she knelt, she aimed toward the entwined bodies. Coldly, willing herself to do what she had always despised, she prepared to kill.

A cry split the air, animal and primitive. Not knowing which one of them it had been torn from, Morgan clutched the gun with both hands and kept it aimed on the now motionless heap in the sand. She could still hear breathing—but only from one. If Dorian stood up, she swore to herself, and to Nick, that she would pull the trigger.

A shadow moved. She heard the labored breathing and pressed her lips together. Against the trigger, her finger shook lightly.

"Put that damn thing down, Morgan, before you kill me."

"Nicholas." The gun slipped from her nerveless hand.

He moved to her, limping a little. Reaching down, he drew her to her feet. "What were you doing with the gun, Aphrodite?" he said softly, when he felt her tremble under his hands. "You couldn't have pulled the trigger."

"Yes." Her eyes met his. "I could."

He stared at her for a moment and saw she was speaking nothing less than the truth. With an oath, he pulled her against him. "Damn it, Morgan, why didn't you stay in the villa? I didn't want this for you."

"I couldn't stay in the house, not after I heard the shooting."

"Yes, you hear shooting, so naturally you run outside."

"What else could I do?"

Nick opened his mouth to swear, then shut it again. "You've stolen my clothes," he said mildly. He wouldn't be angry with her now, he promised himself as he stroked her hair. Not while she was shaking like a leaf. But later, by God, later . . .

"You took mine first." He couldn't tell if the sound she made was a laugh or a sob. "I thought . . ." Suddenly, she felt the warm stickiness against her palm. Looking down, she saw his blood on her hand. "Oh, God, Nicholas, you're hurt!"

"No, it's nothing, I—"

"Oh, damn you for being macho and stupid. You're *bleeding!*"

He laughed and crushed her to him again. "I'm not being macho and stupid, Aphrodite, but if it makes you happy, you can nurse all of my scratches later. Now, I need a different sort of medicine." He kissed her before she could argue.

Her fingers gripped at his shirt as she poured everything she had into that one meeting of lips. Fear drained from her, and with it, whatever force had driven her. She went limp against him as his energy poured over her.

"I'm going to need a lot of care for a very long time," he murmured against her mouth. "I might be hurt a great deal more seriously than I thought. No, don't." Nick drew her away as he felt her tears on his cheeks. "Morgan, don't cry. It's the one thing I don't think I can face tonight."

"No, I won't cry," she insisted as the tears continued to fall. "I won't cry. Just don't stop kissing me. Don't stop." She pressed her mouth to his. As she felt him, warm and real against her, the tears and trembling stopped.

"Well, Mr. Gregoras, it seems you intercepted Mr. Zoulas after all."

Nick swore quickly, but without heat. Keeping Morgan close, he looked over her head at Tripolos. "Your men have the crew?"

"Yes." Lumbering over, he examined the body briefly. He

noted, without comment that there was a broken arm as well as the knife wound. With a gesture, he signaled one of his men to take over. "Your man is seeing to their transportation," he went on.

Nick kept Morgan's back to the body and met Tripolos's speculative look calmly. "It seems you had a bit of trouble here," the captain commented. His gaze drifted to the guns lying on the sand. He drew his own conclusions. "A pity he won't stand trial."

"A pity," Nick agreed.

"You dropped your gun in the struggle to apprehend him, I see."

"It would seem so."

Tripolos stooped with a wheeze and handed it back to him. "Your job is finished?"

"Yes, my job is finished."

Tripolos made a small bow. "My gratitude, Mr. Gregoras." He smiled at the back of Morgan's head. "And my congratulations."

Nick lifted a brow in acknowledgment. "I'll take Miss James home now. You can reach me tomorrow if necessary. Good night, Captain."

"Good night," Tripolos murmured and watched them move away.

Morgan leaned her head against his shoulder as they walked toward the beach steps. Only a few moments before she had fought to keep from reaching them. Now they seemed like the path to the rest of her life.

"Oh, look, the stars are going out." She sighed. There was nothing left, no fear, no anxiety. No more doubts. "I feel as if I've waited for this sunrise all my life."

"I'm told you want to go to Venice and ride on a gondola."

Morgan glanced up in surprise, then laughed. "Andrew told you."

"He mentioned Cornwall and the Champs d'Élysées as well."

"I have to learn how to bait a hook, too," she murmured. Content, she watched as day struggled with night.

"I'm not an easy man, Morgan."

"*Hmm?* No," she agreed fervently. "No, you're not."

He paused at the foot of the steps and turned her to face him. The words weren't easy for him now. He wondered why he had thought they would be. "You know the worst of me already. I'm not often gentle, and I'm demanding. I'm prone to black, unreasonable moods."

Morgan smothered a yawn and smiled at him. "I'd be the last one to disagree."

He felt foolish. And, he discovered, afraid. Would a woman accept words of love when she had seen a man kill? Did he have any right to offer them? Looking down, he saw her, slim and straight in his clothes—jeans that hung over her hips—a shirt that billowed and hid small, firm breasts and a waist he could nearly span with his hands. Right or wrong, he couldn't go on without her.

"Morgan . . ."

"Nicholas?" Her smile became puzzled as she fought off a wave of weariness. "What is it?"

His gaze swept back to hers, dark, intense, perhaps a little desperate.

"Your arm," she began and reached for him.

"No! *Diabolos.*" Gripping her by the shoulders, he shook her. "It's not my arm, listen to me."

"I am listening," she tossed back with a trace of heat. "What's wrong with you?"

"This." He covered her mouth with his. He needed the taste of her, the strength. When he drew her away, his hands had gentled, but his eyes gleamed.

With a sleepy laugh, she shook her head. "Nicholas, if you'll let me get you home and see to your arm—"

"My arm's a small matter, Aphrodite."

"Not to me."

"Morgan." Nick stopped her before she could turn toward the steps again. "I'll make a difficult and exasperating husband, but you won't be bored." Taking her hands, he kissed them as he had on his balcony. "I love you enough to let you climb your mountains, Morgan. Enough to climb them with you if that's what you want."

She wasn't tired now, but stunned into full alertness. Morgan opened her mouth, but found herself stupidly unable to form a word.

"Damn it, Morgan, don't just stare at me." Frustration and temper edged his voice. "Say yes, for God's sake!" Fury flared in his eyes. "I won't let you say no!"

His hands were no longer in hers, but gripping her arms again. She knew, any moment, he would start shaking her. But there was more in his eyes than anger. She saw the doubts, the fears, the fatigue. Love swept into her, overwhelmingly.

"Won't you?" she murmured.

"No." His fingers tightened. "No, I won't. You've taken my heart. You won't leave with it."

Lifting a hand, she touched his cheek, letting her finger trace over the tense jaw. "Do you think I could climb mountains without you, Nicholas?" She drew him against her and felt his shudder of relief. "Let's go home."

Partners

For Bruce, who changed my plans.

CHAPTER 1

Bedlam. Phones rang continuously. People shouted, muttered or swore, sitting or on the run. Typewriter keys clattered at varying paces from every direction. There was the scent of old coffee, fresh bread, tobacco smoke, and human sweat. An insane asylum? Several of the inmates would have agreed with that description of the city room of the *New Orleans Herald*, especially at deadline.

For most of the staff the chaos went unnoticed, as the inhaling and exhaling of air went unnoticed. There were times when each one of them was too involved with their own daily crises or triumphs to be aware of the dozens of others springing up around them. Not that teamwork was ignored. All were bound, by love for, or obsession with, their jobs, in the exclusive community of journalists. Still each would concentrate on, and greedily guard, his or her own story, own sources and own style. A successful print reporter thrives on pressure and confusion and a hot lead.

Matthew Bates had cut his teeth on newsprint. He'd worked it from every angle from newsboy on the Lower East Side of Manhattan to features reporter. He'd carried coffee, run copy, written obituaries and covered flower shows.

The ability to scent out a story and draw the meat from it wasn't something he'd learned in his journalism courses; he'd been born with it. His years of structured classes, study, and practice had honed the style and technique of a talent that was as inherent as the color of his eyes.

At the age of thirty, Matt was casually cynical but not without humor for life's twists and turns. He liked people without having illusions about them. He understood and accepted that humans were basically ridiculous. How else could he work in a room full of crazy people in a profession that constantly exposed and exploited the human race?

Finishing a story, he called out for a copy boy, then leaned back to let his mind rest for the first time in three hours. A year ago, he'd left New York to accept the position on the *Herald*, wanting, perhaps needing, a change. Restless, he thought now. He'd been restless for . . . something. And New Orleans was as hard and demanding a town as New York, with more elegant edges.

He worked the police beat and liked it. It was a tough world, and murder and desperation were parts of it that couldn't be ignored. The homicide he'd just covered had been senseless and cruel. It had been life; it had been news. Now, he wiped the death of the eighteen-year-old girl out of his mind. Objectivity came first, unless he wanted to try a new profession. Yet it took a concentrated effort to erase her image and her ending from his mind.

He hadn't the looks of a seasoned, hard-boiled reporter, and he knew it. It had exasperated him in his twenties that he looked more like a carefree surfer than a newsman. Now, it amused him.

He had a lean, subtly muscled body that was more at home in jeans than a three-piece suit, with a height that only added a feeling of ranginess. His dark blond hair curled as it chose, over his ears, down to the collar of his shirt. It merely added to the image of a laid-back, easygoing male who'd rather be sitting on the beach than pounding the pavement. More than one source had talked freely to the façade without fully comprehending the man beneath the image. When and if they did, Matt already had the story.

When he chose, he could be charming, even elegant. But the good-humored blue eyes could turn to fire or, more dangerous, ice. Beneath the easy exterior was a cold, hard determination and a smoldering temper. Matt accepted this with a shrug. He was human, and entitled to be ridiculous.

With a half smile lingering around his mouth, he turned to the woman seated across from him. Laurel Armand—with a face as romantic as her name. She had an aura of delicacy that came from fine bones and an ivory skin that made a man want to touch, and touch gently. Her hair fell in clouds of misty black, swept back from her face, spilling onto her shoulders. Hair made for a man to dive his fingers into, bury his face in. Her eyes were the color of emeralds, dark and rich.

It was the face of a nineteenth-century belle whose life revolved around gracious indolence and quiet gentility. And her voice was just as feminine, Matt mused. It turned vowels into liquid and smoothed consonants. It never flattened, never twanged, but flowed like a leisurely stream.

The voice, he reflected as his smile widened, was just as deceptive as the face. The lady was a sharp, ambitious reporter with a stubborn streak and a flaring temper. One of his favorite pastimes was setting a match to it.

Her brows were drawn together as she finished the last line of her copy. Satisfied, Laurel whipped the sheet from her typewriter, called for a copy boy, then focused on the man across from her. Automatically, her spine straightened. She already knew he was going to bait her, and that—damn it—she would bite.

"Do you have a problem, Matthew?" Her tone was soft and faintly bored.

"No problem, Laurellie." He watched the annoyance flare into her eyes at his use of her full name.

"Don't you have a murder or armed robbery to go play with?"

His mouth curved, charmingly, deepening the creases in his face. "Not at the moment. Off your soapbox for the day?"

She gritted her teeth on a spate of furious words. He never failed to dig for the emotion that seeped into her work, and she never failed to defend it. Not this time, Laurel told herself as she balled her hands into fists under her desk. "I leave the cynicism to you, Matthew," she returned with a sweetness belied by the daggers in her eyes. "You're so good at it."

"Yeah. How about a bet on whose story makes page one?"

She lifted one fragile, arched brow—a gesture he particularly admired. "I wouldn't want to take your money, Matthew."

"I don't mind taking yours." Grinning, he rose to walk around their desk and bend down to her ear. "Five bucks, magnolia blossom. Even though your papa owns the paper, our editors know the difference between reporting and crusading."

He felt the heat rise, heard the soft hiss of breath. It was tempting, very tempting, to crush his mouth onto those soft, pouting lips and taste the fury. Even as the need worked into him, Matt reminded himself that wasn't the way to outwit her.

"You're on, Bates, but make it ten." Laurel stood. It infuriated her that she had to tilt her head back to meet his eyes. It infuriated her more that the eyes were confident, amused, and beautiful. Laurel fell back on the habit of imagining him short, rotund, and balding. "Unless that's too rich for your blood," she added.

"Anything to oblige, love." He curled the tips of her hair around his finger. "And to prove even Yankees have chivalry, I'll buy you lunch with my winnings."

She smiled at him, leaning a bit closer so that their bodies just brushed. Matt felt the surprising jolt of heat shoot straight through his system. "When hell freezes over," Laurel told him, then shoved him aside.

Matt watched her storm away; then, dipping his hands into his pockets, he laughed. In the confusion of the city room, no one noticed.

D amn!" Laurel swore as she maneuvered her car through the choking downtown traffic. Matthew Bates was the most irritating man she'd ever known. Squeezing through on an amber light, she cursed fate. If her brother Curt hadn't met him in college, Matthew would never have accepted the position on the *Herald*. Then he'd be insufferable in New York instead of being insufferable two feet away from her day after day.

Honesty forced her to admit, even when it hurt, that he was the best reporter on the staff. He was thorough and insightful and had the instincts of a bloodhound. But that didn't make him any easier to swallow. Laurel hit the brakes and swerved as a Buick cut her off. She was too annoyed with Matt to be bothered by traffic warfare.

His piece on the homicide had been clean, concise, and excellent. She wished she'd stuffed the ten dollars down his throat. That would've made it difficult for him to gloat over it.

In the twelve months she'd known and worked with him, he'd never reacted toward her as other men did. There was no deference in him, no admiration in his eyes. The fact that she despised being deferred to didn't make her resent him any less.

He'd never asked her out—not that she wanted him to, Laurel reminded herself firmly. Except for missing the pure pleasure of turning him down. Even though he'd moved into her apartment building, virtually next door to her, he'd never come knocking at her door on the smallest of pretenses. For a year she'd been hoping he would—so she could slam the door in his face.

What he did, she thought as she gritted her teeth, was make a nuisance of himself in a dozen other ways. He made cute little observations on her dates—all the more irritating because they were invariably true. These days his favorite target was Jerry Cartier, an ultraconservative, somewhat dense city councilman. Laurel saw him because she was too kindhearted not to, and he occasionally gave her a lead. But Matt put her in the intolerable position of having to defend Jerry against her own opinion.

Life would be simpler, she thought, if Matthew Bates were still hustling newsprint in Manhattan. And if he weren't so impossibly attractive. Laurel blocked Matt, and her ten dollars, out of her mind as she left the traffic behind.

Though the sun was hanging low, the sky was still brilliant. Warmth and light filtered through the cypresses and streamed onto the road. Deep in the trees were shadows and the musical sound of insects and birds, creatures of the marsh. She'd always known there were secrets in the marshes. Secrets, shadows, dangers. They only added to the beauty.

There was something exciting in knowing another way of life thrived—primitive, predatory—so near civilization.

As she turned into the lane that led to her ancestral home, Laurel felt the familiar mix of pride and tranquility. Cedars guarded each side of the drive, arching overhead to transform the lane into a cool, dim tunnel. The sun filtered through sporadically, throwing patches of light on the ground. Spanish moss dripped from the branches to add that timeless grace so peculiar to the South. As she traveled down the drive of Promesse d'Amour, the clock turned back. Life was easy.

At the end of the drive, Laurel stopped to look at the house. There were two rambling stories of whitewashed brick surrounded by a profusion of azaleas, camellias and magnolias. The colors, vivid and delicate, the scents, sweet and gentle, added to the sense of Southern style and indolence. With the window down, she could smell the mix of heat and fragrance.

There were twenty-eight Doric columns that added dignity rather than ostentation. Ivy clung to each corner post. The grillwork on the encircling balcony was as delicate as black lace and French doors led to it from every room. The effect of the house was one of durability, security, and grace. Laurel saw it as a woman who had coped with the years and emerged with character and gentility. If the house had been flesh and blood, she couldn't have loved it more.

She took the side steps to the porch and entered without knocking. Her childhood had been spent there, her girlhood, her adolescence. A wide hallway split the building in two, running from front door to back. Lingering in the air was the scent of beeswax and lemon, to mix with the fragrance from a bowl of camellia blossoms. The hall would have held the same scent a century before. Laurel paused only briefly in front of a cheval glass to brush the hair away from her face before she walked into the front parlor.

"Hello, Papa." She went to him, rising on her toes to kiss a cheek rough from a day's growth of beard. William Armand was lanky and handsome with dark hair just hinting at gray. While he ran his daily paper with verve, temper, and tenacity, he chose an easier pace for his personal life. He smelled of good whiskey and tobacco. In an old habit, he mussed the hair Laurel had just straightened.

"Hello, princess. Good story on the mayor." He lifted a brow in puzzlement as he saw the quick flash of irritation in her eyes.

"Thanks." She smiled so quickly, her father thought he'd imagined that dangerous light. Turning, she studied the woman who sat in a royal-blue tufted chair.

The hair was pure white, but as full and thick as Laurel's. It surrounded a face layered and lined with wrinkles and unashamedly rouged. Olivia Armand wasn't ashamed of anything. Eyes as sharp and green as the emeralds in her ears studied Laurel in turn.

"Grandma." With a sigh, Laurel bent to kiss her. "Will you never grow old?"

"Not if I have anything to say about it." Her voice was raspy with age and stunningly sensual. "You're the same," she continued, taking Laurel's hand in her strong, dry one. "It's good Creole blood." After giving Laurel's hand a quick squeeze, she sat back in her chair. "William, fix the child a drink and top mine off while you're at it. How's your love life these days, Laurellie?"

Grinning, Laurel dropped down on the hassock at her grandmother's feet. "Not as varied as yours." She caught her father's wink as he handed her a glass.

"Hogwash!" Olivia tossed back her bourbon. "I'll tell you what's wrong with the world today, too much business and not enough romance. Your problem, Laurellie—" she paused to jab a finger at her granddaughter "—is wasting time on that spineless Cartier. Not enough blood in him to warm a woman's bed."

"Thank God," Laurel said with a grateful look at the ceiling. "That's the last place I want him."

"Time you had someone there," Olivia retorted.

Laurel lifted a brow while her father tried not to choke on his drink. "Not all of us," Laurel said smoothly, "have your, shall we say, bawdy turn of mind."

Olivia gave a hoot of laughter and smacked the arm of her chair. "Not everyone admits it, that's the difference."

Unable to resist her grandmother's outrageousness, Laurel grinned. "Curt should be here soon, shouldn't he?"

"Any minute." William eased his tall, angular frame into a chair. "He called just before you came in. He's bringing a friend with him."

"A woman, I hope," Olivia said irrepressibly before she polished off her bourbon. "Boy's got his nose stuck in too many law books. Between the two of you," she added, rounding on Laurel again, "I'll never be a great-grandmother. The pair of you're too wrapped up in law and newspapers to find a lover."

"I'm not ready to get married," Laurel said tranquilly as she held her glass up to the light.

"Who said anything about marriage?" Olivia wanted to know. Heaving a sigh, she looked at her son. "Children nowadays don't know anything."

Laurel was laughing when she heard the sound of the front door closing. "That'll be Curt. I believe I'll warn him about the frame of mind you're in."

"Damned pretty girl," Olivia muttered when Laurel strolled out.

"She's the image of you," her son commented as he lit one of his cigars.

Olivia cackled. "Damned pretty."

The moment she entered the hall, Laurel's smile faded and her jaw tensed. Her eyes flicked over her brother to the man beside him. "Oh, it's you."

Matt took her hand, raising it to his lips before Laurel could jerk it away. "Ah, Southern hospitality." Good God, he thought as his gaze roamed over her, she's beautiful. All that passion, all that fire, under ivory and roses. One day, Laurellie, he promised silently, we're going to set it all loose. My way.

Ignoring the warmth that lingered on her knuckles from his lips, Laurel turned to her brother. He had the angularity and aristocratic features of their father, and the eyes of a dreamer. As Matt watched, the restrained temper on her face softened with affection.

"Hi." She put her hands on her brother's shoulders, leaving them there after she'd kissed him. "How are you?"

"Fine. Busy." He gave her an absent smile, as if he'd just remembered where he was.

"The busy might be an issue tonight," she told him with a chuckle. "Grandma's in one of her moods."

He gave her such a pained look that Laurel laughed and kissed him again. Poor Curt, she thought, so shy and sweet. Turning her head, she looked directly into Matt's eyes. He was watching her coolly, with something undefinable flickering behind the aloof expression. A tremble skidded up her spine, but she kept her eyes level. Who is he really? she wondered, not for the first time. And why, after an entire year, am I still not sure? It always puzzled her how a man with his energy, wit, and cynicism should remain such good friends with her gentle, dreamy brother. It puzzled her, too, that she couldn't pin him down to a type. Perhaps that was why he invaded her thoughts so often. Involuntarily, her gaze slipped down to his mouth. It curved. Silently, she swore.

"I guess we'd better go in," Curt said, oblivious to the undercurrents around him. He smiled in a quick, boyish way that animated his soft eyes. "Having Matt along should distract her. Distracting women's one of his best talents."

Laurel gave an unladylike snort. "I'll bet."

As Curt started into the parlor, Matt took Laurel's hand and tucked it into his arm. "Another wager, Laurellie?" he murmured. "Name the stakes."

There was something insolent in the softly spoken words. She tossed her head back in an angry gesture that pleased him enormously. "If you don't let go of my hand, I'm going to—"

"Embarrass yourself," Matt finished as they crossed the threshold into the parlor.

He'd always liked the room—the faded colors and polished old wood. There were times when he was here that Matt forgot the years he'd spent in a cramped third-floor walk-up with a radiator that let off more noise than heat. That part of his life was over; he'd seen to it. Yet snatches of it crept up on him in spite of success. Shoes that were too small, a belly never quite full—an ambition that threatened to outdistance opportunity. No, he'd never take success for granted. He'd spent too many years fighting for it.

"So, you've brought the Yankee, have you?" Olivia sent Matt a sparkling look and prepared to enjoy herself.

Curt greeted his father, dutifully kissed Olivia's cheek, then busied himself mixing drinks. Grandma had that look in her eye.

"Miss Olivia." Matt took the offered hand and lifted it to his lips. "More beautiful than ever."

"Rascal," she accused, but the pleasure came through. "You haven't been to see me for a month—a dangerous amount of time at my age."

Matt kissed her hand again while his eyes laughed into hers. "I only stay away because you won't marry me."

Laurel struggled not to smile as she chose a chair across the room. Did he have to be so damned charming?

Olivia's laugh was a sound of pure, feminine appreciation. "Thirty years ago, you scoundrel, I'd have given you a chase, even if you are a Yankee."

Matt took the offered glass, and the grateful look, Curt gave him before he turned back to Olivia. "Miss Olivia, I wouldn't have run." He perched on the arm of her chair, much, Laurel thought resentfully, like a favored nephew.

"Well, the time's passed for that," she decided with a sigh before she aimed a look at Laurel. "Why haven't you taken up with this devil, Laurellie? He's a man to keep a woman's blood moving."

Color, as much from annoyance as embarrassment, rose in Laurel's cheeks as Matt sent her a wolfish grin. She sat in stony silence, cursing the fairness of her skin.

"Now that's a fine, feminine trick," her grandmother observed, tapping Matt on the thigh. "Good for the complexion, too. Why, I could still call out a blush on demand after I'd had a husband and three lovers under my belt." Pleased with the deadly stare her granddaughter aimed at her, Olivia lifted her face to Matt's. "Good-looking girl, isn't she?"

"Lovely," Matt agreed, enjoying himself almost as much as Olivia was.

"Breed fine sons."

"Have another drink, Mother," William suggested, observing the war signals in his daughter's eyes.

"Fine idea." She handed over her empty glass. "You haven't seen the gardens, Matthew. They're at their peak. Laurellie, take this Yankee out and show him what a proper garden looks like."

Laurel shot her grandmother an icy glare. "I'm sure Matthew—"

"Would love to," he finished for her, rising.

She switched the glare to him without any effort. "I don't—"

"Want to be rude," he supplied quietly as he helped her out of her chair.

Oh, yes, she did, Laurel thought as she swung through the garden doors. She wanted very badly to be rude. But not in front of her family, and he knew it. "You really enjoy this, don't you?" she hissed at him the moment the door closed behind them.

"Enjoy what?" Matt countered.

"Infuriating me."

"It's impossible not to enjoy something one's so good at."

She chuckled, then despised herself. "All right, here's the garden." She made a wide gesture. "And you don't want to see it any more than I want to show it to you."

"Wrong," Matt said simply, and took her hand again.

"Will you stop that!" Exasperated, Laurel shook her hand but failed to free it. "That's a new habit you've picked up."

"I just found out I like it." He drew her off the terrace onto one of the narrow paths that wound through the flowers. "Besides, if you don't make a good showing at this, Olivia'll just think of something else."

Too true, Laurel admitted. She'd tolerate the man beside her. After all, the sun was splashing red on the horizon and the garden smelled like paradise. It'd been too long since she'd taken the time to see it at dusk. They walked under an arched trellis with wisteria dripping like rain. The birds of the sunlight were beginning to quiet, and those of the night had yet to wake.

"I've always loved it best at this time of day," Laurel said without thinking. "You can almost see the women with their hooped skirts swishing along the edges of the paths. There'd have been musicians in the gazebo and strings of colored lanterns."

He'd known she had a streak of romance, a touch of her brother's dreaminess, but she'd been so careful not to show either to him before. Instinctively, he knew she hadn't meant to now, but the garden had weakened her. He wondered, as he trailed his thumb lightly over her knuckles, what other weaknesses she might have.

"It would've smelled the same then as it does tonight," Matt murmured, discovering just how exquisite her skin looked in the golden light of sunset. "Hot and sweet and secret."

"When I was a girl, I'd come out here sometimes at dusk and pretend I was meeting someone." The memory made her smile, a little dreamy, a little wistful. "Sometimes he'd be dark and dashing—or he'd be tall and blond, but always dangerous and unsuitable. The kind of man a young girl's papa would've whisked her away from." She laughed, letting her fingers trail over a waxy, white camellia. "Strange that I would've had those kinds of fancies when my papa knew I was much too ambitious and practical to fall for a . . ."

Laurel trailed off when she turned her head and found him close—so close it was his scent that aroused her senses rather than the blossom's; his breath she felt on her skin rather than the sultry evening air. The light was touched with gold, blushed with rose. Hazy, magical. In it, he looked too much like someone she might have dreamed of.

Matt let his fingers play lightly with the pulse at her wrist.

It wasn't steady, but this time it wasn't anger that unsettled it. "A what?"

"A rogue," Laurel managed after a moment.

They were talking softly, as if they were telling secrets. The sun slipped lower, and the shadows lengthened.

His face was so lean, she thought suddenly. Not predatory, but the face of a man who wouldn't step aside if trouble got in his way. His eyes were guarded, but she'd noticed before how easily he concealed his thoughts. Perhaps that was why he nudged information from people without appearing to nudge at all. And his mouth—how was it she'd never realized how tempting, how sensual his mouth was? Or had she simply pretended not to? It wouldn't be soft, she thought as her gaze lingered on it. It would be hard, and the taste essentially male. She could lean just a bit closer and . . .

Laurel's eyes widened at the drift of her own thoughts. Beneath Matt's fingers, her pulse scrambled before she yanked her hand away. Good Lord, *what* had gotten into her? He'd tease her for months if he had any idea how close she'd come to making a fool of herself.

"We'd better go back in," she said coolly. "It's nearly time for dinner."

Matt had an urge to grab her and take the kiss she'd very nearly given him. And if he did that, he'd lose whatever inching progress he'd made. He'd wanted her for a long time— too long—and was shrewd enough to know she would have refused ordinary advances from the first. Matt had chosen the out of the ordinary, finding it had its amusements.

Patience, Matt reminded himself, was a crucial element of success—but she deserved one small dig for making him pound with desire and frustration.

"So soon?" His voice was mild, his expression ironic. "If

Olivia had sent you out here with Cartier, I doubt you'd have cut the tour so short."

"She'd never have sent me out here with Jerry," Laurel said before the meaning of her statement sank in.

"Ah." It was a sound designed to infuriate.

"Don't start on Jerry," Laurel snapped.

Matt gave her an innocent grin. "Was I?"

"He's a very nice man," she began, goaded. "He's well mannered and—and harmless."

Matt threw back his head and roared. "God save me from being labeled harmless."

Her eyes frosted and narrowed. "I'll tell you what you are," she said in a low, vibrating voice. "You're insufferable."

"Much better." Unable to resist, he stepped closer and gathered her hair in one hand. "I have no desire to be nice, well mannered, or harmless."

She wished his fingers hadn't brushed her neck. They'd left an odd little trail of shivers. "You've gotten your wish," she said, not quite evenly. "You're annoying, rude, and . . ."

"Dangerous?" he supplied, lowering his head so that their lips were only inches apart.

"Don't put words in my mouth, Bates." Why did she feel as though she were running the last leg of a very long race? Struggling to even her breathing, Laurel took a step back and found herself against the wall of the trellis. She would have sidestepped if he hadn't moved so quickly, blocking her.

"Retreating, Laurellie?" No, it wasn't just temper, he thought, watching the pulse hammer at the base of her throat. Not this time.

Something warm moved through her, like a lazy river. Her spine snapped straight. Her chin jutted up. "I don't have to retreat from you. It's bad enough that I have to tolerate you day after day at the *Herald*, but I'll be damned if I'll stand

here and waste my *own* time. I'm going in," she finished on
a near shout, "because I'm hungry."

Shoving him out of her way, Laurel stormed back toward
the house. Matt stayed where he was a moment, looking after her—the swinging hair, the long, graceful strides, the
simmering fury. That, he thought, was one hell of a woman.
Making love to her would be a fascinating experience. He intended to have it, and her, very soon.

CHAPTER 2

Because she was still seething from the night before, Laurel decided to walk to the paper. Half an hour in the warm air, shifting her way through people, pausing by store windows, listening to snatches of casual conversation from other pedestrians would go a long way toward soothing her agitation. The city, like the plantation house outside it, was an old, consistent love. Laurel didn't consider it a contradiction that she could be drawn to the elegant timelessness of Promesse d'Amour and the bustling rush of downtown traffic. For as long as she could remember, she'd straddled both worlds, feeling equally at home in each. She was ambitious—she was romantic. Practicality and dreaminess were both a part of her nature, but she'd never minded the tug-of-war. At the moment, she felt more comfortable with the noise and hustle around her than with the memory of a twilight garden.

What had he been up to? she asked herself again, jamming her hands in her pockets. Laurel felt she knew Matt well enough to understand that he rarely did anything without an underlying purpose. He'd never touched her quite like that before. Scowling into a shop window, Laurel recalled that Matthew Bates had rarely touched her at all in an entire year. And last night . . . last night, Laurel remembered, there had been something almost casual about the way his fingers had brushed the back of her neck and skimmed over her wrist. *Almost* casual, she repeated. But there'd been nothing casual about her response to it.

Obviously, he had caught her off-balance—intentionally, Laurel added with a deeper scowl. What she'd felt hadn't been excitement or anticipation, but simply surprise. She was fully recovered now. The garden had been moody, romantic. She'd always been susceptible to moods, that was why she'd found herself telling him foolish things. And why, just for a minute, she'd wanted to feel what it would be like to be held against him.

Blossoms and sunsets. A woman might find the devil himself attractive in that kind of a setting. Temporarily. She'd pulled herself back before she'd done anything humiliating, Laurel reminded herself.

Then there was her grandmother. Laurel gritted her teeth and waited for the light to change. Normally, Olivia's outlandish remarks didn't bother her in the least, but she was going too far when she insinuated that Matthew Bates was exactly what her granddaughter needed.

Oh, he'd lapped that up, Laurel remembered, glaring straight ahead. He was easily as impossible as the old girl herself—without her charm, Laurel added loyally. She took a deep breath of the city—exhaust, humanity, heat. Right now, she appreciated it for what it was: genuine. She wasn't going to let an absurd incident in a fantasy world spoil her day. Determined to forget it, and the man who'd caused it, she started to step off the curb.

"Good morning, Laurellie."

Surprised, she nearly stumbled when a hand shot and grabbed her arm. Good God, wasn't there anywhere in New Orleans she could get away from him? Turning her head, she gave Matt a long, cool look. "Car break down?"

Haughtiness suited her, he mused, as well as temper did. "Nice day for a walk," he countered smoothly, keeping her arm as they started to cross the street. He wasn't fool enough to tell her he'd seen her start out on foot and followed the impulse to go after her.

Laurel made a point of disengaging her arm when they reached the sidewalk. Why the hell hadn't she just gotten into her car as she would have any other morning? Short of making a scene on the street, she was stuck with him. When she gave him another glance, she caught the amused look in his eye that meant he'd read her thoughts perfectly. After rejecting the idea of knocking him over the head with her purse, Laurel gave him a cold smile.

"Well, Matthew, you seemed to enjoy yourself last night."

"I like your grandmother, she's beautiful," he said so simply, she stopped short. When her brows drew together, he smiled and ran a finger down her nose. "Isn't that allowed?"

With a shrug, Laurel began to walk again. How was she supposed to detest him when he was being sweet and sincere? Laurel made another stab at it. "You encourage her."

"She doesn't need any encouragement," he stated all too accurately. "But I like to anyway."

Laurel wasn't quite successful in smothering a laugh. The sidewalk was crowded enough to make it necessary for their arms to brush as they walked. "You don't seem to mind that she's setting you up as my . . ."

"Lover?" he suggested, with the annoying habit of finishing her thoughts. "I think Olivia, for all her, ah, liberated ideas, has something more permanent in mind. She threw in the house for good measure."

Stunned, Laurel gaped at him. He grinned, and her sense of the ridiculous took over. "You'd better be sure she tosses in some cash; it's the devil to maintain."

"I admit, it's tempting." He caught the ends of Laurel's hair in his fingers. "The . . . house," he said when her gaze lifted to his, "isn't something a man turns down lightly."

She slanted a look at him, one she'd never aimed in his direction before. Under the lashes, sultry, amused, and irresistible. "Matthew," Laurel said in a soft drawl, "you'll put me in the position of considering Jerry more seriously."

Then, he thought as desire crawled into his stomach, I'd have to quietly kill him. "Olivia'd disown you."

Laurel laughed and, without thinking, linked her arm through his. "Ah, the choices a woman must make. My inheritance or my sensibilities. I guess it's just too bad for both of us that you're not my type."

Matt put his hand on the glass door of the Herald Building before Laurel could pull it open. "You put *me* in the position, Laurellie," he said quietly, "of having to change your mind."

She lifted a brow, not quite as sure of herself as she'd been a moment before. Why hadn't she noticed these rapid mood swings in him before? The truth was, she admitted, she'd dedicated herself to noticing as little about him as possible. From the first moment he'd walked into the city room, she had decided that was the safest course. Determined not to lose the upper hand this time, she smiled as she pushed through the door. "Not a chance, Bates."

Matt let her go, but his gaze followed her progress through the crowded lobby. If he hadn't already been attracted to her, her words would have forced his hand. He'd always liked going up against the odds. As far as he was concerned, Laurel had just issued the first challenge. With an odd sort of smile, he moved toward the bank of elevators.

Laurel's entire morning involved interviewing the director of a highway research agency. A story on road repair and detour signs wasn't exactly loaded with fire and flash, she mused, but news was news. Her job was to assimilate the facts, however dry they might be, and report. With luck she could get the story under the fold on page two. Perhaps the afternoon would yield something with a bit more meat.

The hallways, rarely deserted, were quiet in the late-morning lull. Other reporters returned from, or were on their way to, assignments, but most were already in the field or at their desks. Giving a perfunctory wave to a colleague hurrying by with an on-the-run lunch of a candy bar, she began to structure her lead paragraph. Preoccupied, she turned toward the city room and jolted another woman. The contents of the woman's purse scattered onto the floor.

"Damn!" Without glancing over, Laurel crouched down and began to gather things up. "Sorry, I wasn't looking where I was going."

"It's all right."

Laurel saw a very small hand reach out for a plain manila envelope. The hand was shaking badly. Concerned, she looked over at a pale blonde with pretty features and red-rimmed eyes. Her lips were trembling as badly as her hands.

"Did I hurt you?" Laurel took the hands in hers instinctively. A stray, an injured bird, a troubled stranger—she'd never been able to resist anything or anyone with a problem.

The woman opened her mouth, then closed it again to shake her head violently. The fingers Laurel gripped quivered helplessly. When the first tears rolled down the pale face, Laurel forgot the noise and demands of the city room, the notes scrawled in the book in her bag. Helping the woman up, Laurel led her through the maze of desks and into the glass-walled office of the city editor.

"Sit down," she ordered, nudging the blonde into a faded leather chair. "I'll get you some water." Without waiting for an agreement, Laurel strode out again. When she came back, she noted that the woman had swallowed her tears, but her face hadn't lost that wounded, bewildered expression. "Come on, sip this." After offering the paper cup, Laurel sat on the arm of the chair and waited.

Inside the office, she could hear the muted echo of activity from the city room. It was early enough in the day that desperation hadn't struck yet. Deadline panic was hours away. What desperation there was came from the blonde's efforts to steady her breathing. Hundreds of questions buzzed in Laurel's mind, but she gave the woman silence.

"I'm sorry." She crushed the now empty paper cup in her fingers before she looked up at Laurel. "I don't usually fall apart that way."

"It's all right." Laurel noticed the woman was slowly, systematically tearing the paper cup to shreds. "I'm Laurel Armand."

"Susan Fisher." Blankly, she looked down at the scraps of paper in her lap.

"Can I help, Susan?"

That almost started the tears again. Such simple words, Susan thought as she closed her eyes against them. Why should they make her feel all the more hopeless? "I don't know why I came here," she began jerkily. "I just couldn't think of anything else. The police . . ."

Laurel's reporter's drive rose to tangle with her protective instincts. Both were too natural to her for her to even notice them. She laid a hand on Susan's shoulder. "I work here; you can talk to me. Would you like to start at the beginning?"

Susan stared up at her. She no longer knew whom to trust, or if indeed *trust* was a word to believe in. This woman looked so confident, so sure of herself. She'd never had her life shattered. Why would this poised, vibrant-looking woman listen, or believe?

Susan's eyes were blue, soft and light and vulnerable. Laurel didn't know why they made her think of Matt, a man she thought had no sensitivity at all, yet they did. She put her hand over Susan's. "I'll help you if I can."

"My sister." The words tumbled out, then stopped with a jerk. With an effort, Susan swallowed and began again. "My sister, Anne, met Louis Trulane a year ago."

Louis? The name shot through Laurel's mind so that the hand over Susan's stiffened. Bittersweet memories, loyalties, growing pains. What could this tearful, frightened woman have to do with Louis? "Go on," Laurel managed, making her fingers relax.

"They were married less than a month after they met. Anne was so much in love. We had—we were sharing an apartment at the time, and all she could talk about was Louis, and moving here to live in the fabulous old house he owned. Heritage Oak. Do you know it?"

Laurel nodded, staring off into nothing more than her own memories. "Yes, I know it."

"She sent me pictures of it. I just couldn't imagine Anne living there, being mistress of it. Her letters were full of it, and of Louis, of course." Susan paused as her breath came out in a shudder. "She was so happy. They were already talking about starting a family. I'd finally made arrangements to take some time off. I was coming to visit her when I got Louis's letter."

Laurel turned to take Susan's hand in a firmer grip. "Susan, I know—"

"She was dead." The statement was flat and dull, with shock still lingering around the edges. "Anne was dead. Louis wrote—he wrote that she'd gone out alone, after dark, wandered into the swamp. A copperhead bite, he said. If they'd found her sooner . . . but it wasn't until the next morning, and it was too late." Susan pressed her lips together, telling herself she had to get beyond the tears. The time for them was over. "She was only twenty-one, and so lovely."

"Susan, it must've been dreadful for you to hear that way. It was a terrible accident."

"Murder," Susan said in a deadly calm voice. "It was murder."

Laurel stared at her for a full ten seconds. Her first inclination to soothe and comfort vanished, replaced by a whiff of doubt, a tingle of interest. "Anne Trulane died of a snakebite and exposure. Why do you call it murder?"

Susan rose and paced to the window. Laurel hadn't patted her hand, hadn't made inane comments. She was still listening, and Susan felt a faint flicker of hope. "I'll tell you what I told Louis, what I told the police." She took an extra moment to let the air go in and out of her lungs slowly. "Anne and I were very close. She was always gentle, sensitive. She had a childlike sweetness without being childish. I want you to understand that I knew Anne as well as I know myself."

Laurel thought of Curt and nodded. "I do."

Susan responded to this sign of acceptance with a sigh. "Ever since she was little, Anne had a phobia about dark places. If she had to go into a room at night, she'd reach in and hit the light switch first. It was more than just habit, it was one of those small fears some of us never outgrow. Do you know what I mean?"

Thinking of her own phobia, she nodded again. "Yes, I know."

Susan stepped away from the window. "As much as Anne loved that house, having the swamp so near bothered her. She'd written me that it was like a dark closet—something she avoided even in the daytime. She loved Louis, wanted to please him, but she wouldn't go through it with him."

She whirled back to Laurel with eyes no longer calm, but pleading. "You have to understand, she adored him, but she wouldn't, couldn't do that for him. It was like an obsession. Anne believed it was haunted—she'd even worked herself up to the point where she thought she saw lights out there. Anne would never have gone in there alone, at night."

Laurel waited a moment, while facts and ideas raced through her mind. "But she was found there."

"Because someone took her."

In silence, Laurel measured the woman who now stood across from her. Gone was the defenseless look. Though the eyes were still puffy and red-rimmed, there was a determination in them, and a demand to be believed. An older sister's shock and loyalty perhaps, Laurel mused, but she let bits and pieces of the story run through her mind, along with what she knew of Anne Trulane's death.

It had never been clear why the young bride had wandered into the swamp alone. Though Laurel had grown up with swamps and bayous, she knew they could be treacherous places, especially at night, for someone who didn't know them. Insects, bogs . . . snakes.

She remembered too how Louis Trulane had closed out the press after the tragedy—no interviews, no comment. As soon as the inquest had been over, he'd retreated to Heritage Oak.

Laurel thought of Louis, then looked at Susan. Loyalties tugged. And pulling from both sides was a reporter's instinct she'd been born with. The whys in life always demanded an answer.

"Why did you come to the *Herald*, Susan?"

"I went to see Louis last night as soon as I got into town. He wouldn't listen to me. This morning I went to the police." She lifted her hands in a gesture of futility. "Case closed. Before I had a chance to think about it, I was here. Maybe I should hire a private investigator, but . . ." Trailing off, she shook her head. "Even if that were the right way to go, I don't have the money. I know the Trulanes are a powerful, respected family, but there has to be a way of getting at the truth. My sister was murdered." This time her voice quivered

on the statement and the color that had risen to her cheeks
from agitation faded.

Not as strong as she wants to be, Laurel realized as she
rose. "Susan, would you trust me to look into this?"

Susan dragged a hand through her hair. She didn't want
to fall apart now, not now, when someone was offering the
help she needed so badly. "I have to trust someone."

"There're a few things I have to do." Abruptly, Laurel became brisk. If there was a story, and she smelled one, she
couldn't think of old ties, old memories. "There's a coffee
machine in the lobby. Get a cup and wait for me there. When
I've finished, we'll get something to eat—talk some more."

Asking no questions, Susan gathered up her purse, watching the torn bits of the paper cup drift to the floor. "Thank
you."

"Don't thank me yet," Laurel advised. "I haven't done anything."

Susan paused at the door to glance over her shoulder. "Yes,
you have."

Mouth pursed in thought, Laurel watched Susan wind her
way through the desks in the city room. Anne Trulane, she
thought, and let out a sigh. Louis. Good God, what kind of
wasp's nest was she poking into?

Before she could formulate an answer, the city editor came
in, his thin face creased into a scowl, his tired eyes annoyed.
"Damn it, Laurel, this is a newspaper, not a Miss Lonely-
hearts service. When one of your friends has a fight with her
boyfriend, find someone else's office to flood. Now move it."
He flopped down behind his cluttered desk. "You've got a
story to write."

Laurel walked over to the desk and perched on the corner. Don Ballinger was her godfather, a man who had often
bounced her on his knee. If it came to a toss-up between personal affection and news copy, the copy'd win hands down.

Laurel expected no less. "That was Anne Trulane's sister," she said mildly when he opened his mouth to swear at her.

"Trulane," he repeated as his wispy brows drew together. "What'd she want?"

Laurel picked up a hunk of fool's gold Don used as a paperweight and shifted it from hand to hand. "To prove her sister was murdered."

He gave a short bark that might have been a laugh or a sound of derision. Don took a cigarette out of the desk drawer and ran it lovingly through his fingers. He stroked it, caressed it, but didn't light it. He hadn't lit one in sixteen days, ten hours . . . twenty-two minutes. "Snakebite," Don said simply, "and a night's exposure don't add up to murder. What about the story on the highway agency?"

"The sister tells me that Anne had a phobia about the dark," Laurel continued. "Anne supposedly mentioned the swamp where she died in her letters. She hadn't set foot in it, and didn't intend to."

"Obviously she changed her mind."

"Or someone changed it for her."

"Laurel—"

"Don, let me do some poking around." Laurel studied the glittering paperweight as she spoke. Things weren't always as they seemed, she mused. Not nearly always. "It couldn't hurt. If nothing else, I could work up a human interest piece."

Don scowled down at his cigarette, running a finger from filter to tip. "Trulane won't like it."

"I can deal with Louis," she said with more confidence than she felt. "There's something in this, Don. There was never any clear reason why Anne Trulane went out there alone. She was already dressed for bed."

They both knew the rumors—that she'd been meeting a lover, that Louis had bracketed her to the house until she'd simply gone out blindly, then lost herself. Don put the cigarette in his mouth and gnawed on the filter. The Trulanes were always good copy. "Nose around," he said at length. "It's still fresh news." Before Laurel could be too pleased that she'd won the first round, he dropped the bomb. "Bates covered the story, work with him."

"Work with Bates?" she repeated. "I don't need him. It's my lead, my story."

"His beat," Don countered, "and no one's story until there is one."

"Damn it, Don, the man's insufferable. I'm not some junior reporter who needs a proctor, and—"

"And he has the contacts, the sources and knows the background." He rose while Laurel simmered. "We don't play personality games on the *Herald*, Laurel. You work together." After shooting her a last look, he stuck his head out the door. "Bates!"

"You can't play personality games with someone who has none," Laurel muttered. "I'm the one who knows the Trulanes. He'll just get in my way."

"Sulking always was a bad habit of yours," Don commented as he rounded his desk again.

"I am not sulking!" she protested as Matt sauntered into the room.

He took one look at Laurel's furious face, lifted a brow and grinned. "Problem?"

Laurel controlled the urge to hiss at him, and sank into a chair. With Matthew Bates around, there was always a problem.

"Cheer up," Matt advised a few minutes later. "Before this is over, you might learn something."

"I don't need to learn anything from you." Laurel swung toward the elevator.

"That," he murmured, enjoying the way her lips formed into a pout, "remains to be seen."

"You're not taking on an apprentice, Bates, but a partner." She jammed her fists into her pockets. "Don insisted on it because you'd covered the investigation and the inquest. You could make it easy on both of us by just giving me your notes."

"The last thing I do," Matt said mildly, "is give anyone my notes."

"And the last thing I need is to have you breathing down my neck on this. It's *my* story."

"That really stuck where it hurts, didn't it?" Casually, he pushed the button on the elevator, then turned to her. "Didn't your papa ever tell you that sharing's good for the soul?"

Fuming, Laurel stepped into the car and pushed for lobby. "Go to hell."

She didn't know he could move quickly. Perhaps this was her first lesson. Before she had an inkling what he was doing, Matt punched a button and stopped the car between floors. Even as her mouth fell open in surprise, he had her backed up against the side wall. "Watch how far you push," he warned softly, "unless you're willing to take a few hard shoves yourself."

Her throat was so dry it hurt. She'd never seen his eyes frost over like this. It was frightening. Fascinating. Odd, she thought she'd convinced herself he didn't have a temper, but now that it was about to grab her by the throat, she wasn't surprised. No, it wasn't surprise that had the chill racing over her skin.

She was frightened, Matt observed. But she wasn't cringing. Common sense told him to back off now that his point had been made. But a year was a very long time. "I think I'll just get this out of my system now, before we get started."

He saw her eyes widen, stunned as he lowered his mouth

toward hers. A twist of amusement curved his lips as he allowed them to hover a breath from hers. "Surprised, Laurellie?"

Why wasn't she moving? Her body simply wouldn't respond to the commands of her brain. She was almost certain she was telling her arms to push him away. Good God, he had beautiful eyes. Incredibly beautiful eyes. His breath whispered over her skin, trailing into her mouth through lips that had parted without her knowledge. He smelled of no more than soap—basic, simple. Wonderful.

In an effort to clear her senses, Laurel straightened against the wall. "Don't you dare—"

The words ended with a strangled sound of pleasure as his lips skimmed over hers. It wasn't a kiss. No one would consider such a thing a kiss: a breath of a touch without pressure. It was more of a hint—or a threat. Laurel wondered if someone had cut the cables on the elevator.

She didn't move, not a muscle. Her eyes were wide open, her mind wiped clean as he stepped fractionally closer so that his body made full contact with hers—firm, lean, strong. Even as her system jolted, she didn't move. His mouth was still whispering on hers, so subtly, so impossibly light she might have imagined it. When she felt the moist tip of his tongue trace her lips, then dip inside to touch, just touch, the tip of hers, the breath she'd been holding shuddered out.

It was that quiet, involuntary sound of surrender that nearly broke his control. If she'd spit and snarled at him, he could have dealt with it easily. He'd been angry enough to. He hadn't expected stunned submission, not from her. Over the anger came a tempting sense of power, then an ache—gnawing and sweet—of need. Even as he nipped his teeth into her soft bottom lip he wondered if he'd ever have her at quite such a disadvantage again.

God, he wanted to touch her, to slip that neat little blouse off her shoulders and let his hands mold slowly, very, very slowly, every inch of her. That skin of hers, pale as a magnolia, soft as rainwater, had driven him mad for months. He could have her now, Matt thought as he nibbled ever so gently at her lips. He was skilled enough, she off guard enough that he could take her there on the floor of the elevator before either of them had regained their senses. It would be crazy, wonderfully crazy. Even as she stood still, he could all but taste that passion fighting to overcome her surprise and reach out for him. But he had different plans for the seduction of Laurel Armand.

So he didn't touch her, but lazily backed away. Not once during those shivering two minutes had she taken her eyes off his. Laurel watched that clever, torturous mouth curve as he again pressed the button for the lobby. The elevator started with a rumble and jerk.

"A pity we're pressed for time," Matt commented easily, then gave the elevator car a careless glance. "And space."

Layer by layer the mists that had covered her brain cleared until she could think with perfect clarity. Her eyes were glimmering green slits, her ivory skin flushed with rage as she let out a stream of curses in a fluid, effortless style he had to admire.

"Did you know you completely drop your *Rs* when your temper's loose?" Matt asked pleasantly. "It's an education in regional cadence. Truce, Laurel." He held up his hand, palm out as she drew breath to start again. "At least a professional one until we run down this lead. We can take up the private war when we're off duty."

She bit back a retort and smoldered as the elevator came gently to a stop. It wouldn't instill much confidence in Susan Fisher if the two of them were taking potshots at each other. "An armed truce, Bates," she compromised as they stepped into the lobby. "Try anything like that again, and you'll be missing some teeth."

Matt ran his tongue over them experimentally. "Sounds reasonable." He offered his hand, and though she didn't trust that sober expression on his face, Laurel accepted. "Looks like I buy you lunch after all."

Removing her hand, Laurel straightened the purse on her shoulder. "Big talk on an expense account."

Grinning, he swung a friendly arm around her as they moved toward the rear of the lobby. "Don't be cranky, Laurellie, it's our first date."

She snorted, and tossed her head—but she didn't push his arm away.

CHAPTER 3

Matt chose a noisy restaurant in the French Quarter because he always found it easier to make people talk if they weren't sure they could be heard. He'd sensed, from the introduction, that while Susan Fisher had given her trust to Laurel, she was withholding judgment on him. For the moment, he'd decided to let Laurel lead the way.

He was amiable, sympathetic, as he filed away Susan's every word and gesture. She was a woman, Matt decided, who had buckled under pressure and was fighting her way back up. She still had a long way to go, but on one point she wouldn't be swayed. She'd known her sister. Susan wasn't going to let Anne's death rest until all the facts were laid bare. Perhaps Matt admired her for it all the more because her hands weren't quite steady.

He glanced at Laurel and nearly smiled. She'll take in any stray, he mused, though he didn't doubt she'd bite his head off if he suggested it. She didn't want to be considered soft or vulnerable, particularly by him. They were colleagues or, more accurately, competitors. He'd always enjoyed going head to head with her, reporter to reporter. And after that two minutes between floors on the elevator, he didn't think she'd forget he was a man. He wasn't going to give her the chance to.

Pouring more coffee into Susan's cup, Matt sent Laurel a silent signal that it was his turn. Her slight shrug showed him that the truce was still on. "Your sister died nearly a month ago, Susan." He said it softly, watching her face. "Why did you wait so long before bringing all this up?"

She dropped her gaze to her plate, where she'd been pushing food around for twenty minutes. Over her head, Laurel's eyes met Matt's, brows raised. He could almost hear the question in them. *What the hell's this?* But she knew her job. He felt they were already partners without having stated the ground rules. I question. You soothe.

"Susan." Laurel touched her arm. "We want to help you."

"I know." Setting down her fork, she looked up again, skimming over Matt to settle on Laurel. "It's hard to admit it, but I didn't cope with Anne's death well. The truth is, I just fell apart. I stopped answering my phone—didn't leave my apartment. Lost my job." She pressed her lips together. When she spoke again, they had to strain to hear her over the cheerful din in the restaurant. "The worst is, I didn't even come down for the funeral. I suppose I was pretending it wasn't happening. I was the only family she had left, and I wasn't here."

"That isn't important. No, it's not," Laurel insisted when Susan began to speak. "You loved her. In the end, love's all that really matters." Looking over, she saw Matt watching her steadily. For a moment, Laurel forgot Susan, suspicions, the noise and scents of the restaurant. She'd expected to see cynicism in his eyes, perhaps a very faint, very mocking smile. Instead, she saw understanding, and a question she didn't know how to answer. Without speaking, he lifted her hand to his lips, then set it down again.

Oh no, she thought, panicking. *Not him*. That wasn't just impossible, it was ludicrous. Dazed, she picked up her coffee, then set it back down when she saw her hand wasn't quite steady. That one long look had scattered her wits more effectively than the odd kiss that wasn't a kiss, on the elevator. As from a distance, she heard Susan's voice and forced herself to tune into it.

"It all hit me last week. I guess the first shock had passed and I started to think about her letters. It didn't fit." This time she looked up at Matt, demanding he understand. "Whenever she'd mention that swamp, it was with a kind of loathing. If you'd understand just how much she hated the dark, you'd see that she would never have gone into the place alone, at night. Never. Someone took her there, Mr. Bates. Someone made her go."

"Why?" He leaned forward, and while his voice wasn't hard, it was direct. "Why would someone want to kill your sister?"

"I don't know." Her knuckles went white on the edge of the table as she fought the urge to just lay down her head and weep. "I just don't know."

"I covered the inquest." Taking out a cigarette, Matt reached for the pack of restaurant matches. He didn't want to be tough on her, but if she was going to fold, it would be better if she did it now, before they got too deep. "Your sister'd been here less than a year and knew almost no one, as she and her husband rarely socialized. According to the servants, she doted on him, there was rarely a cross word between them. The basic motives for murder—jealousy, greed—don't apply. What else is there?"

"That doesn't matter." Susan turned back to Laurel again. "None of that matters."

"Let's take it a step at a time," Laurel suggested. "Do you still have your sister's letters?"

"Yes." Susan let out an unsteady breath. "Back at my hotel."

Matt crushed out his cigarette. "Let's go take a look at them."

When Susan was out of earshot, Laurel brushed close to Matt. "The shock may be over," she murmured, "but she's still not too sturdy. Matthew, I have a feeling about this."

"You've got too many feelings, Laurel."

She frowned at him as they skirted between tables. "Just what does that mean?"

"We have to deal with facts. If you want to play Girl Scout, you're going to cloud the issue."

"I should've known better," she said between her teeth. "For a minute back there, I thought I saw some small spark of sensitivity."

He grinned. "I'm loaded with sensitivity. We can talk about it over drinks later."

"In a pig's eye." Laurel swung out the door behind Susan and made a point of ignoring Matt through the cab ride to the hotel.

It was seedy—the streets were narrow, the concrete was chipped, the banisters were peeling. Condensation gathered and dripped from the rusting balconies. The paint on the buildings was cracked and coated with layers of grime and moisture from the constant humidity. All the colors seemed to have faded into one—a steamy gray.

The alleyways were shadowed and dank. At night, Laurel knew, the street would be mean—the kind of street you avoided, or walked on quickly while glancing over your shoulder. From the open window across the street the sounds of an argument overpowered a scratchy jazz recording. A bony cat lay over the stoop and made a low, unfriendly sound in his throat when Susan opened the door.

When Laurel cautiously stepped around it, Susan offered an apologetic smile. "This place has its own . . . atmosphere."

Matt grinned as he cast a look around the dim lobby. "You should've seen the apartment where I grew up in New York."

The strained smile relaxed as Susan turned toward the stairs. "Well, it was here, and it was cheap."

Following them, Laurel frowned at Matt's back. She'd caught another glimpse of sensitivity. Odd. And, though she hated to admit it, the careless comment about his youth piqued her interest. Who had he been? How had he lived? She'd always been very careful not to allow herself to speculate.

The place was so quiet, so empty, that their footsteps echoed on the uncarpeted steps. Cracked paint and graffiti. Laurel studied Susan's profile as she unlocked the door. I'm going to get her out of here, she promised herself, by this afternoon. Catching the amused, knowing look Matt sent her, Laurel glared at him.

"After another merit badge, Laurellie?" he murmured.

"Shut up, Bates." While he chuckled, Laurel stepped into Susan's cramped, shadowy room. It had a narrow bed, a scarred dresser, and no charm.

"That's funny, I know I left the shades up." Crossing the room, Susan jerked the cord so that the dusty white shade flapped up and the sun poured into the room. She flicked a switch that had a squeaky ceiling fan stirring the hot air. "I'll get the letters."

Laurel sat on the edge of the bed and looked up at Matt. "What part of New York did you come from?"

His brow lifted, as it did when he was amused—or evasive. "You wouldn't know it." His lips curved as he moved to sit beside her. "Ever been north of the Mason-Dixon line, Laurel?"

"I've been to New York several times," she began testily, then made a sound of frustration when his smile only widened. "Twice," she amended.

"The Empire State Building, Ellis Island, the U.N., tea at the Plaza, and a Broadway show."

"You love being smug and superior, don't you?"

He ran a fingertip down her jaw. "Yeah."

She fought back a smile. "Did you know you become even more insufferable with prolonged contact?"

"Be careful," Matt warned. "I've a weakness for flattery."

With his eyes on her laughing ones, Matt lifted her hand, palm up, and pressed his lips to the center. He watched, pleased, when confusion replaced the humor in her eyes. Behind them, Susan began to pull out drawers frantically. They didn't notice.

"They're gone!" Susan swept a handful of clothes onto the floor and stared at the empty drawer. "They're gone, all of them."

"What?" A little dazed, Laurel turned to her. "What's gone?"

"The letters. All of Anne's letters."

Immediately Laurel was on her feet and sorting through Susan's jumbled clothing. "Maybe you put them somewhere else."

"No—there is nowhere else," she said with a dangerous edge of hysteria in her voice. "I put them all in this drawer. There were twelve of them."

"Susan." Matt's voice was cool enough to stiffen her spine. "Are you sure you brought them with you?"

She took long, deep breaths as her gaze shifted from Laurel to Matt. "I had every one of Anne's letters with me when I checked into this hotel. When I unpacked, I put them in that drawer. They were there when I dressed this morning."

Her hands weren't steady, Matt noticed, but her eyes were. He nodded. "I'll go check with the desk clerk."

As the door closed, Susan stared down at the crumpled

blouse she held. "Someone was in this room," she said unsteadily. "I know it."

Laurel glanced at the shade Susan had lifted. "Are you missing anything else?"

"No." With a sigh, Susan let the blouse fall. "There isn't anything in here worth stealing. I suppose they realized that. It doesn't make any sense that they'd take Anne's letters."

"Matthew and I'll sort it out," Laurel told her, then was annoyed with herself for linking herself with Matt so easily. "In the meantime . . ." Bending, she began to gather Susan's clothes. "Can you type?"

Distracted, Susan stared at her. "Well, yes. I work—I worked," she corrected, "as a receptionist in a doctor's office."

"Good. Where's your suitcase?" she asked as she folded Susan's clothes on the bed.

"It's in the closet, but—"

"I have a place for you to stay, and a job—of sorts. Oh, this is lovely." She shook out the blouse Susan had crumpled.

"A job? I don't understand."

"My grandmother lives outside of town. Since my brother and I moved out, she's been lonely." The lie came out too easily to be questioned.

"But I couldn't just stay there."

"You'd pay for it." Laurel grinned as she turned back. "Grandma's been threatening to write her memoirs and I've just about run out of excuses for not typing them up for her. You won't be bored. She's eighty-two and didn't give up men until . . . Actually, she hasn't given them up at all. If I weren't so busy, I'd love to do it myself. As it is, you'd be doing me quite a favor."

"Why are you doing this for me?" Susan asked. "You don't know me."

"You're in trouble," Laurel said simply. "I can help."

"Just that easy?"

"Does help have to be complicated? Get your suitcase," Laurel ordered before Susan could work out an answer. "You can pack while I see what Matthew's come up with." As she slipped into the hall, Laurel bumped into him. She let the door click shut behind her. "Well?"

"The clerk didn't see anyone." Matt leaned against the wall and lit a cigarette. "But then he's more interested in cheating at solitaire in the back room than covering the desk." He blew out a stream of smoke that rose to the ceiling and hung there. "I spoke to the woman who does the rooms. She didn't pull the shades."

"Then someone was in there."

"Maybe."

Laurel ignored this and stared at the opposite wall. "Susan thinks it was just a break-in. In her state of mind, that's all for the best."

"You're playing mama, Laurel."

"I am not." Angry, she looked back at him. "It'll be a lot easier to sort through this if she doesn't start thinking someone's deliberately trying to stop her."

"There's no reason for her to think that at this point," Matt said dampeningly. "What's she doing?"

"Packing," Laurel muttered.

He nodded. It wasn't wise for her to stay where she was. "Where's she going?"

Laurel angled her chin. "To my grandmother."

Not quite suppressing a smile, Matt studied the tip of his cigarette. "I see."

"You couldn't see through barbed wire. And don't start spouting off about my getting too personally involved, or—"

"All right." He crushed out the cigarette on the dusty, scarred floor. "And I won't comment that you're a very sweet, classy lady. I'll get a cab," he added when Laurel only stared at him.

Just when I think I understand him, she mused, he throws me a curve. If I'm not careful, Laurel added as his footsteps echoed off the stairs. If I'm not very, very careful, I'm going to start liking him. On that uncomfortable thought, she went back in to hurry Susan along.

In under ten minutes, Laurel was in the back of a cab with Matt, glancing behind her at the taxi that would take Susan to her grandmother.

"Stop worrying about her," Matt ordered. "Olivia'll keep her mind off her sister, and everything else."

With a shrug, Laurel turned back around. "I don't doubt that. But I'm beginning to doubt that Anne Trulane walked into that swamp alone."

"Let's stick with the facts. Motive." Absently, he wound a lock of Laurel's hair around his finger—a habit he'd recently developed and rather enjoyed. "There doesn't seem to be any. Women aren't lured into swamps for no reason."

"Then there was one."

"No sexual assault," Matt continued, half to himself. "She didn't have any money on her own—and her only heir would've been Susan in any case . . . or her husband. He has a sister, but I can't see any benefit there."

"The last people I'd consider as murder suspects would be Louis or Marion Trulane. And there are other motives for murder than sex and money."

He lifted a brow at her tone but continued to toy with her hair. "True, but those always spring to mind. Most of us are fond of both."

"Some think beyond your scope, Matthew. There's jealousy, if we go back to your two favorites. Louis is rich and attractive. Someone might have pictured herself in Anne's place."

He caught something—the drift of something he didn't quite understand. And didn't like. "Do you know him well?"

"Louis?" A smile touched her mouth, a gentle one. It reminded him that Laurel had never once looked at him that way. "As well as anyone, I suppose—or I did. He taught me to ride when I was a girl, let me tag along after him when I was ten and he was, oh, twenty-one or twenty-two. He was a beautiful man—and very patient with a girl's infatuation."

When he discovered his fingers were no longer relaxed, Matt released the tendril of hair. "You got over it, I suppose."

Hearing the cynicism in his voice, Laurel turned, the half smile still on her face. "Weren't you ever in love, Matthew?"

The look he gave her was long and guarded while several uncomfortable emotions moved through him. Her eyes were soft; so was her mouth, her skin. If they'd been alone, he might not have answered the question at all, but would simply have taken what he found he needed so badly. "No," he said at length.

"It softens something in you, something that never quite goes away for that particular person." With a sigh, she sat back against the seat. It had been a long time since she'd let herself remember how sweet it had been, and how hurtful. She'd only been a child, and though her dreams had been fairy tales, she'd believed them. "Louis was very important to me. I wanted a knight, and I think he understood that well enough not to laugh at me. And when he married . . ." She lifted her hands and let them fall. "It broke my heart. Do you know about his first wife?"

Matt was staring down at the hands in her lap; small, elegant hands with the nails painted in the palest of corals and a smoky emerald in an intricate old setting on her finger. An heirloom, he thought. She would have heirlooms, and genteel ancestors—and memories of riding lessons from a tall young man, dashing enough to be a knight.

"Bits and pieces," Matt mumbled as the cab pulled to the curb. "Fill me in later."

Laurel climbed out of the cab, then meticulously brushed off her skirt. "That's perilously close to an order, Bates. Since Don didn't lay down any ground rules, maybe you and I should take care of that ourselves."

"Fine." He didn't know why he was angry. He studied her with eyes narrowed against the glare of the sun. "This is my beat."

With an effort, Laurel smothered the flare of temper. "And it's my lead."

"If you want to get anywhere with it," he said evenly, "you'll leave certain areas to me. When's the last time you fought your way through the red tape in there?" Matt jerked his head toward the station house beside them.

"I've untangled red tape before."

"Not in there," he countered before he took her arm.

"Just a minute, Bates." Laurel pushed his hand away and faced him. "The one thing you're going to understand, is that I may have no choice but to work with you on this story, but the operative word is *with*, not *for*. For the moment, however much it galls me, we're partners."

This seemed to amuse him as the temper turned into an odd little smile. "A nice ring to that. Partners," he agreed, taking her hand. "It might become a habit."

"The danger of that's slim to none. Would you stop touching me?"

"No," he said amiably as they climbed the steps.

Voices boomed off the walls of the station house. Disgruntled voices, insolent voices, irate voices. It smelled dankly, stalely of humanity. Sweat, coffee, cigarettes, alcohol. Five members of opposing street gangs leaned against a wall and eyed each other. A woman with a badly bruised face huddled in a chair and spoke in undertones to a harassed-looking officer who nodded and typed out her statement with two fingers. A young girl in snug shorts snapped her gum and looked bored.

He'd seen it all before—and more. After a cursory glance around, Matt moved through the people and desks. The officers, the victims, the accused, paid no more attention to him than he to them.

A slim brunette in a wilting uniform cupped a phone on her shoulder and lifted a hand in salute. Matt perched on the corner of her desk. Laurel stood beside him, watching as two elderly men nearly came to blows before they were pulled apart.

"Well, Matt, what brings you to paradise?" The brunette set down the phone and smiled at him.

"How you doing, Sarge?"

The brunette tipped back in her chair to give him a long, thorough look. "I haven't changed my phone number here—or at home."

"The city keeps us both pretty tied up, doesn't it? Been to the Nugget lately?"

She picked up a pen and tapped it lightly against her mouth. "Not since last month. Want to buy me a drink?"

"You read my mind, but I have a little business."

Letting out a quick laugh, the sergeant dropped her pen onto a blotter crisscrossed with scrawled names and numbers. "Sure. What do you want, Matt?"

"A quick glimpse at the file on a case—a closed case," he added. "Need to do a little backtracking on a story I did, maybe a follow-up."

Her eyes narrowed. "What case?"

"Anne Trulane."

"Sensitive ground, Matt." Her eyes drifted past his to Laurel's.

"Laurel Armand, Sergeant Carolyn Baker. Laurel and I

are on assignment together," Matt said smoothly. "She's an old family friend of the Trulanes. Thought maybe we'd do something a little more in depth. Case is closed, Sarge, and hell, I covered the thing from start to finish."

"You've already seen the report."

"Then it can't hurt for me to see it again." He gave her a charming smile. "You know I play it straight, Carolyn, no printing privileged information, no hints in a story that messes up an investigation."

"Yeah, you play it straight, Matt." She shot him a look that Laurel thought had more to do with personal feelings than professional ones, then shrugged. "It was all public knowledge at the inquest." Rising, she walked away to disappear into a side room. Beside them, the two old men hurled insults at each other.

"You always work that way, Matthew?"

Matt turned to give Laurel a bland smile. "What way?" When she remained silent and staring, he grinned. "Jealous, love? You've got my heart in your hand."

"I'd rather have it under my foot."

"Vicious," he murmured, then pushed off the desk when Carolyn came back in.

"You can look at the file, take it in the first holding room. It's empty." She gave a quick glance around at the cramped room. "For now," she added dryly. Opening a book, she turned it to face him. "Sign for it."

"I owe you one, Sarge."

She waited until he'd scrawled his signature. "I'll collect."

Chuckling, Matt turned to work his way through to the holding room. An interesting woman, Sergeant Baker. Strange that it was never she who crept into his mind at odd moments. Not her, nor any of the other . . . interesting women he knew. Just one woman.

"Have a seat," Matt invited, closing the door and shutting

out most of the din. The chair he chose scraped over the floor as he pulled it away from a long, battered table.

"Cheerful place," Laurel muttered, glancing around at the dull white walls and dingy linoleum.

"Stick with City Hall if you want tidy offices and white collars." Opening the file, he began to scan it briskly.

He fits here, Laurel realized with a grudging kind of respect. For all his easygoing manner, there was a hard, tough edge underneath she'd only glimpsed briefly. The man on the elevator. Yes, she mused, he'd shown her that ruthless, searing temper there. And more. Laurel didn't want to think of that just yet.

But there was no getting around the fact that there were more facets to him than she'd wanted to believe. It was safer to consider him a shallow, inconsequential man who just happened to be a hell of a reporter. Seeing him now, completely at ease in the grim little room, made her wonder just how much he'd seen, how much he'd experienced. He dealt with the troubles, the griefs, the viciousness of people day after day, yet he didn't seem hard or cold, or overwhelmed by it. What made Matthew Bates tick? she wondered. And what made her suddenly so sure she had to find out?

"Nothing much here," he muttered, skimming the papers. "Autopsy report . . . no sexual abuse, contusions, lacerations attributed to her wandering through the swamp. Copperhead got her on the left calf. Cause of death snakebite, complicated by exposure. Time of death between 12:00 and 4:00 a.m." He handed the sheet to Laurel before going on to the investigator's report.

"Trulane was working late in his study. According to him, he thought his wife was upstairs in bed. He went up around two, found the bed empty. He searched the house, then woke his sister and the staff, searched the house again and the grounds."

Absently, he reached for a cigarette, found the pack empty and swore without heat. "None of her clothes were missing, all the cars were there. His call to the station came through at 2:57 a.m." He glanced over at Laurel. "Nearly an hour."

Her fingers were a bit damp on the autopsy report. "It's a big house. A sensible person doesn't call the police until he's sure he needs them."

After a slow nod, Matt looked back down at the report. "The police arrived at 3:15. The house was searched again, the staff questioned . . ." He mumbled for a moment, skimming the words. "Anne Trulane's body was found at approximately 6:00 a.m., in the southeast section of the swamp."

He'd been there. Matt remembered the gray light, the hot, humid smells, the nasty feel of the swamp even before they'd come across death.

"No one could account for her being out there. According to Marion Trulane, the sister-in-law, Anne had a phobia about the place. That fits with Susan's claim," he murmured. "Trulane stuck with his story about working late, and wouldn't elaborate."

"Have you ever found your wife dead?" Laurel demanded as she took the report from Matt. "It's just possible that he was upset."

He let the scathing words slip off him. "The conclusion is she felt compelled to go in—maybe to face her fears, got lost, bitten, and wandered around until she lost consciousness." He glanced over at Laurel. Her brows were drawn together as she read the report for herself. "You still buddies enough to get us into the house, ask some questions?"

"Hmm? Oh, yes, I suppose so. They'll talk to me. You, too," she added, "if you spread some of your charm around."

His mouth twisted into a grin. "I didn't think you'd noticed."

"I noticed that you can pull it out rather successfully when you put your mind to it. It's a bit deliberate for my tastes, but effective enough."

"Please, Laurellie, compliments are so embarrassing."

Ignoring him, Laurel set the investigator's report aside. "Louis hasn't had an easy time. He's closed himself in since his first marriage failed, but I think he'll talk to me."

Idly, Matt twisted the empty pack of cigarettes into a mass of foil and cellophane. "His wife ran off with his brother?"

"It was horrible for Louis." She slipped the next paper from the file as Matt gazed up at the ceiling, lost in thought.

Her skin went to ice, her stomach knotted, but she couldn't look away. The police photo was black and white and grim. She'd seen death before, but not like this. Never like this. Appalled, transfixed, she stared down at Anne Fisher Trulane. Of what she had come to.

Oh, God, Laurel thought as her head went light and her stomach rolled. It's not real. It's a gruesome joke. Just someone's twisted idea of a joke.

"How long ago did—" Matt broke off as he shifted his gaze to Laurel. Her skin was dead white, her eyes full of horror. Even as he swore, he whipped the photo away from her, then pushed her head down between her knees. "Breathe deep," he ordered sharply, but his hand was abruptly gentle on the back of her head. Hearing her breath shudder in and out, he cursed himself more savagely. What the hell had he been thinking of? "Easy, love," he murmured, kneading the tension at the base of her neck.

"I'm all right." But she wasn't so sure. Laurel took an extra moment before she tried to straighten in the chair. When Matt's arms came around her, she let her head rest on his shoulder. "I'm sorry, that was stupid."

"No." He tilted her head back. "I'm sorry." Very slowly, very carefully, he brushed the hair away from her face.

She swallowed, hard. "I guess you're used to it."

"God, I hope not." He drew her close again so that her face was pressed against his neck.

She felt safe there. The chill was passing. Laurel relaxed, letting him stroke her hair, allowing the warm, real scent of him to block out the institutional smell of the waiting room. She could feel the steady beat of his heart against her. Life. When his lips brushed her ear, she didn't move. It was comfort he offered and comfort she felt. She told herself that was all, as she held on to him as if she'd just discovered him.

"Matthew . . ."

"Hmmm?"

"Don't be too nice to me."

With her eyes closed, her face buried at his throat, she felt the smile. "Why not?"

"Just don't." A bit more steady, she drew away because it was much too easy to stay.

He cupped her face in his hand. "You're beautiful," he murmured. "Have I told you that before?"

Cautiously she moved out of reach. Treat it light, she warned herself. And think about it later. "No." She smiled and rose. "I always jot things like that down."

"Beautiful," he repeated. "Even if your chin is just a bit pointed."

"It is not." Automatically, she tilted it.

"Especially from that angle."

"I have very delicate features," Laurel told him decisively as she picked up her purse. No, damn it, her fingers were not steady yet. God, she had to get out of this place, get out and breathe again.

With his back to her, Matt slipped the photo back in the file folder, closing the cover before he turned around. "Except for the chin," he agreed, putting an arm around her shoulders as he started for the door.

With her hand on the knob, Laurel stopped and looked up at him. Her eyes were dark and more aware than they'd been before they'd come into that room. "Matthew." She leaned against him for a moment, just for a moment. "No one deserves to die that way."

He tightened his grip on her for a moment, just for a moment. "No."

CHAPTER 4

The bar was dim and cool. It was too early for the evening rush, too late for the afternoon regulars. With his mind still on Anne Trulane's file, Matt steered Laurel inside. No, no one deserved to die that way, but then life, and death, didn't always play according to the rules. He'd learned to accept that a long time ago.

Matt had been as quiet as Laurel since they'd walked out of the station house. He was thinking, analyzing. Remembering.

The phone had rung in the early hours of the morning—his source at the station house tipping him on Anne Trulane's disappearance. He'd arrived at Heritage Oak moments after the police. There'd been a mist, he recalled, thinner and nastier than a rain, and an air of silence. He'd sensed Louis Trulane hadn't wanted to call the outside for help. His answers had been clipped, his expression remote. No, he hadn't looked like a harried, concerned husband, but like a man who'd had his evening interrupted.

His sister, and the entourage of servants, had gathered around him a few paces back, in a move that had seemed like a defense before the search had spread into the marsh. It was a winding, humid place with shadows and small, secret sounds. Matt had felt a distaste for it without knowing why. He'd only known he'd rather have been searching the streets and alleyways than that steamy, dripping maze of shadow and bog.

They'd found her, too late, curled on the ground near a sluggish stream when dawn was just breaking. Mist, gray light, wet pungent smells. He'd heard a bird, a lark perhaps, calling in the distance. And he'd heard the crows. Matt remembered Louis Trulane's reaction. He'd been pale, cold and silent. If there'd been anger, grief or despair, he'd closed it inside. His sister had fainted, the servants had wept, but he'd simply stood. . . .

"I'm going to call Louis."

"What?" Matt glanced over to find Laurel watching him.

"I'm going to call Louis, ask if he'll see us."

Slowly, he tore the wrapper from a fresh pack of cigarettes. "All right." He looked after her as she weaved her way through tables to the pay phone in the corner. It wasn't easy for her, Matt thought, and struck a match with more force than necessary. She was too close, too open. Whatever childhood feelings she'd had for Louis Trulane were still too important to her to allow her to see him objectively.

What about you, Bates? he asked himself as he blew out a stream of smoke. You detest him because of the way Laurel says his name. It was time, he told himself, that they both remembered their priorities. The story came first. It had to. If Laurel's relationship with the Trulanes got them in, so much the better. He'd been in the game too long to be under any illusions. People like the Trulanes could toss obstacles in a reporter's way until getting through them was like walking through a minefield.

Not that it would stop him from getting the story—it would only add to the time and the legwork. Either way, Matt mused, either way he was going to poke some holes into that sanctified wall the Trulanes had around themselves and their name.

He saw Laurel coming back, the sadness lingering in her eyes, the color only a hint in her cheeks. She'd get over it, he told himself as something seemed to tear inside him. Because she had to. He waited until she slid into the booth across from him.

"Well?"

"He'll see us at ten tomorrow."

Matt crushed out his cigarette, warning himself not to touch her. "You don't sound too thrilled about it."

"I used the pressure of an old friendship." She looked up then, meeting his eyes with a kind of weary defiance. "I hated it."

"You've got a job to do," he muttered, and found he'd reached for her hand before he could stop himself.

"I know. I haven't forgotten." Instinctively she tightened her fingers on his. "I don't have to like it to do it well." She knew she'd never be able to back off now, not after seeing that picture—not after imagining what Susan Fisher would have felt if she had seen it.

When the waitress stopped beside her, Laurel glanced up. She had to dull the image. Maybe it was weak, but she had to. "Martini," she said on impulse. "A dry martini with an illusion of vermouth."

"Two," Matt ordered, sending Laurel an off-center smile. "It only helps temporarily, Laurellie."

"That's good enough for now." Resting her elbows on the table, she leaned forward. "Matthew, I'm going to consume great quantities of alcohol. This is totally preplanned and I offer no excuses. I will promise, however, not to get sloppy. Naturally, I'll regret this tomorrow, but I think it'll be a lesson well learned."

He nodded, grinning because he saw she needed it. "Since

I'm joining you, I'll try to maintain your high standards. In any case . . ." He leaned a bit closer. "I've often wondered what it would be like to get you drunk and have my way with you."

She laughed for the first time in hours. "There isn't enough gin in this place for that, Matthew."

"We'll see how you feel in a couple hours." Leaning back, he lit another cigarette. "Why don't you tell me about the Trulanes?"

"What about them?"

"Everything."

She sighed, then, picking up the glass the waitress set in front of her, sipped. "This might just be the only thing in New Orleans completely lacking in humidity."

Matt acknowledged this by tapping the rim of his glass against hers. "The Trulanes, Laurellie."

"All right—and don't call me that. Ancient history first," she began. "Heritage Oak was built in the early nineteenth century. The plantation was vast and rich. The Trulanes still own more land than anyone else in this part of Louisiana. Besides cotton and cattle, they were shipbuilders. The profits from that kept the plantation alive after the war. As far back as anyone would remember, the Trulanes've been an important part of New Orleans, socially, financially, and politically. I'm sure Grandma has a large repertoire of stories."

"Undoubtedly," Matt agreed. "Let's just speed up the passage of time a bit. Something in this century."

"Just laying the groundwork." Laurel took a sip from her glass, then toyed with the stem. "Beauregard Trulane—"

"Come on."

"There's always a Beauregard," she said loftily. "Inherited Heritage Oak right after his marriage. He had three children: Marion, Louis, and Charles." Her eyes smiled over the rim of her glass. "He was an enormous man, bellowing, dramatic.

Grandma loved him. In fact, I've sometimes wondered . . . well." She grinned and shrugged. "His wife was beautiful, a very quiet, serene sort of woman. Marion looks a great deal like her. Aunt Ellen—I called her that—died less than six months after my mother. I was around six . . . I've always mixed them a bit in my mind."

With a shrug, she emptied her glass, not noticing that Matt signaled for another round. "In any case, after she died, old Beau went into a steady decline. Louis began to take over the business. Really, he was too young to face those kinds of pressures, but there wasn't much choice. He would've been about eighteen or nineteen at the time, and I suppose I already worshiped him. To me, he was a cross between Prince Charming and Robin Hood. He was kind to me, always laughing and full of fun. That's how I like to remember him," she murmured, and stared into her fresh drink.

"Things change," Matt said briefly. How did a man compete with a childhood memory? he asked himself, frustrated by the look on Laurel's face. Damned if he would. "You're not a child anymore, Laurel."

She shifted her gaze to his and held it steady. "No, but a good deal of my perspective on Louis is that of a child."

He inclined his head and told himself to relax. "Tell me about Marion."

"She's a couple years older than Louis, and as I said, has her mother's looks. When I was young, I thought of her as my personal fairy godmother. She was always so poised, and so beautiful."

A picture of dark elegance and flawless skin ran through his mind. "Yes, I noticed."

"She's too old for you," Laurel said without thinking, then looked over with a frown when Matt burst out laughing. "Shut up, Bates, and let me finish."

"I beg your pardon," he said with his tongue in his cheek.

"Marion used to have me over," Laurel continued, rashly finishing off her second martini. "She'd give me tea and cakes in the parlor. She knew I adored Louis and used to tell me to hurry and grow up so Louis could marry me. I adored her, too."

"She never married?"

"No. Grandma said she was too choosy, but I think she had a love affair that didn't work out. Once I was there on a gray, gloomy day and she told me if a woman had one great love in her life, it was enough. Of course, at the time I thought she was talking about Louis and me, but when I got older and remembered how she'd looked . . ." On a sigh, Laurel reached for her glass. "Women like Marion are easily hurt."

He looked at her, the soft skin, soft mouth, soft eyes. "Is that so?"

"Charles was different." Shaking off the mood, Laurel leaned back with her drink. "I suppose he was a bit like Curt, and I thought of him as an extra brother. He was dreamy and abstracted. He was going to be an artist, and when he wasn't sketching, he was studying or hanging around Jackson Square. They'd hung some of his paintings in the main hall—until he left."

"With the first Mrs. Trulane," Matt finished.

"Yes, twelve years ago. It was a nasty scandal, the sort that causes a lot of pain and fabulous headlines." She shook her head over the opposing loyalties and sighed. The martinis were taking the edge off. "Grandma could tell you a great deal more, but from what I remember, Louis came back from a business trip to find Elise and Charles gone. The rumor that buzzed from servants' wing to servants' wing was that there was a note. Most of their clothes and all of Charles's painting gear were gone."

Laurel looked beyond him, unaware that the bar was filling up with people and noise. Someone was playing on the piano in the rear. "That's when Louis changed. He closed himself off from everyone. The few times I did see him, all the laughter was gone. As far as I know, he's never heard from Charles or Elise. About four years ago, he finally filed for divorce. Marion told me he'd done it strictly as a legality, that he was bitter, very bitter. She worried about him. His second marriage was a surprise to everyone."

Idly, she watched the smoke from Matt's cigarette curl toward the ceiling. The fans spun gently, slicing at the smoke, stirring the air. He hadn't spoken in some time, but she didn't realize it was the quality of his listening that made it so easy to speak. "I called him, first because I really hoped he was happy, and second, because Louis Trulane's remarriage meant a good story. He sounded almost like his old self—older, certainly, but some of the spark was back. He wouldn't give me an interview, he said . . ." She frowned as she searched back for his words. "He said he'd married a child and he needed to keep spring to himself for a little while."

God, did she know what she did to him when her eyes took on that vulnerable, young look? He wanted to take her away somewhere, anywhere, so that nothing could hurt her. And if he tried, she'd think he was out of his mind. Matt crushed out his cigarette with deliberate care. "What do you know about the first Mrs. Trulane?"

"Nothing really." Looking up again, she smiled wryly. "Except I was horribly jealous of her. She was lovely in that soft, kind of misty style that no one can emulate. I do remember the wedding—pink and white magnolias, a huge, frothy wedding cake and beautiful dresses. Elise wore silk and lace with miles of train. She looked like a porcelain doll—gold and white and tiny. She looked like . . ." She trailed off, eyes wide, with her glass halfway to her lips. "Oh God, she looked like—"

"Like the second Mrs. Trulane," Matt finished. Leaning back, he signaled the waitress again. "Well, well."

"It doesn't mean anything," she began in a rush. "Only that Louis was attracted to a certain type of woman. The resemblance to his first wife doesn't add up to a motive for murder."

"It's the closest we've got. And we're still a long way from being certain Anne Trulane was murdered." Matt lifted a brow as he studied Laurel's face. "You're quick to rush to his defense, Laurellie. It's going to be difficult for you to think clearly if you don't let go of your childhood infatuation."

"That's ridiculous."

"Is it?" His lips curved without humor.

"Listen, Bates, I always think clearly, and whatever my feelings for Louis, they won't interfere with my work." She looked down at her empty glass. "I finished my drink."

"So I see." This time the amusement leaked through. Indignation was one of her most appealing expressions. She'd had enough of the Trulanes for the day, Matt decided. So had he. Unobtrusively, the waitress replaced empty glasses with fresh ones. "Well, that's for tomorrow. Why don't you bring me up to date on our favorite city councilman? I'm keeping a scrapbook."

"Why don't you leave Jerry alone?" Laurel demanded, starting on the next drink.

"Everyone's entitled to a hobby."

"Don't be so smug and superior," she mumbled into her glass. "Jerry's a very—very . . ."

"Pompous ass?" Matt suggested blandly, then grinned when she burst into a fit of giggles.

"Damn you, Matthew, if my brain weren't numb, I'd have thought of something." Blowing the hair out of her eyes, she set down her drink and folded her hands. "I find your continually rude comments on Jerry's personality annoying."

"Because I'm right?"

"Yes. I really hate it when you're right."

He grinned, then, tossing a few bills on the table, rose. "I'll walk you home, Laurel. Let's hope the fresh air doesn't clear your brain—you might just be receptive to a few of my baser instincts."

"It'd take more than three martinis to do that." She stood, letting out a long breath when the floor tilted gently under her feet.

"Four," he murmured as he took her arm. "But who's counting?"

"I'm only holding on to you because I have to," Laurel told him as they stepped outside. "After a couple blocks, I'll get my rhythm back."

"Just let me know when you want to go solo."

"How many did you have?"

"The same as you."

Laurel tilted her head back to study him and found the martinis spun not too unpleasantly in her head. "Well, you're taller, and heavier," she added with a smirk. "I have a very delicate build."

"So I've noticed."

She lifted a brow as they passed a sidewalk trumpeter. The sound of jazz was mellow and sad. "Have you really?"

"You could say I've made a study of it—journalistically speaking."

"What's that supposed to mean?"

He paused long enough to touch his lips to hers. "Don't press your luck."

"You have a funny way of kissing," she muttered as her head tilted onto his shoulder. "I don't know if I like it."

To his credit, Matt didn't slip a hand around her throat and squeeze. "We can have a debate on that subject later."

"I really thought you'd have a different technique," she went on. "You know, more . . . aggressive."

"Been spending time thinking about my technique?" he countered.

"I've given it some thought—journalistically speaking."

"It'd be safer to table this discussion until you can walk a straight line." He turned into the courtyard of the building they shared.

"You know, Matthew . . ." Laurel gripped the banister as they climbed the stairs. The steps weren't as steady as they'd been that morning. "You're not really so bad after three martinis."

"Four," he mumbled.

"Don't nitpick now that I've decided to tolerate you." Unzipping her purse, she began to fish for her keys. "Here, hold this."

Matt found himself holding a wallet, compact, notebook, broken earrings, and several ticket stubs. "Anything else?" he said dryly.

"No, here they are—they always sink to the bottom."

Unceremoniously, he dumped the contents back in her purse and took the keys from her. "Are you going to let me in?" A pot of coffee, he mused as she leaned back against the door. A couple of aspirins and a dark room. He wasn't at all certain she could manage any of the three by herself. "We've been neighbors for nearly a year and I haven't had an invitation."

"What appalling manners." Giving him a misty smile, Laurel gestured him inside.

The room, like the woman, had soft edges, elegance and wit. There was the scent of potpourri with a touch of lavender. The colors were creams and roses. Lace at the curtains, velvet on the sofa. On the wall above a gleaming tea cart was a framed burlesque poster from the 1890s.

"It suits you."

"Really?" Laurel glanced around, unaccountably pleased with herself. "'S funny, even if I'd seen your place, I wouldn't know if it suited you." Laurel dragged a hand through her hair as she tried to focus on him. She held it there as she swayed, only a little. "I don't really understand you at all. Framed newsprints or Picassos. In an odd sort of way, you're a fascinating man."

She was smiling at him, only an arm's length away. At the moment, Matt wasn't certain if she was being deliberately provocative or if the martinis were doing it for her. Either way, it wasn't any easier on him. He didn't have many rules, but one of them dealt strictly with making a move on a woman who might not remember it the next morning.

"Coffee," he said briefly and took her arm.

"Oh, did you want some?"

"You do," he said between clenched teeth. "Black."

"Okay." In the kitchen, she stared at the automatic coffee-maker, brows knit. She'd have sworn she knew what to do with it.

"I'll make it," Matt told her, grinning again. "Can you handle the cups?"

"Certainly." Laurel rummaged in a cupboard, and though she rattled them dangerously, managed to set violet-trimmed china cups in their saucers on the counter. "I don't have any beignets."

"Coffee's fine."

"Guess if you *really* wanted some, I could make 'em."

"I'll take a rain check."

"You're a good sport, Matthew." Laughing, she turned and tumbled into his arms. With a smile, she curled her arms around his neck. "You've got fabulous eyes," she said on a sigh. "I bet just everyone tells you that."

"Constantly." He put his hands on her waist, intending to

draw her away. Somehow, she was pressed against him with his fingers spread over the thin material of her blouse. Desire curled inside him like a fist. "Laurel . . ."

"Maybe you should kiss me again, so I can figure out why I always think I don't want you to."

"Tomorrow," he murmured as he lowered his mouth toward hers, "if you remember, you're going to hate yourself for saying that."

"Mmmm, I know." Her lashes lowered as his lips brushed over hers. "That's not a kiss." She drew a long sigh as her nerve ends began to tingle. "It's fabulous." Her fingers crept into his hair to tangle and explore. "More . . ."

The hell with rules, Matt thought savagely. If he had to pay for what he took now, then he'd pay. And by God, it would be worth it. On an oath, he dragged her against him and crushed her mouth with his.

Instant fire. It flared from her into him—or him into her. The source didn't matter, only the results. She moaned. The sound had nothing to do with pain or with wonder, and everything to do with raw desire. Her body strained into his with a certainty. This is right, this had always been right. She found his tongue with hers and let passion and intimacy merge blindingly, then struggled for more.

At that moment, with her head spinning and her body humming, it no longer mattered that it should be he who touched off all the sparks, all the secrets raging in her. No one else ever had. No one else ever could. Again, above all the whirling thoughts in her mind was one simple demand: more.

He was losing. Perhaps he'd been losing since he'd first seen that face. Bits and pieces of himself were being absorbed and he no longer cared. She could have whatever she wanted as long as he could have her like this. Heated, melting, hungry.

Her taste wasn't delicate like her looks, but wild and daring. Her scent was airy, romantic, her mouth ripe with passion. Though he could feel her breasts yield against him, her hands demanded and took. Muttering threats, promises, pleas, he pressed his mouth to her throat and began to please himself.

Her pulse hammered. He could feel it beneath his lips, strong, fast. With a nip of his teeth it scrambled and raced to war with the low sound she made. Then his hands were on her, hard, rushing, urgent until the sound became his name. There was nothing casual about him now, not a trace of the easygoing, faintly amused man who sat across from her day after day. There was the aggression he'd carefully glossed over. The ruthlessness. The excitement.

He wanted her—too much for comfort. Too much for sanity. Perhaps she was all he'd ever wanted, the silkiness, the fire. When she was pressed against him like this, there was no past, no future, only now. Now was enough for a lifetime.

How could her mind be so clouded and her body so alive? Laurel thought she could feel her own blood racing through her veins. Is this what she'd been waiting for? This mindless freedom? It was enough—it was more than she'd ever dreamed of, more than she'd ever understood. She was far from understanding now, but her body was so busy controlling her mind, she didn't care. With a sound of possession and the strength of greed, she dragged Matt's mouth back to hers. It seemed as though her legs dissolved from the knees down.

She heard him swear against her mouth before he clutched her closer. Then he drew her away while she gripped his shoulders in protest, and for support. "Matthew . . ."

"The door." His voice wasn't any more steady than the rest of him. No, he wasn't steady, Matt realized as he held Laurel away from him. And maybe not quite sane. "Someone's at the door, Laurel. You'd better answer it."

"The door? Whose door?" She stared up at him, aroused, dazed.

"Your door." A faint smile touched his lips.

"Oh." She looked around the sun-washed kitchen as though she'd never seen it before. "I should answer it?"

He nearly dragged her back. Her flushed, bemused expression had his fingers tightening convulsively on her arms. Carefully, he released her. "Yeah." Disoriented, Laurel walked away. He'd come too close, Matt thought, too damn close to yanking her to the kitchen floor and taking her like a maniac. He turned to the hissing coffeepot, not sure whether to be grateful to whoever was banging on the door, or to murder them.

Laurel felt as though she'd been swimming underwater and had come up much too quickly. Drunk? She pressed her fingers to her temple as she reached for the doorknob. Whatever the martinis had started, Matt had finished. She shook her head, hard, and when it didn't clear, gave up and opened the door.

"Laurel, you took so long answering I nearly went away." Jerry Cartier, three-piece-suited and vaguely annoyed, stared at her,

"Oh." Her blood was cooling, but the alcohol still swam in her head. "Hello, Jerry."

Because she stepped back, swinging the door wider, he came in. "What were you up to?"

"Up to?" she repeated . . . and remembered. Laurel let out a long breath. "Coffee," she murmured. "I was making coffee."

"You drink too much coffee, Laurel." He turned as she closed the door and leaned back on it. "It isn't good for your nerves."

"No." She thought of Matt. She hadn't realized she had so many nerves until a few moments ago. "No, you're probably right about that." She straightened as it occurred to her what Jerry would have to say if he realized just what she'd been drinking, and how much. The last thing she wanted was a twenty-minute lecture on the evils of alcohol. "Sit down, Jerry," she invited, thinking just how much she wanted to lie down—in a dark room—in silence. If she were lucky, very lucky, she could cross the room and get to the sofa without weaving. She took one hesitant step.

"You're not ready."

Laurel stopped dead. He was right, of course, but crawling wasn't such a good idea. Neither was standing still. "Ready?"

"For dinner," Jerry told her as his brows drew together.

"Hello, Jerry." Carrying a tray of steaming coffee and cups, Matt strolled in.

Jerry crossed one leg over the other. "Matthew."

After setting down the tray, Matt walked casually to where Laurel still stood. "Condemn any good buildings lately?" In an unobtrusive move, he took Laurel's arm and led her to the couch. As she sank down, she shot him a grateful look.

"That's not my jurisdiction," Jerry stated, lacing his fingers together. "The mayor did tell me just the other day about a building on the other side of town. Appalling plumbing."

"Is that so?"

"Coffee?" Laurel interrupted. Martinis or not, she couldn't sit there and let Matt calmly execute an unarmed man. Besides, if she didn't have some coffee, she was going to quietly lay her head on the arm of the sofa and doze off.

"Only a half cup," Jerry told her. "Are you sure you should have any more?"

She made a grab for the handle of the pot and prayed she could pour it. "I haven't had any for hours."

"So, how was your day, Jerry?" Matt asked him as he

closed his hand over Laurel's on the handle. Hearing her small sigh of relief, he nearly grinned.

"Busy, busy. There never seems to be enough hours to get everything done."

Matt's gaze slid down to Laurel's, brushing over her mouth. "No, there doesn't."

Jerry reached for the cup Laurel passed him and had to lean to the right when she missed his hand. "Laurel," he began, giving her an oddly intent look. "Have you been . . . drinking?"

"Drinking?" She set her heel down hard on Matt's foot when he chuckled. "Jerry, I just poured." Lifting the cup to her lips, she drank half the contents. "Why did you say you'd dropped by?"

"Dropped by?" He shook his head as Laurel leaned back, clutching her cup in both hands. "Laurel, we're supposed to go out to dinner."

"Oh." He was probably right, she thought vaguely. If Jerry said they had a dinner date, they had a dinner date. He kept a very precise appointment book.

"Laurel and I are working on a story," Matt put in more for his own amusement than to rescue Laurel. "We've run into some overtime on it. As a matter of fact, we were, ah, covering ground when you knocked on the door." Not by the slightest flicker did he betray the fact that Laurel's heel was digging into his foot. "Reporting really does interfere with a social life."

"Yes, but—"

"You know what it's like to be on deadline, I'm sure." Matt gave him an easy smile. "Laurel and I probably won't have time for anything more than a cold sandwich. We could be tied up on this for . . . weeks. You'll give Jerry a call when things calm down, won't you, Laurel?"

"What? Yes, yes, of course." She drained her coffee and

wished he'd go so that she could pour another. "I'm awfully sorry, Jerry."

"I understand. Business before pleasure." Matt stopped himself before he choked over his coffee. Jerry rose, setting down his cup before he straightened his tie. "Just ring my office when things are clear, Laurel. And try to cut down on that coffee."

"Mmm-hmmm" was the best she could manage as her teeth were digging into her bottom lip. The door closed quietly behind him. "Oh, God!" Not sure whether she wanted to laugh or scream, Laurel covered her face with her hands.

"Tacky, Laurellie," Matt murmured, pouring out more coffee. "Leaving it to me to untangle you."

It would be satisfying to throw the coffee in his face, but she needed it too much. "With everything that happened today—the story," she emphasized firmly when his grin broke out, "I simply forgot about dinner. And I didn't ask you to untangle me."

"That's gratitude." He tugged on her hair until she looked at him. "Not only do I let you break three of my toes, but I help you cover up your . . . impaired condition from your boyfriend."

"He's not." Laurel drank cup number two without a pause, then set down the cup with a snap.

"You're stringing him along."

"That's not true." She started to rise, found it took too much effort and stayed where she was. "We have a perfect understanding. We're friends. Damn it, he's a very nice man, really, just a little . . ."

"Don't say harmless again, the poor guy doesn't deserve it. Then again, he doesn't seem to be in danger of having his heart broken."

"Jerry doesn't see me that way," Laurel began.

Looking at her, sulky-mouthed and sleepy-eyed, Matt

leaned closer. "In that case, you can leave the pompous off of my earlier description of him."

Laurel put her hand firmly on his chest. She wasn't about to risk letting the room spin around her again. "I'm going to bed."

The corner of his mouth tilted. "I love aggressive women."

"Alone," Laurel told him, fighting back a laugh.

"Terrible waste," he murmured, taking the hand she held against him to his lips. Turning it over, he brushed them over her wrist and felt the wild beat below the skin.

"Matthew, don't."

He looked at her. It would be easy, so very easy. He had only to draw her to him and kiss her once; they both knew it. She wanted, he wanted, yet neither of them was quite sure how it had come to this. "Years from now, I'm going to hate myself for handling it this way," he murmured as he rose. "I'd take some aspirin now, Laurellie. You're going to need all the help you can get with that hangover in the morning."

Cursing himself all the way, Matt walked to the door, then shut it firmly behind him.

CHAPTER 5

D amn you, Bates."
Laurel stared at the pale, wan reflection in her bathroom mirror while hammers pounded dully in her head. Why did he have to be right?

Grabbing a bottle of aspirin, she slammed the door of the medicine cabinet closed. This was followed by a pitiful moan as she clutched her head. Laurel knew it wasn't going to fall off; she only wished it would.

She deserved it. Laurel downed the two aspirins and shuddered. Anyone who drank four martinis in an afternoon deserved what she got. She might have accepted it with some grace if he just hadn't been right.

It didn't help her mood that she could remember what had happened after the drinking. She'd practically thrown herself at him. God, what a fool! He wasn't going to let her forget it. Oh, no, he'd tease and torment her for months. Maybe she deserved that, too, but . . . Oh, Lord, did she have to remember how wonderful it had been, how unique? Did she have to stand here knowing she wanted it to happen again?

Well, it wouldn't. Dragging both hands through her hair, she willed the pounding in her head to stop. She wasn't going to fall for Matthew Bates and make an idiot out of herself.

She might be stuck with him on the story, but personally it was going to be hands off and keep your distance. She'd chalk up her reaction to him to an excess of liquor. Even if it wasn't true.

With a sigh, Laurel turned toward the shower. She'd do the intelligent thing. She'd soak her head. As she reached for the tap, the pounding started again—at the front door and inside her temples. Whoever it was deserved a slow, torturous death, she decided as she trudged out to answer.

"Good morning, Laurellie." Matt leaned against the doorjamb and grinned at her. His gaze slid down her short, flimsy robe. "I like your dress."

He was casually dressed, as always, but fresh and obviously clearheaded. She felt as though she'd walked through a desert, eating a few acres along the way. "I overslept," she muttered, then folded her arms and waited for him to gloat.

"Had any coffee yet?"

She eyed him warily as he closed the door. Maybe he was just waiting for the perfect moment to gloat. "No."

"I'll fix it," he said easily and strolled into the kitchen.

Laurel stared after him. No smart remark, no smirk? How the hell was she supposed to keep up with him? she demanded as she dragged herself back to the shower.

She'd been ready to battle, Matt thought as he reached for the glass container of coffee. And all she really wanted to do was crawl back into bed and shut down. A hell of a woman, he thought again. A great deal like her grandmother.

His thoughts traveled back to the evening before. Because he'd known better than to stay in his apartment, one thin wall away from Laurel, Matt had gotten in his car. A little legwork to take his mind off the woman. Olivia Armand would be a fount of information, and her opinion of the Trulanes was bound to be less biased than Laurel's.

Olivia greeted him on her terrace with a look that held

both speculation and pleasure. "Well, well, now the evening has possibilities."

"Miss Olivia." Matt took the gnarled, ringed hand in his and kissed it. It smelled of fresh jasmine. "I'm mad about you."

"They all were," she said with a lusty laugh. "Sit down and have a drink, Matthew. Have you softened that granddaughter of mine up yet?"

Matt thought of the fiery woman he'd held only an hour before. "A bit," he murmured.

"You're slow, boy."

"I've always thought a man's more successful if he covers all the angles first." He handed her a drink before he sat down beside her.

"Not joining me?"

"It's hard enough to keep a clear head around you." While she laughed, he sat back and lit a cigarette. "Where's Susan?"

"Upstairs, being shocked by my journals."

"What'd you think of her?"

Olivia took a slow sip. Little fingers of moonlight danced over the diamonds on her hands. Insects buzzed around the hanging lantern by the door, tapping against the glass. The scents from the garden beyond rose up lazily. "Bright girl. Well-bred, a bit shaky and sad, but strong enough."

"She claims her sister was murdered."

The thin white brows rose, more, Matt observed, in thoughtfulness than surprise. "So that's what this is all about. Interesting." She took another sip, then tapped her finger against the glass. "The poor girl was bitten by a snake in the swamps behind Heritage Oak. Tell me why Susan's thinking murder."

In the brisk, concise style he used in his reporting, Matt ran through the entire events of the day. He saw a bat swoop low over the trees, then disappear. The air was full of the sounds of crickets and the occasional croak of a frog. Palm fronds rustled overhead. The breeze carried a teasing scent of magnolia. A long way from New York, he mused.

"Not as cut and dried as the Trulanes like to keep things," Olivia commented. "Well, Matthew, murder and mystery keep the blood moving, but you're not telling me this to keep my arteries from hardening."

He grinned. She could always make him grin. Leaning back, he listened to the sounds of the night. "I know the general background on the Trulanes, and Laurel gave me a few more details—through rose-colored glasses," he added.

"A touch of jealousy's a healthy thing," Olivia decided. "Might get you on your horse."

"The point is," Matthew said dryly, "I'd like you to tell me about them."

"All right. We'll walk in the garden. I get stiff sitting so long."

Matt took the hand she held out and helped her up. She was tiny; it always surprised him. She walked lightly. If there was any pain or discomfort in her joints, she gave no sign of it. He hadn't lied when he'd said he was mad about her. Within five minutes of their first meeting, he'd fallen for her, and had had no trouble understanding why she'd been the most sought-after girl, then woman, then widow, of the parish.

"Marion was finished in France," Olivia began. "There were rumors of an ill-fated love affair, but she'd never talk about it. She's quiet, but she's sharp, always was. For all her good works and elegant airs, she's also a snob. I'm fond enough of the girl, but she's not her mother, as some would like to think."

Matt laughed, patting the hand tucked through his arm.

"I knew I could count on you for a straight shot, Miss Olivia."

"Can't stand pussyfooting around. Now Charles was like his mother," she continued. "Good-looking boy, head in the clouds. But he had talent. He was shy about it, but he had talent. One of his watercolors hangs in my sitting room."

Then he was good, Matt mused. Olivia might buy the attempt of a poor neighbor, but she wouldn't hang it in Promesse d'Amour unless it deserved it.

"I was disappointed in him for running off with his brother's wife." Catching the ironic look in Matt's eye, she wagged a finger at him. "I have my standards, Yankee. If Louis's wife and brother wanted each other, they should have been honest about it instead of sneaking off like thieves in the night. Louis would have dealt with it better."

"Tell me about him."

"Laurel's first love." She cackled at Matt's expression. "Simmer down, Matthew, every woman's entitled to one fairy tale. When he was young, he was a vibrant, exciting man. He was devoted to his family, and his family's business, but he wasn't serious or stuffy. I'd never have abided that. I believed he loved his first wife deeply and the betrayal destroyed him. It didn't help when the rumors started that she'd been carrying Charles's baby."

"Did you ever meet Anne Trulane?"

"No, Louis was selfish with her, and I felt he was entitled." She sighed and broke a blossom from an azalea. "They were planning a party in September. Marion told me it was going to be a huge, splashy affair, introducing Anne to New Orleans society. She said the poor child was torn between excitement and terror at the idea. I admit, I was looking forward to getting a close look at her. They said she resembled Elise."

"They?" Matt prompted.

"The servants. Bless them." She turned back toward the

house, fleetingly remembering a time when she could have walked and run in the garden for hours. "If I want to know what's going on at Heritage Oak, I ask my cook. She'll tell me what their cook told her." She gave a gusty sigh. "I love espionage."

"You remember what Elise Trulane looked like?"

"My memory's twice as old as you are." She laughed, relishing rather than regretting the years. "More."

Despite the lines time had etched, her face was beautiful in the moonlight. The hand under his was dry with age. And strong. "Miss Olivia, where can I find another like you?"

"You've got one under your nose, you slow-witted Yankee." She settled back in her chair with a little sound of pleasure. "Ah, Susan, come out." She gestured to the woman hesitating at the garden doors. "Poor child," she said to Matt, "she's still blushing. How did you like my journals?"

"They're very—colorful. You've had a . . ." How did one put it? "A full life, Mrs. Armand."

Olivia gave a hoot of laughter. "Don't water it down, child. I've sinned and loved every minute of it."

"A drink, Susan?" Matt steered her to a chair.

"No, thanks. Laurel's not with you?"

"I don't like to bring her when I'm courting Olivia," he said easily, pleased to see that she could smile. "Since I'm here, I wonder if you can remember any names Anne might have mentioned in her letters, anything unusual or out of place she might have written about."

Susan lifted her hands, then let them fall. "She wrote mostly of Louis and the house . . . and Marion, of course. She'd grown fond of Marion. The servants . . . Binney, a Cajun woman Anne said ran the place." Susan thought back, trying to find the details he wanted. "I got the impression she hadn't really taken over as mistress yet. Anne was a bit overwhelmed by having servants."

"Anyone outside the family?"

"She didn't really know anyone else. Oh, there was one of Louis's accountants, Nathan Brewster. She mentioned him a couple of times. I think he'd come to the house to go over papers with Louis. He made Anne nervous." Susan smiled again, this time with sadness. "Anne was very shy of men. Other than that it was all Louis. He was teaching her to ride. . . ."

"Nathan Brewster," Olivia murmured. "I've heard of him. Sharp boy. Your age, Matthew. Supposed to have a nasty temper, nearly killed a man a couple years back. Seems the man was too friendly with Brewster's sister."

"Anything you don't know, Miss Olivia?"

"Not a damn thing." She grinned and gestured for a fresh drink.

He turned to pour it for her. "Susan, do you have a picture of Anne?"

"Yes, do you want it?"

"I'd like to see it."

When she'd risen to go inside, Matt handed Olivia her drink. "Know anything about the Heritage Oak swamp being haunted?"

"Don't be smug, Matthew," she advised. "We Creoles understand the supernatural more than you Yankees. Most of the swamps are haunted," she said with perfect calm as she swirled her bourbon. "The ghosts in Heritage Oak's date back to before the war."

Matthew settled back down, knowing there was only one war Olivia would feel worth mentioning. He remembered Laurel had done precisely the same thing. "Tell me."

"One of the Trulane women used to meet her lover there. Damned uncomfortable place for adultery," she added practically. When Matthew only laughed, she went on blandly.

"When her husband found them, he shot them both—the gun's under glass in their library—and dumped the bodies in quicksand. Since then, occasional lights've been seen or someone'll hear a woman sobbing. Very romantic."

"And terrifying to someone like Anne Trulane," he added thoughtfully.

"It's only a wallet-size," Susan said as she came back out. "But it was taken less than a year ago."

"Thanks." Matt studied the picture. Young, sweet, shy. Those were the words that came to his mind. And alive. He could remember how she'd looked the morning they'd found her. Swearing under his breath, he handed the picture to Olivia.

"I'll be damned," she muttered, tapping the photo against her palm. "She could be Elise Trulane's twin."

The sound of Laurel rummaging in the bedroom brought him back to the present. Matt shifted his thoughts. There was another interview that day. Louis Trulane. He took the coffee out on the gallery and waited for Laurel.

She liked pink begonias, he mused. Pinching off one of the blossoms that trailed over the railing, Matt let the fragrance envelop him. Pink begonias, he thought again. Lace curtains. Where did a man who'd grown up with holes in his shoes fit into that? Strange, he thought more about his beginnings since he'd gotten involved with Laurel than he had in years.

He was staring down into the courtyard when she came out, but Laurel didn't think he was seeing the ferns and flowers. She'd only seen that expression on his face a few times when she'd happen to glance up and see him at his typewriter, immersed in a story. Intense, brooding.

"Matthew?" It was an encompassing question. She wanted to ask what troubled him, what he was thinking of, or remembering. But the look stayed in his eyes when he turned to her, and she couldn't. Then it cleared, as though it had never been.

"Coffee's hot," he said simply.

She went to it, dressed in a sheer cotton skirt and blouse that made him hope the heat wave continued. "No I-told-you-so?" she asked before she sat on one of the white wrought-iron chairs.

"People in glass houses," he returned, leaning back against the railing. "I've had my share of mornings after. Feeling better?"

"Some. I'm going to call the house before we leave. I want to make sure Susan's settling in all right."

"She's fine." Matt speculated on what a woman like Laurel would wear under a summer dress. Silk—very thin silk, perhaps. "I saw her and your grandmother last night."

The cup paused on its way to Laurel's lips. "You went out there last night?"

"I can't keep away from your grandmother."

"Damn it, Matthew, this is my story."

"Our story," he reminded her mildly.

"Either way, you had no business going out there without me."

Walking over, he helped himself to a cup of coffee. "As I recall, you weren't in the mood to socialize last night. If you had been," he added smoothly, "we wouldn't have found ourselves at your grandmother's."

Her eyes narrowed at that, and she rose. "Just because my mind was fuzzy yesterday, Bates, don't get the idea in your head that you attract me in the least." Because he only smiled, she plunged on. "*Any* man might look good after four martinis. Even you."

He set down his cup very carefully. "Mind clear this morning, Laurellie?"

"Perfectly, and—" She broke off when he pulled her against him.

"Yes, I'd say your mind was clear." He lowered his mouth to her jawline and nibbled. "You're a woman who knows exactly what she wants, and what she doesn't."

Of course she was, Laurel thought as she melted against him. "I don't want—oh." Her breath shuddered out as he nuzzled her ear.

"What?" Matt moistened the lobe with his tongue, then nipped it. "What don't you want?"

"You to—to confuse me."

She felt the brush of his lashes against her cheek as he made a teasing journey toward her mouth. "Do I?"

"Yes." His lips hovered just above hers. Laurel knew exactly what would happen if they met. She took a step back and waited for her system to level. "You're doing this to take my mind off the story."

"We both know—" he caught her hair in his hand "—this has nothing to do with any story."

"Well, the story's what we have to concentrate on." She spoke quickly, had to speak quickly until she was certain the ground was steady again. "I don't want you digging without me. I found Susan in the first place, and—"

"Damn it, if and when there's a story, you'll get your half of the byline."

It was easier to be angry than aroused so she let her temper rise with his. "It has nothing to do with the byline. I don't like you probing Grandma and Susan for leads without me. If you'd told me what you wanted to do, I'd have had some more coffee, a cold shower and pulled myself together."

"Maybe you could have." Sticking his hands in his pockets, he rocked back gently on his heels. "The point is, I wanted to talk to someone about the Trulanes, someone who has a little objectivity."

She flared at that, then subsided, hating him for being right. "Let's just go," she muttered, whirling away.

"Laurel." Matt took her arm, stopping her at the doorway. "It's not a matter of the story," he said quietly. "I don't want you to be hurt."

She stared at him while her guards began to shift on their foundations. Trouble, she thought. I'm really going to be in trouble. "I asked you before not to be nice to me," she murmured.

"I'll give you a hard time later to make up for it. The way you feel about Louis—"

"Has nothing to do with any of this," she insisted, no longer certain either of them were speaking of the story. "Let me deal with it myself, Matthew. I can."

He wanted to press her, for himself, for what he needed from her. The time would come when he would have to. "Okay," he said simply. "Let's go."

The breeze helped. It whispered soothingly through the windows as they drove out of town. With her head back and her eyes shut, Laurel listened to Matt's accounting of his visit to her grandmother the evening before.

"I take it from that scornful tone in your Yankee voice that you don't believe in the Trulane ghosts?"

"And you do?" Grinning, he sent her a sidelong look. When she didn't answer right away, he slowed down to look at her more carefully. "Laurel?"

She shrugged, then made a business out of smoothing her skirts. "Let's just say I've got Creole blood, Matthew."

He couldn't stop the smile, on his lips or in his voice. "Ghosts, Laurel?"

"Atmosphere," she corrected, goaded into admitting something she'd just as soon have kept to herself. "I've been in that swamp. There're flowers where you least expect them, small patches of prairie, blue herons, quiet water." She turned in her seat so that the breeze caught the tips of her hair and carried them out the window. "There's also quicksand, nasty little insects, and snakes. Shadows." Frustrated, she turned to stare through the windshield. "I never liked it there. It's brooding. There're places the sun never reaches."

"Laurel." Matt stopped the car at the entrance to Heritage Oak. "You're going by childhood impressions again. It's a place, that's all."

"I can only tell you how I feel." She turned her head to meet his eyes. "And apparently how Anne Trulane felt."

"All right." Shifting into first, he maneuvered the car between the high brick pillars. "But for now, let's concentrate on human beings."

The oaks lining the drive were tall and old, the Spanish moss draping them gray green and tenacious. It hadn't changed. And, Laurel realized at the first sighting, neither had the house.

The brick had aged before she'd been born. There were subtle marks of time, but they'd been there as long as she could remember. The lines of the house were sharp and clean, not fluid like Promesse d'Amour's, but no less beautiful. The brick was a dusky rose, the balconies were soft black. Their delicacy didn't detract from the arrogance of the house. If Laurel saw her own ancestral home as a woman, she saw Heritage Oak as a man, bold and ageless.

"It's been a long time," she murmured. Emotions raced through her—memories. Knights and tea parties, filmy dresses and pink cakes. She'd been a child the last time she'd seen it, daydreamed in it.

With a sigh, Laurel turned and found her eyes locked with

Matt's. There were new emotions now, not so soft, not so tender. This was reality, with all its pain and pleasure. This was real. Too real. Giving in to the panic of the moment, Laurel fumbled with the door handle and got out of the car.

What was happening to her? she asked herself as she took three long, deep breaths. It was getting to the point where she couldn't even look at him without wanting to run—or to reach out. A physical attraction was no problem. She'd managed to submerge that feeling for a year. This was something else again and it promised not to be so easily dealt with. She was going to have to, Laurel told herself, just as she was going to have to deal with her feelings for the Trulanes.

"Matthew, let me handle this." Calmer, she walked with him to the wide, white porch. "I know Louis and Marion."

"Knew," he corrected. He hadn't missed the way she'd looked at the house. Or the way she'd looked at him. "People have the inconsiderate habit of changing. I won't make you any promises, Laurel, but I won't interfere until I have to."

"You're a hard man, Bates."

"Yeah." He lifted the knocker and let it fall against a door of Honduras mahogany.

A tall, angular woman answered the door. After a brief glance at Matt, her nut-colored eyes fastened on Laurel. "Little Miss Laurel," she murmured, and held out both thin hands.

"Binney. It's so good to see you again."

Josephine Binneford, housekeeper, had weathered the decade with little change since Laurel had last seen her. Her hair was grayer but still worn in the same no-nonsense knot at the back of her neck. Perhaps there were more lines in her face, but Laurel didn't see them.

"Little Miss Laurel," Binney repeated. "Such a fine, beautiful lady now. No more scraped knees?"

"Not lately." With a grin, Laurel leaned over to brush her cheek. She smelled of starch and lilac. "You look the same, Binney."

"You're still too young to know how fast time goes." Stepping back, she gestured them inside before she closed out the brilliant sunshine and heat. "I'll tell Miss Marion you're here." With a gait stiffened by arthritis, she led them to the parlor. *"Revenez bientôt,"* she murmured, turning to Laurel again. *"Cette maison a besoin de jeunesse."* Turning, she headed up the stairs.

"What did she say?" Matt asked as Laurel stared after her.

"Just to come back again." She cradled her elbows in her hands as if suddenly cold. "She says the house needs youth." She crossed into the parlor.

If people change, she thought, this remains constant. The room could have been transported back a century; it would look the same in the century to come.

The sun gleamed through high windows framed with royal-blue portieres. It shone on mahogany tables, drawing out the rich red tints. It sparkled on a cut-glass vase that a long-dead Trulane bride had received on her wedding day. It lay like a lover on a porcelain woman who'd been captured for eternity in the swirl of a partnerless waltz.

Matt watched Laurel's long, silent survey of the room. The play of emotions on her face had him dealing with frustration, jealousy, need. How could he get her to turn to him, when so much of her life was bound up in what had been, who had been?

"Memories are nice little possessions, Laurel," he said coolly. "As long as you don't ignore the present when you take them out to play."

He'd wanted to make her angry, because her anger was the easier thing for him to deal with. Instead, she turned to him, her eyes soft, her face stunning. "Do you have any, Matthew?" she asked quietly. "Any of those nice little possessions?"

He thought of a roof that leaked and icy floors and a plate that never had enough on it. He remembered a woman hacking, always hacking, in her bed at night, weakening already-weak lungs. And he remembered the promise he'd made to get out, and to take the woman with him. He'd only been able to keep the first part of the promise.

"I have them," he said grimly. "I prefer today."

She'd heard something there, under the bitterness. Vulnerability. Automatically, Laurel reached out to him. "Matthew . . ."

Not that way, he told himself. He'd be damned if he'd get to her through sympathy. He took the hand she held out, but brought it to his lips. "Life's a ridiculous cycle to be involved in, Laurellie. I've always thought making memories has more going for it than reliving them."

She dropped her hand back to her side. "You're not going to let me in, are you?"

"Today." He ran his fingers through her hair. "Let's concentrate on today."

Unaccountably hurt, she turned from him. "There isn't any without a yesterday."

"Damn it, Laurel—"

"Laurel, I'm sorry to keep you waiting." Marion glided in as only a woman taught to walk can do. She wore filmy dresses in pastels that always seemed to float around her. As Laurel took her hands, soft and small, she wondered how anyone could be so coolly beautiful. Marion was nearing forty, but her complexion was flawless, with a bone structure that spoke of breeding. Her scent was soft, like her hands, like her hair, like her eyes.

"Marion, you look lovely."

"Sweet." Marion squeezed her hands before releasing them. "I haven't seen you since that charity function two months ago. It was odd seeing you there with your pad and pencil. Are you happy with your career?"

"Yes, it's what I've always wanted. This is a colleague of mine, Matthew Bates."

"Nice to meet you, Mr. Bates." Marion held his hand an extra moment, hesitating while her eyes searched his face. "Have we met?"

"Not formally, Miss Trulane. I was here when your sister-in-law was found last month."

"I see." Briefly, her eyes clouded with pain. "I'm afraid I don't remember too much of that day clearly. Please sit down, Binney is seeing to some refreshments. Louis will be along in a moment." She chose a Hepplewhite for herself, straight-backed and dully gleaming. "He's tied up on the phone. Actually, I'm glad to have a moment with you before he comes." Marion folded her hands on her lap. "Laurel, you haven't seen Louis in a very long time."

"Ten years."

"Yes, ten years." Marion gazed out of the window a moment, then sighed. "One loses track of time here. I had to stop having you over after Charles and Elise . . . went away. Louis wasn't in a proper state for an impressionable young girl."

Ten years, Laurel thought, and it still hurts her. What has it done to him? "I understand that, Marion. I'm not a girl anymore."

"No, you're not." Her gaze shifted back, away from the trim lawn and oaks. "Laurel, you saw only the beginnings of a change in him, but as the months passed, as the years passed, he became bitter," she said briskly. "Given to flashes of temper, of absentmindedness. There were times he wouldn't remember—" She stopped herself again, unlacing her hands.

"He didn't forget," she corrected with a wistful smile. "He simply chose not to remember. He and Charles were—well, that's done."

"Marion, I know how difficult it must've been for him." Laurel reached out to lay a hand on hers. "I always knew. The truth is, I didn't stay away because you didn't ask me to come, but because I knew Louis wouldn't want me here."

"You always understood a great deal," Marion murmured. With a sigh, she tried to shake off the mood. "When he brought Anne home, no one was more surprised, more pleased than I. She'd taken that hard edge away."

"I felt that, too." She smiled when Marion sent her a questioning look. "I phoned him a few weeks after he was married."

Nodding, Marion laced her hands again. Her nails were oval, unpainted and buffed. "Perhaps he was overprotective, possessive, but Anne was so young, and he'd been hurt so badly. I'm telling you this now because I want you—" her gaze shifted to Matt "—both of you to understand the state Louis is in now. There's been so much pain in his life. If he seems cold and remote, it's only his way of dealing with grief." She turned her head as Binney wheeled in a tea tray. "Ah, iced tea. Do you still take too many sugars, Laurel?"

She smiled. "Yes. Oh." She glimpsed the tiny pink cakes arranged on the tray. "How sweet of you, Binney."

"I only told the cook Miss Laurel was coming for tea." She gave Laurel a quick wink. "Don't eat more than three, or your grandmother will scold me."

Laughing, Laurel bit into one as the housekeeper left the room. The light, sweet taste brought back a new flood of memories. She heard ice tinkle in the glasses as Marion poured. "Binney hasn't changed. The house, either," she added with a smile for Marion. "I'm so glad."

"The house never changes," Marion told her as she offered Laurel fresh, cold tea in a Waterford glass. "Only the people in it."

Laurel didn't hear him, but sensed him. Carefully, she set down the glass she held. Turning her head, she looked into Louis's eyes.

CHAPTER 6

C an ten years be so long? she thought with a jolt. She'd thought she was prepared. She'd hoped she was. There was gray in his hair now, near the temples. That she would have accepted. There were lines in his face going deep around his mouth and eyes. She could have accepted them, too. But the eyes had none of the warmth, none of the humor she'd loved so much.

He was thin, too thin. It made him look older than thirty-six. She rose, and with a mixture of pain and pity, went to him. "Louis."

He took her hand and the ghost of a smile touched his mouth. "Grown up, Laurel? Why did I expect to find a child?" Very lightly, he touched a fingertip to the underside of her chin. She wanted to weep for him. "You always promised to be a beauty."

Laurel smiled, willing the warmth to come to his eyes. "I've missed seeing you." But the warmth didn't come, and his hand dropped away. She felt his tension even before she felt her own. "Louis, this is my associate, Matthew Bates."

Louis's eyes flicked over Matt and grew colder. "I believe we've met."

"Some tea, Louis?" Marion reached for the pitcher.

"No." His voice was curt, but Marion made no sign other than a quick compression of lips. Neither man noticed, as their eyes were on Laurel. "We're not here for tea and cakes this time, are we, Laurel?" Louis murmured before he crossed the room to stand in front of the empty hearth. Over it was an oil of his mother. Laurel remembered it well. It had been there for years, except for a brief period when Elise Trulane's portrait had replaced it. "Why don't we get on with this?" Louis suggested. "I agreed to see you and Mr. Bates to put an end to this rumor Susan started." He gave Laurel a long look. "Ask your questions. I used to have all the answers for you."

"Louis . . ." She wanted to go to him, soothe him somehow, but the look in Matt's eyes stopped her. "I'm sorry to intrude this way. Very sorry."

"It isn't necessary to be sorry." Louis drew out a thin cigar, eyeing it for a moment before lighting it. "Nothing ever remains as it was. Do what you came to do."

She felt her stomach tighten. The power in him was still there, a power she'd recognized even as a child. It had driven him to take up the reins of a multimillion-dollar firm before he'd finished college. It had enabled him to enchant a young girl so that the woman could never forget him. But it was so cold now. Laurel stood where she was in the center of the parlor while the gap between memory and today grew wider.

"Susan is certain that Anne would never have gone out into the swamp alone," she began, knowing she began badly. "Susan claims that Anne had a terror of dark places, and that the letters she'd written expressed a specific fear of the place."

"And she believes Anne was forced to go in there," Louis finished. "I know all of that already, Laurel."

She was a journalist, she had an assignment. She had to remember it. "Was Anne afraid of the swamp, Louis?"

He drew on his cigar and watched her through the cloud of smoke. "Yes. But she went in," he added, "because she died there."

"Why would she have gone in?"

"Perhaps to please me." Carelessly he flicked cigar ash into the scrubbed hearth. "She'd begun to feel foolish about this fear she'd dragged along since childhood. When I was with her," he murmured, "she wouldn't need a light on in the hallway at night." Abruptly, his head lifted again, to the arrogant angle Laurel remembered in a young man. "The story about the ghosts in the swamp had her imagining all sorts of things. I was impatient." He drew on the cigar again, harder. "She had a . . . need for my approval."

"You think she might have gotten up in the middle of the night and gone out there to please you?" Laurel asked him, taking a step closer.

"It makes more sense than believing someone broke in, dragged her out and left her without myself or any of the servants hearing a sound." He gave her another cool, uncompromising look. "You read the police report, I imagine."

"Yes." She moistened her lips as she remembered the photograph. "Yes, I did."

"Then there's no need for me to go over that."

"Did your wife often have trouble sleeping?" Matt put in, watching as a very small muscle worked in Louis's jaw.

"Occasionally. Particularly when I was working." He glanced over Matt's head, out the long windows. "She thought she'd seen lights in the swamp."

"Did anyone else see them?"

Louis's mouth twisted into something like a smile. "Over the years, dozens of people have claimed to—usually when they've kept company with a bottle of bourbon."

"Mr. Bates," Marion broke in. "Anne was afraid of the swamp, but she was also fascinated with it. It's not unusual for someone to be fascinated by something they fear. She'd become obsessed by the legend. The problem . . . the blame," she amended slowly, "comes from none of us taking her seriously enough. She was so young. Perhaps if we'd insisted she go in during the daylight, she wouldn't have felt compelled to go in at night."

"Do you think she was capable of going in there alone, at night?" Laurel asked her.

"It's the only explanation. Laurel, we all loved her." She sent Louis a quick, misty look. "She was sweet and soft, but she was also highly strung. I thought her nerves came from the plans we were making for the party."

"What difference does it make now?" Louis demanded and tossed his cigar into the hearth. It bounced, then lay, smoldering. "Anne's gone, and neither Susan nor her letters can change it."

"The letters were stolen from Susan's room," Laurel said quietly.

"That's ridiculous. Who would steal letters? She misplaced them." Louis dismissed them with an angry shrug.

"You were married for nearly a year," Matt said casually. "Yet none of your closest neighbors had met your wife. Why?"

"That's my business."

"Louis, please." Laurel took another step toward him. "If we could just understand."

"Understand?" he repeated, and stopped her with a look. "How can you? She was hardly more than a child, the child you were when I last saw you. But she didn't have your confidence, your boldness. I kept her to myself because I wanted to. I had to. There was a generation between us."

"You didn't trust her," Laurel murmured.

"Trust is for fools."

"Isn't it odd," Matt commented, drawing Louis's fury from

Laurel to himself, "how much Anne resembled your first wife?"

The only sound was Marion's sharp intake of breath. Though his hands clenched into fists, Louis stood very still. Without another word, another look, he strode out.

"Please, Louis just isn't himself." Marion fiddled nervously with the glasses. "He's very sensitive about comparisons between Anne and Elise."

"People are bound to make them," Matt returned, "when the physical resemblance is so striking."

"More than physical," Marion murmured, then went on in a rush. "It was a natural observation, Mr. Bates, but Louis won't discuss Elise and Charles. If there's nothing else . . . ?"

"Do you know Nathan Brewster?" Laurel asked abruptly.

Marion's eyes widened before her lashes swept down. "Yes, of course, he's one of Louis's accountants."

Matt's brow lifted before he exchanged a look with Laurel. "His was one of the few names Anne mentioned in her letters."

"Oh, that's natural, I suppose. He came to the house a few times on business. It's true Anne didn't meet many people. Well." She rose, sending them both an apologetic smile. "I'm sorry I couldn't be of more help, but perhaps you can put Susan's doubts to rest now." She held out her hands to Laurel again. "Come back soon, please, just to talk like we used to."

"I will. Tell Louis . . ." Laurel sighed as she released Marion's hands. "Tell him I'm sorry."

They walked out of the house in silence, drove away in silence. As the frustration, the anger built, Matt swore to himself he'd say nothing. Whatever Laurel was feeling was her own business. If she let her emotions get in the way, let herself grieve, there was nothing he could do about it.

On an oath, he yanked the wheel, skidded to the side of the road and stopped.

"Damn it, Laurel, stop."

She kept her hands very still in her lap and stared straight ahead. "Stop what?"

"Mourning."

She turned her head then, and though her eyes were dry, they were eloquent. "Oh, Matthew," she whispered, "he looked so lost."

"Laurel—"

"No, you don't have to say it. He's changed. I expected it, but I wasn't ready for it." She drew a deep breath that came out trembling. "I wasn't ready to see him hurting so much."

Cursing Louis Trulane and all he stood for, Matt gathered Laurel close. She didn't protest when he cradled her against him, but held on. The sun streamed into the car. She could hear birds calling and chattering in the trees beyond the car. As he stroked her hair, she closed her eyes, letting herself draw from the comfort he offered.

"I am mourning," she murmured. "I don't know if you can understand just how important Louis was to my childhood, my adolescence. Seeing him like this today . . ." With a sigh, she kept her head on his shoulder and watched the patterns sun and shade made on the road.

"You're thinking of him as a victim, Laurel. We're all victims of what life deals out. It's how we handle it that's important."

"When you love someone, and you lose them, it kills something in you, too."

"No." He let himself breathe in the scent of her hair. "Damages. We all have to deal with being damaged one way or the other."

He was right, of course he was right. But it still hurt. She said nothing, but sat quietly with her cheek on his shoulder while his hand trailed through her hair. His body was so firm, his heartbeat so steady. She could lose herself here,

Laurel realized, in the front seat of his car with the sun pouring through and the sound of birds calling lazily from tree to tree.

"I keep telling you not to be nice to me," she murmured.

He tilted his head back to look at her. His eyes were intense again, seeing too much. His fingers spread to cup her face. When her mouth opened, he tightened them. "Shut up," he told her before he pressed his lips to hers.

Not so light this time, not so gentle. She tasted frustration and didn't understand it. But she also tasted desire, simmering, waiting, and couldn't resist it. Her body went fluid, every bone, every muscle, as she surrendered to whatever it was they needed from each other. The need was there, she knew. Had always been there. The more she had resisted it, fought it, ignored it, the stronger it had become, until it threatened to overpower every other. Food, air, warmth, those were insignificant needs compared to this. If she was seduced, it wasn't by soft words or skilled kisses, but by the emotions that had escaped before she'd been able to confine them.

"Matthew." She dropped her head on his shoulder and tried to steady her breathing. "This isn't—I'm not ready for this."

Smoldering with impatience and desire, he forced her head back. "You will be."

"I don't know." She pressed her hands to his chest, wishing he could understand—wishing she could. "I told you that you confuse me. You do. I've never wanted a man before, and I never expected it to be you."

"It is me." He drew her closer. "You'll just have to get used to it." His expression changed slowly from barely restrained temper to intentness. "Never wanted a man," he repeated. "Any man? You haven't—been with any man?"

Her chin came up. "I said I never wanted one. I don't do anything I don't want to."

Innocent? Dear God, he thought, shouldn't he have seen

it? Sensed it? Gradually, he loosened his grip until he'd released her. "Changes the rules, doesn't it?" he said softly. Matt took out a cigarette while she sat frowning at him. "Changes the rules," he repeated in a whisper. "I'm going to be your lover, Laurellie. Take some time to think about it."

"Of all the arrogant—"

"Yeah, we'll get into that in depth later." He blew out a stream of smoke. She was steadier now, he thought ruefully. He was wired. He'd better give them both some time to think about it. "Let me throw a couple of theories at you on Anne Trulane."

He started the car again while Laurel struggled to control her temper and to remember priorities. The story, she told herself, and forced her jaw to unclench. They'd deal with this . . . personal business later. "Go ahead."

He drove smoothly, ignoring the knot of need in his stomach. "Louis married Anne Fisher because she looked like his first wife."

"Oh, really, Matthew."

"Let me finish. Whether he cared for her or not isn't the issue. Once they were married he brought her back to Heritage Oak and kept her there, away from outsiders. Men. He didn't trust her."

"He'd been hurt before, in the cruelest possible way."

"Exactly." Matt pitched his cigarette out the window. "He was obsessed with the idea that she might find a younger man. He was possessive, jealous. What if Anne rebelled? What if she gave him a reason to doubt her loyalty?"

"You're suggesting that Louis killed her because he thought she'd violated his trust." She didn't like the chill that brought to her skin, and turned on him. "That's ridiculous. He isn't capable of killing anyone."

"How do you know what he's capable of?" he tossed back. "You didn't know that man in the parlor today."

No, she didn't, and the truth stung. "Your theory's weak," she retorted. "Look at the timetable. Anne died between 12:00 and 4:00 a.m. Louis woke the household sometime between two and three."

"He could've taken her in before two," Matt said mildly. "Maybe he never intended for her to die. He might've wanted to frighten her, taken her in and left her there."

"Then why would he call out a search party?"

Matt turned his head, letting his gaze skim over her face before he shifted it back to the road. "He could've forgotten he'd done it."

Laurel opened her mouth and closed it again. Absentminded, Marion had said. He'd been absentminded, angry, bitter. She didn't like the picture it was drawing in her mind.

Laurel remained silent as he drove through downtown traffic. No man forgot he'd left his wife alone and lost. No sane man. Matt swung over to the curb and stopped. "Where are we going?"

"To see Nathan Brewster."

Laurel glanced up at Trulane's, one of the oldest, most prestigious buildings in the city. Perhaps they'd find something in there that would shift the focus from Louis. "Marion didn't want to talk about Nathan Brewster."

"I noticed." Matt stepped out of the car. "Let's find out why."

"I know what you're thinking," she murmured as they walked toward the front doors.

"Mmmm. That could be embarrassing."

She shot him a look as they walked inside. "Anne was attracted to Nathan Brewster, acted on it and Louis found out. Rather than dealing with it or divorcing her, he drags her into the swamp in the middle of the night and dumps her."

Matt checked the board on the wall and located Accounting. "It crossed my mind," he agreed.

"You've got your own prejudices against Louis."

"You're damned right," he muttered, and took her hand to pull her to the elevator. "Look," Matt began before she could retort. "Let's talk to the man and see what happens. Maybe he's just been embezzling or having an affair with Marion."

"Your ideas get more and more ludicrous." She stepped into the elevator and crossed her arms.

"You're sulking."

"I am not!" Letting out an exasperated breath, she glared at him. "I don't agree with your theory, that's all."

"Give me yours," Matt suggested.

She watched the numbers flash over the elevator door. "After we talk to Brewster."

They stepped out on carpet, thick and plush. Without giving Matt a glance, Laurel crossed to the receptionist. "Laurel Armand, Matthew Bates, with the *Herald*," she said briskly. "We'd like to see Nathan Brewster."

The receptionist flicked open her book. "Do you have an appointment?"

"No. Tell Mr. Brewster we'd like to speak with him about Anne Trulane."

"If you'll have a seat, I'll see if Mr. Brewster's available."

"Nice touch, Laurellie," Matt told her as they crossed the reception area. "Ever think about the military?"

"It's gotten me into a lot of city officials." She took a seat under a potted palm and crossed her legs.

He grinned down at her. There wasn't a trace of the sad, vulnerable woman who'd rested her head on his shoulder. "You've got style," he decided, then let his gaze sweep down. "And great legs."

Laurel slanted him a look. "Yeah."

"Mr. Brewster will see you now." The receptionist led them down a hallway, past an army of doors. After opening one, she went silently back to her desk.

Laurel's first impression of Nathan Brewster was of sex. He exuded it, ripe, physical. He was dark, and though he wasn't tall, he had a blatant virility no woman could miss. Good looks, though he had them, didn't matter. It was his primitive masculinity that would either draw or repel.

"Ms. Armand, Mr. Bates." He gestured toward two small leather chairs before taking a seat behind his desk. "You wanted to talk to me about Anne Trulane."

"That's right." Laurel settled herself beside Matt as she tried to reason out what kind of reaction a woman like Anne would have had to Nathan Brewster.

"She's dead," Brewster said flatly. "What does the press have to do with it?"

"You met Anne at Heritage Oak," Laurel began. "Not many people did."

"I went there on business." He picked up a pencil and ran it through his fingers.

"Could you give us your impression of her?"

"She was young, shy. My business was with Mr. Trulane; I barely spoke to her."

"Strange." Matt watched Brewster pull the pencil through his fingers again and again. "Yours was one of the few names that came up in Anne's letters." The pencil broke with a quiet snap.

"I don't know what you're talking about."

"Anne wrote to her sister about you." Matt kept his eyes on Brewster's now, waiting, measuring. "Her sister doesn't believe Anne's death was an accident."

Matt watched the little ripple of Brewster's throat as he swallowed. "She died of a snakebite."

"In the swamp," Laurel put in, fascinated by the waves of

frustration and passion pouring out of him. "Did you know she was frightened of the swamp, Mr. Brewster?"

He shot Laurel a look, molten, enraged. Matt's muscles tensed. "How would I?" he demanded. "How would I know?"

"Why would you suppose she'd go into a place that terrified her?"

"Maybe she couldn't stand being locked up anymore!" he exploded. "Maybe she had to get out, no matter where, or how."

"Locked up?" Laurel repeated, ignoring the tremor in her stomach. "Are you saying Louis kept her a prisoner?"

"What else can you call it?" he shot back at her. His hands clenched and unclenched on the two jagged pieces of pencil. "Day after day, month after month, never seeing anyone but servants and a man who watched every move she made. She never did anything without asking him first. She never stepped a foot beyond the gates of that place without him."

"Was she unhappy?" Laurel asked. "Did she tell you she was unhappy?"

"She should've been," Nathan tossed back. "Trulane treated her more like a daughter than a wife. She needed someone who'd treat her like a woman."

"You?" Matt said softly. Laurel swallowed.

Brewster's breathing was labored. The temper Matt had been told of was fighting to get free. He'd have to struggle to control it. And, Matt mused, he wouldn't often win.

"I wanted her," Brewster said roughly. "From the first time I saw her out on the lawn, in the sunlight. She belonged in the sunlight. I wanted her, loved her, in a way Trulane couldn't possibly understand."

"Was she in love with you?"

Matt's quiet question drew the blood to Brewster's cheeks. "She would have left him. She wouldn't have stayed in that— monument forever."

"And come to you?" Laurel murmured.

"Sooner or later." The eyes he turned on Laurel were penetrating, filled with passion and feeling. "I told her she didn't have to stay locked up there, I'd help her get away. I told her she'd be better off dead than—"

"Better off dead than living with Louis," Laurel finished as his harsh breathing filled the room.

"It must've been frustrating," Matt continued when Brewster didn't answer. "Loving your employer's wife, rarely being able to see her or tell her how you felt."

"Anne knew how I felt," Brewster bit off. "What difference does it make now? She's dead. That place killed her. He killed her." Brewster sent them both a heated look. "Print that in your paper."

"You believe Louis Trulane killed his wife?" Matt watched Brewster sweep the remains of the pencil from his desk.

"He might as well have held a gun to her head. She got away," he murmured as he stared down at his empty hands. "She finally got away, but she didn't come to me." The hands curled into fists again. "Now leave me alone."

Laurel's muscles didn't relax until they'd walked out into the sunlight. "That was a sad, bitter man," she murmured.

"And one who takes little trouble to hide it."

She shivered, then leaned against the side of his car. "I can understand why he made Anne nervous."

Matt cupped his hands around a match as he lit a cigarette. "Give me a basic feminine reaction."

"Passion, virility, primitive enough to fascinate." She shook her head as she stared up at the ribbons of windows. "For some women, that would be irresistible simply because it's rather frightening. A woman like Anne Trulane would've seen him as one of her dark closets and stayed away." With a short laugh, she dragged a hand through her hair. "I'm not a psychiatrist, Matthew, but I think a certain kind of woman

would be drawn to a man like Brewster. I don't believe Anne
Trulane would've been."

Letting out a long breath, she turned to him. "It's my turn
to write a scenario."

"Let's hear it."

"Brewster's in love with her—or thinks he is, it wouldn't
matter with a man like him. He tells Anne, asks her to leave
Louis for him. How would she feel? Frightened, appalled. A
little flattered perhaps."

He cocked a brow, intrigued. "Flattered?"

"She was a woman," Laurel said flatly. "Young, unsophis-
ticated." She glanced back up at the windows, thinking of
Brewster. "Yes, I believe she might have felt all three emotions. It confuses her, he pressures her. He's very intense,
dramatic. She loves her husband, but this is something she
doesn't know how to cope with. She can't even write her sister about it."

Matt nodded, watching her. "Go on."

"Suppose Brewster contacts her, demands to see her.
Maybe he even threatens to confront Louis. She wouldn't
have wanted that. Louis's approval and trust are important
to her. Anne had to know about his first wife. So . . ."

Laurel's eyes narrowed as she tried to picture it. "She
agrees to see him, meets him outside, late, while Louis
is working. They argue because she won't leave Louis. He's
a physical man." She remembered his strong fingers on the
pencil. "He's convinced himself she wants him but is afraid
to leave. He drags her away from the house, away from the
light. She's terrified now, of him, of the dark. She breaks
away and runs, but it's dark and she's in the swamp before
she realizes it. She's lost. Brewster either can't find her or
doesn't try. And then . . ."

"Interesting," Matt murmured before he flicked his cigarette away. "And, I suppose, as plausible as anything else. I

wish we had those damn letters," he said suddenly. "There must be something there or they wouldn't've been taken."

"Whatever it was, we won't find it there now."

Matt nodded, staring past her. "I want to get into that swamp, look around."

Laurel felt the shudder and repressed it. "Tonight?"

"Mmmm."

She supposed she'd known it was bound to come down to this. Resigned, she blew the hair out of her eyes. "Let's go get some mosquito repellent."

He grinned and ran a finger down her nose. "Only one of us has to go. You stay home and keep a light burning in the window."

The brow went up, arrogant, haughty. "My story, Bates. I'm going; you can tag along if you want."

"Our story," he corrected. "God knows if there'll be anything in there but a bunch of filthy insects and soggy ground."

And snakes, Laurel thought. She swallowed, tasting copper. "We'll have to see, won't we? Matthew, we're running out of angles."

They stared at each other, frowning. Dead end—for now.

"Let's get some lunch," Laurel suggested as she swung around to get into the car. "And get back to the paper before we're both out of a job."

CHAPTER 7

Laurel spent over an hour with Matt in the newspaper morgue, going through files and crosschecking until her neck ached. With luck, the *Herald* would be on computers within the year. Laurel might miss the ambience of the cavernous morgue with the smell of dust and old paper, but she wouldn't miss the inconvenience. Some of the staff might grumble about having to learn the tricks of a terminal, the codes, the ways and means of putting in and taking out information at the punch of a button. She promised herself, as she rubbed at a crick in the back of her neck, she wouldn't be one of them.

"Brewster made page two with his fists," Laurel murmured as she scanned the story. "Two years ago last April." She glanced up briefly. "No one's memory's quite like Grandma's."

"She mentioned a sister."

"That's right. His sister'd been seeing a man who apparently liked his bourbon a bit too well. He'd seen her in a bar with another man and made a scene—tried to drag her out. Brewster was there. It took roughly ten men to pull him off, and before they did, he'd broken a couple of tables, a mirror, three of the guy's ribs, his nose and jaw, and his own hand."

Matt lifted a brow at her cool recital of the violence. "Charged?"

"Assault headed the list," Laurel told him. "Ended up paying a fine when his . . . ah . . . opponent wouldn't press charges." She scrawled a note on her pad. "Apparently once Brewster's temper is lost, it's lost. I think I'll see if I can trace the sister. He might have talked to her about Anne."

"Mmm-hmm."

She glanced over to see Matt scribbling quickly in his own book. "What've you got?"

"Speculation," he murmured, then rose. "I have a few calls to make myself."

"Matthew," Laurel began as they started down the corridor, "weren't you the one who had all the big talk about sharing?"

He smiled at her, then pushed the button for the elevator. "After I make the calls."

"Make up your own rules as you go along?" she muttered when they stepped inside the car.

He looked down at her, remembering her passion in his arms, the vulnerability in her eyes. Her innocence. "I might just have to."

Laurel felt the quick chill race up her spine and stared straight ahead. "Let's stick with the story, Bates."

"Absolutely." Grinning, he took her arm as the elevator opened. They walked into the city room and separated.

Reporters have to get used to rude replies, no replies, runarounds. Laurel dealt with all three as she dialed number after number in an attempt to trace Kate Brewster. When she finally reached her, Laurel had to deal with all three again.

Brewster's sister flatly refused to discuss the barroom brawl and had little to say about her brother. At the mention of Anne Trulane, Laurel sensed a hesitation and caught a slight inflection—fear?—in Kate's voice as she claimed she didn't know anyone by that name.

Laurel found herself dealing with another hazard reporter's face. An abrupt dial tone in the ear. Glancing up, she saw Matt cradling his own phone between his shoulder and ear as he made notes. At least one of us is getting somewhere, she thought in disgust as she rose to perch on the corner of his desk. Though she tried, it wasn't possible to read his peculiar type of shorthand upside down. Idly, she picked up the foam cup that held his cooling coffee and sipped. When she heard him mention the name Elise Trulane, she frowned.

What the hell's he up to? Laurel wondered as he easily ignored her and continued to take notes. Checking up on Elise . . . he's hung up on the similarity in looks, she decided. What does a runaway first wife have to do with a dead second one? As an uncomfortable thought raced into her mind, Laurel's eyes darted to Matt's. *Revenge?* But that would be madness. Louis wasn't—Louis couldn't . . . From the way he returned the look, she realized Matt read her thoughts while she wasn't able to penetrate his. Deliberately, she turned away to stare into Don Ballinger's office. The information they'd given their editor might have been sketchy, but it had been enough to give them the go-ahead.

Matt hung up and tapped his pencil on the edge of his desk. "What'd you get?"

"Zero, unless you count the impression that Anne Trulane's name made Brewster's sister very nervous. And another impression that she treads very carefully where her brother's concerned. What're you up to, Matthew?"

He ran the pencil through his hands, but the gesture had none of the nervous passion and energy that Brewster's had. His hands were lean, not elegant like Louis's, she thought, or violent like Brewster's. They were capable and clever and strong—just as he was. Disturbed, she shifted her gaze to his face. It was becoming a habit for thoughts of him to get in the way of what they had to do.

"Matthew?" she repeated as he looked beyond her.

"It seems the two Mrs. Trulanes had one or two things more in common than looks," he began. He dropped the pencil on his desk and drew out a cigarette. "They each had only one relative. In Elise's case, it's an aunt. I just spoke with her."

"Why?"

"Curiosity." He blew out a stream of smoke as a reporter behind them swore and hung up his own phone. "She describes her niece as a shy, quiet girl. Apparently Elise loved Heritage Oak, and unlike Anne, had already begun to take over the position of lady of the manor. She enjoyed the planning, the entertaining, had ideas for redecorating. The aunt was astonished when Elise ran off with Louis's brother—hasn't seen or heard from her since. She thought Elise was devoted to her husband."

"So did everyone else," Laurel commented. "Things like that do happen, Matthew, without anyone on the outside being aware. I don't imagine Elise would've told her aunt or anyone else that she was having an affair with Charles."

"Maybe not. There is something I find interesting," he murmured, keeping his eyes on Laurel's. "Elise inherited fifty thousand dollars on her twenty-first birthday. She turned twenty-one the month after she left Heritage Oak. The money," he said slowly, "was never claimed."

Laurel stared at him while ideas, answers, spun through her mind. "Maybe she—she might've been afraid to claim it thinking Louis could trace her."

"Fifty thousand buys a lot of courage."

"I don't see what digging into Elise's business has to do with Anne."

His eyes were very calm, very direct. "Yes, you do." She

looked pale again, drained as she had that morning. Smothering an oath, Matt rose. "It's something to think about," he said briskly. "For now, we'd better concentrate on what we have to do tonight. Let's go home. We can catch a couple of hours' rest before we have to get ready."

"All right." She didn't want to argue, and though it was cowardly, she didn't want to think about what he'd just told her. There'd been enough that day. If she was to win out over her emotions, she needed the time to do it.

Matt didn't press her, but made easy, innocuous conversation on the drive home. He was good at falling back on a relaxed style to conceal his inner thoughts and feelings. It was one of his greatest professional weapons, and personal defenses. If he was furious with Laurel's automatic and unflagging defense of Louis Trulane, it wasn't apparent. If he harbored frustrating, near-violent urges to take her to some dark, private place until she forgot Louis Trulane existed, he didn't show it. His voice was calm, his driving smooth. His muscles were tight.

"A nap," Laurel said as they left his car to cross the courtyard, "sounds like heaven. It's been a long two days."

A long year, he thought as needs crawled in him. "And it's going to be a long night," he said easily.

She smiled at him for the first time since they'd left the *Herald*. "What time do we go on safari?"

"Midnight's the accepted hour, I believe." He touched the tips of her hair, then started up the steps.

"Garlic doesn't work against ghosts, does it?" Laurel mused. "No silver bullets, wooden stakes. What does?"

"Common sense."

She gave a windy sigh. "No romance."

At the top of the steps, he grinned at her. "Wanna bet?"

Laughing, she bent to pick up a wrapped box at the base of her door. "I don't remember ordering anything."

"From Jerry, no doubt—a box of number-two pencils."

She tried to glare at him and failed. "Midnight, Bates." After a brief search, she found her keys and unlocked the door. With a final arch look, she closed the door in his face.

His grin faded as he started down to his own apartment. The woman was driving him crazy. She had to be blind not to see it, he thought as he jabbed his key into the lock. Maybe he'd been too cautious. As he walked into the kitchen, Matt stripped his shirt over his head and tossed it aside. Then again, it had taken him weeks to get used to the fact that he'd been struck by lightning the first time she'd lifted those dark green eyes and looked at him.

At that point, he'd told himself it was impossible, the same way he'd told himself it was impossible for him to lose his head over the neatly framed photograph Curt had put on their shared desk in their college dorm.

"My sister," Curt had said in his abstracted way. "Runs copy at my father's paper during the summer. Guess you'd know about things like that."

The words hadn't registered because Matt had to concentrate on just breathing. There he'd been—a senior in college, a man who'd already seen and worked his way through more than many men do in a lifetime—rooted to the spot with one of the shirts he'd been unpacking dangling from his hand, head swimming over a girl who couldn't have been more than fifteen. Impossible.

Matt grabbed some orange juice from the refrigerator and chugged straight from the bottle. He'd gotten over that first . . . whatever it had been quickly enough. Or he'd told himself he had. But when William Armand had written him, all those years later, mentioning his relationship to Matt's senior-year college roommate and offering a position on the *Herald*, Matt hadn't hesitated. And he hadn't asked himself why.

It would've helped, he thought as he tossed the empty bottle in the trash, if he'd found a slow brain underneath that fabulous face. Or a bland or too-sweet personality. It would've helped if he hadn't sat next to her for a full year knowing she was everything he'd ever wanted.

He intended to have her, though her innocence urged him toward a traditional courtship—quiet dinners, candlelight, a gentle touch. Matt felt the stir of desire, and swore. He hoped he had the control he was going to need.

He intended to have her, though the difference in their backgrounds sometimes reared up to mock him. He'd already pushed his way through a lot of doors; now he had to make sure his luck held.

He was going to have her.

Matt stuck his hands in his pockets and headed for the shower. And he heard her scream.

Later, he wouldn't remember bursting out of his own apartment and rushing to hers. He'd remember hearing her scream again, and again, but he wouldn't remember beating on her door and finally, in desperation, knocking it in. What he would remember, always, was the way she'd looked, standing frozen with her hands at her own throat, her face like parchment and her eyes terrified.

"Laurel!" He grabbed her, spinning her around and into him where she stood in his arms, rigid as a stone. "What? What is it?"

He could feel the beat of her heart. Was it possible for a heart to beat that fast? Her skin was like ice, dampened by a sheen of sweat, but she didn't tremble. Not yet. "The box," she whispered. "In the box."

With one hand still on her arm, he turned and looked into the box on the table. The oath ripped out under his breath, pungent. "It's all right, Laurel. It's dead, it can't hurt you." His body trembled with fury as he lifted a portion of the

copperhead from the box. "It can't hurt you now," he repeated, turning back to see her staring, transfixed at what
he held in his hand. Sweat pearled on her forehead. Through
her parted lips, her breath came harsh and quick.

"Matthew . . . please."

Without a word, he covered the box and carried it from
the apartment. He returned—twenty, thirty seconds later—to
find her leaning, palms down on the table, head lowered,
weeping. He still didn't speak as he picked her up to carry
her to the sofa and cradle her like a baby. Then the trembling
started.

Five minutes . . . ten, and he said nothing, only holding
her as she wept into his bare shoulder and shuddered. She
seemed so small. Even when he'd seen those flashes of vulnerability he would never have imagined her like this—totally
helpless, without the slimmest defense against anything or
anyone. As he held her close, Matt promised himself when
he found out who'd sent the box, he'd make them pay for it.

Safe. She knew she was safe now, though the fear kept
threatening to bubble up again—that awful, strangling fear
that couldn't be described but felt only. She could feel his
heartbeat under her hand, and the warm flesh. He was holding her, and the world would settle again.

"I'm sorry," she managed, but continued to cling to him.

"No, don't." He kissed her hair, then stroked it.

"It's always been like that. I was bitten once. I can't remember it, or being sick, but I can't, I just can't handle—"

"It's all right. It's gone now, don't think about it anymore." The trembling had nearly stopped, but he could feel
the occasional spasm that passed through her. Her breath
still came in hitches. His skin was damp from her tears. He
wanted to make her forget—he wanted to get his hands on
whoever had done this to her. "Let me get you a brandy."

"No." She said it too quickly, and the hands against his chest balled into fists. "Just hold me," she murmured, hating the weakness, needing his strength.

"As long as you want." He heard her sigh, felt her fingers relax. The minutes passed again, long and silent so that he thought she slept. Her breathing had evened, her heartbeat slowed and she was warm again. He knew if she'd needed it, he could have held her just so for days.

"Matthew . . ." His name came on a sigh as she tilted her head back to look at his face. Her eyes were still puffy, her skin was still pale. He had to fight the wave of emotion to keep his fingers from tightening on her. "Don't go."

"No." He smiled and traced a finger down her cheek. Her skin was still damp, still warm from her weeping. "I won't go."

Laurel caught his hand in hers and pressed it to her lips. Matt felt something wash over him, warm and sweet, that he didn't yet recognize as tenderness. She saw it move in his eyes.

This was what she'd been waiting for, Laurel realized. This was what she'd needed, wanted, refused to consider. If he would ask her now—but he wouldn't, she knew it. The asking would have to come from her.

"Make love with me," she whispered.

"Laurel . . ." Her words stirred him, impossibly. How could he take her now, when she was utterly without defense? Another time, oh, God, another time, he'd have given any-thing to hear her say those words. "You should rest," he said inadequately.

He's not sure of himself, she realized. Strange, she'd thought he was always so sure. Perhaps his feelings for her were as confusing as hers for him. "Matthew, I know what I'm asking." Her voice wasn't strong, but it was clear. "I want you. I've wanted you for a long time." She slipped her hand up over his chest and neck to touch his cheek. "Love me— now." She brought her lips to his as if quietly coming home.

Perhaps he could have resisted his own need. Perhaps. But he couldn't resist hers. He drew her closer with a moan, gathering her against him as his mouth told her everything in silence. She was boneless, so pliant it seemed she might simply melt out of his arms like a mirage he'd traveled to over endless, impossible days and nights only to find it vanished. He deepened the kiss with something like panic, but she remained, warm and real against him.

Her mouth tasted of woman, not of visions, so warm and sweet he had to fight the urge to devour it. Her tastes, that small hand that remained on his cheek, the airy scent, merged together to make his senses swim. He couldn't afford the luxury now, not this first time.

Matt buried his face at her throat, struggling to hold on to some slim thread of control, but his lips wouldn't be still. He had to taste her. His hands roamed up and over subtle curves. He had to touch her.

"Laurel . . ." He slipped her loosened blouse off one shoulder so that his lips could wander there. "I want you—I ache with it."

Even as he told himself to move slowly, he was drawing the blouse from her. She shifted to help him, murmuring, then only sighed.

"Not here." He closed his eyes as her lips brushed his throat. "Not here," he said again, and rose with her still in his arms. This time she'd let herself be led. She rested her head on his shoulder as he carried her into the bedroom.

The lights slanted through wooden shutters. It highlighted his eyes, so suddenly intense, as he laid her on the bed. "I won't hurt you."

She smiled and reached for him. "I know."

The mattress sighed as he lay beside her. With her eyes just open, she could see the play of light while his lips traced over her face. It was so easy. She should have known that with him it would be so easy. Running her palms, then her fingertips over his back, she felt the ripple of muscle, the taut skin, the strength. This had attracted her from the beginning, and she had struggled to ignore it. Now, she could take her fill.

He caressed her with his lips. Caressed. She hadn't known such a thing was possible with lips alone. He showed her. Her skin softened, then tingled from it.

Lazily . . . thoroughly . . .

His mouth moved over her throat and shoulders while his hands tarried nowhere but in her hair. A gentle nip, a soft flick of tongue and she was floating.

She heard the bluesy sound of a trumpet from outside. The sound drifted into the room to mix in her mind with Matt's murmurs. He nuzzled into her throat so that she turned her head to give him more freedom and breathed in the sweet scent of vanilla from her bedside candle. She made some sound, a long, low sigh, but had no way of knowing that this alone had his pulses hammering.

His lips pressed onto hers with the edge of desperation under the gentleness. She felt it, yielded to it, as she drew him yet closer.

When he touched her, a lean, hard hand over the silk of her camisole, her sigh became a moan. She arched, feeling the aching fullness in her breasts she'd never experienced. Needs sprang up from everywhere, all at once, to pulse under her skin. But he wouldn't be rushed—by her or himself. His fingers trailed, aroused, but stopped just short of demand. He wanted the demand to come from her own needs, not his.

Slowly, inch by inch, he drew the swatch of silk down to her waist, finding her skin no less luxurious. With openmouthed kisses he explored it, listening to the shuddering sound of her breathing that meant the loss of control. He wanted that from her, for her, while he desperately hung on to his own. When his mouth closed over her breast, the muscles in his back relaxed. God, she was sweet.

While Laurel went wild beneath him, he lingered, drawing out their mutual pleasure, drinking in her tastes and textures. He caught her nipple between his teeth, holding it prisoner, tormenting it with the play of his tongue until he knew she was utterly steeped in passion, in the dark, mindless pleasures. Then he went on.

She knew only sensations now—there were no thoughts, no sane thoughts, as flames leaped inside her and fire shivered along her skin. The movements of her body were instinctive, offering, pleading. His lips continued to roam over her as he slipped the rest of her clothes from her. The feel of hot flesh against hot flesh had her gasping. With each trembling breath she took, the scent they made together overwhelmed her. Intimate, earthy. Glorious.

Her body was molten—fluid, fiery—but she was helpless. Whatever he wanted from her he could have taken in whatever way he chose. The choices she had made—first to resist him, then to accept him—no longer applied. There were no choices in this world of dazzling light and radiant heat. Her body craved. Her spirit hungered. She was his.

He knew it. And, knowing, fought to remember her innocence when her passion was tearing at his control. She was agile and slim, and at the moment as abandoned as a sleek young animal. Her hands sought him without hesitation, her lips raced to take whatever he'd allow. With his breath rasping, his blood pounding, he struggled to keep the pace as he'd begun. Easy.

When he touched her, she jolted beneath him, shuddering and shuddering with the first peak. Through his own desire,

Matt could feel her stunned, helpless delight. No one else had given her this, no one else had taken this from her. No one.

He buried his face at her throat, groaning. So moist, so warm. So ready. He shifted onto her. "Laurel . . ."

Suspended on shaft after shaft of sensation, she opened her eyes and looked into his. If her body was fluid, his was tight as a bowstring. Over the waves of passion came one clear certainty. He thought only of her. She couldn't speak, drowned by needs and the sharply sweet newness of love just discovered. Laurel drew his mouth down to hers.

At the touch of her lips, she gave up her innocence as easily, as gently, as sliding down a long, cool bank toward a warm river.

She slept. Matt lay beside her and watched the light through the window slats go from white to rose to gray before the moonlight drifted thinly in. His body was exhausted, from the strain of control, from the ultimate loss of it, but his mind wouldn't rest.

There'd been times over the last months when he'd nearly convinced himself that once he'd had her, the lingering need would pass. Now, as he lay in her bed, with moonlight slanting across her body, with her head nestled against his shoulder, he knew the need would remain as basic and essential as the need for air.

Physically, he knew, she was his. He could touch off her passion, exploit her needs and keep her. It wasn't enough. He wondered if he could draw out her emotions, her love, with the same deliberate care with which he'd drawn out her desire. He wondered if he had the patience he'd need.

Turning his head, he looked down at her as she slept against him. Her skin was like porcelain with the dusky lashes shadowing her cheeks. Delicate . . . He traced a finger down her cheekbone. Yes, she had delicacy, which at times made him feel like an awkward boy staring at pastries in a bakery window. But she had verve, and energy and ambition. These he understood, as they matched his own.

Partners, he thought, and his eyes glinted with something between amusement and determination. Damn right they were. Bending down, he crushed his mouth to hers.

Head swimming, body throbbing, Laurel came awake on a wave of passion. Her skin leaped under his hands as they raced over her, taking and demanding with a speed that left her giddy. She moaned against his mouth, tossed so quickly from gentle sleep to ruthless desire that she could only cling. He set the pace again, but it was nothing like the first time. She catapulted from peak to peak, swept along, driven, until he took her with all the urgency he'd blocked out before.

Spent, stunned, she waited for her breath to return as he lay over her, his face buried in her hair. Should she have known it would be like this? Could she? More than anything, that quick, desperate loving showed her just how careful he'd been with her the first time.

I love him, she thought as she tightened her arms around him. Wouldn't that knock him off his feet? With a wry smile, she toyed with the hair that curled over his neck. Matthew Bates, I'm going to play a very careful hand with you—and I'm going to win.

She gave a long, luxurious sigh. Did loving make the body feel so wonderfully lazy? "Were you trying to tell me it's time to get up?" she murmured.

Lifting his head, he grinned at her. "I don't think so."

"This wasn't supposed to happen."

"Yes, it was." He kissed her brow lightly, lingeringly. "We're just a little ahead of schedule."

Her brow arched, but the haughty gesture had to compete with the soft, just-loved flush of her skin. "Whose schedule?"

"Ours," he said easily. "Ours, Laurel."

It was difficult to argue with something that seemed so

reasonable. Laurel linked her hands at the base of his neck and tilted her head. "You look good, Bates."

Amusement flickered in his eyes. "Yeah?"

"Yeah." She ran her tongue over her teeth. "I guess I'm getting used to those beachboy looks and that Yankee speech pattern. Or maybe—" she caught her bottom lip between her teeth, but the laughter shone in her eyes "—maybe I just like your body. You work out?"

He braced himself comfortably on his elbows. "Now and again."

Experimentally, Laurel pinched his bicep. "Weights?"

"No."

"Well, I've never cared for obvious muscles." She ran a hand down to his wrist, then back again. "You seem to be in good enough shape to handle our plans for the evening."

He nipped at her bottom lip. "Which are?"

"A little hike through the swamp."

He rubbed his lips over hers easily, while his mind did some quick calculations. He could distract her, wait until she slept again, then go without her. "I was thinking we could . . . postpone that."

"Were you?" Though her body began to soften, her mind was much too sharp. "Until you could sneak out there on your own?"

He should've known better. "Laurel . . ." He slid a hand up to her breast.

"Oh, no." She shifted quickly until she lay on top of him. "You can forget the idea of going out there without me, Bates. We're a team."

"Listen." He took her firmly by the shoulders while her hair dipped down to brush his. "There isn't any need for you to go. It's just a matter of poking around anyway. It'll be faster and easier with only one of us."

"Then you stay here." She kissed him briskly and sat up.

"Damn it, Laurel. Think."

"About what?" she tossed back as she rose, naked, to rummage through her drawers.

"No one left a nasty little box at my door."

She bit down hard on her lip, then turned with a T-shirt and a pair of panties in her hand. "No, they didn't," she said calmly enough. "They left it at mine, obviously for a reason. We're making someone nervous, Matthew. And that someone is damn well going to have to deal with me."

He looked at her, small and straight with her naked skin glowing in the moonlight. At the moment, she looked perfectly capable of avenging herself. "Okay, tough guy," he drawled as he swung his legs out of bed. "When we find out who it was, you can go a few rounds. In the meantime, you might remember there're snakes in that swamp—and they're not dead in a box."

He knew he'd been deliberately cruel, he'd meant to be. But when he saw her fingers tighten on the shirt she held, he cursed himself.

"I won't look." Jaw set, she wriggled into the panties. "You'd better get dressed."

"Stubborn, hardheaded, obstinate," he began furiously.

"Yeah." Jerking the shirt over her head, Laurel glared at him. "But not stupid. Whoever dropped that thing at my door wanted me to back off. That points to Brewster or—or the Trulanes," she managed after a moment. "If they wanted us to back off, there's a reason, and the reason might just be in that swamp."

"You won't get any argument on that from me," he said evenly. "But it doesn't follow that you have to go."

"If I let that kind of threat steer me away, I'll have to turn in my press badge. Nobody's going to put me in that position." She gave him a long, level look. "Nobody."

Matt's temper struggled toward the surface, then subsided. She was right—that was one point he couldn't get around. In silence, he pulled on his jeans. "I've got to get a shirt, and a flashlight," he said briefly. "Be ready in ten minutes."

"All right." She made a business of searching through her drawers until she was sure he'd gone.

Laurel pressed her fingers to her eyes and let the fear out. It was a sticky, cloying sensation that rolled over her and left her light-headed. As it ebbed, she rested her hands against the dresser and just concentrated on breathing. She had to go—now more than before she'd looked in that box. If a threat wasn't answered, then it was buckled in to. If there was a threat, it meant someone was afraid.

Anne Trulane had been afraid of the swamp. Laurel pulled on worn jeans with hands that were almost steady again. She understood that kind of fear, the kind that has no true explanation but simply is. Laurel didn't believe Anne had voluntarily walked into that dark, secret place any more than she herself would voluntarily walk into a snake exhibit. The full certainty of it hadn't struck until tonight, with the burgeoning of her own fear. And, by God, she was going to prove it.

Matt . . . Laurel switched on the bedroom light and began to search through the disorder of her closet for boots. He was only being unreasonable because he was concerned for her. While she could appreciate it, she couldn't allow it. Love might urge her to give in to him on this one thing—but then how many other things might she give in to once she started?

However he felt about her, she mused as she located one boot, he felt about her because of the way she was. The best thing she could do for both of them was to stay that way.

Swearing at her own disorganization, Laurel shouldered her way into the closet for the other boot.

When he returned, Matt found her sitting on the floor of her room, fighting with knotted laces. He was wearing an outfit very similar to hers, and his more customary amiable expression. He'd calmed down considerably by rationalizing that she'd be safer with him in any case—and by promising himself he'd watch Laurel like a hawk every moment they were in the swamps of Heritage Oak.

"Having a problem?"

"I don't know how this happened," she muttered, tugging on the laces. "It's like somebody crawled in there, tied these in knots, then buried the boot under a pile of junk."

He glanced at her littered floor. "I'm disillusioned. I always thought you were very precise and organized."

"I am—at work. Damn!" She scowled at a broken nail, then fought with the laces again. "There—now I just need a flashlight." Springing lightly to her feet, she dashed past him and into the kitchen.

"You know, Laurellie," Matt commented as he followed her. "A few more molecules missing and you wouldn't have a seat in those pants."

"It'll be dark."

He patted her bottom. "Not that dark."

Grinning, she pulled a flashlight from the kitchen drawer and tested it. "Then you'll have to walk in front and keep your mind off my anatomy."

"I'd rather watch your back pockets jiggle." Swinging an arm around her, he walked to the door.

"They don't jiggle." She stopped, frowning at the splintered wood. "How did that—"

"You were too busy screaming to open the door," Matt said easily, nudging her outside. "I called the super about it."

"You broke it down?" Laurel turned to stare at him.

He grinned at her expression before he tugged her down the stairs. "Don't make doors like they used to."

He broke it down. The thought of it stunned her, sweetly. At the foot of the stairs she stopped and wrapped her arms around his waist. "You know, Matthew, I've always had a soft spot for knights on white chargers."

He framed her face with his hands before he kissed her. "Even tarnished ones?"

"Especially."

CHAPTER 8

Matt parked his car in the shadow of the wall that encircled the Trulane estate. The moment he cut the engine, silence fell. He could sense, though she climbed from the car as he did, Laurel's regret over the one thing they'd carefully not talked about. Trespassing, in secret, on what belonged to Louis. He also knew it was something that would continue to remain unsaid. He slipped his flashlight, base first, into his back pocket.

"I'll give you a leg up first."

Nodding, Laurel placed a foot in his cupped hands and reached for the top of the wall. She shinnied up nimbly, then, bracing herself on her stomach, reached a hand down for his. The grip was firm and dry, holding briefly until they lowered themselves on the other side.

"Somehow, I think you've done this sort of thing before," she murmured, dusting her hands on the back of her jeans.

He grinned. "Let's just say I've had to scale a few walls in my career."

"And not all metaphorical," she concluded.

"You'll force me to mention that you went up and over like a veteran yourself."

Laurel took one brief look around, letting her gaze linger

on the shadow of the house in the distance. "I don't suppose you've considered the legal repercussions if we're caught."

It was as close as she'd come, he knew, to speaking of Louis. Matt took her hand, drawing her away from the wall. "Let's not get caught," he said simply.

They moved, as quietly as shadows themselves, over the north lawn. Flashlights weren't needed here. The light of the half-moon was thin, but clear enough to guide the way. The air was still, but far from silent. Night birds rustled in the trees, their whisperings punctuated now and again by the hoot of an owl. Overlaying all was the incessant music of crickets.

Fireflies glimmered with their sporadic gold-toned light. It smelled thickly of summer blossoms and green grass.

Already Laurel could see the gloomy silhouette of the edge of the swamp. The aversion was so ingrained she had to force herself not to hesitate. But her fingers curled tightly around Matt's. His palm was cool and dry against hers.

Doesn't he feel it? she wondered as the chill raced over her skin. Doesn't he feel the *darkness* of the place? It held secrets best left alone—secrets that bred in the soggy grasses. She shuddered as the lawn gave way to it.

"It's a place," Matt said quietly. "It's just a place, Laurel."

"It's evil," she said, so simply he felt a tremor of unease. Then she stepped under the first overhang of trees.

Determination made her force back the fear. Though her fingers remained in his, their grip lightened. "Hard to believe," she began in an easier voice, "even driven by love—or lust—that one of the Trulane women would have picked this place to cheat on her husband. I think her name was Druscilla."

Matt gave a choked laugh as he pulled out his light. "Maybe Druscilla had a thing for humidity and mosquitoes. Now . . ." He didn't switch the light on, but looked behind him where the outline of the house could just be glimpsed through the trees. "I'd say this is about the most direct spot where someone would enter the swamp if they were coming from the house."

Laurel followed his gaze. "Agreed."

"Then it follows that Anne would most likely have come in somewhere around this point."

"It follows."

"Okay, let's go see what we can find. Stick close."

"An unnecessary warning, Matthew," Laurel said loftily as she unpocketed her flashlight. "If you feel something crawling up your back, it's just me."

They hadn't gone more than three yards when the thick, fat leaves dimmed the moonlight. The shadow of the house was lost behind the tangled hedge of other shadows. Already the wild cane sprang up to block what was within, and what was outside, the swamp. The twin beams of their flashlights cut a path through the dark.

It was a world of clinging dampness, of shadows and whispering sounds that made the flesh creep. Even the smell was damp, with the ripe odor of rotting vegetation. Matt began to understand why Anne Trulane might have been terrorized in there. He wouldn't care to lose his way, alone, in the dark. But he wondered why she'd only gone deeper rather than turning back. Blind panic? He scowled at the crude, overgrown path. Maybe.

She should've gotten the hell out.

"Doesn't make sense," he muttered.

Laurel shone her light off the path where something rustled. Her fingers closed over Matt's wrist and let the light, steady pulsebeat soothe her. "What doesn't?"

"Why didn't she get out?"

Carefully, Laurel turned her light back to the path. It was

probably only a possum, not every sound meant snakes. She remembered, uncomfortably, that black bears had often been seen in the northern, forested part of the swamp. "Whatever theory we go by, Matthew, Anne was frightened in here. She panicked, lost her sense of perspective."

"Are you frightened?" He glanced down to where her fingers dug into his wrist.

"No." Sending him a rueful smile, Laurel loosened her hold. "No, I'm way past fear, closing in on terror."

"Could you get out of here?"

"Well, I—" She broke off, seizing his hand again. There was a time and place for dignity—and this wasn't it. "You're not leaving me in here, Bates."

"What would you do if I did?"

"I'd murder you the minute I got out."

Grinning, he took her arm as they began to walk again. "How?"

"Poison, I imagine, it's the slowest, most painful way."

"No, how would you get out?"

"I'd—" She swallowed on the notion of having to find her way out alone, then turned around. Shadows, rustling, and the cloying smell of wet earth and rotted grass were all around. There was quicksand, she knew, to the east and to the southwest. "I'd head that way in a dead run," she said, pointing, "hang a right at that stump and keep on going."

"And you'd be out in five minutes," he murmured. He turned his face back to hers. The moonlight caught in his eyes, glinting. "Why did she keep going deeper?"

If she tried to think like Anne, Laurel realized, she'd end up losing what courage she had and bolting. Dragging a hand through her hair, she tried to think coolly instead. "She'd been bitten—maybe she was sick, delirious."

"How fast does the poison work, I wonder." He shrugged,

making a note to check on it if it became necessary. "It seems she'd've had time to get out, or at least get closer to the edge."

"They found her by the river, didn't they?"

"Yeah." He looked down at her again. "Dead center. When we were searching the place, we'd come across her tracks now and again where the ground was wet enough to hold them. There didn't seem to be any pattern."

Blind panic, he thought again. Yet she hadn't been as frozen as Laurel had been that afternoon. She'd been running, in what had appeared to be a random flight, deeper into what she feared most . . . or running away from something she found more terrifying.

Laurel jolted as the bushes beside them rustled. Matt aimed his light and sent a raccoon scurrying back into the shadows.

"I hate making an ass of myself," she mumbled as her heart slipped back out of her throat. "Let's go on." Annoyed at the blow to her pride, she started ahead of him.

They moved in silence, going deeper. Laurel kept her flashlight trained on the uneven ground to guide their way while Matt shone his from side to side, searching for something neither of them could have named. But they'd both followed hunches before.

"Don't laugh," Laurel ordered, coming to an abrupt halt.

"Okay," he said amiably.

She hesitated, gnawing at her lip. "I mean it, Bates, don't laugh."

"Cross my heart?" he ventured.

"I feel like—something's watching."

"Another raccoon?"

"Matthew—"

"Relax." He cupped the base of her neck in his hand and rubbed, deliberately treating it lightly because he'd felt that trickle between his shoulder blades, as well. Ghost stories, he told himself. He was letting Laurel's feelings about the place get to him.

If he'd believed such things he'd have said there was something evil in the twisting shadows, something that would shrink from the sunlight. But he didn't believe in such things. Evil, when it came, came from the human element.

"Too many people have died here," she said, and shuddered.

He touched her neck again, and his hand, his voice were gentle. "Do you want to go back?"

Oh, God, yes, she thought, but squared her shoulders. "No, let's go on. You can smell the river now."

As they came near the banks, she could smell the wet leaves, vegetation, but the river made no sound as it flowed slowly. Cypress trees made lumpy shadows. A few slivers of moonlight worked through the overhanging trees and fell palely on the water, but only made it seem darker. A frog plopped into the river as they approached.

There were alligators in there, Laurel thought, wrinkling her nose. Big ones.

"It was here." Matt shone his light on the ground. "Laurel, could you still get out of this place if you had to?"

As she followed the play of his light, she was remembering the picture from the police file. Clamping down on her lip, she forced the image from her mind. "Yes, the way we came's the easiest, I imagine, but almost any direction from here would get you out eventually."

"Yeah." He moved around, playing his light on the ground. "Strange that she picked the core of the swamp to give up." He swore in frustration. Nothing here, he thought, nothing here. What the hell had he expected to find? "I'd like to get my hands on those letters."

"Whoever took them would've destroyed them by now if there was anything in them to work with."

"I wonder if Susan—" He broke off as the beam of his light picked up a glimmer. Bending, Matt worked a small piece of metal from the ground.

"What is it?"

"Looks like a broken piece of jewelry. Seen better days." Rising, he turned it over in his hands. "Anne's?"

Laurel took it from him, wiping away some of the caked-on dirt. "I don't know, a month in this place . . ." She shone her light on it as some nagging memory teased the back of her mind. "It looks like the front of a locket—expensive, look how intricate the carving is." The memory lunged toward the front of her mind, then retreated. Laurel shook her head in exasperation. "It's familiar," she murmured. "Maybe it was Aunt Ellen's—Louis could've given it to Anne after they were married."

"We might be able to check it out, for what it's worth." Taking it from her, he slipped it into his pocket. Frustrated, he shone his light to the right and down the bank of the river. "Stay here a minute, I want to get a closer look down there."

"For what?"

"If I knew, I wouldn't feel like I was chasing wild geese."

"I'll go with you."

"Laurel, it's a bog down there. You've been lucky avoiding snakes this far. Don't press your luck."

She remembered the water moccasins that swam in the river. With a gesture of indifference, she shrugged. "You've got two minutes, Bates. Any longer and I'm coming after you."

"Two minutes." He kissed her lightly. "Stay here."

"I'm not moving."

She watched the beam of his light as he walked away, then made his slippery way down the bank. He didn't know what he was looking for, but she understood his need to do something. All they'd found so far were more questions, and a broken piece of jewelry.

She frowned again, thinking of it. A childhood memory? she wondered, pushing the hair away from her face. Had she seen that locket when it had been bright and clean—against a white dress? Laurel pressed her fingers to her temple as she tried to bring the image into focus. One of Aunt Ellen's lacy party dresses? Frustrated, she dropped her hand.

Another minute, Bates, she told him silently. Why was it the small night noises seemed to grow louder now that he wasn't standing beside her? She shifted uncomfortably as a bead of sweat trickled down her back, leaving a chill in its wake.

It's just this place, she told herself, refusing the urge to look over her shoulder. In an hour we'll be back home and I'll be able to laugh at how I stood here shivering in the heat and imagining goblins at my back. In an hour . . .

The soft rustle at her back had her stiffening. Damn raccoons, Laurel thought on a wave of self-disgust. She opened her mouth to call for Matt when an arm locked around her throat.

Shock registered first, seconds before her body reacted to it, or the abrupt lack of air. In an instinctive move of self-preservation, Laurel jabbed back with her elbow, only to meet empty space as she was shoved away. Her flashlight spun out of her hand as her body whooshed through wild cane. She landed hard, her head slamming back into the base of a cypress.

At the edge of the river, Matt saw the arch of light, then darkness where he'd left Laurel. He plunged up the bank, cursing the slick grass and shouting her name. When he saw her sprawled, his heart stopped—with the vivid picture of Anne Trulane leaping in his mind's eye. He grabbed her, not gently, and hauled her against him. At her moan, he began to breathe again.

"What the hell're you doing!" he demanded, rolling with the fury fear had given him.

"I'm having a concussion," she managed, and shook her head to clear it—a mistake as the ground tilted under her. "Someone pushed me—came up from behind." She reached gingerly to test the bump at the back of her head, then gripped Matt's shirtfront with sudden strength as he started to rise. "Oh, no, you're not leaving me here again."

Simmering with rage, straining at impotence, he settled beside her again. "All right, just sit a minute." He ran his fingers through her hair to lift her face to his. "Are you hurt?"

She saw the anger, the concern, the frustration in his eyes. "Not really." She smiled—her head was throbbing, but that was all. "Just a bump. It didn't knock me out; I just saw stars—not unlike the ones I saw the first time you kissed me."

That helped, she thought, feeling the grip of his fingers on her arm relax slightly. But that brooding look was still in his eyes as he searched her face.

"I shouldn't have left you alone."

"Matthew, if you're going to start being macho and guilty, I'll get cranky." Leaning forward, she kissed him. "Let's see if I can stand up."

With his hands cupping her armpits, he pulled her gently to her feet. No dizziness, she thought, waiting a moment. The throbbing was subsiding to an ache.

"It's okay, really," she said when he continued to study her face. "I've had worse bumps."

You won't have any more while I'm around, he swore to himself viciously, but smiled. "I won't make any remarks about hard heads. Now, what did you see—besides stars?"

"Nothing." She let out a frustrated breath. "I was so busy

telling myself I wasn't going to be a fool that I wouldn't look around when I heard something rustling in the bushes. The next thing I knew someone had an arm around my throat. I hadn't even started defensive move 21-A when they pushed me into that tree. By the time the stars stopped exploding, you were here and they were gone."

Whatever grim thoughts of revenge worked in his mind, his touch was gentle as he felt the back of her head. "You'll have a bump," he said easily as he forced his jaw to unclench, "but the skin's not broken."

"There's good news."

Tilting her head back to his, he gave her one long, hard kiss. His hands were steady again, but his temper wasn't. "Sure you can walk?"

"If you mean as in out of here, absolutely. I lost my flashlight."

"Buy a new one," he advised as he picked up his own. "It went in the river."

"Oh, that's just great. I only bought it a month ago." She scowled over this as they started back the way they'd come. "Well, I guess we found something after all," she murmured.

"Yeah. Someone who knows what we're up to doesn't like it one damn bit. Lovelorn ghosts don't shove people into trees, do they, Laurel?"

"No." And she was thinking, as he was, that the house was close. The people in it knew the swamp.

They walked back in silence, each of them more cautious than before, listening to every sound, second-guessing the shadows. Matt kept Laurel at his side, his hand on hers until they walked into the clear. There wasn't the faintest glimmer of light from the house in the distance.

The lingering distaste for where they'd been clung to him even after they'd dropped on the other side of the wall. He wanted a shower—a long one.

Laurel didn't speak again until Heritage Oak was miles behind them.

"We'll have to talk to Louis and Marion again."

"I know." Matt punched in the car lighter. Maybe if he filled his lungs with smoke he'd stop tasting the air of the swamp. "Tomorrow."

Leaning back, Laurel closed her eyes. And tomorrow was soon enough to think about it. "I don't know about you, but I'm starving."

He turned his head to look at her. She was still a bit pale—but even that could've been the moonlight. Her voice was steady, her breathing calm. He hadn't sensed fear in her, not even when she'd been half-dazed and sprawled on the ground. Frustration, yes, annoyance with herself for being caught unaware. But no fear.

With her head back and the shadows dancing over her face, she reminded him forcibly of Olivia. Unique, indomitable, fascinating. Laughing, Matt grabbed her hand and pressed it to his lips.

"We'll order a pizza and take it back home."

Though she hadn't a clue what had lightened his mood so abruptly, Laurel went with it. "With everything," she demanded.

It was after two when Laurel pushed away from Matt's smoked-glass table, stuffed. She couldn't say his apartment wasn't what she'd expected because she'd had no idea just what to expect. She did know it showed an easy mode of living—deep, plump cushions, thick carpet, soothing colors all mixed together with a flair for style and a penchant for comfort.

There were neither framed newspapers on his walls nor Picassos, but a set of oils done by an artist she didn't recognize. Both were of New York, one a cityscape showing its elegance and glitz, the other a street scene with crumbling buildings and cracked sidewalks. Both were excellent in their way, and the contrasts intrigued her. She supposed, in his career there, he'd have seen both sides.

"I've reached my limit," she said when Matt started to slide another piece onto her plate.

"Big talk about eating it, box and all." Matt bit into the slice he'd offered her.

Picking up her wineglass, Laurel rose to wander the room. Her feet sank into the carpet. "I like your place. You like—" she wiggled her bare toes "—to be comfortable."

"Most people do." He watched as she wandered to his stereo to sort through his album collection.

"Mmmm. But not everyone makes an art out of it." Laurel set a record aside to study the paintings more closely. "These are very good," she commented. "I don't recognize the artist, but I have a feeling I'll be seeing his work again."

"He'd be glad to hear it." Matt picked up his own glass, studying her over the rim. The wine was heavy and sweet. "We grew up in the same neighborhood."

"Really?" Laurel tilted her head, even more interested. "Do you miss it? New York?"

Matt's gaze flicked up to the painting, then back to the wine in his glass. "No."

"But you carry it with you."

"We all carry our baggage around," he murmured, then got up to stick what remained of the pizza in the refrigerator.

Laurel frowned after him. What brought that on? she wondered, then looked back at the paintings. The same neighborhood, she mused, seeing the soiled streets and tired buildings. When he came out of the kitchen, she was still facing them. "You grew up here."

He didn't have to see which painting she was looking at

to know what she meant. "Yeah." He pulled his shirt over his head as he walked. "I need a shower."

"Matthew." Laurel went after him, catching his arm outside the bathroom door. She recognized impatience and ignored it. "It was hard, wasn't it?"

"I survived," he said indifferently. "Not everyone does."

Her sympathy was automatic and reflected in her eyes, the touch of her hand on his arm, her voice. "Tell me about it."

"Just leave it."

She stared at him, the hurt unexpected and brutally sharp. Her step back was a retreat from it before she straightened her shoulders. "All right, I'm sorry. Thanks for the pizza, Bates. I'll see you in the morning."

He took her arm to stop her. "Laurel, you know you can't stay in your place until the door's fixed."

She met his eyes calmly. "Not all of us need locks and bolts, Matthew."

"Damn it—" He broke off, making a savage effort to keep his temper. He knew he was wound up, still tense from what had happened to her in the swamp, still dazed by what had happened between them in her bed. Emotions were crowding him, and he wasn't dealing with them well. "Listen, I grew up in a tough little neighborhood on the East Side. It has nothing to do with you. Nothing."

A dash of salt for the wound, Laurel thought as she stared up at him. "That's clear enough," she said evenly. "Let's just call it professional curiosity and leave it at that."

"Damn it, Laurel." He grabbed her by the shoulders when she started to leave again. "You're not staying in that place alone tonight."

"Don't you tell me what I'm going to do."

"I *am* telling you," he tossed back. "And for once you're going to *do* what you're told."

She gave him a cold, neutral look. "Take your hands off me."

He started to get angry, but even through his own anger he could see beneath hers to the hurt. On a sigh, he dropped his forehead to hers. "I'm sorry."

"You don't owe me an apology," she said carefully.

"I do." When he lifted his head, his eyes were dark and thoughtful. "I hurt you, I didn't mean to."

"No, it's all right." Without fuel, her temper vanished, leaving only a faint echo of the hurt. "I was prying."

"No, I—" Matt hesitated, then let it go. He wasn't ready to drag it all out and look at it again, not with Laurel. "I don't want to argue with you, Laurel. Look, it's late, we've both had enough to deal with today. I can't dig back there tonight."

Her arms went around him. Even if the anger had still lashed at her, she couldn't have stopped them. "No more questions tonight."

"Laurel . . ." He covered her offered mouth with his. The tension began to drain, degree by degree, as he filled himself with her. "Stay here," he murmured. "Stay with me."

With a sigh, content, accepting, she rested her head on his shoulder. "Do I get shower privileges?"

She heard his low laugh as he nuzzled at her throat. "Sure. But we have to double up. You've heard about the water shortage."

"No, not a word."

"Really?" He tugged her into the bathroom. "It's at a crisis stage. Let me tell you about it."

She was laughing as he drew her shirt over her head.

When she got out of the shower, Laurel was flushed and tingling. Clutching a towel at her breasts, she looked up at Matt. "I'm so impressed." When his grin tilted, she went on blandly, "With the fact that you're such a conservationist."

"Conservation is my life." He tugged the towel from her, smiling easily when she gasped. "Gotta cut back on the laundry, too. You know how many gallons of water a washing machine uses?" His eyes swept down her, then up again. "Better get you into bed, you'll catch a chill."

Regally, she walked away, leaving Matt to admire the view. "I suppose turning on a light would go against your values."

"Civic duty," he corrected, then surprised her by grabbing her around the waist and tumbling onto the bed with her.

Winded, she glared up at him. "Now listen, Bates—"

He silenced her quickly, completely and effectively. He'd meant to tease her, continue the half torturous, half pleasurable game they'd begun under the cool spray of the shower. But her legs were tangled with his, her body yielding, and her mouth . . .

"Oh, God, Laurel, I need you." His mouth crushed back on hers with a savagery the night seemed to have worked on him.

He forgot patience, and she, the need for it. He forgot gentleness, and she, the need for it. His tongue dived deep into her mouth as if there were some taste, some hint of flavor he might be denied. But she would have denied him nothing. Her passion raced from tingling arousal to raging desire, and her mouth was as greedy, as insistent, as his. She was not to be seduced this time, or to be swept helplessly along, but to take as much as she gave.

She hadn't known passion could strip every remnant of civilization away, but she learned. Glorying in the abandon, she touched and tasted where she would with hands and lips that moved quickly, with no more patience than his. He smelled of the soap she'd lathered on him herself. The sharp, clean scent played with her senses, swam in her head while her needs delved in darker places.

They were only shadows in the bed, tangling, clinging,

but their passion had substance and form. Perhaps the whispering threats of the past hours drove them both to take, and take hungrily, all that could be found between man and woman. Damp skin, thundering pulses, breathless moans. For both of them it was the moment, the heady present, that mattered. Yesterday and tomorrow were forgotten.

He knew he was rough, but control had vanished. Heat seemed to pour out of her, drawing him deeper and deeper into his own furious passion. Her body was as it had been when he'd first taken her hours—oh, God, had it only been hours?—before. Sleek and smooth and agile. But the change came from within. There was no pliancy in her now, but an urgency and demand that raced with his.

His lips rushed over her, running low on her stomach with hungry kisses. But his need to taste wasn't any stronger than her need to experience. She wanted all there was to have this time, everything he'd already given her and whatever secrets were left. She wanted to learn whatever desire had left to teach.

She opened for both of them, eager, urging him down until he found her. She arched, stunned and only more desperate at the play of his tongue. He whipped her up and over the first crest, never pausing, relentless, as she shuddered with her nails digging into his shoulders.

Wave after wave of heavy, molten pleasure swept her, but he continued as if he would keep her, keep them both, spinning on the very verge of fulfillment. There couldn't be so much. But even as the thought raced through her mind there was more. And still more. She should have been sated from it, but she pulsed with energy. She should have been overwhelmed, but it was as if, somehow, she'd always known it would be like this. His heart raced with hers, beat matching beat. Passion poured out of her, but as it poured it was replenished.

"Matthew." His name was a moan, a gasp. "I want you."

As his mouth hurried back, skimming over her, she felt his tremors and the hammer-thrust beat of his heart. Each rasping breath seemed to merge with her. She saw his eyes glimmer once in the pale light of the moon, then tasted the mixture of soap and salt on his flesh.

"I need you. . . ." They spoke together. She arched to meet him.

CHAPTER 9

The sky hung low. Thick pewter clouds trapped the heat and humidity so that rain wouldn't have been a threat, but a blessed relief. The leaves didn't stir, or turn their pale undersides up in anticipation, but hung limply.

Laurel leaned back and let the sticky air coming through the car window do what it could. Along the sides of the road the trees stood, casting shade that could offer only slight relief to the throbbing heat. Glancing at them, she wished she were sitting under one, near a cool river on soft, damp grass.

She was traveling the road to Heritage Oak for the third time in two days. Each time, it was just a bit more difficult to face the kind of answers she might find there.

Louis would be angry, she had no doubt of it. The man she'd seen yesterday would be furious at being disturbed again—if he spoke to them at all. And Marion . . . Marion would be hurt, Laurel thought with a flash of guilt. Hurt that she persisted in pursuing something Marion found distasteful and distressing to both herself and her brother.

I won't think about it, Laurel told herself, and turned her head to stare, brooding, out the window. What choice do I have? Questions have to be asked, things have to be said. It's gone too far to turn back now. If anything, it should be easier to have the questions come from me. But it wasn't, she thought miserably. Not for any of us.

She knew why Matt was silent. He was giving her time to pull herself together, sort out her emotions for herself before they arrived at Heritage Oak. Considerate. Strange, she thought with a small smile, a week before she'd have sworn Matthew Bates hadn't a considerate bone in his body. She'd learned quite a bit about him in the last few days. Not quite all, Laurel mused, thinking of the paintings in his apartment. But still, a great many important things—the most important of which was that she loved him.

They'd yet to speak seriously about what had happened between them. In an odd way, she felt they'd both been reluctant to probe the other's emotions. Treat it light—don't press. Those were the words that ran around in her head. She wondered if they ran in his as well.

It had all happened so fast. A year? That's fast? she thought with a faint smile. But it had. Whatever had been building between them over the months had been so cleverly ignored that the sudden blaze of passion had been totally unexpected. And that much more exciting. But was that all it was for him? Laurel wished she had the confidence, or the courage, to ask.

Turning back, she studied his profile. Strong, casually handsome, with an easygoing smile and amused eyes. Yet he wasn't quite all those things. From his writing she'd already known him to be savvy, ironic, insightful. She'd also discovered that he was only laid-back when he chose to be. That wasn't his true nature. He was an impatient, restless man who simply played the game his own way. Over and above the love that had crept up on her, Laurel had discovered to her own amusement, that quite simply she liked his style.

Partners, she thought as her smile widened. You'd better

get used to it, Bates, because we're going to stay that way for a long, long time.

"See something you like?" he asked dryly.

Laurel tilted her head and continued to study him. *Play it light.* The words ran through her mind yet again. "As a matter of fact, I do—and it still surprises me."

He chuckled, and with his eyes on the road reached over and tugged on her hair. "I'm crazy about your compliments, Laurellie. A man never knows if he's been pumped up or slapped down."

"Keeps you on your toes, Bates."

"You did tell me once I had fabulous eyes."

Her brow lifted. "I did?"

"Well, you'd had four martinis at the time."

She laughed as he swung between the pillars of Heritage Oak. "Oh, well, who knows what a person might say in that condition? What color are they, anyway?"

He narrowed them as he turned toward her.

"Blue," she said, catching her tongue between her teeth. "Blond hair, blue eyes—rather an ordinary combination, but you do the best you can with it."

"Yeah. And it is a pity about your chin."

Laurel lifted it automatically. "My chin," she said as he stopped the car, "is not pointed."

"I hardly notice it." Matt jingled the keys in his hand as he stepped from the car. He'd lightened her mood, he noticed, but only temporarily. Already, as she glanced up at the house, he could see the struggle between her emotions and her profession. Laurel being Laurel, the profession won, but not without cost.

"Matthew, Marion will see us because her upbringing wouldn't allow her not to, but . . ." She hesitated as they climbed the porch. "I doubt if Louis will talk to us."

"We'll have to convince him otherwise," he said flatly, and let the knocker fall heavily on the door.

"I don't want to push him too hard right now. If—"

It was the way his head whipped around, the way his eyes flared, that stopped her. "When?" he demanded.

She opened her mouth, but the annoyance and impatience on his face had her biting back the first reckless words. "All right," she murmured, turning to face the door again. "All right."

Guilt. He felt the sting and wasn't quite sure what to do about it. "Laurel—"

The door opened, cutting off whatever he might have said. Binney glanced at both of them while a flicker of surprise—and something else—came and went in her eyes. "Miss Laurel, we didn't expect to see you again so soon."

"Hello, Binney. I hope it's not inconvenient, but we'd like to speak to Louis and Marion."

Her eyes darted to Matt, then came back to Laurel. "Mr. Louis has a black mood. It's not a good time."

"Black mood?" Laurel repeated. "Is he ill?"

"No." She shook her head, but hesitated as if the denial had come too quickly. "He is . . ." Binney stopped as if searching for a phrase. "Not well," she finished, lacing her long, bony fingers together.

"I'm sorry." Laurel gave her an easy smile and hated herself. "We won't keep him long. It's important Binney." Without invitation, she stepped into the hall.

"Very well." Laurel caught the quick, accusing glance before the housekeeper shut the door. "Come into the parlor, I'll tell Miss Marion you're here."

"Thank you, Binney." Laurel caught her hand at the entrance to the parlor. "Is Louis often . . . not well?"

"It comes and goes."

She closed her other hand over the thin, hard one as if

willing Binney to understand. "Did he have these black moods when Anne was—when he was married to Anne?"

Binney's lips compressed until there was nothing but a tight line. In the way of a woman well used to the house she lived in, and the people she lived with, Binney let her gaze sweep down the hall and up the stairs in a gesture so quick it was hardly noticeable. When she spoke, her words were hurried, low and French.

"You knew him, Miss Laurel, but there have been so many changes, so much pain. Nothing is as it was when you came for your tea parties and riding lessons."

"I understand that, Binney. I'd like to help him."

Binney's gaze swept the hall again. "Before," she began, "during the time between when Mr. Charles left and when Mr. Louis brought the girl home, he had many . . . hard moods. He might roam the house and speak to no one, or lock himself in his study for hours. We worried but . . ." Her shrug was eloquent. "Later, he began to go away on business and it would be better. The years, they weren't easy, but they were . . . quiet. Then he brought the girl back, his wife."

"And things changed again?" Laurel prompted.

"Only better." The housekeeper hesitated. Laurel thought she understood perfectly the tug-of-war her loyalties were waging. "We were surprised. She had the look of the first one," Binney said so quietly Laurel strained to hear. "It was strange to see her, even her voice. . . . But Mr. Louis was happy with her, young again. Sometimes, only sometimes, he would brood and lock himself away."

Ignoring the knot in her stomach, Laurel pressed on. "Binney, was Anne afraid when Louis would . . . brood?"

Her mouth became prim again. "Perhaps she was puzzled."

"Was she happy here?"

The nut-brown eyes clouded. Her mouth worked before her

face became still again. "She said the house was like a fairy tale."

"And the swamp?"

"She feared it. She should have stayed away. What's there," she said in a low voice, "is best left alone."

"What's there?" Laurel repeated.

"Spirits," Binney said, so simply Laurel shivered. There was no arguing with old beliefs, old legends. She let it pass.

"Did Anne see Nathan Brewster often?"

"She was a loyal wife." Her tone changed subtly, but enough that Laurel knew the automatic defense of the estate and all in it had been thrown up. Laurel took what she knew might be the final step.

"Did Louis know that Brewster was in love with Anne?"

"It is not my place to say," Binney replied stiffly and with disapproval. *Or yours to ask.* Laurel heard the unspoken words very clearly. "I'll tell Miss Marion you're here." Coolly, she turned her back on them both and walked away.

"Damn," Laurel breathed. "I've lost her, too."

"Sit down," Matt ordered, steering her to a chair. "And tell me what that was all about."

Sitting, Laurel began to speak in the flat tone of recital. "She told me that Louis was prone to black moods and brooding after Charles and Elise left. Understandable enough," she added automatically—too automatically for Matt's liking. "The servants worried about him. Then he apparently pulled out of it a bit when he began to travel on business. They weren't expecting him to bring Anne back and obviously her resemblance to Elise caused some talk, but Binney seemed fond of her. She said Louis was happy, less moody, that Anne was happy, too."

She sighed, leaning back in the chair, but her fingers drummed on the arms. "She holds to the local feeling about the swamp."

"Ghosts again?"

"Don't be so literal-minded," Laurel snapped. "It's the . . . essence of the place," she finished lamely.

As Laurel had with the housekeeper, Matt let it pass. "Didn't I hear Brewster's name mentioned?"

"She'd only say that Anne was a loyal wife. I tried to press." She lifted her eyes to his. "That's when I lost her."

"Forget your feelings for a minute and use your head." He spoke sharply because he'd rather face her annoyance than her vulnerability. "If the housekeeper knew about Brewster—and from the way she clammed up she must have—who else knew?"

"You don't hide things from servants, Matthew. They'd all know."

"Yet not one of them mentioned his name when they were questioned by the police."

Laurel linked her hands in her lap to stop her fingers from drumming. "To have mentioned it would've cast a shadow on Anne's reputation and therefore Louis's. Remember, too, the investigation led to nothing more than a verdict of accidental death. It would've seemed pointless to stir all that up then."

"And now?"

"The servants are loyal to Louis," she said wearily. "They're not going to gossip to outsiders about something that would bring him more pain."

"I have connections downtown," Matt mused. "I could probably get someone out here to ask a few questions."

"Not yet, Matthew, a few more days." Laurel caught Matt's hand in hers as he stood next to her chair. "I don't want to push the police on Louis until there's no other choice. We don't have enough to justify reopening the investigation in any case. You know it."

"Maybe, maybe not." He frowned down at her and bit back a sigh. "A few days, Laurel. That's all."

"Laurel, Mr. Bates." Marion came in with her hands already extended for Laurel's. "Please, sit down, Mr. Bates. I'm sorry I've kept you waiting, but we weren't expecting you."

Laurel caught the faint disapproval and acknowledged it. "I'm sorry, Marion, I hope we didn't catch you at a bad time."

"Well, I'm a bit pressed, but . . ." She squeezed Laurel's hands before choosing the brocade love seat across from her. "Would you like some coffee? A cold drink, perhaps. It's such a dismal day."

"No, thank you, Marion, and we won't keep you long." Party talk, she thought in disgust. How easy it is to cover ugliness with party talk. "It's important that we speak to you and Louis again."

"Oh." Marion's gaze swept from Laurel to Matt and back again. "Louis is out, I'm afraid."

"Will he be back?" Matt asked her, without accepting her invitation to sit.

"I can't say. That is, I can't say when. I'm sorry." Her expression altered subtly, brow creasing as if she were forced to say something unpleasant. "The truth is, Laurel, I'm not sure he'll agree to talk to you again."

That hurt, but she'd expected it. Laurel kept her eyes level. "Marion, Matthew and I went to see Nathan Brewster yesterday."

They both saw, and registered, each flicker of expression on Marion's face. Distress, agitation, annoyance, doubt; all came quickly and were as quickly gone. "Did you? Why?"

"He was in love with Anne," Laurel returned. "And apparently made little secret of it."

Marion's eyes cooled, the only hint of annoyance now. "Laurel, Anne was a lovely child. Any man might be attracted to her."

"I didn't say he was attracted," Laurel corrected. "I said

he was in love with her, in his way. He wanted her to leave Louis."

Laurel saw Marion's throat work before she spoke. The thin gold chain she wore around it glittered with the movement. "What Mr. Brewster may have wanted doesn't mean anything. Anne loved Louis."

"You knew about this." Laurel watched Marion's eyes, pale gray like her brother's.

For a moment Marion said nothing, then the only sound she made was a sigh. "Yes," she said at length. "I knew. It would've been impossible not to see by the way the man looked at her. Anne was confused." Her hands lifted, linked, then fell. "She confided in me because she just didn't know how to deal with it. Anne would never have left Louis," she murmured as her fingers unlinked to knead the material of her skirt. As the nervous gesture continued, her eyes remained level and nearly calm, as if her hands were controlled by something else entirely. "She loved him."

"Did Louis know?"

"There was nothing for him to know," Marion said sharply, then struggled to regain her composure. "Anne only spoke to me because the man upset her. She told her sister that he made her nervous. Anne *loved* Louis," Marion repeated. "What difference does it make now?" She looked at both of them with suddenly tormented eyes, her fingers clutching the filmy material of her skirt. "The poor child's dead, and rumors, nasty rumors like this, will only make it more difficult on Louis. Laurel, can't you stop this? You must know what this continued pressure does to Louis."

"If things were just that simple," Matt began, breaking in before Laurel could speak. "Why do you suppose someone sent Laurel a warning?"

"Warning." Marion shook her head as her nervous fingers finally stilled. "What warning?"

"Someone left a box on my doorstep," Laurel said with studied, surface calm. "There was a dead copperhead inside."

"Oh, my God! Oh, Laurel." She stretched her hands out to grip Laurel's. They trembled ever so slightly. "Why would anyone have done something so nasty? When? When did this happen?"

"Late yesterday afternoon. A few hours after we'd left Heritage Oak."

"Oh, my dear, you must have . . . Anne was bitten by a copperhead," she murmured, as if she'd just remembered. "You think—Laurel, you don't believe that Louis would do such a thing to you. You can't!"

"I can't—I don't want to believe it of Louis," Laurel corrected. "We thought it best if both of you knew about it."

With a steadying breath, Marion released Laurel's hands. "It must have been dreadful for you. My own nerves—Louis's . . ." She broke off with a shake of her head. "Of course I'll tell him, you know I will, but—"

"Miss Marion?"

Distracted, Marion looked over her shoulder to the doorway. "Yes, Binney."

"Excuse me, but Mrs. Hollister's on the phone, about the hospital charity drive. She's insistent."

"Yes, yes, all right, tell her I'll just be a moment." She turned back, playing with the collar of her dress. "I'm sorry, Laurel, about everything. If you'd like to wait here, I'll take care of this and come back. But I don't know what else I can say."

"It's all right, Marion, go ahead. We'll just let ourselves out."

"Once you put your teeth into it," Matt commented when he was alone with Laurel, "you chomp down nicely."

"Yes, didn't I?" Without looking at him, she picked up her bag and rose. "Professional hazard, I suppose."

"Laurel." Matt took her shoulders until she looked up at him. "Stop doing this to yourself."

"I would if I could," she murmured, then turned away to stare out the window. "I didn't like the way Marion came apart when I mentioned Brewster."

"She knows more than she's saying." He touched her hair, and would have drawn her back against him.

"Louis is outside," Laurel said quietly. "I want to talk to him alone, Matthew."

He took a step back, surprised that such an ordinary request would hurt so much. "All right." When she walked out the French doors, he stuffed his hands in his pockets and moved closer to the window. Without the least compunction, he wished Louis Trulane to hell.

The heat outdoors was only more stifling after the coolness of the parlor. The air tasted of rain, but the rain wouldn't come. What birds bothered to sing, sang gloomily. She smelled the roses as she passed them, and the scent was hot and overripe. As she came closer to him, Laurel could see the damp patches on Louis's shirt.

"Louis."

His head jerked up when she called him, and he stopped. There wasn't any welcome in his face or in his stance, nor was there the cool indifference she'd seen the day before. He was furious. "What're you doing here?"

"I have to talk to you."

"There's nothing to say."

"Louis." She took his arm when he started to go on without her. Though he stopped again, he spun back to her with a look that made her drop the hand.

"Leave us both with a few decent memories, Laurel, and stay away from me."

"I still have the memories, Louis, but I have a job to do." She searched his face, wishing there was something she could do, something she could say, to prevent what she knew could be the final breach between them. "I don't believe Anne went into that swamp freely."

"I don't give a damn what you believe. She's dead." He looked over her head, out to the edge of the north lawn, where the marsh took over. "Anne's dead," he said again, shutting his eyes. "That's the end of it."

"Is it?" she countered, hardening herself. "If there's the slightest possibility that someone lured or frightened her into that place, don't you want to know?"

He broke off a thin branch of crape myrtle. Laurel was reminded forcibly of Brewster's hands on a pencil. "What you're saying's absurd. No one did—no one would have a reason to."

"No?" She heard the quiet snap of wood between his fingers. "Someone doesn't appreciate our probing into it."

"*I* don't appreciate your probing into it," Louis exploded, tossing down the mangled wood and blossoms. "Does it follow that I murdered my wife?" He spun away from her to stare at the edge of the north lawn. "For God's sake, Laurel. Why do you interfere in this? It's over. Nothing can bring her back."

"Does my interference bother you enough that you'd leave a dead snake on my doorstep?"

"What?" He shook his head as if to clear it. "What did you say?"

"Someone sent me a dead copperhead, all done up nicely in a box."

"A copperhead—the same as . . ." His words trailed off as he slowly turned back to her. "A nasty joke," he said, tossing the hair back from his face in a gesture she remembered. "I'm afraid I haven't been up to jokes of any kind lately, though I hardly see . . ." He broke off again, staring down at her. His expression altered into something she couldn't quite read. "I remember. Poor little Laurel, you were always terrified of them. I nearly strangled that cousin of mine the day he stuck a garter snake under your nose at one of Marion's garden parties. What were you? Nine, ten? Do you remember?"

"I remember."

His face softened, just a little. "Have you outgrown it?"

She swallowed. "No."

"I'm sorry." He touched her face in the first gesture of friendship. She found it hurt more than his angry words. "You never liked the swamp because of them."

"I never liked the swamp, Louis."

"Anne hated it." His eyes drifted back. "I used to try to tease her out of it—just as I used to tease you. Oh, God, she was sweet."

"You never let me meet her," Laurel murmured. "Why didn't you let anyone meet her?"

"She looked like Elise." His hand was still on her face, but she knew he'd forgotten it. "It stunned me the first time I saw her. But she wasn't like Elise." His eyes hardened, as slate gray as the sky. "People would've said differently just by looking at her. I wouldn't tolerate it—the comparisons, the whispers."

"Did you marry her because she reminded you of Elise?"

The fury came back at that, so sudden and fierce Laurel would've backed away if his hand hadn't tightened. "I married her because I loved her—needed her. I married her because she was young and malleable and would depend on me. She wasn't a woman who'd look elsewhere. I stayed with her through the year we had so that she wouldn't grow bored and discontent, as Elise claimed she had in that damned note."

"Louis, I know how you must feel—"

"Do you?" he interrupted softly, so softly the words hung on the stagnant air. "Do you understand loss, Laurel? Betrayal? No," he said before she could speak. "You have to live it first."

"If there had been someone else." Laurel moistened her lips when she found her mouth was dry. "If there'd been another man, Louis, what would you've done?"

He looked back at her, cool again, icy. "I'd have killed him. One Judas is enough for any man." He turned, walking away from her and the house again. Laurel shivered in the sticky heat.

He'd seen enough. Matt crossed to the French doors and, fighting the urge to go after Louis and vent some of his frustration, went to where Laurel still stood, looking after him.

"Let's go," he said briefly.

She nodded. The mood—hers, Louis's, Matt's—seemed to match the tightness in the air. A storm was brewing in all of them. It wouldn't take much to set it off. In silence, they walked across the neatly trimmed lawn to Matt's car, then drove away from Heritage Oak.

"Well?" Matt touched the car lighter to the tip of a cigarette and waited.

"Binney was right about his mood," Laurel said after a moment. "He's on edge, angry, with nothing to strike out at. He still dismisses Anne's death as an accident. The way he looked out at the swamp . . ." Laurel glanced up at Matt, seeing the hard, set profile that wasn't so very different from the expression Louis had worn. "Matthew, I'd swear he loved her. He might've gotten involved with her because of her resemblance to Elise, even married her with some sort of idea about having a second chance, but Louis loved Anne."

"Do you think he always kept them separated in his mind?"

"I told you before, I'm not a psychiatrist." Her answer was sharp, and she set her teeth. Nothing would be accomplished if she and Matt started sniping at each other again. "I can only give you my own observations," she said more calmly, "and that is that Louis loved Anne, and he's still grieving for her. Part of the grief might be guilt—that he'd teased her about being afraid of the swamp," she told him when he sent her a quick look. "That he didn't take it seriously enough."

"You told him about the box?"

"Yes." Why doesn't it rain? she thought as she pulled her sticky blouse away from her shoulder blades. Maybe the rain would wash everything clean again. "He didn't put it together at first, then when he did, I'd say he was more disgusted than anything else. Then . . . then he remembered I'd always been terrified of snakes. For a couple of minutes, he was just like he used to be. Kind, warm." Swallowing, Laurel looked out the side window while Matt swore, silently, savagely.

"I asked him why he hadn't let Anne meet anyone. He said he didn't want the comparisons to Elise he knew would crop up. He kept close to her because he didn't want her to grow bored and—"

"Look elsewhere," Matt finished.

"All right, yes." Laurel's head whipped back around. "Aren't you forgetting about those glass houses now, Matthew? Haven't you any compassion at all? Any understanding as to what it's been like for him?"

He met her heated look briefly. "You've got enough for both of us."

"Damn you, Matthew," she whispered. "You're so smug, so quick to judge. Isn't it lucky you never lost anyone you loved?"

He hurled his cigarette out the window. "We're talking about Trulane, not me. If you're going to start crusading again, Laurel, do it on your own time. Not when you're my partner. I deal in facts."

She felt the rage bubble up and barely, just barely, suppressed it. Her voice was frigid. "All right, then here's another one for you. Louis said he would've killed any man that Anne was involved with. He said it with a cold-bloodedness I'm sure you'd admire. Yet Nathan Brewster still works for him."

"And here's another one." Matt pulled into a parking space at the *Herald* and turned on her. "You're so hung up on Trulane you've made some kind of Brontë hero out of him. You refuse to see him any other way. He's a ruthless, bitter man capable of cold violence. His first wife chose his younger brother. Haven't you ever asked yourself why?"

She jerked her arm out of his hold. "You know nothing about love and loyalty, Matthew."

"And you do?" he tossed back. "If you'd grow up, you'd see that you don't love Trulane, you're obsessed with him."

She paled, and as the blood drained from her face, her eyes grew darker, colder. "I do love him," she said in a low, vibrating voice. "You haven't the capacity to understand that. You want things black-and-white, Matthew. Fine, you stick with that and leave me the hell alone."

She was out of the car quickly, but he had her by the shoulders before she could dash into the building. "Don't you walk away from me." The anger spilled out, with something very close to panic at the edges. "I've had enough of Louis Trulane. I'll be damned if I'm going to have him breathing down my neck every time I touch you."

Laurel stared up at him, eyes dry. "You're a fool. Maybe you'd better take a good look at the facts again, Matthew. Now leave me alone." When her voice broke, they both swore. "Just stay away from me for a while."

This time when she turned from him, Matt didn't stop her. He waited until she'd disappeared inside the building before he leaned against the hood of his car. With the heat

shimmering in waves around him, he drew out a cigarette and
tried to pull himself together.

What the hell had gotten into him? He'd attacked her. Matt
dragged a hand through his hair. An emotional attack wasn't
any prettier than a physical one. The heat? He shifted his
shoulders beneath his damp, sticky shirt. That might be part
of it, it was enough to set anyone's nerves on edge.

Who was he trying to kid—himself? Matt blew out a long
breath and watched the smoke hang in the thick, still air. The
crux of it was, she'd spent the night with him, giving herself
to him, bringing him all the things he'd needed, wanted . . .
then he'd seen Louis put a hand to her cheek.

Idiot. Laurel couldn't have cursed him more accurately
than he did himself. He'd let jealousy claw at him until he'd
clawed at her. He hadn't been able to stop it. No, he corrected,
he hadn't tried to stop it. It'd been easier to be angry than to
let the fear take over. The fear that he'd had for her since he'd
looked in the box on her table—the fear that he had of her
since he'd discovered he was hopelessly in love with her. He
didn't want to lose her. He wouldn't survive.

Maybe he'd sniped at her hoping she'd back off and let
him take over the investigation. If he'd found a way to prevent her going with him into the swamp, she wouldn't have
been hurt.

Maybe he'd used Louis as an obstacle because he'd been
afraid to risk telling Laurel how he felt about her. He'd
planned things so carefully—he always had. Yet things had
gotten out of hand from the moment he'd started to work with
Laurel on this story. How was he supposed to tell her that
he loved her—perhaps on some level had loved her from
the moment he'd seen that picture propped against Curt's
books? She'd think he was crazy. Matt crushed the cigarette
under his heel. Maybe he was.

But he was still a reporter, and reporters knew how to

follow through, step by step. The first thing was to give Laurel the space she'd demanded. He owed her that. In giving it to her, he could do a little digging on his own. The next thing was to find a way to apologize without bringing Trulane into the picture again.

The last thing, Matt thought as he crossed the parking lot, the last thing was to get it into her thick head that he loved her. Whether she liked the idea or not.

CHAPTER 10

Laurel considered it fortunate that she'd been sent back out on an assignment almost immediately after coming into the city room. She was able to grab a fresh pad, hook up with a photographer and dash out again before Matt was even halfway up on the elevator.

She didn't want to see him, not until the anger and the hurt had faded a bit. The three-car pileup at a main intersection downtown, with all the heat, noise, and confusion it would generate, should distract her from her personal problems. Temporarily.

He was being unreasonable, she told herself with gritted teeth while the photographer cruised through a yellow light and joined a stream of traffic. Unreasonable and unyielding. How could anyone be so utterly lacking in compassion or empathy? How could a man who had shown her such unquestioning support and comfort when she'd been frightened feel nothing for someone who'd been through what Louis Trulane had? Didn't he recognize pain? How could she love someone who . . . That's where she stopped, because no matter how or why, she loved Matt. It was as simple as that.

Because she loved him, his lack of feeling and his words had cut that much deeper. To accuse her of being obsessed by Louis. Oh, that grated. Any rational person would understand that Louis Trulane had been her childhood hero. She'd loved him freely, with a child's heart and in a child's way. In the course of time, the love had changed, not because Louis had changed but because she had.

She still loved Louis, perhaps not quite objectively. She loved Louis the way a woman loves the memory of the first boy who kissed her, the first boy who brought her a bouquet. It was soft and safe and passionless, but it was so very sweet. Matt was asking her to turn her back on that memory. Or to dim it, darken it with suspicion.

To a woman like Laurel, the memory of a young man who'd treated a child and her infatuation gently should have no shadows. But Matt was using it to swipe at her for something she couldn't understand. He'd even implied that she might be thinking of Louis when they were together. How could he possibly believe . . .

Here, her thoughts broke off again as a new idea crept in. A fascinating one. Matt was plain and simply jealous.

"Ha!" Laurel uttered the syllable out loud and flopped back against the car seat. Her photographer sent her a sidelong look and said nothing.

Jealous . . . well, that was certainly interesting, even if it was still unreasonable and asinine. But if he was jealous, didn't it follow that his feelings for her were more involved than she'd let herself believe? Maybe. Or maybe he was just being typically insufferable—as she'd almost forgotten in the first heady waves of love that he was. Still, it was something to think about.

They had to stop the car in a thick tangle of traffic and bad-tempered blasting of horns. "I'll get out here and go up on foot," Laurel told her photographer absently. "Pull over as soon as you can." Stepping out, Laurel went to work.

Matt was out on the street as well. The noise in the Vieux Carré might have been a great deal more pleasant than what Laurel was dealing with, but the heat was only slightly less intense. He could smell the river and the flowers, a combination that had come to mean New Orleans to him. At the moment, he hardly thought of them. For the past hour, he'd been very busy.

A trip to the police station and a few carefully placed questions had earned him the information that no official search had ever been issued for Elise or Charles Trulane. A missing-persons report had never been filed on either of them. The note, the missing clothes and painting gear had been enough to satisfy everyone. Matt wasn't satisfied.

When he'd questioned further, he'd hit a blank wall of indifference. What did it matter how they'd left town or if anyone had seen them? They *had* left, and ten years was a long time. There was plenty of other business in New Orleans to keep the force busy other than an adultery that was a decade old. Sure, the lab boys would play with his little chunk of metal when they had the time, and what was he up to?

Matt had evaded and left with fewer answers than he'd had when he'd gone in. Maybe he'd draw a few out of Curt.

Turning a corner, Matt strolled into a dim little bar where a trio was playing a cool, brassy rendition of "The Entertainer." He spotted Curt immediately, huddled in a corner booth with papers spread all over the table. There was a glass of untouched beer at his elbow. Matt had a quick flashback of seeing Curt exactly the same way during their college days. The smile—the first one in hours—felt good.

"How's it going, Counselor?"

"What?" Distracted, Curt looked up. "Hi." He tipped the papers together in one neat, economical movement and slid them into a folder. "What's up, Matt?"

"The same," he told the waitress, indicating Curt's beer. "A little legal advice," he said when he turned back to Curt.

"Oh-oh." Grinning, Curt stroked his chin, the only resemblance to his sister Matt could see.

"Advice, not representation," Matt countered.

"Oh, well." When the waitress put Matt's beer on the table, Curt remembered his own.

"If I decided to add to my portfolio, would you consider Trulane Shipping a wise investment?"

Curt looked up from his drink, his abstracted expression sharpening. "I'd say that was more a question for your broker than your lawyer. In any case, we both know your portfolio's solid. You're the one who gives me tips, remember?"

"A hypothetical question then," Matt said easily. "If I were interested in speculating with a New Orleans-based company, would Trulane be a wise place to sink my money?"

"All right. Then I'd say that Trulane is one of the most solid companies in the country."

"Okay," Matt muttered. He'd figured that one was a blind alley. "Why do you think no one's touched Elise Trulane's inheritance?"

Curt set down his beer and gave Matt a long, level look. "How do you know about that?"

"You know I can't reveal a source, Curt. Fifty thousand," he mused, running a finger down the condensation on his glass. "A hefty amount. Interest over ten years would be a tidy little sum. I'd think even a man like Trulane would find some use for it."

"He doesn't have any claim on the money. It's a straight

inheritance in Elise's name." He shrugged at Matt's unspoken question. "The firm handled it."

"And the lady just lets it sit." Matt's brow rose at his own statement. "Strange. Hasn't your firm tried to track her down?"

"You know I can't get into that," Curt countered.

"Okay, let's take it hypothetically again. When someone inherits a large amount of money and makes no claim, what steps're taken by the executors to locate the beneficiary?"

"Basic steps," Curt began, not sure he liked the drift. "Ads in newspapers. In all likelihood an investigator would be hired."

"Say the beneficiary had a husband she wanted to avoid."

"The investigation, any correspondence pertaining to it, would be confidential."

"Mmm-hmm." Matt toyed with his beer as the piano player did a quick, hot rip over the keys. "Did Elise Trulane have a will?"

"Matt—"

"Off the record, Curt. It may be important."

If it had been anyone else, Curt would have brushed it off and found some handy legal jargon to evade the question. He'd known Matt too long and too well. "No," he said simply. "Both she and Louis had wills drawn up, but Elise took off before they were signed."

"I see. And the beneficiaries?"

"Standard wills for husband and wife without issue. Marion and Charles have their own money."

"Substantial?"

"Putting it mildly. Marion's a very wealthy woman." Then, because he anticipated the question before it was spoken, he added, "Charles's investments and his savings sit collecting interest as Elise's do."

"Interesting."

Curt kept his eyes level—not emerald like his sister's, but sea green and calm. "Are you going to tell me what all this is about?"

"Just covering all the angles."

"It has something to do with what you and Laurel are working on—for Susan."

"Yeah." Matt swirled his beer as he studied his friend. "You've met Susan?"

"I was out at the house." A faint color rose under Curt's skin, bringing Matt a picture of the time, years before, when Curt had fallen hard for a premed student. "She told me about Anne, and the letters." Curt's gaze came back to Matt's, reminding him that Curt wasn't an impressionable college student any longer, but a man with a sharp legal mind and a quiet strength, despite his dreaminess. "Are you going to be able to help her?"

"We're doing what we can on this end. Since you know her, and she's confided in you, maybe you can keep her calm, and out of it, until something breaks."

"I'd already planned on that," Curt said simply. "You taking care of Laurel?"

Matt grimaced, remembering how they'd parted a few hours before. "Nobody takes care of Laurel," he muttered.

"No, I guess not." Distracted again, Curt slipped his folder into his briefcase. "I've got an appointment, but when there's more time, I'd like a few more details on this."

"Okay. And thanks."

Alone, Matt brooded into his beer. Too many loose ends, he mused. Too many pieces that just don't fit. Two people might turn their backs on friends and relatives, especially in the first impetus of love, but not on more money than most people see in a lifetime. Not for ten years.

Either love made them delirious, he concluded, or they're dead. Dead, to him, made a lot more sense.

Leaning back, he lit a cigarette. If they'd had an accident after leaving Heritage Oak, didn't it follow that they'd have been identified? He shook his head as theories formed and unformed in his mind. It all tied together, somehow, with Anne Trulane. And if one of his theories was right, the one he kept coming back to, then someone had killed not once, but three times.

He studied the thin blue wisp of smoke and swore. It was too late in the day to allow a thorough check of Louis's whereabouts on the day of Elise and Charles's disappearance. And tomorrow was Sunday, which meant he probably couldn't get his hands on the information he needed until after the weekend. Monday then, he thought, and crushed out his cigarette. On Monday, no matter how reluctant Laurel was, they would start digging back, and digging thoroughly.

Rising, he tossed bills on the table and strode out. Maybe it was time they had a talk.

Laurel was totally involved with her story when Matt walked into the city room. He started toward her, glanced at the clock, then went to his own desk. Deadline was sacred. When he sat down across from her, he noticed the expression on her face. Unholy glee was the closest he could come.

Laurel nearly chuckled out loud as she dashed off the story. A three-car pileup, a lot of bent metal. Not normally anything she'd have found amusing, but no one had been hurt. And the mayor's wife had been in the second car.

Better than a sideshow, Laurel thought again as she typed

swiftly. The mayor's wife had dropped all dignity and deco-
rum and very nearly belted the hapless driver who'd plowed
into her from behind, sandwiching her between him and the
car stopped at a light in front of her.

The air, already steaming, had been blue before it was
over. Maybe it was the heat, or the pressure she'd been under
for the last few days, but Laurel found this a much-needed
comic relief. It would've taken a stronger person than she
not to be amused watching a prim, nattily dressed woman
with a wilted corsage grab a man built like a truck driver
by his lapels and threaten to break his nose. And that had
been before her radiator had blown, spewing water up like
a fountain.

Ah, well, she thought as she finished up the report, it
would do every man good to read that people in high places
get their fenders dented and their tempers scraped, too. Page
one, oh, yes indeed.

"Copy," she shouted, glancing at the clock. Just under
deadline. Her smile was smug as she turned back and found
her gaze linked with Matt's. A dozen conflicting emotions
hit her all at once, with one fighting to push aside all the others. She loved him.

"I didn't see you come in," she said carefully and began
to tidy the disorder of her desk.

"Just a few minutes ago. You were working." The bedlam of the city room went on around them with shouts of
"Copy!" and rushing feet and clicking typewriter keys. "Are
you finished?"

"Soon as the copy's approved."

"I need to talk to you. Can we have dinner?"

She hadn't expected that cautious, slightly formal tone
from him, and wasn't sure how to deal with it. "All right. Matthew—" The phone on her desk rang. Still thinking about

what she would say to him, Laurel answered, "City room, Laurel Armand."

Matt watched her expression change, the color fluctuate before her gaze jerked back to him. "I'm sorry," she began, indicating the phone on his desk a split second after he'd already started to reach for it. "You'll have to speak up, it's very noisy in here." She heard the faint click as Matt picked up her extension.

"You've been warned twice." It was a whisper of a voice, sexless, but Laurel didn't think it was her imagination that she sensed fear in it. "Stop prying into Anne Trulane's death."

"Did you send me the snake?" Laurel watched Matt punch another extension on the phone and dial rapidly.

"A warning. The next one won't be dead."

She couldn't control the silver shot of panic up her spine, but she could control her voice. "Last night, you were in the swamp."

"You have no business there. If you go in again, you won't come out."

Laurel heard someone across the room yell out a request for coffee, no sugar. She wondered if she was dreaming. "What are you afraid I'll find?"

"Anne should've stayed out of the swamp. Remember that."

There was a click, then the drone of the dial tone. Seconds later, Matt swore and hung up his own phone. "Not enough time for the trace. Any impressions on the voice? Anything you recognized?"

"Nothing."

He picked up her pad, where Laurel had automatically recorded the conversation in shorthand. "To the point," he muttered. "We're making someone very nervous." Someone, he thought as his own theory played back in his head, who may have killed three times.

"You're thinking about the police again," Laurel decided.

"You're damn right."

Laurel dragged a hand through her hair as she rose. "Listen, Matthew, I'm not saying you're wrong, I just want some time to think it through. Listen," she repeated when he started to speak. "Whoever that was wants us to back off. Well, for all intents and purposes we will be for the weekend. I want some time to go over my notes, to put them together with yours, hash it out. If we do go to the police, on *Monday*," she added with emphasis, "we'd better go with all the guns we have."

She was right, but he didn't like it. Several ideas for nudging her out of the investigation ran through his mind. He'd have the weekend to choose the best of them. "All right, check in with Don. I'll get my notes together."

Instead of the rare steak and candlelight Matt had planned on, they ate take-out burgers and chili fries at Laurel's drop-leaf table. Their notes were spread out—Matt's made up of scribbles Laurel thought resembled hieroglyphics while her own were sketched in precise Gregg shorthand. They hadn't taken the time—and both of them separately agreed it was just as well—to touch on their earlier argument or the reasons for it. For now they were professionals covering every angle of a story.

"I'd say it's safe to assume we have enough circumstantial evidence to conclude that Anne Trulane's death was something more than an unfortunate accident." Laurel wrote in a composition notebook, a valiant attempt to organize their snatches of words and phrases into coherency.

"Very good," Matt murmured. "That sounded like something Curt would say to the jury."

"Don't be a smart aleck, Bates," she said mildly. "Pass

me that soda." Taking it, she sipped straight from the bottle and frowned. "We have Susan's claim that Anne was afraid of dark places—the swamp in particular—which has since been corroborated by Louis, Marion and Binney. We have the stolen letters from Susan's hotel room, my nasty little box, a hefty shove in the swamp, and an anonymous phone call."

Because she was writing, Laurel didn't notice that Matt snapped the filter clean off his cigarette when he crushed it out. "The first interview with Louis and Marion . . . nothing much to go on there but emotion, which you don't like to deal with."

"It can be useful enough," Matt said evenly, "when you look at it with some objectivity."

She opened her mouth to hurl something back at him, then stopped. "I'm sorry. I didn't mean to snipe. Brewster," she went on briskly. "We know he thought he was in love with Anne, wanted her to leave Louis. No conjecture there, since he said so himself." She underlined Brewster's name heavily and continued. "We also have Marion's corroboration of the first part of that, and Anne's reaction to it. My second interview with Louis leads me to believe that he either didn't know about Brewster's feelings or didn't think they were important enough to worry about, as Brewster's still employed by his company."

Laurel rubbed a hand over the back of her neck, the first and only outward sign that she was tired. "The gist of it is that we agree it seems unlikely Anne would've gone into the swamp without some kind of outside pressure—and that it's less likely she would have continued to head deeper unless she had no choice. In my opinion, Brewster's still the obvious candidate."

Matt flipped over his pad to a new set of notes. "I spoke with Curt today."

"Huh?" Laurel looked up at him, trying to tie his statement with hers.

"I wanted some corroboration on a theory I had."

"What does Curt have to do with this?"

"He's a lawyer." With a shrug, Matt lit a cigarette. "As it turns out, I was luckier than I expected, as he works for the firm that handles Elise Trulane's inheritance."

Laurel put down the bottle she'd lifted. "What does that have to do with any of this?"

"I'm beginning to think quite a lot. Listen." He skimmed through his notes. "Fifty thousand dollars, plus ten years' interest, has never been touched. Charles Trulane's money sits moldering. Untouched. There would've been a very discreet, and I'm sure very thorough investigation on behalf of the bank to locate them." He flipped back a few pages, then lifted his eyes to Laurel's. "No missing-persons report was ever filed on either Elise or Charles Trulane."

"What're you getting at?"

Very carefully, he set down his pad. "You know what I'm getting at, Laurel."

Needing to move, she rose from the table. "You think they're dead," she said flatly. "Maybe they are. They could've had an accident, and—" She broke off, and he knew her thoughts had followed the same train his had. Laurel turned back to him, her eyes very steady. "You think they were dead before they left Heritage Oak."

"It's more than a possibility, isn't it?"

"I don't know." Pressing her fingers to her temples, she tried to think logically. "They could've taken off, changed their names, gone to Europe or Asia or God knows where."

"Could've," he agreed. "But there's enough room to doubt that, isn't there?"

"All right, yes." She took a deep breath. "And if we go that route, figuring they were tied with Anne's death somehow, it'd put Brewster in the clear. But why?" Laurel demanded. "Who'd have had a motive but Louis, and he was out of town."

"Was he?" Matt rose, knowing they had to tread carefully around Louis Trulane. "He has his own plane, doesn't he? Flies himself—or did. You know what the possibilities are there, Laurel."

She did. An unexpected arrival, the lovers caught, unaware. A moment's madness. In a small private plane the bodies could've been taken anywhere. Pale, she turned back to face Matt. He was expecting her to argue, or to back out. Of course, she could do neither now.

"It won't be easy—maybe impossible," she added in a calm, professional voice, "to check the incoming and outgoing flights on a night ten years ago."

"I'll get started on it Monday."

She nodded. "I'll work on Curt. We might be able to get the name of the firm that looked for Elise and Charles."

"No."

"No?" she repeated blankly. "But it makes sense to try that angle if we're going at it this way."

"I want you to back off." He spaced his words very evenly as he rose. "I don't want you asking any more questions."

"What the hell are you talking about? You don't get a story without asking questions."

"Whatever we get out of this, whatever the outcome as far as the paper is concerned, we'll split down the middle. But from now on I take over."

Laurel tilted her head. "You're out of your mind."

Maybe it was the very calm, very mild way she said it that tripped the last button. Every reasonable argument, every carefully thought-out method of persuasion, deserted him. "I'm out of *my* mind!" he threw back. "That's rich."

He paced, deliberately walking away from her so that he wouldn't just grab her by the collar and shake. "It's not a game, damn it. We're not playing who can hit page one."

"I've never considered my profession a game."

"I don't want you in my way."

Her eyes narrowed. "Then I'll stay out of it. You stay out of mine."

"It's dangerous!" he shouted. "Use your head. You're the one who's been threatened, not once, but three times. Whoever's behind Anne's death isn't going to hesitate to kill again."

Her brow lifted—that damned, beautiful, haughty black brow. "Then I'll have to watch my step, won't I?"

"You idiot, no one called me and told me to back off. No one threatened me." There was panic in his voice now, raw panic, but she was too busy fuming to notice.

"You want to know why, Bates?" she hurled out at him. "Because I'm a woman and obviously would buckle under. The same way you figure if you shout enough and throw your weight around I'll do the same thing."

"Don't be any more stupid than you have to."

"But the one thing they forgot," she continued furiously, "the one thing *you* forgot, is that I'm a reporter. And to get a story, to get the truth, a reporter does what's necessary. Most of us deal with being in jeopardy in one form or another. That's the business."

"I'm not in love with most reporters," Matt tossed back. "I'm in love with you!" He stormed right past her as he said it, not stopping until he'd reached the table and his cigarettes.

Laurel stared at him while he pushed aside papers in search of a match. She was winded, as though she'd raced up flight after flight of stairs two at a time. Now that she'd reached the top, she simply forgot why she was in such a hurry in the first place. It wasn't until he'd stopped swearing and muttering to turn to her that she felt the glow, the warmth, the pleasure.

Matt set down the unlit cigarette and stared at her. What the hell had he said? Oh, God, had he just blown everything by laying his cards on the table before he'd covered his bet? And just how was he going to handle this one? He decided to give her a way out if she wanted one.

"Did I . . . just say what I think I said?"

Laurel didn't smile, but folded her hands neatly in front of her. "Yes, I have a witness."

His brow lifted. "There's no one here."

"I'll bribe someone."

He hooked his hands in his pockets because he wanted so badly to touch her. "Is it what you want?"

She gave him an odd look, then took a step closer. "I wonder why I thought you were insightful and observant. It's a general sort of rule, Matthew, that when a woman's in love with a man, she likes it better if he's in love with her, too."

His heartbeat was very light and fast. He couldn't remember ever feeling like that before. "Tell me," he murmured. "Don't make me beg you."

"Matthew . . ." A little dazed that he couldn't see what must have been glowing on her face, she reached for him. "You're the only man I've made love to because you're the only man I've been in love with. Neither of those things is ever going to change."

"Laurel." But he couldn't say more because her mouth was on his, giving, just giving. His arms came around her to draw her closer as thoughts spun in his head. So long—it's been so long. He could hardly remember a time when he hadn't

wanted it to be like this. A time when he hadn't wanted to
have those words still lingering on the air. "Again," he demanded. "Tell me again."

"I love you. Only you." Her arms curved up his back until
she could grip his shoulders. "I thought if I told you before,
even an hour ago, you'd think I was crazy. When?" Giddy,
she clung to him. "When did it start?"

"You wouldn't believe me." Before she could disagree, his
lips were on hers again.

He took her deep, and still deeper, quickly. If he'd thought
he'd loved her to the point of madness before, it was nothing
compared to what stormed through him now. His love was
met, and matched. Everything was washed from his mind but
Laurel.

She could lose herself in a kiss from him, lose herself
in that soft, velvet-edged darkness he'd first taken her to.
To know that he wanted her was exciting. To know that he
loved her was glory. Words, there were so many words she
wanted to say. But they would wait until this first overriding
need was satisfied. As she felt her bones melting, she drew
him with her to the floor.

Quickly, quickly. Neither spoke, but each knew the other's
mind. Hurry. Just to feel one another's flesh. Clothes tangled,
untangled, then were discarded. Oh, the sweetness of it, the
sweetness that came from only a touch. She could smell
the hot muskiness of the day on him with the lingering scent
of soap. She wallowed in it with her lips pressed against his
throat. His pulse beat there, fast and light.

He murmured against her ear, only her name, but the sound
of it drifted through her softly. The slow, liquefying pleasure
made everything she'd ever felt before seem hollow. Then
his tongue dipped inside to follow her name.

A long, lingering stroke, a whispering caress. There was
no need to hurry now. Passion was filled with wonder. I'm

loved, I'm wanted. Spirits are fed on this alone. She could feel it pouring from him—contentment—even as his heart-beat hammered against hers. Desire, when mixed with such emotions, has more power. And at times, more patience. They'd woo each other.

His lips moved over her shoulder, down, lazily down, to linger on the pulse point at the inside of her elbow. She felt the answering beat from a hundred others. Her hand ran through his hair, the curling thickness of it, before she let her fingers stroke beneath to his neck. He lifted his head to look at her and the look held—long, silent—until, smiling, their lips joined again.

The change happened so slowly, perhaps neither of them noticed. Not yet urgent, not yet desperate, but desire grew sharper. Gradually, quiet sighs became quiet moans. With his mouth at her breast he heard her breathing quicken. His senses were clouded—her scent, her taste, the satin that was her skin. Hunger seeped into them, and the excitement that came from knowing the hunger would be satisfied. His hands journeyed down.

The inside of her thighs was as warm and alluring as vel-vet. He let his fingers linger there, then his mouth. Though she shuddered, the first crest came easily, a gentle lifting up and up, a quiet settling. Her body throbbed with anticipa-tion of the next while her mind was filled with him. Head whirling, she shifted to lie over him, to give to him all the pleasures he'd given to her.

How warm his flesh was, how firm his body. Her hands wandered down to his hips, skimmed over his thighs. She felt the quiver of muscle beneath her.

She was floating, but the air was thick and syrupy. Her limbs were weighted, but her head was light and spinning. She felt him grasp her, heard him hoarsely mutter her name. Then he was inside her and the explosion went on and on and on. She had only enough sanity left to pray it would never stop.

He watched her. He struggled to hold back that seductive darkness so that he would always have this image of her. The light fell over her brilliantly. With her head thrown back, her hair streamed down her back. She knew only pleasure now— his pleasure. He held her there for an instant with perfect clarity. Then the darkness, and all its savage delights, overcame him.

CHAPTER 11

It was dark. Matt had no idea of the time, and cared less. They were snuggled close in Laurel's bed, naked and warm. Like careless children, they'd left their clothes in heaps in the living room. It was pleasant to imagine they could stay just as they were for the whole weekend—dozing, making love, saturating themselves with each other.

He knew all there was to know about her, what pleased her, what annoyed, what made her laugh. He knew where she'd come from, how she'd grown up, snatches of her childhood that he'd drawn out of Olivia or her father and Curt. She'd broken her ankle when she was nine, and she'd worked on her high school paper. She'd slept with a one-eared stuffed dog until she was seven.

It made him smile to think of it, though he wasn't certain she'd be pleased to learn he knew.

There was so much he hadn't told her. Matt could remember the hurt on her face when he'd pushed her questions away. There was so much he hadn't told her—but she loved him anyway.

Laurel shifted against him, her eyes open and adjusted to the dark, her body quietly content. "What're you thinking?"

He was silent for a moment, then lifted a hand to touch her hair. "I grew up in that painting." Laurel put her hand in his and said nothing. "Old people stayed off the street at night and anyone else traveled in groups. Too many alleys and broken streetlights. Cops patrolled in pairs, in cars. I can't remember a night when I didn't hear the sirens."

She was so warm and soft beside him. The room was so quiet. Why was he bringing it all back? Because it never really goes away, he answered himself. And I need to tell her.

"I worked for a guy who ran a newsstand. One summer we were robbed six times. The last time he was fed up enough to put up a fight. I was out of the hospital in two days, but it took him two weeks. He was sixty-four."

"Oh, Matthew." Laurel pressed her face into his shoulder. "You don't have to talk about it."

"I want you to know where I came from." But he fell silent again as two long minutes passed. "In the apartment where I lived, the halls smelled of old cooking and sweat. It never went away. In the winter it was cold, drafts through the windows, icy floors. In the summer it was a furnace. You could smell the garbage from the alley three floors down. At night you could hear the street—dealers, prostitutes, the kids who looked for both. I stayed away from the dealers because I wanted to stay healthy and used the prostitutes when I could scrape up the extra money."

He waited, wondering if he'd sense her withdrawal. Her hand stayed in his. Laurel was remembering her impression of his apartment. He'd made an art out of comfort. How much he must have hated growing up without the basic rights of warmth and security. And yet . . . he'd brought the painting with him. He hadn't forgotten his roots, nor was he ignoring that part they'd had in forming him. Neither would she ignore them.

"I lived with my aunt. She took me in when my mother

died and my father took off. She didn't have to." He linked his fingers with Laurel's. "She was the most unselfish person I've ever known."

"She loved you," Laurel murmured, grateful.

"Yes. There was never enough money, even though she worked too hard and when I was old enough I brought in more. The rent would go up in that filthy place or . . ." He broke off and shrugged. "Life," he said simply. "I swore I was going to get us out of there. One way or the other I was going to get us the hell out. I knew what I wanted to do, but it was like pie in the sky. A reporter, a job on one of the big New York papers and a salary that would move her out to some nice little place in Brooklyn Heights or New Rochelle.

"So I ran copy and studied until my eyes hurt. There were other ways," he murmured, "quicker ways, to get the kind of money I wanted, but that would've destroyed her. So when the scholarship came I took it, and I got out. When I'd come back during the summer, it was so hot I'd forget what it was like to live in that place in January. By the middle of my senior year I had nearly enough saved to move her out—not to a house in Brooklyn Heights, but to a decent apartment. By that summer I'd have gotten her out. She died in March."

Laurel turned her head so that her lips could brush over his skin, lightly, easily. "She would've been proud of you."

"If I'd have taken another way, she might still be alive."

"If you'd have taken another way," Laurel said slowly, rising on her elbows to look at him, "you'd have killed her yourself."

His eyes glinted in the filtered light of the moon. "I've told myself that, but other times I think I might've given her even six months of comfort." He caught Laurel's hair in his hand, feeling the fine silk of it. "She used to laugh. Somehow, she'd always find a way to laugh. I owe her just for that."

"Then so do I." Lowering her head, she kissed him. "I love you, Matthew."

"When I've thought of you, and me, I've wondered how the hell I was going to work it." He cupped the back of her neck. "We couldn't have had more different beginnings. There were times I thought I wanted you just because of that."

When she lifted her head, he was surprised to see her smiling. "You ass," she said lovingly.

"So beautiful," Matt murmured. "I'll never forget that picture Curt had of you, the one he kept on his desk in our room."

Surprised, Laurel started to speak, then stopped. He'd said she wouldn't believe it; now, with emotions swamping her, she didn't want to tell him he'd been wrong. She wanted to show him.

"I could see you at one of those long, lazy garden parties in a silk dress and picture hat," Matt said softly. "It made my mouth water. And I could see you with someone bred for the same things."

"I hate to repeat myself," she began, but he didn't smile. "You're thinking of Louis," Laurel said flatly.

"No." He started to draw her back to him. "Not tonight."

"You listen to me." The humor and the softness had fled from her eyes as she pulled away. "The way I feel about you has nothing, *nothing*, to do with the way I feel about Louis. I've loved him since I was a child and in almost exactly the same way. Both he and Marion were an integral, vital part of my childhood. The fairy-tale part. Every girl's entitled to one."

He remembered her grandmother saying essentially the same thing. The muscles in his shoulders began to relax. "I think I understand that, Laurel. It's today that concerns me."

"Today my heart aches for him, for both of them. Today I wish I could help, knowing, at the same time, that what I

have to do might hurt them beyond repair. If my feelings
had been different, don't you think that sometime over the
last ten years, I'd have gone to him? I wonder why," she said
heatedly before he could answer, "when I waited all these
years to fall in love, I had to fall in love with an idiot."

"The luck of the draw, I guess."

"Well, I'll tell you one thing, Bates, I'm not going to explain myself to you on this again. Take it or leave it."

He let out a deep breath and paused as if weighing the
pros and cons of the ultimatum. In the dim light he could
see the angry glare in her eyes, the agitated rise and fall of
her shoulders. She might've been molded in a softer manner
than he, but no one matched wits or wills so well.

"Will you marry me, Laurel?" he asked simply.

He heard the quick hitch of her breath, saw the surprise
rush into her eyes. For a moment, there was quiet. "It took you
long enough," she said just as simply, then dived onto him.

L aurel awoke with the sun streaming over her face and
Matt nibbling on her ear. She didn't have to open her eyes
to know it was a beautiful day. Sometime during the night
the rain had come to wash the heaviness from the air. Without opening her eyes, she stretched and sighed. Matt's lips
moved to her jawline.

"I love the way you wake up," he murmured. He slid a
hand down to cradle her hip.

"Mmmm . . . what time is it?"

"Morning." His lips finally found hers.

With another lazy stretch, she linked her arms around his
neck. "Have I ever told you how much I like you to kiss me
just like that?"

"No." Lowering his head, he did so again while she lay
boneless beneath him. "Why don't you?"

"If I tell you . . . mmmm . . . you'll know how to win every argument."

Laughing, he pressed his lips to the curve of her shoulder. "I'm crazy about you, Laurellie. When're we getting married?"

"Soon," she said definitely. "Although the minute we tell Grandma she'll—" Laurel broke off, eyes flying open. "Oh, God, *brunch!*"

"I wasn't thinking of food just yet," Matt murmured, going back to nibble on her ear.

"Oh, no, no, you don't understand. What time is it?" Shoving him aside, Laurel grabbed the bedside clock. "Oh, boy, we'd better get moving or we'll be in serious trouble."

Matt grabbed her around the waist as she started to hop out of bed. "If we stay right here," he began, pinning her beneath him again, "we can get into serious trouble by ourselves."

"Matthew." Laurel avoided the kiss, but it landed on the vulnerable hollow of her throat. "Sunday brunch at Promesse d'Amour is sacred," she said unsteadily.

"Can you cook?"

"What? Oh, well, yes, that is, if your stomach's very broadminded you could almost call it that. Matthew, don't." Breathless, she caught his wandering hand in hers.

"Why don't we have a private brunch here, somewhere around dinnertime?"

"Matthew—" she shook her head to clear it, then put both hands firmly on his shoulders. "Since you're going to join the family, you might as well get used to certain ironclad rules and traditions. Sunday brunch," she continued when he grinned, "is nothing to play around with."

"I'm an iconoclast."

"Bite your tongue," she told him, and struggled with a grin of her own. "Grandma would forgive me if I took up exotic dancing. She'll even overlook the fact that I'm marrying a Yankee, but she'd never, never let me get away with missing Sunday brunch. Even being late clouds the reputation, and we're pushing that."

Matt gave a long, exaggerated sigh. "For Miss Olivia, then," he agreed, and let Laurel wiggle out from under him.

"I'm going to get a shower," she said, dashing toward the bathroom. "If we move fast, we'll make it before deadline."

"Two can shower as quick as one," he commented as he stepped in with her.

"Matthew!" Laughing, Laurel lifted a hand to his chest. "If we're in here together, we're definitely going to be late for brunch."

He drew her against him. "I'll risk it."

"Matthew—"

"You forget." He lowered his mouth to nibble on hers. "I know how to win arguments."

"Oh, damn," she sighed, and melted against him.

They were late.

"We're really in for it," Laurel muttered as Matt turned the car under the arched cedars.

Matt sent her a quick wolfish grin. "It was worth it."

"Just get that cat-ate-the-canary look off your face, Matthew," Laurel warned. "Try to look suitably humble."

"We could use the one about the flat tire," he suggested.

"No less than a five-car pileup equals pardon," she said grimly. "And you don't have a dent in this car." She shot him a look.

"No," he said positively, "not even for you."

"It's that practical Yankee streak," she said under her breath as the house came into view. "Okay, it probably won't work, but we'll go for it. Turn your watch back."

"Do what?"

"Turn your watch back, fifteen minutes." She fussèd rapidly with her own. "Go on!"

"What's she going to do?" he demanded as he parked his car beside Curt's. "Take you to the woodshed?"

"You'd be surprised," Laurel muttered. "Oh-oh, here she comes. Listen, I know this might be almost impossible for you, Matthew, but look innocent."

"Maybe I'll just drop you off here and see you back in town."

"You do and I'll break your arm," she promised as she stepped from the car. "Grandma!" Laurel went forward with smiles and open arms. She kissed both lined cheeks and pretended she didn't notice the coolness in the sharp emerald eyes. "You look wonderful."

"You're late," Olivia said flatly.

"Oh, no, minutes to spare. I've brought Matthew with me," she added quickly. With luck, a lot of it, it would be enough to distract Olivia.

"Miss Olivia." He took the haughtily offered hand and lifted it to his lips. "I hope I'm not intruding."

"You're late," she repeated while her gaze raked over both of them.

"Why, how could we be?" Laurel countered, glancing down at her watch. "It's only just eleven now."

"That trick's older than I am." Olivia lifted her chin in the manner her granddaughter had inherited. "*Why* are you late?" she demanded, daring either of them to make an excuse.

Laurel moistened her lips. If she had a few more minutes, she could probably come up with a great lie. "Well, you see, Grandma—"

"It's my fault, Miss Olivia," Matt put in, earning a grateful glance from Laurel.

"What," Olivia began regally, "does my granddaughter being late have to do with you?"

"I distracted her in the shower," he said easily.

"Matthew!" Laurel cast him a horrified look that altered into one that promised swift and lethal revenge. His name echoed off into silence.

"I see." Olivia nodded. "That's a reasonable excuse," she decreed as Laurel's mouth dropped open. "Close your mouth, girl," she said absently as she continued to study Matt. "Took your own sweet time about it, but that's worked out for the best. You'll be marrying her soon."

It wasn't a question. Matt could only grin as Laurel began to sputter. "Very soon," he told Olivia.

"Welcome to the family—" she grinned and offered her cheek "—Yankee." With a wink for her granddaughter, she held out a hand for Matt to formally escort her around the house to the terrace.

No one's like her, Laurel thought with a fierce flurry of love and pride. Absolutely no one.

With her usual panache, Olivia dominated the table, with her son at the opposite end and the younger generation between them. As always, she'd made the most out of the Sunday tradition. White linen, gleaming silver and crystal, fresh flowers in bowls that had been treasured before the war.

The talk was quiet, general, easy. Laurel could see that Susan was a much different woman from the one who had fallen apart outside the city room. No more trembling fingers. If there was a sadness in her eyes, it was fading. She cast Laurel one look that spoke of complete trust. With it, Laurel felt the burden grow.

Not now, she told herself as she sipped at cool, dry champagne. Tomorrow was soon enough to bring all that back. For today, she needed to absorb the magic and the timelessness. Where else, she wondered, could six people be sitting with the sun gleaming on silver that was more than a century old? There was birdsong and a precious breeze that might only last a moment. It was too rare to crowd with sorrows and suspicions. And she was in love.

She glanced over at Matt, and her eyes told him everything.

"This will be your job one day, Laurellie," Olivia stated, cutting delicately into the crepe on her plate. "Traditions like this are important—more for the children than their parents. You and Matthew are welcome to the west wing when you're married. Permanently or whenever you feel the need to come. The house is big enough so that we won't bump into each other."

"Have some more coffee, Mother," William interrupted, sending her a telling look that expressed his feelings about matchmaking. "I want to talk to both of you." He nodded to his daughter and to Matt. His glance barely skimmed over Susan, but it was enough to tell Laurel he was referring to Anne Trulane. "Monday morning, my office."

"Business is for Monday." Olivia sent her son back a look every bit as stubborn. "I want to talk about the wedding. The garden couldn't be better suited to a summer wedding. You're welcome to have it here on the terrace."

"How about next weekend?" Matt put in, reaching for his coffee.

"Matt, don't encourage her," William advised. "She'll have Curt suing you for breach of promise."

"Damn right!" The thought made Olivia give a hoot of laughter as her hand came down on Laurel's. "We've got him now, Laurellie. William!" She caught him in the act of smothering a laugh with a cough. "Aren't you going to ask this boy all the rude questions a father's supposed to ask? A father can't be too careful when a man wants his daughter— especially a Yankee."

"The truth is," Laurel began before her father could speak, "Matthew's marrying me for the house, and as a cover so he can dangle after Grandma."

Her father's grin altered into blank astonishment. "Are you joking?"

"No," Laurel said lightly as she dipped a strawberry into cream. "Matthew's crazy about Grandma."

"Laurel—" William began with a half laugh, only to break off without any idea what to say.

"She's not joking," Curt murmured, studying his sister. He glanced over at Matt as he remembered his roommate's fascination with a photograph, the questions. "All this time?" he said softly.

"Yes." Matt looked over at Laurel and smiled. "All this time."

"Well, it's been a cleverly kept secret," her father stated. "And from a veteran bloodhound like me."

Smiling, Laurel reached out a hand to him. "Do you mind?"

He gripped her hand. "Nothing could please me more." His gaze shifted to Matt. "Nothing. The point is—" his fingers relaxed with his smile "—I didn't think the two of you even liked each other. You had one particular adjective for Matt, as I recall."

"Insufferable," Laurel supplied. "It still holds."

"That's what adds spice to a relationship," Olivia declared as she pushed back from the table, a signal that meant the formality of the brunch was over. "Susan, be a sweet child and run up to my room. There's a small locket in my jewelry case, gold, encrusted with pearls."

The moment she'd gone, Olivia turned to Curt. "Going to let this Yankee show you up, Curtis?"

Rising, Curt made a great to-do over removing a piece of lint from his jacket. "Ma'am?"

"*He* lollygagged around for a year. I expect you should be able to snatch that girl up in half the time."

"Mother." William strolled over to place a hand on her shoulder. "Be satisfied with one victory."

"After I'm through with Curtis," she continued irrepressibly, "I'm getting started on you."

He acknowledged that with a nod before he turned to his son. "Every man for himself. Ah, Matt, there's something I've been meaning to talk to you about."

"Coward," Olivia murmured as her son drew Matt away.

"Is this it, Miss Olivia?"

"Yes, thank you." She smiled as Susan handed her the locket. "Curtis, why don't you take Susan through the garden. You like the garden, don't you, Susan?"

"Yes." Susan looked down at her hands, then lifted her eyes to Curt's. "Yes, I do."

"There, you see, she likes the garden. Run along. Now then." Without pausing for breath, she turned to Laurel.

"Grandma." Laurel gave her a long, hard hug. "I adore you."

Olivia let herself enjoy the warmth and scent of youth before she drew Laurel away. In her own masterly way, she studied her granddaughter. "You're happy."

"Yes." With a laugh, Laurel tossed back her hair. "If you'd have asked me a month ago—good God, a week ago—how I'd feel about marrying Matthew Bates on the terrace, I'd've said . . ." She broke off, laughing again. "I'd better not repeat what I'd've said."

"You pretended you weren't attracted to him right from the beginning."

"I did a good job of it."

Olivia gave a hoot. "Ah, but you're like me, child!"

"The highest of compliments."

Olivia dropped the locket into her lap and took Laurel's

hands. "When we love, really love, it's with everything we have, so we don't give it easily. Your grandfather . . ." She looked misty for a moment, young. "God, but I loved that man. Fifteen years with him wasn't enough. When he died, I grieved and grieved hard, but then life—you have to live it as it comes. The others, after him, they were . . ." She shook her head and smiled again. "They were for fun. I cared about every man I've been with, but only one had all of me. You'd understand that," she murmured. "So would your Yankee."

"Yes." Laurel felt the tears swim into her eyes and blinked them back. "I love you, Grandma."

"You'll lead each other a dance," Olivia said after giving Laurel's hands a quick squeeze. "There's nothing better I could wish for you. This is for you now." Olivia lifted the locket from her lap, cupping it in her hand a moment as if warming it. "Your grandfather gave it to me when we were engaged. I wore it when I married him. It would mean a great deal to me if you wore it when you marry Matthew."

"Oh, Grandma, it's lovely." Laurel took the gold, gleaming dully and still warm from her grandmother's hands. It was studded with tiny pearls that carried just a hint of blue under the white. "I've never seen you wear it."

"I haven't since he died. It's time it was worn again and worn by a bride."

"Thank you." Leaning over, Laurel kissed Olivia's cheek, then with a smile turned the locket over in her palm. So lovely, she thought, and it would look so perfect against a floaty, romantic white dress. Maybe something with lace and . . .

As memory jarred, she pressed a hand to her temple.

"Laurellie?"

"No." Absently she patted her grandmother's hand. "I'm all right, I've just remembered something. Or think I have. I have to use the phone."

Jumping up, she dashed into the house with the locket clutched in her hand. From memory, she dialed Heritage Oak. With her eyes on the locket in her hand and her mind on another, she barely heard the answering voice.

"Oh, Binney," she said quickly. "It's Laurel Armand." When there was silence, she leaped into it. "Please, Binney, I know you're angry with me for questioning you. I understand. I'm sorry, truly sorry if I pressed too hard."

"It isn't my place to be angry with you, Miss Laurel," she said quietly. "It isn't my place to answer questions."

"Please, there's something I have to know. It could be very important. A locket." She plowed on into the un-receptive silence. "The locket Louis gave Elise before they were married. She wore it on her wedding day, and, I think, always after that. I can remember that I never saw her when she wasn't wearing it. The gold locket with the etching on the front. Do you remember it, Binney? You must," she went on before there could be an answer. "She kept Louis's picture in it."

"I remember the locket."

Something—not excitement, not fear—began to pound in her chest. Laurel recognized it as disillusionment. "She always wore it, didn't she? It was very small and elegant, something she could wear every day and still wear with evening clothes."

"It was her habit to wear it."

Laurel swallowed and fought to keep her voice steady. "Binney, was Elise afraid of the swamp?" She knew the answer herself, but wouldn't go with childhood memories now. It was time for facts, no matter how they hurt.

"It was a long time ago."

"Please, Binney. You knew her, you were there."

"She did not like it," Binney said flatly. "She knew the legend."

"But sometimes—sometimes—she went in there," Laurel whispered.

"Yes, sometimes she went in, but only with Mr. Louis."

"Yes, yes, I know." Laurel let out a long breath. "Only with Louis. Thank you, Binney."

Hanging up, Laurel stared down at the locket in her hand. She slipped it gently in her pocket and went to find Matt.

He saw her, crossing the lawn. With a brief word to her father, Matt went to meet her. Even from the distance, he'd recognized the look in her eyes. "What is it, Laurel?"

Her arms went around him, her cheek to his chest. For a moment, she just needed that—the strength, the promise. The tug-of-war inside her was almost over. It didn't surprise her that she still loved Louis, or the Louis she'd known. "Matthew, where's the piece of locket you found in the swamp?"

"I took it to the police lab. They're going to run some tests." He drew her away far enough so that he could see her face. "Why?"

Quietly, she drew a breath. Then she straightened and stood on her own. "They're going to find that it was out in the weather, perhaps covered and uncovered by rain and dirt over and over—for ten years."

"Ten—" He broke off as understanding came. "It was Elise's."

"I remembered where I'd seen it. I just called Heritage Oak and spoke to Binney to be sure. Elise wore that locket every day."

Because she was pale, because he loved her, Matt chose to play devil's advocate. "All right, but it's still not proof. She could've lost it in there any time."

"No, it's not proof," Laurel agreed. "But I don't think there's a chance that Elise simply lost it there. First, it was too important to her. And second, she didn't go in there often. She wasn't afraid the same way Anne was, but she had a healthy respect for the legend. The only times she went in, she went in with Louis. Binney just corroborated."

He could see the struggle, the emotion, in her eyes. This time he felt none of the frustration, the jealousy, that had plagued him. Gently, he cupped her face in his hands. "I'm sorry, Laurel."

She caught his wrists in her hands and held tight. "Oh, God, Matthew, so am I."

"I think we should fill in your father before we leave," he said carefully. "But we might want to keep it away from Susan for a while. We still don't have anything solid for the police."

"No." Laurel glanced over as she heard Susan's laugh drift from the garden. "Let's leave her out of it for now. My father can probably put on enough pressure to reopen the investigation on Anne, and stir one up on Elise and Charles."

"We've got enough," Matt agreed, watching the struggle on her face, "to start putting pressure in the right places."

"Oh, God, Matthew, do you realize, if what we're thinking is fact . . . Louis must be terribly ill. With Charles and Elise it might have been a moment of blind fury, but all these years it would've eaten at him. And then to meet Anne." She pressed her fingers to her eyes. Would she ever be able to separate the emotion from the necessity? "He needs help, Matthew. Can you imagine what a dark place he's been living in all this time?"

"He'll get help. But, Laurel . . ." He took her shoulders until she dropped her hands and looked at him. "First we have to prove it. I think if we concentrate on the first—on Charles and Elise," he said carefully, "it'll lead to Anne. It's not going to be easy for you."

"No," she agreed, "not easy, but necessary." Watching

his eyes, she thought she could almost see the idea forming. "What're you thinking, Matthew?"

"Pressure," he murmured. "The right pressure in the right place." He brought his attention back to her. "Louis must already be on the edge, Laurel, ready to go over. He's warned you off three times. Just what do you think his reaction would be if he saw that piece of locket?"

"I think—" Laurel's hand reached automatically for the one in her pocket "—it would break him."

"So do I." He slipped an arm around her shoulders. "We'll have to make another trip to Heritage Oak tomorrow."

CHAPTER 12

The clutter of notes was still spread over Laurel's drop-leaf table with the wrappers and cardboard of their takeout meal. Clothes—hers and some of his—were scattered over the floor. Laurel closed the door behind them and jiggled her keys in her palm.

"You're a slob, Matthew."

"Me? It's your place. Besides—" he nudged his shirt out of his way with his foot and sat down "—you were the one who dragged me to the floor, crazy for my body. And," he continued when she snorted, "you were the one who pulled me out of here this morning like the building was on fire."

He was distracting her—she was distracting him—from what hovered around the verges of both their thoughts: Louis Trulane and what to do about him.

"Well, since I've already had your body, and brunch," she added sweetly, "you can help me clean up this mess."

"Better idea." Rising, he yanked her into his arms. "Let's add to it."

"Matthew!" But his mouth crushed down on hers. His fingers were making quick work of the zipper at the back of her dress. "Stop it!" Half laughing, half in earnest, she struggled against him. "You're crazy. Don't you ever think about anything else?"

"Sometimes I think about eating," he confessed, then nipped, none too gently, at her collarbone.

"Matthew, this is ridiculous." But the quick heating of her blood told her otherwise. "It was only a few hours ago that—oh."

"I'm hungry again," he murmured, then devoured her mouth.

God, he was making her head spin. With her dress already down to her waist, Laurel tried to pull away. "Stop. There's things we have to talk about, and—"

"Mmm, a reluctant woman." He dragged her against him again. "That gets my lust cells moving."

"Your what?" she demanded, choking on a laugh.

"Just watch." Before she realized what he was up to, she was slung over his shoulder.

"Bates! Have you lost your mind?"

"Yeah." He pulled the dress the rest of the way off as he headed for the bedroom. Carelessly, he dropped it at the doorway, sending her shoes to follow. "Blame it on the lust cells."

"I'll tell you what I think about your lust cells," she began, but the wind rushed out of her as she landed on the bed beneath him.

Then he was taking her back to places she'd been, but so swiftly, so immediately, she couldn't keep up. Relentless, he wouldn't allow her to fall behind. Bright streams of color seemed to burst inside her head while her body was consumed with pleasure, such hot, liquid, throbbing pleasure.

No thought. No words. She could only feel and feel and feel. The rest of her clothes were gone. Had she heard something rip? Did it matter? Her body was wild to be touched, tasted, to experience all the mad things he seemed determined to do.

Emotions exploded in her, poured out of her. Oh, God, she was so free, so wonderfully free. Pleasure was an absence of pain, and she felt only pleasure in his hands, his lips, the taste of his tongue inside her mouth, the feel of his flesh beneath her fingers.

Excitement, heady, steamy excitement. Liberation. Soaring, half crazy with delight. The knowledge that her life would be splashed with moments like this made her laugh aloud. The next moment he had her gasping. She locked her arms around him as her world rocked and spun.

He took her on a roller coaster of sensations, plummeting down, climbing, climbing, only to whip blindly around a turn to fall again. Weightless, helpless, with the air rushing in her lungs and her heart thundering in her ears.

Then he plunged into her, driving her over that last, giddy hill.

When she could breathe again without gasping, when she could think without pooling all her concentration onto one word, Laurel slid a hand across his chest. He was lying on his back, possibly, she thought, just possibly, as enervated as she.

Laurel turned her face into his shoulder. "You did that more for me than yourself."

Matt gave a weak laugh. "I'm a real Samaritan. No lengths I won't go to to serve my fellow man."

"Matthew." Laurel shifted, so that she lay over him, her head supported just under his by her folded arms. "You knew I was tense, trying not to be. You knew I didn't want to think about what's going to happen, even though I have to. I was being a coward."

"No." He brushed the hair back from her face. "You were

being human. You needed to wipe it away for a little while, blank it out. I did, too." He smiled, with the touch of irony in the lifted brow. "This was better than an aspirin."

She managed to match the smile. "You'll have to keep yourself available every time I have a headache." She lowered her face to kiss his chest, then lifted it again. "Matthew, I can handle this. I can."

Maybe, he thought. Maybe not. But he'd give her the first test. "Okay. I want to run over to the lab and get the locket back whether it's been tested yet or not. I'd feel better if I had it."

Laurel nodded, accepting. "And in the morning, we take it out to see Louis."

I take it out, he corrected silently, but merely nodded. That was something he'd deal with when the time came. "If he doesn't just fall apart at that, we'll have a lot of legwork to do, but we bring the uniforms in."

"Agreed," she said simply. Her heart was already numb.

He sat up, wondering just where he'd tossed his clothes. "Do you want to come with me now?"

"No." She let out a deep breath. What had her grandmother said? Life—you have to live it. "I'll tell you what I'm going to do for you, Bates, and believe me, you're the first man I've offered this to."

He was standing, pulling on his slacks. The grin tilted. "Fascinating."

"I'm going to cook you dinner."

"Laurel, I'm—overwhelmed."

"You might be a great deal more than that after you eat it," she murmured.

"We could always eat out."

"Don't be a coward," she said absently, wondering just what she had in the freezer that could be used. "Better pick up some wine." Kneeling, she buttoned up the rest of his shirt for him herself. "And some bicarbonate," she added, laughing up at him.

"Bicarbonate," he murmured. "That doesn't inspire confidence."

"No, but it'd be a smart move."

"I shouldn't be long."

"Take my door key in case I'm involved in the kitchen. And, Matthew," she murmured, sliding her arms around his neck, "make sure you control those lust cells until you get back."

He kissed her, then gave her a friendly pat on the bottom. "An hour," he promised before he strolled out.

An hour, Laurel mused, and stretched her arms to the ceiling as she heard the front door close. That should give her time enough to try her hand at being domestic.

It didn't take her long to deal with the disorder of the apartment, or to realize just how smoothly Matt had eased out of helping. She decided that having to eat her cooking would be punishment enough for him. Going to the kitchen, she poked in the refrigerator.

A little juice, less milk, two pounds of butter. *Two* pounds, Laurel mused. How had that happened? Still, there was the makings for a salad in the vegetable bin. A start. Maybe a casserole, she decided. She was almost sure she had a cookbook around somewhere.

Fifteen minutes later, she was elbows deep in the beginnings of a tuna-and-macaroni dish that the cookbook promised was foolproof. With a glance around the now cluttered and disarranged kitchen, she smirked. Whoever wrote the book didn't know Laurel. She was going over the next step when the phone rang.

Matt, she thought, dusting off her hands as she went to answer. He probably wants to know if I'd like him to pick up some take-out Chinese. You're not getting off that easy, Bates. Grinning, she answered.

"Hello."

"Oh, Laurel, thank God you're home."

Tension banded the back of her neck immediately. "Marion? What is it?"

"Laurel, I didn't know what to do. Who else to call. It's Louis."

"Is he hurt?" Laurel asked quickly. "Has he been hurt?"

"No—I don't know. Laurel . . ." Her voice broke and she began to weep.

"Marion, calm down and tell me what's happened."

Her breathing rasped into the phone. "I've never seen him this bad before. All day, he wouldn't speak to anyone, but that happens sometimes. Oh, God, Laurel," she said on a sudden burst of emotion, "it's been such a strain, worse since Anne . . . Laurel," she began again, nerves quivering in her voice. "I need help."

"I'm going to help," Laurel said as calmly as she could. "What's happened?"

"Just now, a few minutes ago." Laurel heard her take a steadying breath. "He flew into a rage. He wasn't—wasn't making any sense. He was saying things about Elise, and about Anne. I don't know—it was as though he'd gotten them mixed up in his mind."

Laurel pressed her lips together. She had to be calm, had to think straight. "Where is he now?"

"He's locked himself in his room. He's raging up there, I can hear the furniture . . . Laurel, he won't let me in."

"Marion, call a doctor."

"Oh, God, Laurel, don't you think I've tried that before? He won't see one, and he's never been as—as out of control as this. Please, come. You were always our friend. Louis was so close to you before—before all of this. You might be able to calm him down, and then if I could just figure out what to do so that he'd—he'd get help," she finished in a whisper. "Laurel, please, I just can't expose him to strangers the way he is now. I don't know who else to trust."

"All right, Marion." She pictured Louis locked in his room, on the edge of madness. "I'll be there as quickly as I can."

"Laurel . . . as a friend, not as a reporter, please."

"As a friend, Marion." After hanging up the receiver, Laurel pressed the heels of her hands to her eyes.

Matt shifted the bag he carried and slipped Laurel's key into the lock. "I got red and white," he called out. "You didn't say what we were having." A glance at the living room showed him that Laurel had already tidied up. He was going to hear about that, Matt mused, grinning. "I don't smell anything burning."

He swung into the kitchen and lifted a brow. Whatever she was making, it apparently required every inch of counter space. Matt set the wine in the sink—the only place left for it—and shook his head. This was the woman whose notes were always in perfect order? Whose desk was clear and ordered at the end of each day? Dipping his hand into a bowl he drew out a cold, spongy elbow of macaroni.

"Ah, Laurel," he began, dropping it again. "There's this little place on Canal Street, great seafood. Why don't we . . ." He paused at the entrance to the bedroom. Empty. He felt the first prickles of unease. "Laurel?" Matt repeated, pushing open the bathroom door. Empty. Fear washed over him; he pushed it back. She'd just gone out for something she was missing for the recipe. She probably left a note.

When he hurried back into the living room, he found it by the phone. But even before he read it, he didn't feel relief, only more fear.

Matthew—Marion phoned, very upset. Louis is losing control, talking about Elise and Anne. He's locked himself in the bedroom. She needs help. I couldn't say no. Laurel.

"Damn it!" Matt tossed down the note and raced for the door. The fear was still with him.

Shadows were lengthening as Laurel turned down the drive toward Heritage Oak. The air was still again in the late-afternoon hush. A bird called out, as if testing the silence, then was quiet again. Even as she stopped the car at the end of the drive, Marion was running down the front steps toward her.

Her hair was loose, her face pale and tear-stained. It ran through Laurel's mind quickly that she'd never seen Marion so totally lacking in composure.

"Oh, God, Laurel." Marion grabbed her as if she were a lifeline. "I couldn't stop him. I couldn't stop him!"

Laurel's head whipped up, her eyes fixing on the window of Louis's room. She had a sickening picture of him lying dead by his own hand. "From what? Marion, what has he done?"

"The swamp. He's gone in the swamp." She covered her face with her hands and sobbed. "I think he's lost his mind. The things he was saying—he pushed me."

Not dead, Laurel told herself. Not dead. You have to be calm. "What did he say?"

Marion lowered her hands. Her eyes were wide, stricken. "He said," she began in a whisper, "he said he was going to find Elise."

"Elise," Laurel repeated, forcing herself not to give in to the horror of it.

"We have to do something!" Marion grabbed her again. "Laurel, we have to do something, go after him—*find* him. He's having a breakdown or—"

"Marion, how can we find him in there? We should call the police."

"*No!* Not the police. It's Louis." She seemed to come to grips with herself as she released Laurel. "I can find him. I know the swamp as well as he does. You don't have to come with me—I asked too much."

Laurel dragged both hands through her hair as Marion started across the lawn. He'd put her up on her first pony, she remembered. Played patient games of chess, listened to her rambling stories. Whatever he'd done, how could she walk away without trying to help?

"Marion, wait. I'm coming with you."

Marion stopped and held out a hand.

They moved quickly toward the swamp. The instant revulsion came as she stood at the edge of it, but she forced it back. It was just a place, she told herself. And Louis was in it.

The shadows were long on the ground now. Daylight was thinning. They'd have an hour, maybe a bit longer, Laurel reassured herself, before it was too dark to see. By then, they'd have found him. She moved into the swamp without hesitation.

"I think he might have gone to the river—to where Anne was found." How much did Marion know or suspect, Laurel wondered. At the moment, she didn't think Marion was in any shape for questions or theories. "Are you going to be all right?" she asked, looking at Marion's flowing pastel skirts and elegant pumps. "It's hard going through here."

"It doesn't matter," Marion said impatiently. "Louis is my brother."

"It's going to work out for the best," Laurel told her, almost believing it herself.

"I know." Marion managed a smile.

They moved slowly, side by side, and then with Laurel

just ahead as the path narrowed. The place was alive with noise—birds, insects. Once she saw a blue heron rise up gracefully and glide. They were coming to the river.

"Maybe we should call to him, let him know we're here," Laurel suggested. "It might frighten him if we're too quiet."

"He won't hear you."

"Not if he's gone the other way, but if he's anywhere near the river, then—" Laurel broke off as she turned around.

Marion held a gleaming old gun in her hand. A sliver of sunlight dashed against the chrome. For a moment, as her gaze rested on it, Laurel's mind went blank. Then, slowly, she looked up into Marion's face. Despite the red-rimmed eyes, the tracks of tears and disordered hair, her expression was calm and composed. There was something buzzing in her ears that Laurel didn't yet recognize as terror. She kept her eyes on Marion's face.

"Marion." The name came out calmly enough. Calmly and very soft. "What are you doing?"

"What I have to do," she said mildly.

Was the gun for Louis? Laurel thought frantically. If it was for Louis, then why was it pointed at her? She wouldn't look at it—not yet—she'd look only into Marion's clear gray eyes. "Where's Louis, Marion? Do you know?"

"Of course, he's working in his study. He's been working all afternoon."

"All afternoon," Laurel repeated, trying to hold back the trickle of fear that was eating at her wall of control. "Why did you call me?"

"I had to." Marion smiled. It was a gentle one. "After I spoke to you this morning about Elise's locket, I knew it had gone too far. You'd gone too far."

"Spoke to me? But I talked to Binney . . ." She trailed off. "It was you?"

"I'm surprised you didn't remember that Binney spends

her Sundays with her sister. You made it terribly simple, Laurel. You expected Binney, so I was Binney." The smile faded. Marion's brows drew together, delicately, as they did when she was annoyed. "I'm very disappointed in you, Laurel. I warned you to stay out of this. Can you imagine the trouble you'd have caused if it had been Binney? Questioning a servant about family matters." She shook her head as a flicker of irritation darkened her eyes. "You've been raised better than that."

Raised better? Laurel thought giddily. Was she mad? Oh, God, she thought as fear washed over her. Of course she was mad. "Marion, what are you going to do?"

"You'll have to be punished," Marion told her calmly. "Just like the others."

Matt's car skidded to a halt next to Laurel's. He hadn't stopped cursing since he'd tossed her note aside. Cursing helped hold off the fear. If he's hurt her, Matt thought as he sprinted up the steps. By God, if he's touched her . . . Lifting a fist, he pounded on the door.

"Trulane!" He pounded again, sick with fear. When the door opened, he was through it in seconds, with his hands gripping hard on Louis's shirt. "Where's Laurel?"

"What the hell do you think you're doing?" Louis stood rigid, his eyes burning with fury.

"What have you done with Laurel?" Matt demanded.

"I've done nothing with Laurel. I haven't seen her." He looked down at the hands gripping his shirt. "Get your hands off me, Bates." He'd like a fight, Matt realized. He'd like the simple release of a purely physical explosion—fist against flesh. Matt saw it in his eyes.

"We'll go a few rounds, Trulane," Matt promised grimly.

"There's nothing I'd like better—after you tell me what you've done with Laurel."

Louis felt something bubbling inside of him. The emotion, for the first time in weeks, had nothing to do with grief. It was pure fury. Somehow it was cleansing. "I told you I haven't seen her. She isn't here."

"You can do better." Matt flung a hand toward the open door. "Her car's out front."

Louis followed the gesture and frowned. Some of the pent-up anger gave way to puzzlement. "She must've come to see Marion."

"Marion called her." Matt shoved him back against the wall, catching him off-balance. "She told her to come because you were out of control, locked in your room."

"Are you crazy?" Louis pushed him away, and they stood eyeing each other, both tall men, both ready, anxious, for blood. "Marion would hardly call Laurel if I were locked in my room. As it happens, I've been working all afternoon."

Matt stood, breathing fast, trying to hold on. If he hit Trulane, even once, he might never stop. He could feel the violence bubbling up inside him. Not until he saw Laurel, he promised himself. And after that . . .

"Laurel left me a note that she was coming here after a phone call from Marion concerning your unstable condition."

"I don't know what the hell you're talking about."

"Laurel's car's out front," Matt said between his teeth. "And you're here."

Louis gave him a cold stare. "Perhaps you'd care to search the house."

"I'll do just that," Matt tossed back. "While I'm at it," he continued as he reached in his pocket, "why don't you take a look at this and see what explanation you can come up with?"

Opening his palm, he held out the piece of locket. Louis gripped his wrist, fingers biting into flesh. "Elise—where did you get that?" His eyes whipped up to Matt's, dark, tormented. "Where in hell did you get that?"

"In the swamp." Matt closed his hand over it. "Laurel recognized it, too, then confirmed it with your housekeeper on the phone this morning."

"Binney?" Louis stared down at Matt's closed hand. "No, Binney isn't here. The swamp? In the swamp?" Again Louis lifted his head. His face was white. "Elise never went in there without me. She always wore that, always. She had it on the day I left for New York, before she—" He shook his head, color rushing back to his face. "What the hell are you trying to do?"

Matt tried to take it step by step. A new fear was crawling in. "Laurel told me she called here—around noon—and spoke with your housekeeper."

"I tell you Binney isn't here, hasn't been here all day! She goes to her sister's. All the servants are free on Sundays. There's only Marion and I."

"Only Marion?" Matt murmured. Marion who had called—Marion who had, by her nervous distress, sent them after Brewster. And Marion, Matt remembered all at once, who had said Anne had told Susan that Brewster made her nervous. How would she have known that unless—unless she'd seen the letters. "Where is she?" Matt demanded, already halfway down the hall. "Where's your sister?"

"You just wait a damned minute." Louis grabbed Matt by the arm. "What are you getting at? Where did you get that locket?"

"In the swamp!" Matt exploded. "Damn you, don't you understand Marion's got her!" His face became very still and very pale. "In the swamp," he repeated. "She has her in the swamp, just like the others."

"What others?" Louis was on him before Matt could move. *"What others?"*

"Your sister's a murderer," Matt flung back at him. "She's killed three times, and now she has Laurel."

"You're crazy!"

"I'm not crazy." He opened his fist again so that the locket sat dully in the center of his palm. "We were in the swamp the other night—someone attacked her. The same person who sent her the dead snake, and the one who threatened her over the phone yesterday. The same person," he said evenly, "who called her here now. Laurel came here for you," Matt told Louis, watching his eyes. "Are you going to help me?"

Louis stared down at the locket, his breath unsteady. "We'll go in. Wait here."

Turning, he walked into a room across from the parlor. Seconds later, he came back with a small pistol. The color had drained from his face again. In silence, he handed it to Matt. "She's taken the gun." His eyes met Matt's. "The antique we've kept under glass."

D on't panic, don't try to run. Laurel ran the words over and over in her mind as she watched Marion. She looks so calm now, as if any minute she'd smile and offer me tea and cakes. How long has she been mad? Laurel swallowed slowly, careful to make no movement at all. Talk—she wants to talk about it.

"Punish," Laurel repeated. "You punished the others, Marion?"

"I had to."

"Why?"

"You were always a clever child, Laurel, but not clever enough." She smiled again, old friend to old friend. "After all, look how easily I threw your attention onto Brewster, just by telling the truth. Anne would never have left Louis. She adored him."

"Then why did you punish her, Marion?"

"She shouldn't have come back." Marion let out a little, shuddering sigh. "She should never have come back."

"Come back?" Laurel repeated, allowing herself a quick glimpse over Marion's head. If she could distract her, get just a few seconds' head start, could she lose herself in the brush?

"She didn't fool me," Marion said, smiling again. "Oh, she fooled the rest of them—especially Louis—but I knew. Of course, I pretended I didn't. I'm very good at pretending. She was afraid of the swamp," Marion said absently. "I knew why, of course I knew why. She died here before, she had to die here again."

Laurel stared as the horror of what was in Marion's mind washed over her. Keep talking, keep talking, keep talking, she told herself as a thrush began to sing in the cypress behind her. "Why did you kill Elise the first time?"

"She had no right!" Marion exploded so that Laurel gave a quick, involuntary jerk back. "She had no right to the house. It was mine, always it's been mine. Louis was going to will it to her. To *her*! She didn't have Trulane blood, wasn't one of us. *I'm* the oldest," she raged. "By rights, the house was mine. Father was wrong to leave it to Louis."

Her chest began to shudder, but when Laurel looked down, she saw the gun was still steady. "It's always been mine. I love it. All of this." Her eyes skimmed the swamp and softened. "It's the only thing I've ever loved."

"But why Elise?" Laurel interrupted. A house, she thought frantically. Did someone kill for a house, a plot of grass and dirt? It had been done before, she reminded herself. Over and over again, since the caves. "Why didn't you kill Louis, Marion? Then you'd have inherited."

"Laurel." Her voice was soft. "Louis is my brother."

"But—but Charles," she began.

"I never wanted to hurt Charles." Tears sprang and swam in her eyes. "I loved him. But he saw us, he interfered." A single tear drifted down her cheek. "I didn't have a choice. Elise and I went for a walk—she was lonely without Louis. When we were far enough away from the house, I took out the gun. This gun," she said, lifting it higher. "Do you recognize it, Laurel?"

She did. She'd seen it under glass in the library. The same gun another Trulane had used to kill—to punish. "Yes."

"I knew I had to use this." She ran a fingertip down the barrel. "It was as if it was waiting for me, as if someone was telling me that it was right that I punish Elise with this. Do you understand?"

"I'm trying to."

"Poor Laurel," Marion murmured. "Always so understanding, so caring. That's how I knew you'd come today when I called."

Laurel felt her knees start to shake. "You were telling me about Charles."

"Yes, yes. He saw us, you see. Saw me leading Elise into the swamp at gunpoint. At least, he must have—I didn't have time to ask, everything happened so quickly. We were here when he found us. Just here."

She glanced around as if they might not be alone after all. Laurel took a very slow, very small step to the right. "Don't, Laurel," Marion murmured, lifting the gun a fraction higher. Laurel stood still. "Elise went wild—that must have been when her locket was broken. I should've been more careful. I had to shoot her. Then Charles was pushing me down. My own brother—shouting at me. The gun seemed to go off again, all by itself. Then he was dead."

Her tears were dry now, her eyes clear. "I didn't know what

to do at first, and then, it just came. They'd been lovers, like the other two who'd died here. I'd have to forge another note. This time Elise would tell Louis she'd left him for Charles. It was better," she muttered. "Really, it was better that way. I had to drag them to the quicksand."

"Oh, God." Laurel closed her eyes, but Marion didn't notice.

"I packed some of their clothes. All the servants were gone because it was Sunday. Charles's paints, too—I nearly forgot them. Of course, he'd never have left without his paints. They went in the quicksand, too. Then it was done. It was simple. Of course, Louis was hurt. He suffered." Her eyes clouded for a moment. "I know he blamed himself, but I could hardly tell him it was all for the best. The house was mine again, he was busy with his work. But sometimes," she whispered. "Sometimes I'd hear them in here. At night."

Laurel swallowed the metallic taste of horror. "Charles and Elise?"

"I'd hear them—it would wake me up and I'd have to come out, come look. I never saw them—" Again, she looked around as if expecting someone. "But I heard."

It's driven her mad, Laurel thought. How is it no one saw, no one suspected? She remembered Marion at a charity function only months before—delicate, elegant, with a spray of violets pinned to her lapel. She looked down at the gun again.

"Then she came back," Marion said flatly. "She said her name was Anne, and Louis believed her. I knew. She'd look at me with those soft, shy eyes, and she was laughing! I let her think she'd fooled me."

"And you brought her in here again."

"I had to be more careful this time. Louis hardly let her out of his sight, and she'd never, never go near the swamp. That night, he was working late. I heard her in the study with him. He told her he'd probably be a couple hours more, to go up to bed without him. I knew it was time. I went into her room, put a pillow over her face. Oh, I had to be careful, I couldn't kill her then. It had to look like an accident this time. She was very small, and not strong. It only took a minute until she was unconscious. Then I carried her out here."

Marion smiled, remembering. "I had the gun, but she didn't know I couldn't afford to use it. When she came to, she was terrified. Elise knew she was going to die again. She begged me to let her go, but I made her get up. I thought it best if she drowned in the river. When she started to run, I let her. It would be simpler if she exhausted herself first and I kept close. Then I heard her scream. The snake, a young one, Elise had walked right over the nest. You see, it was meant," Marion told her. "It was right. All I needed then was enough time for the poison to work—and a night, a whole night out in that damp air. I waited until she stopped running, until she was unconscious, here, right here where she'd died before. Then I went home." Marion smiled, but now her eyes were blank. "She won't come back this time."

"No," Laurel said quietly. "She won't come back."

"I've always been fond of you, Laurel. If you'd only listened, this wouldn't have happened."

Laurel moistened her lips and prayed her voice would be steady. "If you shoot me, Marion, they'll take you away from Heritage Oak."

"No!" Her hand tightened on the gun, then relaxed. "No, I'm not going to shoot you, unless I have to. If I do, I'll have to place the blame on Louis. I'll have to, you'll be responsible for that."

It was so hard to breathe, Laurel discovered. So hard to make the air come in and go out. If she concentrated on it, she'd keep herself from screaming until Marion made her stop. "I won't walk into the river, or the quicksand for you."

"No," Marion agreed. "You're not like the others, not so easily frightened. But there's one thing . . ." Holding the gun level, she sidestepped toward the wild cane. "You came in here to snoop around, you couldn't leave it alone. And you met with a tragic accident. Just like Elise—Anne." She drew a wicker hamper out of the bush. "This one," she said quietly, "isn't dead."

She knew, and the fear wrapped around her. Tight. With a long, smooth stick, Marion pushed the hamper closer, then flicked off the lid. Laurel froze, feeling the weightlessness in her head, the ice in her stomach as the snake slithered out. Then another one.

"I didn't want to take any chances," Marion murmured. Setting down the gun, she held the stick with both hands. She looked up at Laurel and smiled. "You've always been terrified of them, haven't you? How well I remember you fainting dead away over a little garter snake. Harmless creatures." She poked her stick at the copperheads until they coiled and hissed. "These aren't."

She wanted to run, to scream. The gun would've been better. But her voice was trapped by the fear, her legs imprisoned by it. As if her consciousness had floated off, she felt her skin spring damp and clammy.

"It won't matter if you don't move," Marion told her easily. "They're angry. I can make them angrier." She prodded them again, nudging them closer to Laurel. One lashed out at the stick, and Marion laughed.

It was the laugh Matt heard. It chilled him to the bone. When he saw them, the snakes were less than a foot away from Laurel, hissing, coiling, enraged, as Marion continued to prod at them. Matt gripped the gun in both hands, prayed, and fired.

"*No!*" Marion's scream was long and wild as the body of one snake jerked, then lay still. She spun around, stumbling, not even feeling the fangs that sank into her ankle before Matt pulled the trigger again. And she ran, bursting through the wild cane like an animal, hunted.

"Laurel!" Matt had his arms around her, dragging her against him. "You're all right." Desperate, he closed his mouth over hers. "It's over. I'm getting you out."

"Matthew." The sobs were heaving in her chest and she fought against them. "She's mad. She killed them all—all of them. My God, Matthew. The snakes—"

"Gone," he said quickly, pulling her closer. "They're gone. You're all right."

"For the house," Laurel said into his chest. "Dear God, she killed them for the house. Louis—"

Matt turned his head. Only a few yards away, Louis stood staring at them. There was no color in his face. Only his eyes seemed alive. "She's been bitten," Louis said, so quietly Matt barely heard. "I'll go after her."

"Louis—" Matt looked back at him, finding there was nothing, absolutely nothing, that could be said. "I'm sorry," he murmured.

Nodding, Louis walked into the cane. "Just get Laurel out of here."

"Come on." Matt pressed his lips to her temple. "Can you walk?"

"Yes." The tears were streaming down her face, but she found them a relief. "Yes, I'm all right."

"When I'm sure of that," he said as he held her close by his side, "I'm going to strangle you."

He waited until they were in the clear, then drew Laurel down on the grass. Her head sank to her knees. "I'll be all right in a minute, really. We'll have to call the police."

"Louis took care of it before he left the house. They'll be here any minute. Can you tell me now?"

At first, she kept her head on her knees as she spoke.

Gradually, as the horror and the dizziness faded, she lifted it. When she heard the sirens, her hand slipped into Matt's and held tight.

So much confusion—with the police in the swamp, all the questions. A hell of a story, Laurel thought on a bright bubble of hysteria. Though she swallowed it, she gave in to the need to press her face into Matt's shoulder. Just a few more minutes, she told herself. I'll be all right in just a few more minutes. She let Matt lead her back to the house, then drank the brandy he urged on her.

"I'm better," she told him. "Please, stop looking at me as though I were going to dissolve."

He stared at her a minute, then, pulling her into his arms, buried his face in her hair. "Damn you, Laurel." And his voice trembled. "Don't ever do that to me again. I thought I was too late. Another five minutes—"

"No more," she murmured, soothing him. "No more, Matthew. Oh, I love you." She drew his face back. "I love you so much."

She met the aggressive kiss, feeling all the fears drain. He was here, holding her. Nothing else mattered. She lifted a hand to his face as the front door closed. "It's Louis," she said quietly.

He came in slowly. His hair and clothes were streaked and disheveled. His eyes, Laurel saw, were not cold, were not remote, but weary and vulnerable. Without hesitation, she rose and went to him. "Oh, Louis."

He slipped his arms around her, holding on. His face dropped to the top of her head. "We found her. She's—they're taking her to the hospital, but I don't know if . . . She's delirious," he managed, and drew away. "Did she hurt you, Laurel?"

"No, no, I'm fine."

His gaze shifted to Matt. "I owe you much more than an apology."

"No, you don't."

Louis accepted this with a nod and walked to the brandy. "Are you up to telling me the whole story now?"

He kept his back to them as Laurel related everything Marion had said. Once, when she saw his shoulders shudder, she faltered. He shook his head and gestured for her to finish.

"I need to talk to Susan," he said when Laurel fell silent.

"She's with my grandmother."

Pouring another brandy, Louis nodded. "If she'll see me, I'll go out tomorrow."

"She'll see you, Louis," Laurel murmured. "Please, please, don't take the blame for this."

He turned around slowly. "Do something for me?"

"Of course, you know I will."

"Yes," he said with a faint laugh. "Yes, I know you will. Write your story," he said in a stronger voice. "And make it good. Everything, I want everything out. Maybe then I can live with it."

"Matthew and I'll write it," Laurel told him, and rose to take his hand. "And you'll live with it, Louis. I'm coming back and see that you do." She touched his cheek. "I love you."

With a ghost of a smile, he kissed her. "You're well matched with him, Laurel," he murmured, looking over at Matt. "You're as stubborn as he is. Come back," he agreed, squeezing her hands. "I'm going to need you."

When they walked from the house a few minutes later, Laurel breathed deep. Just the scent of night. The scent of life. "It's beautiful, isn't it?" She threw her face up to the stars. "We'd better call my father, let him know we have one hell of an exclusive on the way."

"Next time you decide to go for one," he said dryly, "remember we're partners. No more solo meets."

"You got it," she agreed. "Let's take your car," she decided, too keyed up to drive. "I can get mine tomorrow. Oh, God, Matthew!" Dropping down inside, she leaned back against the seat. "I never want to go through another night like this, even for a Pulitzer."

"That's what you get for taking off before you fixed dinner." His hands were finally steady, he noted as he turned the key. "Makes a man wonder what kind of wife he's getting."

"A gem," she assured him. "You're getting a gem, Bates." Leaning over, she kissed him. "I haven't thanked you for saving my life."

"No." He smiled, cupping the back of her neck so he could linger over the kiss. "What'd you have in mind?"

"Doing the same for you." She grinned at him. "We're eating out."